'The Fear is a moving read. It tackles every parent's nightmare, that of a stricken child, all woven into a fast-moving plot. It's about confronting life's perils. The pivotal chapter is particularly powerful.'
Henry Winter – Chief Football Writer at The Times

'An extraordinary book about an ordinary family
– really interesting and absorbing.'
Jo Brand

Four stars: '...a powerful read.' FourFourTwo magazine

Based on true events in his life, Mark Cunnington's eighth novel is both a compelling and emotive read. Tackling a tragic family backstory, his parents' dementia and son's unique football story, The Fear is a must-read novel for any parent.

Available in paperback from
www.triopublishing.co.uk, Amazon and bookshops.
Available as an ebook on Amazon, Apple Books and Google Play.

Strait Sets

Mark Cunnington

Trio Publishing

First published 2021

Published by Trio Publishing

www.triopublishing.co.uk

ISBN 978 1 8382918 0 8

Published in electronic edition by Trio Publishing 2021

Printed and bound in Great Britain by Clays Ltd, Elcograf S.p.A.

Thanks to Karen and Paula

Strait Sets takes place in a contemporary England where Covid-19 has never existed. Everything is 'old normal' rather than 'new normal'. Times are not unprecedented.

STRAIT SETS

Part 1

AD (After Divorce)

I moved my head closer to the window and peered through the large rain-splattered pane of glass, scanning the properties for sale – a selection of flats, chalet bungalows and houses – before spotting it. Exactly the same image as I had seen online, the photo stark and almost square on, cropped tight with zero artistic input. For once the camera hadn't been trying to lie or distort. No fake news here, I thought, just a simple holiday snap of a simple holiday dwelling. I tilted my head slightly to one side, scrunching my face and wondering what else could be said of it to make it more appealing. Very little, I concluded. It was what it was. Where it was that was the crucial bit. Well, not exactly where it was, everybody knew where it was, the giveaway clue being in the description. It was *where* the where was that drove the desirability and with it the breath-taking, sharp-slap-around-the-face asking price. Location, coupled with the associated traditional quintessential Englishness of the structure, and there you had it. One hell of a price tag.

One hell of a price tag I might be willing to meet? It certainly looked like I was seriously considering it – given the one proviso of haggling a few grand off, an act of self-validation rather than anything to do with the money – seeing as I had made a viewing appointment *and* driven the best part of a hundred miles to be here. To view it in the flesh. In all its gloss-coated, lap boarded, veranda with twin pitched felt-tiled roof, lurking-by-the-shore glory.

Despite appreciating the absurdity of the numbers underneath the photo of the beach hut, I stoically viewed them with only mild

9

animosity. I was over regarding sums of money with rage and frustration. What was the point? It hadn't changed anything in the past and I didn't want it to become an issue of the present. Time to move on from any number negativity and clamber free from the train-crash wreckage of my current situation.

I eased my head away from the window and turned to face the wind and horizontal rain howling in from the North Sea. The road, on whose pavement I stood, was the small seaside town's main thoroughfare and home to many of its retail outlets and coffee shops. This morning it was completely empty and devoid of movement. No people. No cars. Not even a hateful seagull to splatter corrosive white guano on either. Nuclear/zombie apocalypse personified. And it was only two weeks until Easter. What the hell must it be like in January? What did everybody *do* over the winter in such a seasonal environment?

In answer to my mental conundrum, I pictured the indigenous population slipping into collective hibernation sometime around November, shortly after the excitement and high jinks of Halloween and Bonfire Night. Behind locked doors, in a host of bedrooms surprisingly resourced with ultra-sophisticated, hi-tech equipment, en masse and at the designated time, the town's residents dutifully climbed into their assigned stasis pods to ride out the months of little daylight. Desolate and deserted, the small coastal town bided its time, waiting for its inhabitants to awaken in springtime.

Few things look as forlorn and desperate as the English seaside in the depths of winter – although a pathetic, mewling, just-dunked cat crawling sodden from cold water runs it a close second. It's a scenario only the weather has the power to change. With a rise in temperature and lengthening days, gradually our seaside can morph from dull and dreary to bright and beautiful. Unfortunately, the massive flaw in that theory, as I stood chilled to the bone and battered by a ferocious north-easterly, was a winter weather system despite it being April. In my fantasy, I hadn't made the obvious connection between the weather and the town's inhabitants. That was the reason why no one was around. The pods hadn't yet thermally triggered to open.

Dragging myself back in the moment, I fixated on the photo of the beach hut, the one I had found online only a few days ago, and questioned my true reasons for being here, bank details at the ready, strangely eager to see whether I might suffer buyer's remorse. The brutal truth, even if it did make me uneasy, was evident. Essentially, I was here on a quest to seek out the happier times of my life and take solace in nostalgia. A fortifying hug from my past which I hoped would impact positively on my present and transform my future. Undoubtedly, the act of a divorcee buying a beach hut was a classic desperate gambler's last punt. Stalled in my current social cul-de-sac, it felt a wager worth chancing.

The plan, if you could call it a plan, rested on any future shoreline base camp affording me the chance to recharge, re-energise, reorganise and recommence my newly-found single life. The majesty of the English seaside wiping my slate clean of all the blood, snot and gore currently pebble-dashed to it. Here, by the sea, away from all I had been through, I aspired to be as happy as I had been in childhood when holidaying on this section of coast with my mother and grandparents. Owning a beach hut was the first step in the next phase of my life. The phase devoid of *her*. The ex. The woman who had once been my wife.

Unlikely? Maybe. But from my viewpoint it looked worth a punt. Believe me, when your world's been kicked from pillar to post and you've haemorrhaged money, self-worth, self-confidence and several vital organs – including a penis – anything, even the implausible, can look pretty compelling. The only downside I could foresee in my seaside nostalgia strategy was how it pulled the ongoing confrontation with my mother into focus, reminding me of the love I used to have for her which had now turned to contempt. Powerless to influence her, she seemed determined to pursue her new path with vigour, despite my endless protestations.

A curtain of water from the adjacent store's awning suddenly showered me in a mini-deluge, cold-shocking me with icy wetness between my upturned collar and the nape of my neck. It reminded me of the time Chloe and I performed our 'ice bucket challenge' years ago, right at the start of our relationship, and posted the resulting videos on our respective Facebook feeds. Afterwards, laughing and giggling like small children, we peeled off our sodden clothes and in the rush of our nakedness made spontaneous love on the kitchen table. In the throes of my violent orgasm, as I rammed hard and deep into her, dumping my load, the salt cellar careened off the table and deposited its contents on the kitchen floor. Post coitus and ever superstitious, I surreptitiously bent down and, making sure Chloe wasn't looking, grabbed a pinch of salt and threw it over my shoulder before sweeping the rest up.

With hindsight, as an act of warding off evil omens, that hadn't proved especially successful.

Eyeing the rapidly refilling and now bulging awning with trepidation, I stood hunched against the bullying elements, shuffling from one sodden foot to another, running the premise over in my mind for one last last time. Buying the beach hut would eat up all my remaining cash. If I went ahead, my financial safety net would no longer be able to catch me. It would hang slashed to ribbons, holed and gaping, the gaps large enough for me to plunge through should any unforeseen disaster occur. I would be left having to live a more considered month-to-month existence, to budget sensibly and rein in any spendthrift tendencies.

The perversity of the moment steeled me and I finally made up my mind. 2018 had started all 'Beast from the East' and look how that had turned out. Oh to have owned a beach hut through *that* summer. More pertinently, why bother playing it safe? My whole life up until this juncture had been spent playing it safe. And where had it got me? Aged thirty-two, divorced, childless, living in a poky, rented flat and stuck in the same job I had been doing since leaving university. That's where. I walked four brisk strides down the window pane to the estate agent's door, opened it and stepped inside. And not to get out of the wind and the rain.

D Day (Divorce Day)

Mr Anthony Furlington of Forsythe, Furlington & Saunders Solicitors – 'Underhand, Shyster and Judas' as I occasionally referred to them – rotated the A4 invoice on his leather-inlay mahogany desk through one hundred and eighty degrees, saving me the displeasure of having to read upside down. I didn't bother to acknowledge this as a sympathetic gesture as I was pretty confident I had already been charged for it. Stony-faced, I gazed at the swarm of figures printed on it, a single-sided piece of paper financially defining my real-time status in the Game of Life. Obviously, I was losing. The big question, by how much.

Anxious to know, yet fearing the worst, I ignored a swathe of numbers at the top of the page and allowed my eyes to slip uneasily towards the crucial bottom line. An action only briefly interrupted by a quick glimpse at the gruesome figure defining the violent mugging constituting FFS's involvement in my divorce. The last number, the one sitting alongside 'Total monies available', was worse than I had hoped for, despite the good fortune of the house selling for nearly double the price Chloe and I had originally paid for it. As my brain absorbed the disappointment, I actually made a noise. A tiny gasp of pain, as if I had inadvertently stepped on a pebble while walking on a sandy beach.

Mr Anthony Furlington LLB (Licensed Law Bandit) picked up on my discomfort and threw me an unctuous look of concern – one of several he probably kept in the drawer of his desk alongside his useful solicitor-sized box of 'Insincere Platitudes' flashcards. Box ticked on the client emotional engagement front, Furlington set about the professional analysis of my invoice in his drab, monotone speech. The verbal equivalent to watching paint dry in a cold, damp environment, it was a voice I had become gratingly familiar with over the course of our dispiriting engagement.

"If we can just quickly run through your current financial statement, Mr Chambers. This is the figure for the house sale, this is the figure for the cash in your and Ms Chambers' joint account and this is the figure for the money acquired from the sale of the two vehicles," Furlington indicated, running a manicured forefinger over the upper sections of the paper.

Trying to push aside the weird calculation my brain had decided to embark on, namely, the number of sessions FFS's bill could buy Furlington with an austerely attractive Danish nail bar technician, I hauled my stare off the piece of A4 and grunted in a 'What can you do?' manner. Chloe and I hadn't even been able to come to an amicable arrangement over the two vehicles, despite knowing we would lose thousands selling quickly to a main dealer. Furlington pressed onwards and downwards, his voice droning like a fat, lazy bug on a still summer's evening. One I wanted to swat to death with a well-aimed smash of my Babolat tennis racket.

I've always considered myself to possess a decent overhead, even if Chloe never forgave me for missing an easy smash on set point in our club's mixed doubles final two summers ago. Failing to capitalise on an easy put away and go one set up in a best of three final, we then went on to lose to the club's stardust couple, the Winstones, in straight sets. It was where things had started to go wrong. Crazy, really, to be able to pinpoint the failure of a marriage so precisely to one small act, but it has been empirically proven so and my missed smash is now fully appreciated as the Big Bang moment of my adult life. My future universe's moment of birth where all before it became uncreated.

"I'm sorry, Chloe. I was so tight and wanted to beat them *so* much, I choked and mistimed it off the frame," I explained during our rather intense 'why we lost' retrospective.

"Too busy ogling Emily's legs, more like!" she stated in outrage.

"*What*? How can you even say something like that!" I protested.

"Don't bother trying to lie your way out of it, Paul. I've seen how you look at her," she replied witheringly.

Looking back, the sole redeeming circumstance of our acrimonious post-match analysis lay in the fact we had already left the clubhouse and were in the car going home. At least nobody else had to endure the embarrassment of listening to a married pair squabbling over a lost tennis match.

"Moving on to the debit side of matters," Furlington continued, his speech suffocating and dry, taking oxygen from the room like an eager vacuum pump. "We have the matter of the estate agent's fees, we have the matter of the property selling solicitor's fees, we have the matter of the payment required to finalise the existing mortgage commitments on the property. Then the matter of all of the other various sundry items needing to be finalised... All listed for your perusal here." The manicured finger tapped once. "Moving on from that settlement figure, we move to the matter of the agreed split of all remaining monies with Ms Chambers." Furlington looked up. I looked up. I had been shafted, what else was there to say other than goodbye lump sum donated by Daddy, thanks for coming. Furlington's head bowed and he pressed on. "This leads us to the matter of the payment required re our invoice for work conducted in facilitating divorce proceedings and, finally, the matter of the amount we have paid into your individual current account." Furlington raised his head and smiled. "The end of a rather difficult and, most certainly for your part, very challenging journey. I have in my possession, as we discussed earlier," Furlington said, sliding an envelope my way, "your decree absolute."

Furlington paused and worked his face into an expression I suspected he still practised every morning in front of a mirror. "Are there any questions you'd like to ask, Mr Chambers?"

I considered his request and was about to summon up all my remaining energy to shake a tired, disgruntled head when, surprisingly, out of nowhere, a counter question came to me.

"Just out of interest, have you ever managed to successfully talk someone out of a coma?" I asked.

Furlington blinked in mild contemplation, his monobrow forming a brief pencil representation of a seagull. "I don't think I can ever recall having been asked," he replied.

"Well, probably for the best," I remarked.

There. Right there was the tiny spark of hope. The moment when a little bit of the old me crawled out from underneath the boulder where it had been skulking. It marked the turning of the tide, if you like, where the first wave reaches back up the sand a little further than the last. It was that very evening, spent alone in my rented flat, bottle of beer in hand, family-sized bag of Kettle crisps perched between my legs, when the concept of blowing virtually all my remaining cash on a beach hut floated to the top, and then bobbed brightly, on the disturbed waters of my thought process.

AD

"It can't always be as bad as this at this time of year, can it?" I asked Kevin, the estate agent from Ramsbottom & Son who had dealt with my initial enquiry by phone.

"Sorry?" he responded.

"Is it always as bad as this at this time of year?" I repeated, raising my voice in an attempt to stop it being lost on the wind.

"No! Not normally. This is dire! And Easter's only two weeks away!"

"That's what I was thinking," I answered ruefully.

"Ironically, they've only just moved the huts back into position from their 'safe' winter storage. I'm hoping none of them have been damaged."

The two of us were making our way towards the beach hut from the office on foot because the rain had finally stopped and, I had been reliably informed, it was less than a ten-minute walk. Even so, I still got the impression Kevin wasn't exactly ecstatic to be out of the office exposing himself to the elements. Maybe it was some sort of commission thing. As expensive as the beach hut was, it wasn't exactly in the five-bedroom detached price range.

The blanket cloud, rapidly fleeing over our heads in an apparent desperate rush to head inland, as if late for an important meeting, had changed colour from a dark, forbidding grey to something approaching off-white. With it, the day's brightness had increased marginally. Triggered by thoughts of light and shade, I reminisced about the times Mum, her parents and I had spent holidays in Southburgh over twenty years ago. With it came a vivid recollection of my dear grandfather and his ancient Kodak Retinette camera, armed with 35mm 100 ASA slide film and the separate light meter he always kept hanging round his neck. Irrespective of time of day – I think he slept with them – whenever the four of us holidayed on the east coast, the camera and light meter were Grandad's constant companions. The pair hung about him like bulky analogue necklaces.

With his light meter constantly to hand, my grandfather would incessantly aim it at scenery, objects and people, even when not taking photos, as if charting a light reading map of his entire surroundings. At some point during this endless process, either by a reckoning of interest, arbitrariness, or perhaps the passing of some pre-ordained number, Grandad would stop and take an actual photo. Afterwards he would loudly and solemnly pronounce the F-stop setting at which the Kodak's manual lens had been set. Today's conditions were now f4, I reckoned. No more than that. Flashbulbs would definitely have been on standby.

When first trusted to use the brown-cased SLR in a low light situation, aluminium fan flash unit attached, Grandad warned me of the inherent dangers of magnesium filament bulbs. "Don't touch one of them buggers after they've just gone off, young Paul. You'll get your fingers burnt." Goaded by his words, I had been unable to resist the temptation and for the rest of the holiday endured minor burns to the index finger and thumb of my right hand. "That'll learn you," he remarked, shaking his head and holding my hand under a cold tap in a pungent public toilet, tears trickling down my cheeks. Growing up something north of a complete moron, I never did it again. Walking with Kevin, however, I did contemplate if history was about to repeat itself.

"Winter storage?" I shouted, as another squall attempted to hijack my words.

"The huts get moved for the winter to a more sheltered area away from the shoreline to protect them from the elements," Kevin told me with a gesture of his head. "There's a large car park back over the other side of the pier. They get put there," he bellowed.

"I never knew beach huts were migratory," I cracked. "You learn something new every day."

"I guess they do sort of fly. If only on the end of a jib crane cable," Kevin replied.

"Who pays for that?" I asked, wondering if any were flying unaided today.

"The hut owners."

"Okay," I answered in a non-committed tone.

"It's not a huge expense," Kevin assured me. "And the council does give a rebate on the rent to go towards it.

"The rent?"

"I'll explain it all when we get there. It's not too far now, thank goodness. Down that set of steps," the estate agent shouted, pointing some hundred yards in the distance towards a pair of extensive white handrails.

The two ends of the handrails terminated at the junction of two rendered brick piers, four yards apart, before turning through ninety degrees and sweeping downwards towards the sea, following both sides of a set of concrete steps. We pressed on towards them in silence, directly into the full force of the gale now we were out of the narrow streets and it had clear passage to assault us.

"I shouldn't want to be out on the sea today," I loudly remarked, eyeing the towering walls of dark water as we made our way down the set of concrete steps, the physical effort more akin to climbing them such was the wind's desire to push us back. "Not without my waterproof factor fifty," I joked, surprised at being able to now taste seawater on my lips despite our distance from it.

"Yes, it's not *exactly* conducive weather to buying a beach hut, is it?" Kevin agreed as we manfully completed our descent and turned to walk along the promenade, a row of beach huts to our right, a four foot drop to the empty sandy beach on our left. "But when it's summer and it's warm and sunny it's so beautiful. The summer of 2018 was incredible."

"I'll have to take your word for it," I said, keeping my powder dry.

Our pace had increased with the change of direction as we were now wind-assisted, the hoolie buffeting the pair of us along the prom as if an invisible giant was nudging us in the back.

"You don't have to take my word, Mr Chambers. Ask anyone. In summer there's nowhere better to spend your time. You'll have to try and look past this awful weather."

Keen not to let Kevin know he was preaching to the converted, my answer was deadpan.

"I'm trying. Trouble is, the wind keeps making my eyes water.

A bit like the beach hut's asking price, come to think of it."

Kevin threw his head back sharply, as if controlled by a puppet master whose arm had suffered an involuntary spasm, the barest hint of a forced smile grudgingly elbowing its way across his face. He was over twenty years older than me, mid to late fifties at a guess, and had probably heard it all before. Too bad. My first move in the chess game of buyer v seller had been played. I had edged out a pawn. Price negotiations were officially under way.

After passing around ten huts we came to the one bearing the Ramsbottom & Son's 'For Sale' board. Standing back and allowing Kevin to go first, I followed him up the one step to the covered area of decking comprising the hut's veranda. Turning to look at the vicious sea, I leant against the timbered half wall that followed the sides of the veranda's footprint. As each fresh, briny gust slammed into the beach hut's side, my backside felt each miniscule movement of the structure beneath it. It appeared Kevin was suffering equally from the buffeting, acting out his sit-com part of drunkard-attempting-to-put-key-in-lock. Eventually, Kevin got his act together and unlocked the large padlock securing the temporarily shuttered panel glazed double doors.

"There we go," he said, as he fixed one of the double doors wide open on a securing hook.

This time he let me go first. I stepped inside, my eyes taking in the sparse spectacle. My first impression, setting aside the relief of finally getting out of the wind and the odd feeling of lightheadedness that accompanied it, was one of surprise. To be honest, I hadn't been sure what level of finish to expect inside a 21st century beach hut costing tens of thousands of pounds, but whatever I had envisaged it was definitely more than the meagre reality on display before me. Clearly, there was always likely to be a wide spectrum of beach hut internal decor, from top spec to the less salubrious, but this hut appeared to double as a time capsule. The inside looked as if it had been untouched for decades.

The interior walls and ceiling had been gloss painted white at some distant point in the past and had since slid a few notches on the colour chart to something approaching cream. They were bare save for a row of metal coat hangers fixed to the left-hand side wall and a lonely, high level, red fire extinguisher on the other. The far end wall boasted a small, centrally located opening window with a single wall cupboard to its side. Below the window, positioned asymmetrically and hard against the fire extinguisher wall, stood a conjoined double and single floor unit topped by a chipped marble-patterned rolled edge worktop. Three rows of naff tiling, boasting cracked and missing grouting, completed an unappealing splashback of sorts. The four doors attached to the wall and floor units – avocado green to clash hideously with the marble-patterned worktop – were hanging at an angle emanating 'jaunty', if appertaining to headwear, but, in this context, asthmatically gasped 'fucked'.

On the disgustingly scuffed and worn linoleum floor, one looking like it had been danced on for weeks by a horde of sandpaper-shod ravers high on crystal meth, sat a cheap single burner cooking stove. It lay brooding in the corner, in the gap between the left-hand side wall and the end panel of the floor units. It was the type that ran on an internal butane/propane canister and retailed in high-end camping equipment outlets – like Halfords – for under twenty quid. Taking on the air of a naughty schoolboy sent to the corner, the stove nevertheless laid claim to being the hut's one and only appliance.

I viewed the stove with bemusement, wondering what it was doing on the floor. I hazarded the previous owners had left it, rather than bother to lug it anywhere, because it was worthless. The idea of trying to ignite it, considering the composition and close confines of the structure it sat in, brought to mind the actions of a madman or a pyromaniac, irrespective of the presence of a fire extinguisher.

21

"Isn't it wonderful?" Kevin gushed unprovoked, turning on the spot in a gesture I suspected he had perfected over hundreds of repeated property showings, his hands expansive on arms angled up from his elbows.

My time absorbing the dire interior had caused a conversational deficit. I hadn't uttered a single word since entering the beach hut and Kevin, well aware of the universally-accepted fact sales pitches abhor a vacuum, had rushed to fill it. I batted away his enthusiasm with a dour response.

"The interior's pretty tired. It needs a complete refit."

Kevin ignored my comment. "These huts are wonderful. No running water, no electricity and no mains drainage," he enthused, listing the hut's debatable USPs.

"But now you're going to tell me it's still got its own dedicated wi-fi."

"No. *No!* There's no wi-fi. You don't *need* wi-fi. That's the whole point. You don't need *any* of the things I mentioned. All those modern amenities simply aren't necessary. That's the point. That's the *charm* of the place. It's retro. It's staycation, now that Brex…"

"Please! Not the B-word. Don't say the B-word. Everyone's had quite enough of *all* the B-words."

"'Words'?" Kevin queried.

'Boris', I mouthed, like I was saying something indelicate behind the back of an elderly relative.

Kevin's head indicated his acquiescence. "It's the ultimate time warp staycation," he continued, his face now sporting a smarmy grin. "And you *can* get a signal. Phone and internet," he added. "Let's not get too carried away. We're not completely cut off in Southburgh. Everyone needs to keep in touch."

I pulled out my smartphone to check. "Three bars and 4G. Technology lives. Even here. Who would have thought it? Does that mean I can download potable water?" I asked as it dawned on me I hadn't seen a tap anywhere.

22

"Ah, well, you see, there you have it. That is why this particular hut is considered prime location. There's a drinking water tap only fifty yards away," Kevin indicated, pointing further down the promenade "The café, very good food, coffee and cakes, is only another forty."

"Only fifty yards? Do I have to manually pump it up?" I asked with a touch of sarcasm.

"No. Just turn the tap on."

"And boiling a kettle?"

Kevin pointed to the stove. "Not too sure what that's still doing here, but something similar would boil a kettle in no time. If you wanted a fry up and a full English breakfast at the same time as you sat gazing out over a perfect blue sea, it might be worth investing in something a little more modern. One with a double burner?" he suggested.

"What about a fridge? For all those roasting hot summer days, mill pond seas and shimmering cloudless blue skies I'm imagining right now."

"You bring a cool box. Keep it in the back in the shade and your drinks and food will keep all day. Not a problem. You don't *need* electricity. You see, owning a beach hut is all about adjusting and tweaking yourself to a different set of values. It's half the fun. Going back in time a little."

"I guess we'd all like to be able to do that. To go back in time to a simpler age," I conceded.

"Well, in Southburgh, you can. It's the town's speciality," Kevin said earnestly. "It's why people come," he said, getting into his stride for the hard sell. "It's mainly families. Three generations together quite often. They come here to spend a traditional week or two beside the seaside beside the sea. It's often generational, a tradition passed down from one to the other. But shared. That's the important bit. Sharing time *talking* to each other away from all those horrid screens." I nodded, but not too enthusiastically.

23

"People buy, rather than rent, because they want involvement and, let's be honest, the kudos of owning a beach hut in Southburgh." He paused. "How old are your children?" he asked.

"Oh," I answered, feeling my face flush. "I haven't any. Recently divorced. My wife is, was, a few years younger than me. We never thought the time was quite right to start a family. Probably for the best as it turned out."

Kevin's countenance flashed alarm. "I'm sorry..." he replied, his voice trailing off as he grappled with the unsettling reasons why a recently divorced childless man might want to buy a beach hut.

"I'm looking for somewhere to chill," I explained, trying to help us both out of a hole. The last thing I wanted was to come across as... what? A potential mass murderer, a sexual predator, something even worse. "I've always loved the seaside. I came here for several holidays many years ago with my mother and her parents. Three generations, as you rightly say. Now I'm looking for a space to heal. To sort myself out. It's been a very traumatic time... the divorce. And my mother has struggled to come to terms with the recent death of my father. That's affected me greatly too. It's been tough."

Kevin relaxed. "Absolutely," he gushed on an exhalation of breath. "I can imagine. Very difficult. Once you're here, I'm sure your stress and worries will leave you. If you love the seaside, then Southburgh will love you back. That's what I always tell people," he added. "We're a classy seaside resort. You won't find a single slot machine on the whole of the seafront. Nor any tacky shops selling seaside tat. We're a cut above. For someone looking to relax in a refined atmosphere, by the sea, we're unmatchable. It's why our clients are prepared to pay handsomely to own their little slice of it."

"Moving on from the positives, tell me the ugly stuff. The nitty-gritty. Rents, leases, hut migration, insurance. What I can and can't do in my beach hut should I buy it."

"Well, you can't sleep in it overnight," Kevin answered. "But no one's going to mind if you stay an hour or so after dark. Other than that, as long as what you're doing doesn't inconvenience or annoy anyone and your behaviour is socially acceptable, you can pretty much please yourself. As to the nitty-gritty as you term it, the leases on these huts are of thirty years duration and contain an option to renew again nearer the expiry date. The rent is payable to the district council and, as I said earlier, they do offer you a rebate towards the cost of moving the hut to its winter location. The rent is currently around fifty pounds a month including the dreaded VAT. The hut must be insured, be well maintained externally, and initially you have to purchase a Licence to Assign to take possession from the district council freeholder. On the plus side, you are free to rent the hut out to other families and this season over the summer months you'd easily get two hundred and fifty a week. Possibly more. If you were to sell it and make a profit, and I would expect you to do so, even after only a year, that's subject to capital gains tax."

"What about the neighbours?" I asked with a smile.

"Whoever you get will be nice. I can guarantee it."

"So nothing at all sordid or unscrupulous goes on in Southburgh?"

Kevin laughed. "Not unless you regard an art shop asking two hundred and fifty pounds for a framed picture taken by a local photographer as sordid and unscrupulous."

"Remind me of the hut's asking price again."

"Eighty thousand." Kevin's voice took on a harder edge. The end game was approaching.

"Would your client take seventy-five? It *is* in need of a serious revamp."

Kevin's faced creased in mock agony. "Unfortunately, I'm all too aware they wouldn't accept that figure, I'm afraid."

"What if I were to offer another thousand?"

"Seventy-*six*?" Kevin responded.

"Yes."

Kevin nodded. "You know, I think there's a strong chance the owners will run with that. Look, if we're done here, let's go back to the office where I'm certain we can finalise things. A few phone calls and I think we can tie this up pretty rapidly."

I nodded my agreement. Four grand. An ego-boosting saving and ample for me to return at Easter, stay in a local B&B, and revamp the hut internally. My new life was on the verge of starting. All that was left to do now was pay for it. And then live it.

BD (Before Divorce)

"*Here* they are! We thought you weren't coming. You're not still brooding over that missed smash are you, Paul?"

Looking to see where the voice was coming from, I pulled a face and wafted an insouciant hand in its general direction to indicate nothing could be further from the truth. Desperately trying to create a believable smile on my face, Chloe and I had no option other than to walk hand in hand across the busy hotel function room towards the source of the taunting words. The Winstones. Steven, enthusiastically beckoning us towards him, and Emily, cool and motionless alongside, were seated on two barstools with drinks in their hands. As usual, the pair were radiating an aura of good health, good looks and extreme affluence. Rumour had it Steven's annual salary, as the CEO of a mid-sized firm of financial advisors, bested mine as a mere college lecturer by a factor of ten. Emily, his beautiful wife of less than a year – a part-time freelance something or other – had youth on her side. Nine years younger than Steven, Emily had yet to hit thirty.

Once within a couple of yards of them, I experienced the full force of their superiority bubble. A tangible frisson making a small part of me feel in awe of them, desire to be like them and want to be incorporated by them into their social circle. Running parallel to this sat diametric feelings of resentment, envy and dislike. Of Steven, predominantly. The galling truth, especially for those with bigger egos than mine – and there were plenty present tonight – lay in everyone's collective inability to challenge the Winstones' 'Stardust Couple' epitaph. Thanks to that missed smash of mine, Chloe and I couldn't even lay claim to the far less glamorous title of 'Senior Mixed Doubles Champions'.

Emily and Steven had arrived earlier in his brand new company Audi R8 V10. I had spotted it in the car park lording it over all the other cars when our taxi dropped us off. Parked centrally for maximum exposure, it sat there sucking up attention thanks to its audacious looks and design. Ones physically depicting its unquestionable technology, speed, power and expense. Despite the Audi's delicious drivability, if Steven stuck to form, the car wouldn't be making the return journey home when expected. Instead, it would be shunned by its drunken driver as he staggered into an Uber and only retrieved once he had sobered up. The Audi's single-legged role designed only with the sole intention of reflecting an aura of glamour upon its owner. To be conspicuously flashed as an object of desire. One of at least two Steven currently held in his possession.

From close range, I wilfully gave Emily's legs a thorough examination. Bronze, svelte and slick with moisturiser, one long, lithe, tanned limb lay crossed over the other as she sat on her stool sipping her drink. I had little doubt her expensive, long black dress – daring slashes either side to the upper thigh – had been purchased precisely with her current pose in mind. She had probably even rehearsed her current pose in the master bedroom of their wonderful home (valued at two million quid plus as verified by myself, via Zoopla, in a moment of tragic inadequacy two days ago). No one could argue Emily hadn't nailed the pose. She looked stunning.

Happy to have reset the balance sheet somewhat – Chloe accused me without foundation therefore I get a free hit – I lifted my eyes from their leggy feast, only to awkwardly catch Emily's during transition to a more orthodox level.

"What can I get you two runners-up?" Steven asked Chloe, a smug smirk on his lips.

"Glass of red, please, Steven," Chloe responded, upbeat without a trace of humiliation.

"Corona Extra," I answered more sullenly.

"There you go, Paul," Steven said, peeling off a twenty and a ten pound note from a considerable wedge, head nodding towards the bar. "Be a star. Scotch on the rocks for me and a gin and tonic for Emily," he added, waving the notes at me.

"Sure," I responded flatly, taking them from his hand.

Moving off, I made a mental note not to offer him his change back, just to see if he would have the cheek to ask for it.

"My word you're looking gorgeous tonight, Chloe," I heard Steven growl lasciviously as I headed towards the bar, convincing me he wasn't on his first drink of the evening. "Come and stand next to me so I'm completely surrounded by beautiful women. Oi! Don't rush back, Paul. I'm fine here with the girls," I heard him shout towards my back.

I looked over my shoulder to see Steven yank Chloe towards him with a tentacle arm snaked around her waist. In response, she shrieked at being tugged backwards on to his lap. An exclamation, I moodily judged, more shaded by delight than alarm. Shrugging it off, and attempting to ignore the commotion behind me, I pushed further into the mass of bodies waiting at the bar, many of whom were also distracted by the commotion. Despite my sulky mood, I had to concede wherever Steven and Emily deigned to go, heads always turned. At him for his behaviour, at her for her looks.

28

Waiting to be served, I disinterestedly scanned the room and the surrounding bar throng. The odd face I only ever encountered on a tennis court sporadically registering. Jim; a player prone to serial double faulting. Alice; a ladies fourth team player who could lob for England. Dean; a teenager on a crusade to hit every tennis shot he played as hard as possible, irrespective of accuracy. Joyce; a retired old dear who had refined the uncanny knack of incorrect court positioning to an art form, thus ensuring all her shots were half-volleys. Michael; the not-proud-at-all owner of a rally-killing, single-use backhand and Jill; a solid player with iffy spatial aware-ness leading to her specialised trait of baseline volleying.

These players, along with everyone else present, were attending the tennis club's annual prize-giving evening held at The Royale Hotel, as tradition dictated, on the first Saturday evening after club finals day. If past form was anything to go by, the night would pan out into a strange combination of drunken fun and laughter, divi-sion by cliques, uniform dire dancing – with the odd youthful exception – and a clichéd smattering of one-sided sexual attraction. These cases of unreciprocated lust invariably between several of the club's officially ticketed 'Rich Elderly Bored Housewives' – who were *always* terrible players – and the young male coaches who suffered the twice weekly indignation of being their hired eye-candy ball machines.

Occasionally, more reciprocated and less extreme attractions – inter-member infatuation – manifested themselves on awards night. I could recall bearing witness to two major alcohol-fuelled indiscretions over the years. One brief, if extremely boisterous, knee-trembler in a men's toilet cubicle – I had been doing my own business in the adjacent trap – and one blowjob in the hotel grounds. On that occasion, I had rushed outside on the verge of puking and accidentally stumbled across them mid act. It was dark, I was drunk, but I could still recognise who did the sucking and who was the suckee. To be fair, they were a married couple – just

29

not to each other.

Downgrading from those two explicit acts of lust and betrayal, sat a succession of more everyday peccadilloes; stolen kisses, drunken fumbles and a host of flirtatious conversations, acts often committed by people I had previously considered to be rather stilted and reserved. It always fascinated me, watching the membership off court and under the influence of alcohol (or something else) when social constraint veneers weathered off certain members as if captured by time lapse photography. Others noticed it too. The gossip from awards night flew around the club for weeks after, much to the shame and mortification of those involved.

As well as sexual indiscretions, both major and minor, over time I had also been told of many old feuds flamboyantly verbalised to me by a legion of drug-loosened tongues. Feuds caused by long ago, but never forgotten, bad line calls, lost matches (I'm a union card-holding member of that sub-section), the non-inclusion in specific social fours and the non-selection for any number of the club's various teams. Naturally, this being England and tennis being the most polite and middle-class of all sports, none of these grievances were ever uttered to those who had supposedly caused the original offence. Adulterous sex in a cubicle or a blow job in the car park – fine. Inappropriate, politically incorrect sexual behaviour – not a problem. Challenging someone over a bad line call from five years ago, not being asked to play team tennis or not being included in a Wednesday morning four at ten, tea and biscuits after – highly taboo.

Disregarding sexual motive and the unburdening of ancient enmity, the category of braggadocio heralded the last of awards night's three main conversational themes. Name dropping of top universities offspring were attending; fabulous holiday destinations; expensive new cars awaiting pick up in high-end Teutonic showrooms; outlandish materialistic purchases from five figure vinyl turntables to ten figure saucer-sized watches; glorious second properties in dazzling foreign locations; the forensic revelation of vocational bonuses and the general grandstanding of lives all reared their ugly heads. Somehow, for whatever reason – alcohol + captive audience + opulent environment – the charged atmosphere of awards night elicited a turbo-charged version of everyday tennis club life, where all response and actions veered towards the grotesque. Looking to get a handle on how the sharp-elbowed middle classes operate? Come join our club, attend our awards night and watch how we play.

For those members more financially impeded or lacking any bragging rights – me, obviously – the only effective answer in the game of club one-upmanship is to be good at tennis. On court, all social standing is immediately countermanded by the ability to hit a yellow ball over the net with a racket. By losing to Steven and Emily, Chloe and I had missed out on the one opportunity where we could compete and stand a chance of beating them. The fact our Senior Mixed Doubles Final was contested by two married couples had without doubt made matters worse. In the past, Chloe and I had lost to Steven twice before in the mixed final when he had part-nered different women – *always* the club's strongest female player – before his whirlwind romance and marriage to Emily. On those occasions, defeat hadn't cut so deep. One married couple facing another married couple had altered the dynamic completely, ramping up the tension not only between the two pairs, but also *within* each pair. Increased anxiety had made me miss that smash, increased stress had created Chloe's wild accusation and losing had devastated us. Stuck at an awards night with the prospect of me and Chloe picking up yet another gallant runners-up medal, to later put in the attic, while being constantly patronised by Steven Winstone, was not my idea of a fun night out.

Secretly mulling over the defeat, I wondered if Steven's decision to ask Emily to marry him had rested heavily on her tennis skills. A

31

good county senior, Emily staked claim to being the best female player the club had ever seen. Looking back, Steven's interest in her was evident from the minute he saw her play, yet few of us thought it would culminate in marriage. Steven seemed set in his ways as a serial monogamist, chopping and changing his gorgeous women with the same regularity he did his cars. With Emily's arrival those habits stopped dead in their tracks, her strong game presumably ticking the final box. Why she accepted such a rushed proposal from a man nine years her elder was another matter entirely. I doubted it had anything to do with his decent serve-and-volley game.

Returning with the drinks, I saw my best friend, James, engaged in conversation with the three others. Like me, James had been a junior at the club and we had known and played tennis with each other for well over twenty years. To my irritation, I also noticed Chloe had only managed to edge marginally off Steven's lap and his arm was still around her. Not satisfied with getting his hands on the Senior Mixed Doubles trophy, it seemed Steven was keen to run them over my wife.

"James, how's it going? Sorry, I haven't got one for you," I exclaimed trying to be chipper while offering the clutch of drinks clasped in both hands to Chloe, Emily and Steven.

"That's okay. I'm good, thanks," he replied, holding up a near-full glass of lager. "I only came over because I've got something to show you. My Mum found it the other day when she was having a clear out." James extracted a battered and dog-eared six by four colour print from the back pocket of his chinos and passed it to me. "Look at this. Junior finals day 1999."

I took the photo from him and eagerly scanned the faces of twenty or so keen teenage tennis protégés.

"Oh. My. God. Look at us! Look at Jennifer. Melissa and Emma's hair. Your shorts. My crap top."

"Remember that guy?" James asked, poking a finger at the tallest boy.

"Yes. Jason Jeffries. JJ. What a case he was!" I remarked, shaking my head in disbelief at some of the memories flooding back. "You don't remember him, do you?" I asked Chloe. She shook her head. "No. Of course. He left long before you joined."

"I think 'got kicked out' is the technical term you're looking for," James interjected.

"Good point," I replied. "JJ was mayhem personified. He stole his mother's bar key once, when she was social secretary, and they found him the next morning drunk and unconscious on the club-house floor. Unbelievable! Do you remember the time the club chairman caught him riding that stolen moped around the courts with the floodlights on? He'd tried to pull a wheelie and crashed it into one of the nets and got tangled up in it."

James exploded into a cackle of laughter. "Or that time he brought an air rifle up the club and started putting holes in the advertising banners," he said, adding to the list of JJ anecdotes.

"He sounds a bit mental," Chloe commented, unimpressed. "No wonder he got thrown out."

"The thing was," I responded, irritated by her gruff response to my fond memories, "he was a fantastic player. Really talented. He played Junior Wimbledon. He was so good he should have been better," I said, rolling out one of my favourite stock phrases. "It was a shame he got pushed out. I haven't seen him or heard from him since, I don't think anyone has. Everyone liked him despite his crazy behaviour. The juniors that is. I think the committee hated him," I quantified.

James nodded enthusiastically as he took the photo back from me. "Cheers... Well, I'd better leave you four to it," he said. "Catch you later. I've *got* to show this to Emma."

"Cheers, James," I answered.

"Bye, James," Emily said pleasantly.

Steven and Chloe only nodded, appearing less than impressed with my brief wander down memory lane.

Once James was out of earshot, Steven stuck out a hand. "Change, please," he demanded.

"'Change, please'. Give me my fucking change, please. I only earn over 300k a year and need it to buy some lube because I'm a non-stop *wanker*," I complained to Chloe in a whiny voice.

It was three hours later, the presentations had been made and I was pretty drunk. Steven and Emily had held up the silver Senior Mixed Doubles trophy like they had won the Champions League. Grudgingly, I knew the pictures would look fantastic on social media – but not if I remembered to unfriend or unfollow them first.

"Shut up, Paul. What is it with you and Steven?"

"Nothing. Apart from the fact he's an arrogant, conceited dick."

"He's good looking and talented. Business and tennis. Deal with it. We could have beaten them and stolen their moment in the sun, but we didn't. And we both know why."

"Fucking great," I hissed. "Still banging on about that are you? Pleased you think he's so good looking and successful, though. Fancy him do you? Now you've got to sit on his lap for an hour," I slurred. "Was his dick hard?"

"Grow up," Chloe sneered, turning and striding away from the edge of the dance floor where we were standing.

Not quite drunk enough to have lost all self-awareness, I turned and walked off – in the opposite direction. I didn't want to be seen standing solo, staring at the dance floor's sweaty worshippers gyrating to an eclectic mix of decade-spanning music. And I definitely didn't want to follow my wife.

An alcoholic fog, coupled with a juddering mental playback of our dumb argument, saw me stumble out of the function room and into another area of the hotel. The drop in temperature and the relative quietness soon snapped me back into the real world. Blinking, I slowly began to take in reality. To my surprise, I saw Emily sitting on her own on a cream-coloured leather sofa in an otherwise empty reception area. I walked over to her.

"What are you doing out here?" I asked, picking my words out with tweezers in an attempt to hide the fact I was drunk.

"Too hot. Too noisy. Feeling a bit rough. Probably had too much to drink," Emily said in short staccato bursts, her eyelids half closed. "You?"

"Same. Needed some cool," I replied, mimicking her speech pattern. "Steven?" I asked.

"Pissed. Dancing," she replied, flinging a 'whatever' hand in the air.

Her answer gave me licence and, emboldened, I sat next to her. As soon as my arse touched cream-coloured leather I realised my inebriated brain had miscalculated and I had moved in too close. Violating her personal space, I became acutely aware of how one of my thighs was now in direct contact with one of Emily's bare legs. I looked down slowly, mesmerised, for visual confirmation. When I looked back up, I caught Emily's eye for the second time that evening.

"Do you like looking at my legs? That's twice I've caught you," she enquired without malice, her hand lifting a long tress of jet-black hair off her face.

I felt myself glow white hot with embarrassment.

"Sorry," I murmured. "Miscalculated."

"That's okay," she replied casually, the row of z's ending her first word hinting at her alcoholic consumption. "I can't really complain, can I? Not when I'm wearing a dress like this," she explained, motioning the parted fingers of both hands downwards across her midriff and onwards to her thighs. "Pretty much however I walk, however I sit, wherever you look, you see leg." She paused for a few seconds as if weighing up something in her head. "Steven chose this dress for me," she confirmed, tilting her head towards me. "He so wanted me to wear it tonight. He said I'd be the star of the show. He said nobody would be able to take their eyes off me."

"He was right. The man's a genius," I said laughing.

Emily smiled at my joke and my heart did a strange sort of flutter.

"I have noticed, over our short wedded life, how he rather likes to show off his possessions," she admitted, turning her gaze away from me and sending it mid-distance to the far wall.

"Chloe thought I missed that smash on our set point because I was distracted by your legs," I blurted, shocked at my out-of-control loquacious mouth.

Emily's head turned slowly back to me and her inquisitive hazel eyes searched for mine. "And did you?" she asked coquettishly, one corner of her mouth lifted upward in a semi smile.

I could sense I was losing control and becoming further overwhelmed by the close proximity of her beauty. Frantically, I tried to wrestle back my composure. This was precisely how you became tennis club gossip.

"No," I answered slowly and then, as if in an out-of-body experience, heard myself say. "I was... am... more interested in what's between them."

Emily carried on staring at me, her expression unchanged. I braced myself for the inevitable withering riposte/smack in the face/punch in the gonads.

Instead, she put her hand around the back of my neck and pulled me in to kiss her. Her mouth felt warm and velvety to my tongue. It tasted of gin and tonic. For the five minutes we sat alone kissing, I never once mentioned how distraught I had been at losing a tennis match to her.

AD

The Vice-Principal sat behind a pile of documents strewn over a desk only half as plush as the one I saw in Furlington's office a few days earlier. Malcolm Green was probably around the same age as my divorce solicitor, (early sixties), but on this particular Monday morning he looked a decade older. So battered and sleep deprived did he appear, I wondered if someone had set about him in his sleep – a professional cage fighter perhaps.

"I had notification, late on Friday, from whom we are going to be receiving a visit," he declared in his archaic syntax, face haggard and puffy, dark voluminous bags under his eyes, hair side-parted millimetres above a left ear and grown long to fashion a comedy comb-over. A laughable attempt to conceal his pink-domed, male pattern baldness that served only to emphasise it.

I shifted uneasily in my seat. This statement and his beaten up demeanour could only mean one thing.

"The Big O?" I ventured.

"You have it in one, young man," he answered. "*Ofsted* are coming." The first word was virtually spat out. "Not a good time if I'm being honest... Never is, I suppose," he admitted. "But now... Now is particularly difficult." Malcolm let out a sigh and turned his watery eyes to mine. "As you know all too well, there are an awful lot of bubbling pots I need to keep lids on at this juncture. Unfortunately, as of late, there is now another one on the point of boiling over. One you *can't* know about," he said pointedly. "The last thing I need is an external set of prying eyes barging into the kitchen and asking what's cooking."

"When are they due to come?" I asked, mentally noting the enigmatic new bubbler.

"The week after the Easter holiday."

I registered my surprise. "How come you know so early?"

Malcolm looked upwards as if to indicate divine intervention. "I'm very lucky, *very* lucky, to have an old school friend who still works for Ofsted. He's been kind enough to put me in the picture and give me the inside track," Malcolm replied. "Very poor form, of course, as far as they're concerned. He'd be hauled over the coals if it ever came to light."

"So not common knowledge?"

"Good God, no. Only you, me, the principal and the chairman of the governors know about it. It'll be our little secret…" Malcolm said with a feeble simper, his two rheumy orbs searching my face for something.

Mystified, I could only stare back at him, my face as blank as the pieces of paper on which the construction lecturers were supposed to write their lesson plans. The last Mocksted inspection had picked up on it. Construction, in general, weren't too happy about the criticism. The Plumbing Lecturer had been especially forthright when reprimanded, informing his line manager, while menacingly waggling a set of stilsons under his nose, that he could 'Fucking do one. And so can your fucking lesson plans'.

"Don't you remember that seventies western series, Alias Smith and Jones?" Malcolm enquired, his expression hopeful. "It's a line from the opening…" His voice petered out. "No. You wouldn't. Sorry. You're far too young. I'm losing the plot. Only trying to lighten the mood a little," he added, a desperate grin still held on his face as if at gunpoint.

I nodded sympathetically. Malcolm was only giving me a heads up regards Ofsted because I was so close to him. Because he had been such a dear friend and colleague of my late father. Dad and Malcolm had known each other, worked with each other, socialised with each other and played golf with each other for nearly forty years. Since Malcolm had moved to take up his position at my college, a year after Dad's death, the vocational link between the Greens and the Chambers had once again been reinstated. Desperately missing Dad, or so I assumed, Malcolm started to confide in the next best option – me – virtually from the offset. Senior management secrets soon followed.

Dad and Malcolm had been joined at the hip for decades and, in a way, as Dad's best friend, it was fitting Malcolm had been there at the end – to share my father's last few seconds on Earth, cradling him to his scrawny chest, tears in his eyes, as Dad's life quietly and quickly ebbed away on the seventeenth fairway of their favourite golf club. 'The Cardiac Hole', is the name the members blackly give it. Par is a tee shot of over two-hundred yards down into a deep valley followed by a long iron approach to a highly elevated plateau green where two solid putts sees you home and hosed. On the fateful day, Dad hit a nice drive and his second, a good shot by all accounts, landed pin high and twelve feet to the right of the flag. Keen to see what putt he had left for his birdie, Dad strode off up the arduous incline with his half set golf bag slung over his shoulder. Fifty yards later, he collapsed and died. The post mortem revealed he had suffered a massive heart attack, one that would have killed him anywhere in the world apart from inside a modern cardiac ward, let alone isolated from medical care on a golf course. Dad remains the latest fatality, but was still the fifth golfer to lose his life on that hole since the course opened in 1984. My father's commemorative plaque now hangs with four others above the bar in the clubhouse. Not so much a bogey five as a body count of five.

This happened over three years ago, and Mum, apparently released from the shackles of a dull, loveless marriage – according to her – has spectacularly metamorphosised into a new woman. She is now Mum 2.0 and to the amazement of everybody who knows her, and to my utter incredulity, she has resolutely dumped her previous identity – a shy, quiet, slightly dowdy, stay-at-home housewife – and embraced a completely new persona. One who is fiery, assertive, loves foreign travel, expensive clothing and, most shockingly of all, the pursuit of younger men. Her new wardrobe, high end make-up and fuck-me footwear – she's always in heels – combined with her personality change, make her virtually unrecognisable from the sepia version of her past.

Without Dad, but with the money he left to her via his life insurance policies and teaching pension, my mother has dressed up, stepped out and embraced a myriad of sexual dalliances with a seemingly never-ending supply of men at least ten years younger than her. She fritters away money holidaying abroad with them, wining and dining with them and buying designer-labelled clothing, make-up and perfume to make herself more attractive to them. This step change commenced, with indecent haste in my eyes, a mere four months after Dad's funeral. How she's managed to adapt so quickly and so easily into her new world, I'm not too sure. But my word, has she. And each day she does so with the vivacious carpe diem mentality of the person who fears there might not be a tomorrow.

"There might not be a tomorrow for all I know, Paul. I might die in my sleep tonight," she replied when I first tackled her over my concerns about her behaviour. "Look what happened to your father. No one saw that coming."

"I'm sure you won't die in your sleep, Mum," I replied, snidely. "I'm pretty certain all those different men you invite back to the bed you used to share with Dad will keep you awake."

"I was in a loveless marriage for over thirty years. *Now's* the time to make up for it," she countered tartly, taking a sip from her glass of red, the colour of her drink co-ordinated with her nail varnish and lipstick.

"So how come *I'm* here if it was so loveless?" I mocked.

"You? God knows how we managed to produce *you*. The fertility stars must have aligned on that joyous occasion," she said, laughing bitterly before her face slowly clouded with self-reflection. "You know, looking back, now he's dead, I wonder what it was that ever attracted me to your father in the first place." I shrugged sarcastically at her question. "Older man infatuation and his intelligence, I suppose. Your father didn't exactly have much else going for him. Maybe it had more to do with my amazing naivety, at feeling so flattered and grateful for receiving his attention, worthless as it turned out to be," she said nastily, answering

40

her own query before levelling a vindictive index finger at me. "I've never spelt this out before, Paul, but seeing as you brought the matter up, let me inform you that your father was more in love with the golf club than he was with me. He didn't die from a heart attack in a passionate bout of making love to me, he died from one playing *golf*. Now *that* tells you everything you need to know about our relationship. He might have provided financially, but emotionally and sexually, forget it." Another mouthful of red passed her glossed lips. "I'm still in my fifties," she declared. "Remarkably, I've recently discovered I *am* attractive to men. They say I've got a great figure, dress fantastically, look well-groomed and don't look my age at all." My mother let out a self-gratified snort of laughter. "Men… *want* me!" she exclaimed as if it was the most obvious thing in the world. "After all those years of one man *not* wanting me."

"Or they want your money," I countered bitterly.

"No, I can assure you it's not the money, Paul," she told me categorically, a knowing smile on her face. "You see, what you can't appreciate, now I'm finally being treated like a proper woman after all those years of being discarded, is how much I rather like it. I've rediscovered desire. I *want* to be touched. I *have* a libido. A powerful libido. Who would have thought? After it lying dormant for so long." My mother eyed me coolly. "And I shall continue to submit to it whether you like it or not." My mother suddenly erupted with indignant fire. "Do you know, your father never even made love to me on our wedding night? He said he was 'too tired'. How horrible and spiteful of him," she said shaking her head in vehement disbelief. "I was only twenty. Young, impressionable. In love with a man who, it turned out, didn't love me back." She stared at me. "Don't put your father on a pedestal, Paul. Not when he doesn't deserve it. And certainly don't criticise me for grabbing a late-in-life chance of happiness."

"Well, I'm sorry, but I am criticising you, Mum," I replied. "It's

41

all too convenient for you to blame Dad now he's not here to defend himself. Turning him into some kind of monster." I curled my lip in resentment. "Besides, if he was that bad, why didn't you just clear off and leave him years ago?"

My mother snorted derisively. "One day *you* might find out what it's like to be rejected," she said, all too prophetically as it turned out. "To be constantly rebuffed by the one you married, cold-shouldered night after night to the point you lose all self-worth. How do you imagine that *feels*?" My mother's diatribe faded into contemplation. "But, no. You're right. I should have left him. Regretfully, I lacked the conviction. The sad reality is your father whittled my confidence away to nothing. I simply felt too ugly and too frightened to leave."

"Was it *really* like that, though? Or are you just making it up?" I questioned. "I don't remember it like that."

"Yes, it bloody well was like that!" my mother exploded. "And no, I'm not making it up. I might have hidden it from you as you were growing up, very successfully it appears, but your father had *zero* interest in me. Work and golf, yes. But not me." My mother looked pityingly my way. "Truth is, he didn't have a lot of time for you, either. He was the one who insisted on sending you to boarding school, not me. And ask yourself this, did *he* ever take you to tennis lessons when you were back home? Or did I do it? Did he ever play with you when you were little, or was that me too? Why do you think my parents came with us on holiday? Don't you remember how his summer holidays were always taken with the golf club crowd, or have you conveniently forgotten that fact?" I felt my mouth dry and I swallowed nothing into the sickened pit of my stomach. Seeing me on the ropes, my mother went in for the kill. "The only thing your father did for you was *pay* for you. He bought your education, paid for your tennis coaching and gave you a deposit for the house you bought with Chloe. It cost him nothing in terms of time, effort and engagement. It might have impressed you, going to a nice school, having lots of one-to-one tennis coaching and getting on the housing ladder, but the harsh reality is, for all of your life, he bought you off. I even had to twist his arm over the tennis lessons. Your father hated tennis. Hated it because you liked it more than golf."

"That's not true," I argued. "It was Dan Maskell's fault. Dad said he hated tennis because he couldn't stand Dan Maskell's sibilant voice, whistling its way all over the BBC's coverage of Wimbledon."

"Listen to yourself, Paul. An education like yours and you believe that? And you ended up a *teacher*. Your father might have failed to mould your sport choices, but he sure got you career-wise." I felt my bottom lip wobble. Hopelessly, I Googled the search engine in my head for 'pithy comebacks' and got no matching results. "Do you want to know how many times we had sex in over thirty years of marriage?" my mother teased, her voice enamelled with derision.

"No, I don't!"

"Six!" she said gleefully, her expression revelling in the awkwardness of mine. "You're a statistical anomaly. A probability breaker. It's why you're an only child… like me."

Sometimes I dream about my mother and every time I do, I end up killing her. I bludgeon her to death with one of Dad's golf clubs. The blood-splattered six iron the weapon of choice, the one I repeatedly swing to cleave open her skull. In the background, as I'm manically swinging, I hear Dad's voice saying, "Good shot, son. Good shot. You'd never have been able to do that sort of damage with a tennis racket."

The early stages of Mum's new life became an annoying, intermittent background noise, happenstance – the unseen producer – fading it in and out on the mixing deck of my life as it saw fit. Little did I realise, with my mother striding off down a new fork in her life, I would shortly be forced down one of my own. No wonder I got messed up so badly. Her wanton sex life rampaging onwards, cranked to the max, mine marooned like a ship wallowing in the Doldrums – although, admittedly, one manned by a crew with high speed internet access to pornography.

Today, my feelings towards her have shifted slightly and I can't deny Mum's words have had an effect on me. Her continued insistence of the veracity of them and my continued reflection over time have made me reconsider my stance. I do now concede that Dad did go on an awful lot of summer golfing holidays, most of them with Malcolm and other golf club cronies in tow. It's also true to say, as a direct cause, Mum and I did go on the vast majority of summer vacations without him and Mum's parents invariably filled the void Dad left. Mum was the one who always took me to tennis and Dad did get the hump when I opted on picking up a tennis racket as opposed to golf clubs. And it is possible, I guess, she could have successfully hidden her unhappy plight away from me as I grew up. I attended boarding school from the age of seven until eighteen, then went straight to university, and wasn't at home an awful lot throughout that long period of time.

Whenever I returned home, as far as I can recollect, everything seemed fine and nothing appeared overly untoward. It certainly never crossed my mind Mum and Dad might have any issues between them. My thoughts were firmly focussed on playing tennis and any upcoming seaside holidays that might be in the pipeline. Dad didn't come on those holidays, but so what? That was the norm. It was the default situation going right back to my toddler years. In retrospect, it appears I had became conditioned to the status quo to the point of blind acceptance. Maybe Mum had become conditioned to it too, only able to break free once Dad had passed.

After university and teacher training – Dad did vigorously encourage me down the educational career path – I moved into a rented house, which I shared with three other university friends who were all moving into the world of work. My life revolved around teaching, tennis and trying to sleep with women. Not agonising over my parents' relationship or whether they were having sex or not. What child would ever expend energy raking over such a gross subject matter?

The answer to that question, at this point in time, is me.

Despite these admissions, I still can't bring myself to whole-heartedly accept my mother's words. I see them as an exaggeration of a truth I've never recognised with my own eyes. It's only her truth I get to hear now Dad has died and I'm minded to call it a 'justification truth'. A truth spoken by her, for her, to rationalise the fact she's been turned, by Dad's money, into a financially-enriched, head-strong cougar. Thanks to my recent divorce, this present dynamic is not without irony. As it stands, my mother and I are both single, the difference being she's getting it and I'm not. It's now my turn to harbour grave doubts over my attractiveness and to feel rejected, unwanted and unloved. The pair of us exist in a counterintuitive sexual universe; one where I'm constantly left to wonder whether she laughs out loud at me every time she has an orgasm. For the record, I don't laugh out loud at her when I'm having one at the end of masturbating. I don't even crack a smile.

The titbits of privileged college information Malcolm willingly shares with me, whether serious, as today's, or scandalous as in other instances, are not meant for the likes of my ears. They should remain the sole preserve of senior management, for those way above my status and pay grade as a mere lecturer. Often shocking and entertaining in equal measure, these morsels of madness come with strings attached, namely the implicit demand of me keeping them to myself. Frustratingly, the frequently lurid tales of hapless mismanagement, back-stabbing, empire-building, financial inepti-tude and bizarre behaviour among the senior management are exactly the type of anecdote I would love to relate to fellow members of the teaching staff. If only to confirm their complete lack of faith in the senior management's fourth floor administration 'vision' is fully justified and that we are being led into the abyss by a bunch of self-promoting, overpaid chancers.

If I were to reveal college management procedures, to the local press for example, the ramifications would be enormous. Heads would roll. Mine would be the first, despite the governors recently implemented Whistleblowers' Charter. The one decreeing a supposed amnesty on all those prepared to step forward and speak out against poor practice, poor management, bullying, sexual harassment and other issues affecting the college's ability to provide quality teaching and learning. In spite of this promise, no one on the teaching staff is prepared to chance it and a culture of stress and intimidation prevails, thanks to the constant day-to-day slog of coping within an insufficiently funded FE system. The fear of losing a job, with little alternative opportunity of re-employment and the threat of 'performance management', keeps staff in check.

Everyday problems are kept hidden by a middle management determined to only reveal what they want to reveal to a senior management determined to only reveal what they want to reveal to a principal determined to only reveal what he wants to reveal to the board of governors. In short, the college is not a happy workplace and an upcoming Ofsted inspection only serves to exaggerate all its shortcomings.

"I guess the time elapsed since our last visit meant we were likely to get picked soon and the maths fiasco affecting last year's results would also have flagged us up."

"Absolutely," Malcolm agreed. "We were pretty much asking for it after a debacle like that. All we can hope, through the self-inspection process of our earlier Mocksted report, is to pre-empt their criticism and show them what we've put in place to ensure it never happens again."

"How did Graham react to the impending Ofsted visit?"

"The principal was a study of controlled composure."

"I bet he was."

The principal's short fuse and explosive temperament were part of college lore. It was the one character trait of his I didn't have to keep quiet. Unfortunately, the other sleazier ones I did.

"The man's a disaster. The lengths I've had to go to in keeping his 'indiscretions' hushed up are ridiculous." Malcolm stared at me, wordlessly underlining the pact existing between us. "He's our very own Harvey Weinstein. If he hadn't been carrying on with John's wife when she worked in HR, the maths department would still have its head and wouldn't have gone into a tailspin."

John Walker's sudden departure from the A level maths department a week after his wife, Susan, had walked out on HR, both for 'personal' reasons, had left it in dire straits. Unable to recruit quickly, the small team of lecturers tried to plug the gap caused by John's leaving. The additional burden soon took its toll and two of the younger maths lecturers, unable to cope with the workload, signed off sick with stress. From there on everything had imploded. With no money for supply lecturers, makeshift lessons from unqualified staff drafted in saw teaching quality plummet and, unsurprisingly, results with it.

"You don't want to know how much John's package cost us," Malcolm continued. "We had to pay *him* for leaving us in the lurch! All we got in return for five figures was chaos and his silence."

"The staff are dreading another Ofsted inspection," I commented. "It's been like the sword of Damocles hanging over us. Once they get official confirmation of the inspection, stress levels will be through the roof."

"I suspect they'll find it better to get it over and done with rather than being in a state of perpetual limbo. Once they can come to terms with it," Malcolm suggested.

I nodded. There was a slice of truth in the prospective relief of getting the inspection over, however demanding.

"How are you bearing up on a personal level?" Malcolm asked, changing tack. "How's the divorce going?"

"I'm officially single. You can tell by my recently updated Facebook relationship status. On a more mundane, less important level than social media, legalities are finally finished and I've received my decree absolute. I'm back in the game," I cracked, trying to sound jocular and upbeat.

The thought of entering back into the singles market was actually terrifying. Despite sharing her DNA, by any reckoning, I certainly wasn't my mother. She might have super-successfully redefined herself and dived into the sex pool, cracking out lengths of effortless front crawl, but I, the skinny, white kid with arms folded tightly about himself, a tortured host of body image issues, could only creep around the edge fretting over how cold and deep and dangerous the water might be.

"Quite," Malcolm responded. "Where are you living now?"

"I'm renting. A small flat. Only I have recently bought myself a property. A beach hut in Southburgh. I put an offer in over the weekend and it should be mine in time for the Easter holidays."

Malcolm shot me the stare of contempt he normally reserved for the tradesmen of external contractors.

"Really? How much?"

"Seventy-six grand. It's more or less all I've got left after the divorce settlement."

"Are you insane? Nearly eighty thousand pounds for a beach hut? What are you going to do with it?" Malcolm asked, genuinely staggered.

"Sit in it. Sit beside it. Look at the sea. Soak up the sun. Watch the world go by as it saunters up and down the prom. I shall rent it out at some point to rake some money back," I added, not wanting to sound too vacuous.

"Watch the world go by in *Southburgh*?" Malcolm remarked, unimpressed. "Does the world go to Suffolk?"

"You'd be surprised," I replied, hinting at deeper knowledge.

Malcolm's tone turned more conciliatory. "I do remember your father always saying how much you liked the seaside. It was your mother's parents who often accompanied you and her, wasn't it?"

I nodded enthusiastically. "They did. And I loved it. I still do. That's why I bought it... And as a place where I can start to come to terms with my single-status situation."

"You have to admit it's a pretty extravagant way of going about it," Malcolm replied, fingering his comb-over to check if it was still in place. "Talking family, how is your mother? I haven't seen her for some time."

"She's changed so much since Dad died you wouldn't believe it," I replied with candour. "There's no pretty way to say it, and it pains me to do so, but my mother has turned into a cougar." Malcolm's baggy face registered interest, if not comprehension. Maybe he didn't know what a cougar was. "She blames Dad," I continued. "She says her new-found promiscuity is all to do with making up for her 'lost years' and restoring her self-confidence and self-esteem. She claims Dad never had much 'interest' in her, if you see what I mean." I paused, wondering if now was the hour to broach the subject with my father's most intimate friend. I decided to go for it. "You knew Dad better than anyone, Malcolm. Did he ever, at any time, confide anything personal to you? When he was a bit drunk, perhaps? Did he ever mention anything about him and Mum? Their sex life, or lack of it? Why the golf holidays always clashed with our family ones?"

"No," Malcolm answered instantly and dismissively, shaking his head, his attention downward and focussing on the paperwork strewn across his desk. "He never said anything like that." Malcolm lifted his head. "He loved you all very dearly, I'm as certain of it as I can be. I think what you have to remember is that attitudes have changed over the years," Malcolm stated. "I can't deny how golf can be a very obsessive game. It's hardly unique, many men over the years have fallen to the siren call of the course.

49

Your father was one. So was I. Let's be honest, it's the reason why *my* marriage failed. It's not something I'm especially proud of, although I have always believed it's healthy for a man to have an outlet. An escape route. One enabling him to get out of the house. My view has always been that women should learn to live with it and accept it and be content with what we've provided for them. The security of a home. A safe domestic environment." Malcolm pulled a face. "Not very PC, I'm afraid… Ever the old dinosaur, eh?" Malcolm smiled. "Peter was a marvellous man and, I'm sure, a good husband. He was a kind, intelligent and talented teacher who went on to become a brilliant educational administrator. I suspect your mother is bending the truth to suit her own ends, if I may be so bold."

Thanks for the misogynistic bullshit, I thought, unsure whether I could believe a single word Malcolm had told me.

BD

The next time I was due to pick up a racket and partner Chloe occurred the following weekend after the awards night. The competition an inter-club mixed doubles match. Since our spat over the missed smash and Steven's wonderful attributes, the atmosphere between the pair of us had been as healthy as a mouth-breathing cyclist slipstreaming a ten-year-old diesel van ascending a steep incline. So bad, I had wondered if my fraternising with Emily had made club gossip and Chloe, rather than confront me on the issue, had opted to bottle it up.

Much to my frustration, I'd had no opportunity to either confirm or deny my theory by using my usual go-to channels – a sneak peek at Chloe's phone to check her text messages, WhatsApp tennis group or Facebook Messenger account. All I managed to glean from social media came via James's Facebook pictures of me and Chloe receiving our runners-up medals. Chloe had commented, 'Missed out again! Maybe next year!', so no clues there. Eventually, with nothing concrete to back up my theory, I decided, on balance, I had probably got away with it.

Once convinced my kiss with Emily remained a secret, my indignation skyrocketed and I quickly stooped to operating in a bubble of low-level moping and mild ill-will towards Chloe. My morose mood grounded in her unjust accusation over the missed smash, her declared appreciation of Steven's good looks, tennis talents and business acumen and my perception of her enjoying being hauled on to his lap. Co-existing with my irritation of Chloe's behaviour lay my inability to calculate the significance, if any, of the time I had spent with Emily. Blundering around in a circle of my own thoughts, in the end I gave up, settling on seeing what happened the next time I saw her. The only hard fact to emerge was that the last few days with Chloe were definitely the worst of our married life together.

On the morning of the match, the pair of us got ready in silence. Having left the house for the short car journey to the club – it was a home match – with me driving, Chloe dipped the already frosty atmosphere a few degrees lower with the first words she had spoken to me all day.

"I don't think we should play together today," she declared. "I'll partner James and you can play with Vikki."

Bad atmosphere or not, her wanting to opt out of partnering me for a tennis match had not featured on my radar.

"Okaaay. Where's that come from?" I replied, taking my eyes off the road to see her hard-faced, dead-ahead stare.

"Paul, really? Are you that dense?" she answered, a mean-spirited glance flicked my way.

Deciding I couldn't be bothered with an escalation in hostilities, I quickly capitulated. She could keep her reasons for now.

"Fine," I exhaled wearily. "I'll play with Vikki and you can play

51

with James if that's what you want. I don't suppose they'll mind."

"I'm sure they won't and it *is* what I want," she answered, a cutting edge to her voice.

"Jesus," I sneered, performing a sub-conscious one-eighty. "You're in one."

"Oh, come on. Do you genuinely think we're in a good enough place to take part, as a pair, in a competitive match?" she asked, incredulity dripping from her voice. "We've hardly said a word to each other for days."

"I guess it depends on whether you need to take your private life on court or can leave it outside the tramlines," I retorted.

"How can I not take it on court, Paul? You behaved like a child at the awards. And you've been in a petulant mood all week. I'm certainly not feeling very kindly disposed towards you at the moment."

"'Kindly disposed towards me'?" I parroted, mimicking her voice. "What kind of language is that? What does that even mean?"

Chloe ignored my question. "The last thing I want is for us to play so badly it turns out to be an embarrassment."

"How's that work, then?" I asked. "Disregarding the uppermost thought in your head is the worry people will judge us if we lose a tennis match, rather than anything to do with our relationship."

"It's not about losing. I've lost enough times with you on far more important occasions," Chloe stated, clearly referring to the Winstone match. "I simply don't feel as if I can support you on court. I don't want to have to run down a single ball for *you*," she added, as if it was the most heinous chore imaginable.

"Cheers," I said, caustically. "Thanks for that."

"No problem."

I let out a spluttering laugh. "You're unbelievable. Are you *actually* saying you're so pissed off with me you couldn't be bothered to chase down a lob that went over my head? You'd let it bounce twice and lose the point?"

"Pretty much."

"Pathetic," I snapped, losing my temper. "What a joke. It's okay for you to call me out on *your* interpretation of why I missed a smash, one missed shot that apparently caused us to lose the whole match. Like *you* didn't make any unforced errors. But when I do it to you, for sitting on Steven's lap, you don't like it. Nice double standards, hon."

"I was *not* sitting on his lap! He pulled me back on to it and you know it."

"You hadn't moved very much by the time I came back with the drinks."

Driving more aggressively now, anger in direct correlation to the downwards pressure of my right foot, I barrelled the car into the next corner.

"Slow down!" Chloe ordered. Obeying, I braked overly harshly, gaining a little happiness from seeing Chloe's body jerk hard against the restraining seatbelt. "Idiot!" she sniped.

Back to total silence, I remembered Vikki was a leftie. Maybe I ought to ask her if she fancied playing on the ad court and going Australian when she served from the deuce side to force our opponents to hit to her forehand. Both could be smart tactics and help us win. Especially now that me and Vikki winning both our rubbers, or at the very least, bettering James and Chloe's results, had now become paramount. No way was I getting outplayed by my wife and her new partner.

With car parked, racket bags and food for the after-match lunch extracted from the boot, Chloe and I walked the short distance down the narrow pathway towards the clubhouse.

"You can tell them," I said to the back of Chloe's head as we strode down the hedge-lined walkway in single file. "You don't want to play with me, so it's down to you."

"Fine," she barked, not looking back.

Breezing through the clubhouse doorway, an act on both our parts, we found only James inside. Vikki and our opponents had not yet arrived.

"Hi, James," Chloe chimed, switching on the charm.

"All right, mate?" I asked genially, doing much the same.

"Good, thanks," he replied. "You two all fit and raring to go? Nice day for it. Should be a good match, they always put out a useful four."

I nodded. "As always."

"Absolutely," Chloe said positively, placing her racket bag on one of the clubhouse tables, busying herself by unzipping and then rummaging through one of its many sections. "James," she started, her voice higher than usual. "There's one thing we wanted to ask you. How would you feel if we mixed up the pairs today?" she asked, looking up from the bag, a small tube of sun cream now in her hand. "I play with you and Paul plays with Vikki? Our confidence has taken a bit of knock after losing the final last week and we both felt it might be better if we were to split up."

A carefully neutral smile appeared on James's face. "Yeah, sure. No worries. I'm up for that. I can't imagine Emily will mind who she plays with."

"Emily?" Chloe asked.

"Vikki's not well," James explained. "She's got a sickness bug that started overnight. She texted Emily to ask her to step in last minute. I got a message an hour ago to let me know the situation. Emily said she might be a bit late."

"Good… That's settled, then," Chloe said, rubbing a pea-sized dollop of sun cream on her nose. "Just need the loo," she added, self-consciously.

"Everything okay with you two?" James whispered once Chloe was in the toilet.

"Be careful what you wish for," I said cryptically, my stomach churning now I knew I had Emily as a partner. "But, yeah, everything's cool. Her call to split up. Nothing to do with me."

James thrust a bottom lip over his top one and bobbed his head a few times. "Shame. I was rather looking forward to playing with Emily," he said wistfully. "But hey. You enjoy your match with her. Try not to get sidetracked by that body."

"As if."

James fingered his chin. "Seriously, though, I hope you haven't had a fallout over losing the final. That would be silly."

I puffed out my cheeks and expelled some air. "You know the conversations we've had in the past concerning the pitfalls of partnering a partner. It'll sort itself out."

James laughed in response. "Thing is, you needn't have lost. You had your chances. If you hadn't missed that smash and taken the first set…"

"Yeah. Thanks. I don't need reminding by *two* people."

The noise of Chloe making her way out of the toilet killed the conversation.

"Shall we go and have a hit?" she asked, all bubbly and keen.

"Sure," James replied. "I'll get the match balls."

By the time Emily arrived, fifteen minutes late, I was hitting solo against the opposition's second pair. Chloe and James, having finished their knock-up, had already started against the opposition's first pair.

"Sorry I'm late everyone. Just let me hit a few and we'll get started," she sang out to the three of us as she walked quickly down the side of the court.

Dropping her racket bag by the net post, Emily unzipped it, took out one of the three Wilsons ensconced within and propped the racket, head down, against the net. Quickly removing her outer layers of clothing, she picked up the black-strung weapon and athletically glided on court in a short, pale-blue tennis dress.

"When I knew *you* were playing I thought I'd better make the effort and wax my legs, seeing as I know how much you like looking at them," she whispered, her eyes sparkling as she lithely wafted past me to take up her position on the forehand side.

I nodded dumbly, promptly dumping my next two backhands into the bottom of the net. Out of ammo, I jogged forward to retrieve the two miss-hits while Emily cracked a succession of perfect topspin forehands towards her opponent.

"Backhand's going well," she gently chided as I returned to the baseline. "By the way," she informed me as I turned and hit a forehand from the bouncing ball I had just dropped. "I also waxed the bit in between you said you were so interested in."

AD

On Wednesday, my first lesson after lunch – where I once again reined in my yearning to spill Ofsted-flavoured beans all over the staffroom carpet – took the form of a BTEC Level 3 business class. Half an hour into it, the classroom door unexpectedly swung open and partially through it, to stunned silence and one gaping maw (mine), leant Graham Ives, the college principal. Initially unsure whether the figure was real – a prototype hard light hologram conjured up by the science department? – given Graham's legendary dislike of departing his hallowed fourth floor sanctuary and mingling with the lower-level plebs, the vision's command proved human and unambiguous.

"A word in my office. Straight after this lesson," came the terse directive fired my way.

Communiqué dispatched, the principal immediately vanished, the door slamming shut behind him. As soon as it closed, the spell now broken, a clamour of speculation spontaneously erupted from the group of seventeen-year-olds seated before me. They might not have recognised the caller, but the message remained patent.

"You been a naughty boy, Sir?" I heard a singular voice call out over the others.

The background noise changed to a chorus of sniggers. The incident energising a dull lesson with the brief lightning bolt of entertainment where, for once, a member of staff looked to be in trouble rather than a student. I could see it written all over several of the acne-ridden faces in the front row, as if I had the power to visually decipher hormonally-dictated Braille. 'Paul Chambers is in the shit' the message read.

"I'm not too sure," I answered the unknown questioner with honesty, frantically dredging my brain for a faux pas I might have recently committed.

Had there been an Ofsted leak? Had Malcolm cracked and fingered me as the likely source when exposed to one of Graham's violent verbal onslaughts?

"Anyway… That's enough noise, thank you" I said, trying to reassert my authority and clear my mind. "Where were we? Yes... Mass markets and niche markets…"

Forty minutes later, lesson completed, I stood outside Graham's fourth floor office, procrastinating in an empty corridor while desperately attempting to calm and compose myself. With an elevated heart rate and stomach churning in sync with a whirring brain, I struggled to think straight. The primary reason for my panicked state, undeniably, the reason for my being summoned, the disorientating cleanliness and upmarket spec of the college's uppermost tier also taking its toll. It was like being in a different building. Without doubt, I was in a different world.

Graham had never before invited me to his office for a 'chat'. I had always assumed he was barely aware of my existence and I reasoned the chances of this unique invitation turning out to be a socially inclined affair appeared minuscule. As far as I could tell, it looked as if my heckling student had called it correct. One massive bollocking with my name on it lay waiting for me on the other side of the door. I forced myself to knock twice, reluctant to find out why.

"Come."

I entered over the threshold of no return to see Graham reading a Trout & Salmon magazine. I would have been less surprised if it had been a Haynes Workshop Manual given Graham's supposed disdain for cars. The principal always cycled to work whatever the weather, for effect or otherwise nobody was quite sure. Not in a million years did I have him down as an angler.

"I didn't know you fished," I observed, nodding at the magazine.

"I don't. Brother's birthday. He's a fluff chucker and I need a present," he responded, folding the magazine shut and slinging it with irritation on to his desk. "Have you seen the price of the shit they sell in there? Fucking ridiculous."

I shook my head and, as if treading on eggshells, obeyed Graham's non-verbal offer to sit on the chair in front of his desk. Eyes darting, I checked for wires and a switch.

"We have a problem, Paul," Graham said tenting his fingers and knocking the small talk straight out the ground. "I'm afraid, as of this morning, Will Harmer is no longer with us. I've had to let him go."

Gobsmacked, I mentally juggled a bombshell I could never have predicted. Will Harmer, my ultimate boss, Director of Business, Catering and Sport, a stalwart of the college for over fifteen years, had been 'let go'. A management-speak euphemism meaning almost anything.

"Why?" I asked meekly, alarmed I might somehow be collateral damage as a result of the sacking. I had never been one of Will's inner circle and wondered whether he had lashed out, accusing me of a fake transgression via a hate-strewn diatribe unleashed in the aftermath of his dismissal.

"Let me answer that in two very distinct parts," Graham began, his face taking on the menace of a viable IED. "Harmer was removed from his post this morning for gross misconduct. It's been an ongoing investigation, partaken over the last few weeks as we had to make certain correct protocol had been followed. Initially, an incriminating happenstance came to light and we asked IT to take a look into Harmer's movements, in particular his electronic diary. Once we had accessed his account," Graham snorted air down his nostrils like a bull about to charge, "we found out he'd been making appointments with people who didn't exist. Lots of them. For over five years. Almost half the people he was hooking up with were fake."

"What?" I exclaimed staggered.

"Harmer had been making bogus appointments," Graham continued. "Sometimes as many as a dozen a week with non-existent personnel supposedly attached to colleges, educational bodies, suppliers, contractors, you name it."

"Why?" I asked, barely believing what I was hearing.

"So he could get out of his office and while away his time doing fuck all *and* get paid for it. That's *why*," Graham snapped, his face now a deep shade of red, the vein in his temple prominent like a twanging subcutaneous hawser embedded under his skin. "Either that or he was getting an awful fucking lot of college-funded afternoon delight."

I prayed my shields-up poker face had reacted quickly enough to stop me expressing the resentment I felt at Graham's hypocrisy. His affair with John's wife was one Malcolm-supplied card I needed to hold particularly close to my chest when in his presence. So tight the print came off on my skin. Seconds passed. Convinced my visage hadn't betrayed me, and reasoning it was unlikely I was due a bollocking, I felt myself relax.

"For *five* years, you say?" I remarked, perhaps relaxing a bit too much.

"I'm not saying this reflects well, Paul. Don't fucking go there. I can't micro-manage every single prick in the whole fucking building," Graham exploded, droplets of spittle spraying from his mouth. "We were all duped. Harmer severely abused the high-level trust bestowed on him by *all* his colleges. That fucker won't work in education again, I can assure you of that," Graham promised, his whole body straining to break out of his expensive suit like a not-quite-angry-enough Hulk.

Malcolm's irksome new boiling pot, the one he couldn't divulge when we had spoken on Monday must have been the Harmer investigation. Seeing as Graham had now let me in on it, I presumed I had a role to play.

"And my involvement is…?" I asked.

"Hold your horses, Paul. I'm *coming* to that," Graham erupted, his voice bouncing off the office walls.

He paused, held up a hand by way of apology and reset himself, sucking in a huge intake of air. When he resumed, he spoke quietly and with control. A mode of speech so alien to him the effort and strangulated tone of his voice hinted at him fending off an embarrassing unseen giant anaconda attack under his desk.

"Ofsted are due to visit in April, the week after the Easter holiday. Malcolm has a connection who tipped us off. Now, I don't have to spell out how badly it would reflect on a college missing a director during an Ofsted inspection. Questions would inevitably be asked and, quite frankly, the answers would make us a laughing stock. We'll be fire fighting on enough fronts as it is, the last thing we need is them getting a whiff of this Harmer fiasco." Graham pulled the corners of his mouth downwards. "We could misinform and mislead, embark on a method of subterfuge, pull the wool over their eyes. I'd like to think we're above those sorts of shenanigans. I feel there's a cleaner, more practical way of dealing with the situation." Graham straightened himself in his chair. "*That's* where you enter the equation, Paul."

"I get it," I replied, deciding to chance my arm with a bit of black humour. "On the first day of the visit, you want me to set up on the balcony and pick off the Ofsted inspectors with a high-powered assault rifle as they enter the building, one by one, until they're all dead."

A smile flittered across Graham's face and I knew he was picturing the satisfying carnage of motionless blood-soaked Ofsted inspectors littering the entrance to the college.

"Please don't make that offer again, Paul," he said with a cold laugh. "I might be tempted to take you up on it." Humour slid from Graham's face like a fried egg from a Teflon pan. "No, my requirements are a little less dramatic. What the college needs, what I need, is someone who can temporarily step into Will Harmer's shoes. A person who knows the college well and who can act as a safe pair of hands until we're clear of the inspection." Graham locked me rigid with a piercing stare. "Your good friend, Malcolm, has assured me you're trustworthy and have an extremely safe pair of hands. I hope he's right."

"Ah," I began, the request kaleidoscoping through my head. "So," I restarted, wanting to spell it out for my own satisfaction, "you want me to act as a temporary Director of Business, Catering and Sport?"

Graham nodded. "On the plus side, there's unlikely to be a life sentence at the end of it and you won't need to procure an assault weapon from a black market arms dealer," he cracked sardonically. "And it's only for the duration of the inspection. Consider it a brief period of role-play within our senior management structure."

"But aren't we still going to be misinforming and misleading, embarking on a method of subterfuge and pulling the wool over their eyes if I take the role in a temporary capacity?" I asked, throwing Graham's words back at him. "What if they ask me awkward questions? Ones I haven't a clue how to answer."

"I think you're over thinking it. We'll supply you with all the relevant answers you'll need. You'll be fully briefed," Graham non-answered, his irritation beginning to rise again. "It's called noble cause corruption, Paul. It's a few tiny white lies to uphold the greater good. They'll be busy digging hard in other places," Graham said, pulling a grim face. "The maths department, management, teaching, learning and assessment. Fucking value added. You'll be kept low profile."

"What about my classes? I asked.

"You'll still have to run them. We can't have BTEC Level 3 business classes going untaught during an Ofsted inspection, can we?"

"But what if they want to sit in on one of my lessons? I can't be a business lecturer *and* Director of Business, Catering and Sport at the same time, can I? I can't be here, there and everywhere. I can't be omnipresent..." I argued, starting to gabble.

Graham cut me dead. "These. Are. All. Minor. Incidentals," he said, spelling it out loudly. "Unlikely, million-to-one scenarios. It's simple enough, you step up to the plate for us in our moment of need and, let's just say, you won't go unrewarded."

"'Unrewarded'?"

"I'm not saying this will give you a first class ticket to management, Paul, but when the time comes at the end of this school year to hand out the vocational holiday spots, you definitely won't get bumped off the flight."

Sitting in the principal's office, the air of surrealism mounting, I felt caught between a rock and a hard place. Graham had made me the proverbial offer I couldn't refuse. To do so was as sensible as taunting a ravenous scrap yard dog by dangling gravy-dipped genitals inches from its slathering jaws. That said, trying to put a different slant on it, it did sort of fit in with my start-afresh, new me, post-divorce plan of pushing my life forward.

"I'll do it."

"Is the correct option," Graham said matter-of-factly. "Leave it with me for the moment and I'll speak to you closer to the time. Meanwhile, it goes without saying, this is a strictly confidential matter. Tell no one. And I mean no one. Officially, Will has left because of health reasons. Let's pray the little shit contracts something horribly debilitating tomorrow."

Nodding, I pushed myself up from the chair to leave. Graham stopped me with my knees at forty-five degrees.

"One last thing, Mr Paul Chambers, Director of Business, Catering and Sport. You need a new suit. Put in a petty cash claim, with the receipt, directly to me. Three hundred quid tops. Get it over the holiday and wear it on the day we're back. There'll be a meeting. You'll get an email." Graham halted to eye me up and down. "Pick a nice one, eh?"

BD

Friday night social play – the pick'n'mix counter of club tennis. The rules: runs from the first Friday after the clocks go forward to an undetermined date dependent on continued membership enthusiasm and the generosity of the English weather. Open to any member with senior status irrespective of gender, playing ability or age (junior members may be awarded senior status subject to *their* playing ability). Play, starting at six-thirty, is organised into doubles matches of approximately twenty-five minutes' duration. Players for each court to be decided by the non-playing member (on the night) whose turn it is to organise as depicted by the rota. The rota, pinned to the clubhouse notice board early March, comprises the full list of Friday night organisational slots needing to be voluntarily filled. (n.b. some arm-twisting by committee members may be required to fill said spots.) Also incumbent on the organiser of each Friday night is the provision of after-play food.

The amount and type of food to be provided on Friday night is very much open to each organiser's personal discretion. You will be judged, that's all I'm saying. One particular year, a run of compet-

itive home baking created such a conveyor belt of delicious food –
mouth-watering quiches, canapés and cakes – several regular
Friday-nighters blamed it for them putting on weight. The liars. At
the other end of the spectrum, one of the younger male player's
virginal efforts comprised eighteen large packets of supermarket-
brand crisps, seven large baguettes and one giant tub of margarine.
Ten years on he still occasionally gets reminded of it. And not in a
good way.

When it had last been my turn, I had a Eureka! moment and
brought pizzas. Unwrap them, pop them in the oven, keep an eye
on them to make sure they don't burn and job done with minimum
prep. The only problem, it transpired, as everyone tucked in, lay in
my disregard of a vegetarian option. This error of foresight had
been gently pointed out to me by several players. Several stick thin
players. The ones so thin you can see around them to make a line
call even when they're standing right on it.

Friday night social play is generally supported by the more
gregarious section of the club's membership. (The cliques and
control freaks tend to avoid it and arrange their own social play.)
By definition, its open door policy supports a wide range of ages
and playing ability, invariably making for an unpredictable night's
tennis in terms of quality. The best hope for getting decent play on
a Friday night, speaking as one of the stronger team players – not
that I would ever admit it – lies in the organiser slipping you a few
better quality games in amongst the weaker ones. If an organiser is
so inclined, he or she will intermittently pair up the better players
into strong fours, either as a mixed or same-sex doubles. If better
players are thin on the ground, or as a cloaking device to hide elitist
tennis within the Friday night social play remit, opposing two
strong players with a weaker player of a similar standard can work
pretty well.

Some organisers wilfully dismiss this standpoint. Without
exception they're usually the ones who wouldn't know a topspin

backhand if it reared up off a baseline and hit them in the mouth. To their way of thinking it's Friday night *social* play and it can do exactly what it says on the tin. If one of this creed is in charge, as a strong player, you're on your own. Literally. You've no hope there'll be another one on court with you.

Disregarding organisers with pre-conceived agendas concerning the composition of Friday night social play, just as some players are better than others, then so are some organisers better than others. For those less able, getting to grips with nine courts, thirty-six players – not including those having to sit out on a busy night – remembering all their names and then arranging them into fours in an, ideally, gender-equal ratio can be a tricky call. Factor in the headache of having to remember not to put two or three players from an earlier round back on court together fifty minutes later and ensuring any sitting out is distributed fairly, in the hands of the inept, the whole thing can quickly degenerate into chaos. Five players on court 1, three on court 9; three women and one man on court 4 next to three men and one woman on court 5; people sitting out two rounds on the trot and three players playing together three times in a row are all typical organisational faux pas.

These types of administrative errors are genuine mistakes. Simple cases of oversight caused by a swarm of names and courts blurring into a confusing mass on one piece of A4 paper, placed on a clipboard, with string-tethered pencil attached. (The methodology is as old-school as you can get. There is probably an App out there somewhere, but no one has bothered to find it and force a break from tradition). What's less accepted is the husband/wife organiser who gives their partner great games all night.

Worse still, is the disenchantment experienced by the unfortunate sap who gets saddled with the night's weakest player for most of the evening. For all the bluster of the supposedly non-elitist weaker players, forever chiming the mantra that the stronger players must 'mix in', they *always* moan if they get stuck with someone worse than them.

Over the years, I have been that unfortunate sap on several occasions and have ended up stuck on court with ageing, decrepit players boasting all the mobility of the gravestone I presumed they were likely to be buried under in six months' time. The type of players who happily watch the ball sail past them to all corners of the court while shouting 'Yours!' after flashing a well-wide-of-the-mark racket at it. The type of players so deathly slow, watching them move is like seeing photos of them playing tennis in consecutive weekly colour supplements. Players without itchy feet thanks to having never suffered from athlete's foot. Players whose massive, frying-pan-gripped rackets push serves over the net so slowly, should they have been timed by a thirty mph zone speed gun, the display would have flashed up a smiley face.

On the flip side of the deal, what organisers hate most are players finishing their twenty-five minute stint and then casually announcing it's their 'last one', consequently ruining the next round of matches. Organisers also loathe players who can't be bothered to listen when the arrangements for the next round are called out, leading them to field umpteen 'What court did you say I was on?' questions. What's even worse, as an organiser, is being barracked and moaned at by a whining 'We've-only-got-three-on-our-court!' trio only to find, after high volume investigations, the missing player ensconced in the clubhouse ordering a drink.

Despite these moments of frustration, Friday night social play thrives. There are two key factors for this. Firstly, it's enjoyable for members to have a night of organised play with nothing more onerous put on them other than to turn up, get directed to a court and swing a racket on it. Secondly, there are the furtive, secretive personal hopes of who you might get to play with on any given Friday night. This might be because you fancy them, like the aesthetic look of them or are simply attracted to the way they play tennis.

Friday night social play is the only organised night where men and women mix on court. Tuesday night is Ladies' night and Wednesday night is Men's night, both organised by the respective club captains, while Mondays and Thursdays are set aside for junior coaching. Consequently, Friday night social play, for the predominantly heterosexual membership, offers the only organised play with the added dimension of a little unresolved sexual tension. Many of the sexual peccadilloes manifesting themselves at the annual awards night started their fermentation during Friday night social play.

When I had first been awarded senior status, aged sixteen, the nature of Friday night social play easily compensated for its lack of playing standard. For me to have the opportunity to go and mix on court with the way-out-of-my-league, older, sophisticated women of the club was nothing short of thrilling. Positive comments concerning my playing ability soon followed and, buoyed by my reception, I reciprocated their appreciation by lusting over them more than ever. I (wet) dreamt of increasingly bizarre scenarios with any number of them, normally culminating in naked club-house showers, where I repeatedly benefited from their full and extensive repertoire of advanced sexual techniques. Naturally, none of these ever materialised, but, as an insight into the young male psyche, I never once stopped hoping.

When I returned to the club having completed university and teacher training with a steady girlfriend, I felt less enamoured. Despite attending Friday night social play most weeks, my thoughts, ones I kept firmly – and getting firmer by the second – down the front of my tennis shorts, lay elsewhere with my non tennis-playing girlfriend. Moving on in time, once I met Chloe – a good tennis player who had joined from another club – and settled into a long-term term relationship and then married her, the intermittent standard of the tennis on a Friday night became ever more problematic. Happily married, I wasn't interested in the other female players and often missed Fridays, unmotivated by the prospect of the patchy tennis I might have to endure. When I did attend, I often did so only at Chloe's behest not to be such a killjoy.

Things changed and turned full circle when Emily joined. I first heard rumour of her on the club grapevine from fellow male team tennis players who, to a man, eulogised over her play – she could *volley* for Christ's sake – and her amazing looks. The way they described her, as if she was a tennis-playing angel who had fallen from heaven and alighted on our courts, *our* courts, compelled me to see her for myself. My interest in Friday night social play suddenly regrouped and I followed the well-trodden path of hoping to play with a specific female member, just as I had in the past.

I have to say, Emily didn't disappoint. She was every bit as stunning as everyone had said, not only a very attractive woman, but also a beautiful player. One whose quicksilver, D'Artagnan-like poached volleys at the net set her aside from any female club player I had previously witnessed. With a text-book service action, big topspin forehand, a flatter double-handed backhand drive and effortless court speed, she encapsulated all my female tennis-playing perfections. In any physical form she would have been enchanting to watch, purely on the basis of her incredible technique, put within a body of such allure she was devastation on legs. Long, lithe, svelte legs.

Over the first couple of Fridays I watched from afar – well, from the other courts out of the corner of my eye, at least – slyly, surreptitiously and making damn sure Chloe wasn't watching me watching her. Finally, after experiencing a lot of frustration, organisational chance put us on the same court twice in a single evening and I played both against and then with her. Cranking my game up to the max, a rarity on Friday nights, I tried my hardest to impress her. On only the second rally of the match opposing her, I hit a good, deep backhand approach to her forehand, to within inches of the baseline and, with my partner already camped at the net, I stormed in alongside. Emily crashed the resulting forehand down the line on my backhand side, the ball whistling past me before I could get a racket anywhere near it. I praised the shot, instantly judging her the most talented and attractive female tennis player I had ever stepped on court with.

Others were equally smitten and Steven, unsurprisingly, proved no exception. Over the following months, I watched as he moved in on her, like an apex predator stalking its prey – coolly, cunningly, determinedly and with a certain opulent élan. Remarkably, he always seemed to get either paired with or against her at least twice every Friday – except for the time when I organised and spectacularly fucked him over by keeping him as far away from her as possible. Apart from my solitary intervention, so frequent were the match-ups, I could only assume that he had slipped various organisers a few quid here and there to make it happen. Or promised other benefits within his considerable array of powers.

Whatever the true nature of the plan he devised, it had worked. Within eighteen months they were married and the pair of them instantaneously became the club's most beguiling couple; glamorous, wealthy and with a hedonistic lifestyle to die for. To kick off married life, they honeymooned at Four Seasons Resort Bora Bora in French Polynesia after the most wonderful and lavish of weddings staged in the grounds of an elegant Sussex stately home. Those of us club members Steven particularly wanted to impress/rub our noses in it, were invited to the reception. That evening, Steven paraded Emily around as if she were a prized filly being led around a paddock. The king of the club now had his queen.

On a personal note, I had never liked Steven. Once he had successfully ensnared Emily, I found myself liking him even less than before. If that were possible.

Unlike other poisonous tongues wagging in the clubhouse, I

held my counsel over the Stardust Couple and, biting my own, voiced nothing detrimental about Steven. As for Emily, I was less tight-lipped, but only when passing comment on the quality of her tennis playing abilities. Not once did I remark on her physical attractiveness, only other than to James, my most trusted and valued confidant. I never dared flirt with her or even dreamt of making a pass at her – other than ones aimed cross court or down the line. I stuck to playing my best tennis whenever on court with her and kept my admiration for her looks well out of the public arena. When my big chance to impress came along, my one chance to beat her and her odious husband, I fluffed my lines and missed that smash. With it, came not support from my wife, only accusation.

Rather oddly, on the very night Emily and Steven collected the trophy for the match they had won – okay, I admit, partially aided by my overhead error – to my complete stupefaction, I *did* make a pass at Emily. And not a very subtle or sophisticated one. Quite the opposite. Stranger still, Emily responded to it, initiating a kissing session lasting for five whole minutes. Only the unspoken consensus of our vulnerability had curtailed our passions, the pair of us departing to our respective partners with not a further word spoken.

Days of fretting and consternation followed. Cue Vikki's illness, Chloe's call on two mixed-doubles pairings and, suddenly, out of the blue, I'm stepping on court to partner Emily in a competitive match for the very first time. Her first words to me on arrival, a blatant resurrection of my vulgar pass, ones pandering to it, no less, leaving me to wonder just what the hell was going on between us.

With no answers forthcoming during the match, I was desperate to find out.

As I drove to the club for an evening of Friday night social play without Chloe – she had texted to say she was working late and couldn't make it – I recalled how easy it had been playing doubles with Emily compared to with Chloe. Despite my initial knock-up nerves, once we got going, I played pretty well riding the coat-tails of Emily's talent. Very active at the net, Emily poached brilliantly throughout both rubbers, especially on my serve, intercepting and putting balls away without me having to play another stroke. Her service, powerful and accurate, proved easy to hold, often one of the more difficult tasks for the woman to achieve in a mixed doubles match. Solid on return of serve and quick around the court, Emily had the ability to hustle balls back which Chloe would never have got to. Dynamic, energetic and electric, Emily was thrilling to play with and I couldn't stop myself wondering if she put up the same sort of performance in bed.

Emily and I coasted to victory in both rubbers, whereas Chloe and James only managed to win one and narrowly lost the other. The perfect result as far as I was concerned. An overall win with Emily and me comfortably proving to be the superior pair. Not that I mentioned anything so toxic while eating the post match lunch with our opponents, or at home later. Not a scintilla of smugness seeped from my lips. I wasn't that stupid.

Old issues concerning the standard of play on a Friday night were not remotely on my agenda when, ten minutes early for the six-thirty start, I entered an almost empty clubhouse. I didn't care if I ended up on court all evening with the three worst players present, received serves under thirty mph, or if the food turned out to be tins of unheated supermarket-brand baked beans and unbuttered white bread. Just so long as Emily turned up and I got the chance to try and fathom out where, if anywhere, our relationship was going.

Very conscious of my hypertensive state, I took the offer to burn off some excess energy with a quick singles hit while Emma, the organiser for the night, set about her task of listing members as they arrived. Once there were enough, she blew her whistle and, like cows called for dinner, we herded around her to hear our names called for the first round of fours. Emily's wasn't among them.

Going through the motions in my first match, my spirits soared when I saw Emily and Steven arrive and confirm their participation with Emma. Boosted by this, I prayed Emma would come up with the goods and put Emily on court with me at some stage in the evening. After the allotted twenty-five minutes – which felt more like twenty-five hours – the whistle blew and all the players herded in once again. As Emma prepared to announce the pairings for the next round, I felt like the manager of a non-league club attending the third round draw of the FA cup – one hoping to pull a Premiership high-flyer.

"Court five. Emily, Steven, Paul and Vikki," Emma decreed.

Yes! Jackpot! Big home crowd with lucrative TV rights.

"How are you feeling now, Vikki? Better?" I asked the middle-aged left-hander as the four of us made our way to court five.

"Much better, thanks. It was one of those twenty-four hour bugs. I was sick all night," she clarified shuddering. "There was no way I could have played. Lucky Emily could step in for me. I hear you won three-one and you two won both?"

"Paul pulled me through," Emily answered, her perfect white teeth flashing.

"I don't think so," I modestly replied.

"How we going to play?" Steven asked brusquely, unimpressed with our mutual appreciation society.

"I guess we can't have the Senior Mixed Doubles winners playing together, can we Vikki? Far too strong," I suggested, massaging Steven's ego and manipulating him at the same time. "Shall we split up them up?"

"I think so," Vikki concurred.

"Fine. Rough or smooth?" Steven asked, spinning his Head racket, its handle rotating through a loose left hand.

"Smooth, darling," Emily called, a slight edge in her voice.

Steven closed his hand on the racket handle, stopping it spinning and looked down at the strings. "Smooth. Your choice."

This time Emily ceded to me.

"We'll serve," I decided.

"We'll have one down this end," Steven responded.

Emily and I walked to our half of the court, her diverting to gather up some balls that were close to the net. She placed two of them on the strings of the flat racket I offered her and the remaining one she tucked into the pocket of her skirt.

"Right," she said, eyes wide, the edge still in her voice. "You start. Same as Sunday."

I nodded, cracking the code of her message. She wanted to win! On the baseline and ready to serve, I noticed Vikki had positioned herself on the forehand side. Steven's ego evidently not capable of relinquishing the advantage side – the one traditionally taken by the man in mixed doubles – despite Vikki's left handedness and decent forehand. Taking some pace off and slicing my first serve way out wide, Vikki could only hoist up a defensive back-hand lob. One Emily smashed away with venom right at Steven, the ball missing him by inches. No apology followed.

"Nice serve, partner," Emily remarked with little emotion, taking the spare ball from her pocket and throwing it to me.

Reloaded, next serve I went for a big flat one out to Steven's backhand and made it. His cross court return, slightly mistimed and a little off the frame, saw Emily cut it off with a short sliced backhand stop volley that bounced barely a yard from the net. Thirty-love.

"Ball please, Steven. I can't reach," she instructed, forcing him to retrieve her cheeky winner.

Two more first serves saw me hold the first game to love. As we crossed to change ends, Vikki congratulated me on a game well served. Steven said nothing, his mood now surly. A few scruffy points coupled with a couple of half-decent rallies forced Steven's first service game to deuce. On the next point, Steven served hard down the middle into Emily's backhand and Vikki, expecting a cross court reply, was caught completely flat-footed as Emily flicked one down her line for a winner.

"Cover your tramlines, please, Vikki," Steven told her in no uncertain manner.

Break point, with poor Vikki at the net and now positioned virtually in the tramlines, Steven tried to hit a slider down the tee on to my forehand rather than go percentage to my backhand. I picked it and hit a good forehand, one dipping down to his feet forcing him to volley up as he came in behind his serve. Emily didn't hesitate and she stepped across to volley his volley for a winner straight down the middle.

"That'll upset him. Losing his serve," Emily quietly remarked as I gave her a ball for her service.

Next game, Emily underlined the break by holding, hitting solidly from the baseline to force errors from Vikki and Steven. Steven was now forcing points, trying to win them quickly and he netted a couple of attempted interceptions when made at full stretch. Most glorious of all was when he attempted to poach once more, far too early, Emily spotted him and hit an inside out forehand winner down the line into the gaping hole left by his premeditated move.

"Cover your tramlines, please, Steven!" Vikki teased, pulling a cheeky face at me over the net.

Break point in the next game on Vikki's serve, thirty-forty, I hit a backhand service return cross court that Steven left well alone and followed it into the net. In response, Vikki played a nice extreme angled cross court forehand, one I only just managed to reach, and my resulting full-stretch backhand volley floated past Steven and clipped the outside edge of the line.

"Wide," Steven called, gesticulating with a finger pointing off court.

"Are you sure?" I queried.

"The ball was out. Deuce," he confirmed, forcefully ending the conversation.

The next two points Emily and I both hit poor service returns and Vikki held serve, making the score three-one in games with my service up next. I duly held to fifteen and Steven, volleying solidly, held his to thirty. Four-two. Halfway through Emily's service game at thirty-fifteen, the whistle shrilled to end the contest and we played out the final point until Vikki hit a backhand wide. We stopped playing and all four of us approached the net.

"Thank you, Emily," I said, shaking hands with my partner. "Well played."

"Thank *you*," she responded.

"Thanks, Vikki," I said, shaking her hand over the white tape, my peripheral vision catching no sign of anything similar occurring between Emily and Steven.

"Thank you, Paul," Vikki reciprocated.

"Cheers, Steven." I offered my hand and he took it, giving it a cursory solitary pump.

Walking off court behind the chatting Emily and Vikki, thinking the brief game had gone as well as it could, Steven veered over towards me and physically nudged into me altering my stride pattern.

"Who do you think you are questioning my line calls?" he angrily asked.

"Sorry?" I started, shocked at the physical contact.

"You heard," he stated aggressively.

"Look, I only queried it because the ball had gone behind you and wasn't sure if you saw it land. I was looking straight down the line and thought it might have clipped it," I explained, trying to diffuse the situation.

"It was *my* call. *Not* yours."

"All right," I replied, taken aback by his intensity. "You took the point. I didn't exactly argue with you."

The four of us had now reached the courtside gate. Shooting me a filthy look, Steven pushed past the two women in front, opened the gate and strode through it without a backward glance. As the gate swung backwards, I stepped in and caught it, holding it open for Vikki and Emily to walk through.

"Ignore him," Emily advised as she slipped by me. "His firm lost one of their biggest clients to a competitor. He's been in a terrible mood all week."

From there on the evening meandered on in a much more sedate manner. I played three more rounds, nowhere near the standard of the one I had enjoyed with Emily, but, still on a high from earlier, fun nevertheless. In the clubhouse afterwards, ready to eat and eyeing up Emma's impressive spread laid out on a large table constructed by a local artisan from recycled scaffold planks – a showpiece item designed to virtual signal the club's sensibilities, one costing a small fortune – Emily ghosted in alongside me.

"Was it in?" she asked.

"My volley?" I replied. She nodded. "I genuinely thought so. I wouldn't have said anything otherwise."

Emily nodded again, apparently satisfied with my explanation. "No Chloe tonight?"

"She had to work late," I told Emily as I gingerly picked up a hot jacket potato and quickly placed it on my plate.

"That's a shame. She missed a good night's tennis. For a Friday," Emily commented, now reaching out across the wide table to get some food of her own.

"Emma's as good as gold. She'll always give you a good game if she can. Her food's always great as well."

"You're a college lecturer, aren't you, Paul?" Emily asked, somewhat tangentially.

"That's right," I confirmed. "I teach BTEC Level 3 business at the local college."

"I'm a freelance writer," Emily said as if it was a common vocation.

"Oh… right. I knew you were a freelance something or other…" I replied lamely.

"I've recently been commissioned to write an academic piece for a trade magazine on the cutbacks government have made to the funding of education for sixteen to eighteen year olds. They also want me to touch on the success, or rather the lack of it, of the apprenticeship levy scheme," Emily told me. "I wondered if you'd be interested," her eyes flicked towards the bar where Steven was buying a drink, "in doing an interview? To get an insider's take on how it's affected FE."

"Absolutely," I gushed. "If you like, I could commandeer a room and book a time at the college. As long as it didn't clash with my teaching timetable it wouldn't be a problem," I suggested, markedly overstating my influence.

Emily's mouth formed a wry smile as she tucked a section of hair behind an ear. "No, that's okay. I can't have you going to all that trouble on my behalf. I can sort out somewhere a little, shall we say, less public. Somewhere where we can be alone. Then, if you fancy it, you can 'commandeer' the hell out of me instead."

"Sounds good," I managed to croak.

"Perfect. Let me get my phone from my bag so I can add your number."

AD

I knocked on the front door of my mother's house, holding the recently purchased off-the-peg suit by a crooked finger over my shoulder. After a short period, the door swung open to reveal a burly man in a dirty Scruffs Tee shirt, his muscular forearms covered in poor quality tattoos.

"All right, bud?" he enquired with attitude, suggesting my answer would feature well down the list of his priorities.

My prior apprehension, one formulated in response to the sign-written van parked on the drive, appeared justified. My mother had clearly acquired a fresh penchant for animalistic sex and here, towering above me, stood the brutish manual worker providing it. Still, no need for too much involvement. See Mum, ask her what I want to ask her and get the hell out.

"Is... the, er, lady of the house in?" I asked stiltedly.

"Who wants to know?" white van man countered, glowering and edging towards the threshold.

"Is Linda, Mrs Chambers, in," I corrected myself. "I'm, Paul, her son."

White van man's large square face cracked into a relaxed smile, exposing a gold front tooth.

"Sorry, fella," he apologised, holding up a vertical palm. "I thought you were a cold-calling salesman. She's out. Won't be long. I'm Barry. I'm fitting a new boiler for her."

"Oh, right," I replied, realising I had jumped to the most extreme of conclusions. "'Gas Safe'," I commented, jerking a thumb towards the van and the yellow triangular emblems plastered all over it. I knew Gas Safe. I chatted with the plumbing lecturers every now and then.

"Got to be all reg'ed up now, fella. You can't use a fucking shovel nowadays without the right ticket."

"I know," I concurred, my tone conveying sympathy. "The way of the modern world." From my low vantage point I flashed my best smile. "Any chance I can come inside and wait for her?"

"Sorry, bud," Barry said, jumping to one side. "'Course you can. Mind the tools on the deck as you come through. I don't want you tripping over and snapping your neck like a KitKat. My public liability couldn't hack it," he laughed.

Hanging my new suit on the coat rack in the hallway, I followed

Barry into a tool-strewn kitchen where I spotted the brand new boiler hanging on an outside wall.

"Is it a combi?" I asked, trying to talk trade.

"Nah. Heat only. Your mum wanted to keep the cylinder and the airing cupboard for drying her clothes," Barry replied, wading into waters far too deep for my limited scope. "Just got to connect up the gas, fill the system and she's good to go," Barry informed me, his eyes fixed on the white metal box. "Fancy sticking the kettle on?" he asked, turning them back on me with a hopeful look.

"Why not? I could murder a cuppa," I answered, slipping into his vernacular.

"Nice one. Milk and no sugar for me. I'm sweet enough," he said with a wink.

With two mugs of builder's tea brewed, I perched on a kitchen stool like an academic parrot and listened to Barry's take on Premiership football while he worked. A viewpoint he quickly pared down to the bullet points of it being played, managed and coached by 'overpaid, foreign tossers'. More disturbingly, after giving me a perfunctory insight into the plumbing and heating game – how he had to be retested every five years, cowboy operators, VAT returns – he then started to talk about my mother.

"Your mum's a good-looking woman for her age, I'll say that for her," he confided, immediately putting my teeth on edge. "Lovely person, too. Always making me tea, giving me biscuits, feeding me great big slices of cake."

"That's her all right," I replied with non-commitment, fearing where the conversation might be heading next.

"She's helped me out a lot," Barry continued, feeding a length of copper tubing into his bending machine. "I've had a few problems at home and she's given me some well sound advice. I suppose when you've lived through a shit load of hassle yourself, it helps you understand how others feel when they're going through it. You know, all the stuff that went on with your dad."

"She's told you about that, has she?" I asked somewhat shocked.

"Yeah," Barry replied casually, like my mother had told him a passing incidental about a family pet. "All the stuff about him not wanting to go on holiday with you. Always off playing golf."

"Oh, that," I said breathing a sigh of relief.

"And him not wanting to screw her," Barry stated, body-slamming me to the ground without a smidgen of embarrassment.

"Well... It..." I floundered.

"I'm not being funny, fella, and I appreciate he was your dad, not that I'd ever mention it to your mum, but didn't you ever wonder if your old man might have swung both ways? You know, that he liked doing a bit of shirt lifting on the side."

I almost choked on my tea. "No, I didn't," I managed to answer.

Barry noted my unease. "No offence, bud. My gut reaction that's all. Call it as I see it, and all that. Here, take that for a sec." Barry passed me his pipe cutter. "Cheers," he said, asking for it back having measured and marked the pipe.

Tipping forward on my stool, I handed Barry the cutter.

"Look at you two workers," my mother beamed, surprising us both, Star Trek-style transported into the kitchen doorway.

"Christ! You made me jump, Mrs C. We didn't hear you come in," Barry declared laughing, turning his attention to me and pulling a 'that was a close one' face. "I thought I might as well make use of him, what with him hanging around the place making it look untidy."

"Absolutely, Barry. Cup of tea anyone?" she gushed, breezing into the kitchen and deftly waltzing through the assorted mantraps in her patent black leather, stiletto-heeled court shoes.

"Paul's only just made one, but I'll have another. Milk and no sugar..."

"...I'm sweet enough!" my mother chimed in unison with Barry, both of them disintegrating into hilarity.

"Barry," my mother declared, filling the overworked kettle. "I

80

shall miss our tea breaks and little chats once you're gone."

"Me too, Mrs C. Me too," Barry concurred.

"Sure you don't want one, Paul?" my mother asked as the kettle closed in on its task.

"I'm good."

My mother's expression indicated otherwise and, having made herself and Barry tea, she turned on me like I was the least-favoured son.

"I presume there's a reason for you dropping by, Paul?" I agreed there was. "In that case, let's leave Barry in peace and go in the living room."

My mother opted for a seat on the green leather settee placed against the living room's longest internal wall. I sat at right angles to her in one of the suite's armchairs, opting for the one nearest the bay window overlooking the front lawn. From this vantage point, looking down the length of the living room, I noticed all of Dad's golf trophies had been removed from the glass-fronted trophy case. In their place sat several sets of ceramic dog and cat-themed knick-knacks. The old photo of my parents' wedding day, the one usually placed on the mantelpiece, had also disappeared.

My mother sipped her tea. "Well?"

"My divorce has come through. I've got my decree absolute," I stated, my mother's only response a twitch of her mouth. "Also, in another development, I've gone and done something slightly reckless."

My mother perked up at this. "Sounds interesting. Tell me more."

"I've blown nearly all the remaining divorce money on a beach hut."

"A beach hut!" my mother exclaimed excitedly. "How wonderful! Where?"

Feeding off her energy, I couldn't stop myself smiling. "Have a guess."

81

"Not *Southburgh*?" she instantaneously replied.

"Yes! Southburgh! I drove up there after finding it online. You wouldn't believe how hideous the weather was, not that it deterred me. I still fell in love with it and bought it."

"Good for you! Is it one of the ones down from the pier by the promenade?"

"Yes. It's still as you'd remember it. The whole town hasn't changed at all," I told her, the excitement evident in my voice. "I'm going there tomorrow. We've broken up for the Easter holidays now, so I'm staying for a few days to give the interior a revamp."

"Marvellous!" my mother declared wholeheartedly. "Did going back remind you of Nanny and Grandad?" I nodded, a surge of emotion welling inside me. "What a shame they're not here for you to show them."

"I know," I agreed. "The memory that came back strongest was Grandad, his camera and that light meter of his. Pointing it at everything and everyone all day long. Do you remember when I burnt my fingers on a flash bulb after he'd told me not to touch them?"

My mother's eyes had gone misty. "I do," she answered, dreamily.

"And do you remember how exciting it used to be when the photos arrived in the post? Pictures of us on the sand and going in the sea. Eating ice creams and fish and chips. I loved those times, Mum."

"I know you did, Paul. They were special days."

We both sat in muted contemplation for a few seconds and in the quietness, I felt closer to her than I had in years. Looking at her, through what I supposed were fresh eyes, I saw a woman most sons would have been proud of. She looked great and was making the most of her life. What's not to like? Why had I taken such direct umbrage at her high-spirited lifestyle choices? Barry's simplistic, no bullshit, shoot-from-the-hip opinion about Dad had also hit the mark. What if he was right? Why hadn't I ever considered something like it? To stop myself from drowning, I reached out for the rope securely tethered to the reason why I had come to my mother's house in the first place.

"There's something else. I've sort of been promoted at work," I fudged, my mother's mouth forming a 'get you' 'O' shape. "To celebrate, I've bought myself a new suit. It's hanging up in the hallway. Let me quickly go and get it."

Choosing the suit a few hours earlier hadn't been easy. Without Chloe to issue sartorial guidance – I would have called it 'nagging me' during our marriage – it soon dawned on me how clueless I was at buying clothes for myself. Underlining the steep learning curve I needed to climb now flying solo, I had picked a suit, but wasn't sure if I had picked the right one. With Graham's warning echoing in my mind, I had come to my mother's house to seek a second opinion.

"I wanted to ask what you thought," I said, returning with the suit inside its protective cover, hanger hook protruding from the top. "You always dress well. You'll be able to tell whether it fits and looks good."

"Pop it on, then," she purred in response to the compliment. I looked anxiously at the open living room door. "Oh, don't worry about Barry. Don't be so silly. It won't take you a few seconds."

I did as instructed, whipping off my shoes, changing my trousers and putting the new jacket on over the top of the shirt and tie I was already wearing.

"Shoes back on. For trouser length," my mother instructed.

I slipped on my brogues and tied the laces. "What do you think?" I asked now I was once more fully dressed.

"Turn round," she instructed, making little circles with her index finger. "Okay. Lift the jacket up at the back... Trousers fit well and they're the correct length. Now turn back to me. Undo the bottom jacket button. That's better... Now undo the other button

83

and put both hands in your pockets. Turn sideways. Very nice. Good choice, Paul. Well done," she praised without it sounding too patronising.

"You're not just saying?"

"No. Of course not. Whatever makes you say that?"

"I've not been very nice to you since Dad died," I answered meekly. "I haven't taken what you've said very seriously and thought you might…"

"Say you looked nice when actually you looked like Coco the Clown. After being dragged *along* a hedge rather than through it?"

"Something like that."

"You stupid boy," she lightly admonished.

"I'm not Private Pike," I bantered, referencing one of her favourite TV shows.

"No," she said, standing up, walking over to me and running the fingers of her right hand under the inside of one of the jacket's lapels. "You're my son and I love you." She pecked me gently on the cheek – there would be lipstick – and as her head moved back her eyes looked questioningly into mine. "Has something happened that's made you reconsider?"

"Not really. Nothing specific… Maybe going back to where we used to go on holiday sparked it off."

My mother spoke solemnly. "Everything I told you was true. It might be hard for you to accept, but I promise I wouldn't lie over something so important. All I want to do now is have some fun. Is that such a crime?" My head told her it wasn't. "Thank you. You know it's your turn next. Now you're at the start of a new beginning."

"I hope so."

"Go and get life," my mother urged. "Leave the past behind and grasp the future. Go do something crazy and savour *every* minute of it," she stressed. "Promise me."

"I promise."

"Good."

"I'd better change and be off," I said excusing myself. "I need to collect the materials for the revamp. One of the guys in construction has ordered everything for me on his trade account."

"Send me some photos of the beach hut. Before and after. I'll mark you on your DIY skills. Send them on WhatsApp," she added, proud of her new social media skills.

"Will do."

"And don't leave it so long before you call round again."

"Will don't."

"Take care of yourself, Paul. Eat properly," she warned as only a mother can.

"I'll try," I assured her as I started to take off my new suit jacket.

Once I was changed and ready to leave, I popped into the kitchen to say goodbye to Barry.

"See you later, Barry."

"Cheers, bud. Take it easy," he replied.

I carried on down the hallway, opened the front door and turned to wave goodbye to Mum. She didn't notice, her gaze was fixed into the kitchen, a smile on her face. She was taking off her earrings.

Back in the car, I considered Barry's mind-blowing supposition my father might have been bisexual. Tweaking it further, I wondered if an alternative, more accurate, theory rested in the less exotic proposition of Dad being gay. Hardly an original premise, the family man secretly leading a double life to hide his preferences, especially during less enlightened times. A man shackled by society convention, unable, or perhaps unwilling, to have his own Schofield moment of release. If true, no wonder he and Mum only had sex six times. Once I was born, job done. Child in place, created – not through love or desire – but rather as a means to prop up and substantiate the lie lived out by the father. A boy he paid for, but never engaged with, played with, or accompanied on holiday.

85

My god. This was massive. Hello complete life reappraisal! Staggered by this fresh insight, I swore to accept Mum's version of the truth until proven otherwise. A fire of hurt burning inside me, I started the car. I had to get to Malcolm and crowbar open his closet and find out what lurked inside. To try and discover if the pink-domed prick had lied to me when heaping praise on Dad and gainsaying Mum. If he had been economical with the truth, then by definition, he must have had skin in the game. Fucking hell, I thought, as I pulled away, it gets worse! What if Malcolm and Dad were lovers? Malcolm's divorce might have hinged on him committing adultery rather than playing too much golf. Adultery committed with another man. My father!

Shame the Jeremy Kyle Show was cancelled, otherwise I might have got the chance to vent on it.

BD

Despite asking to interview me and swapping mobile numbers, I hadn't heard from or seen Emily in weeks. Frustratingly, our paths never crossed at the club – there had been no more mixed-doubles matches for us to play in – and every subsequent Friday night I had attended had stayed Emily-free. Adding to my irritation, and very much seen as a list of missed opportunities, my club visits had all been unaccompanied. Chloe's firm had apparently landed a global marketing campaign, stretching their capacity to breaking point, and all staff were racking up the overtime in an attempt to cope with the increased workload.

As the period of Emily drought extended, I experienced a directly proportional desire to stop it dead in its tracks by turning on the sprinklers. This nagging impulse, constantly growing and heckling, led me to search for a plausible excuse permitting me to ring her. Despite the strength of these urges, I couldn't manage to conjure up a sufficiently compelling reason and aborted every time I picked up my Samsung with the intention of definitely, no, really definitely, doing it this time.

The rationale jerking me back, like an unruly dog on a choker lead, the realisation everything happening to date had been at her instigation. Emily set the agenda, not me, and I lacked the confidence to break that mould, however desirable the thought. I couldn't force myself to up the ante and take control. Instead, like an actor, or so I imagined, promised a leading part in a Hollywood blockbuster, I waited passively for the phone to ring. And every time it did, adrenalin coursed through my body only to be swiftly displaced by crushing disappointment.

Emily's number on my phone, unused or not, was still an excruciatingly thrilling wonder. As the days slid by into weeks without interaction, either in person at the club or remotely by phone, her number became the single, remaining tenuous link between us. Sometimes, my yearning for her got so strong I would simply sit and stare at her contact details. 'Emily Winstone Mobile' I would read in my head and picture her playing tennis. Other times, I would look at her contact details and picture her doing something else – like giving me a blowjob, riding me reverse cowgirl, or her saying, 'Oh, my, god! *Yes!*' as I ejaculated, porno-style, all over her perfect arse.

What this teenage fantasising quickly led to, apart from heightened feelings of inadequacy, was a severe case of adult paranoia. One caused by the harrowing possibility Chloe might glance at my phone, stumble across Emily's contact details and, by an inexplicable form of android phone telepathy, become immediately aware of the wild, treasonous crap flying around in my head.

If accidental discovery of dangerous innermost thoughts via device-to-human telepathy was one problem, then another lay in the state of our marriage. Chloe and I weren't exactly setting world class standards, even if the raw antagonism of the past few weeks had subsided into the strained ambience of sterile functionality. We weren't right. And we both knew it. Not one episode of intimacy, nor any physical contact come to that, had taken place between us since that missed smash. Our world felt flat and lacking in empathy. A relationship flat-lining through everyday drudgery with no spark to lift it and, thanks to Chloe's workload, now dogged by increasing periods of separation.

Upset by the parallels now existing in my married life with the ones my mother claimed to have existed in hers, I began to feel more and more unhappy. Struggling to apportion blame for the marriage status quo – I knew my Emily infatuation was stupid, but felt tipped into it by Chloe's increasingly distant behaviour – I became confused, entangled in contradictions and unable to work my way clear. Emily's contact details the red button to self-assured destruction.

Feeling guilty, yet somehow justified in equal measures, I realised I couldn't cope with casually leaving my phone lying around the house like an anti-personnel mine – one that blew *me* up if Chloe stepped on it. So, as a response, I implemented regime change. When charging the phone, I only used the socket underneath my bedside table, always at night, so it remained right next to me. When I showered or used the toilet, I took the phone into the bathroom with me. I stopped leaving it unattended on worktops in the kitchen, on the dining room table and on the coffee table. I stopped looking at it when Chloe was around and for the most part, when I was at home, I kept it buried in a pocket. Eventually, unable to stand the stress any more, I put a security lock on it. A first for me because previously Chloe and I had been quite relaxed about looking at each other's phones, reading out messages and answering incoming calls.

Fascinatingly, Chloe initiated a reciprocal response. At more or less the same time as I began moderating my phone behaviour, I started to notice her doing the same. She didn't leave her iPhone lying around like she used to and only charged it from the socket underneath her bedside table, always at night, so it remained right next to her. When she showered or used the toilet she took her phone into the bathroom with her. She stopped leaving it unattended on worktops in the kitchen, on the dining room table and on the coffee table. She stopped looking at it when I was around and for the most part, when she was at home, she kept it buried in a pocket or a bag. Whether she had put a security lock on hers like I had on mine, I hadn't a clue. I suspected she had.

Initially, I put her actions down to an extremely mild version of the tit-for-tat murders committed in Northern Ireland during The Troubles. One side instigates an unsavoury act of aggression and, in response, the other retaliates with one of equal brutality. Not the most charming analogy for a husband and wife relationship, equating it to two opposing paramilitary forces locked in a decades-long murderous political life-and-death struggle, but there you go. Then, one evening, as we were sitting watching Netflix, Chloe's phone rang and the look on her face told me all I needed to know. Fielding the call, she immediately left the living room, only returning after she had hung up.

"Who was that?" I casually asked.

"Work," she answered. "It's crazy at the moment. I don't know why we took them on. They're too big. We'll all burn out at this rate."

"More overtime?"

"All weekend."

The penny, at last, dropped with a satisfying clunk. She wasn't hiding her phone away in a juvenile strop because I had started hiding mine. She was hiding her phone away because she was up to something she didn't want me to know about. It was so obvious. How could I have missed it before? That's why *I* had started doing it for fuck's sake. How dumb of her to think I wouldn't notice, even if I had been a bit slow on the uptake. In the immediate birth of my fresh lucidity, a voice gravely warned me to adopt the brace position. Chloe's affair, if that indeed was what she was up to, might well be considerably further advanced than my pathetic situation. What did I have? A five minute kiss, a bit of flirting and a phone number given in order to facilitate a workplace task. The truth was, I had nothing. Only what my wayward mind projected on it.

That night in bed, I wanted angry sex – as in, angry because I hadn't been getting any. I decided to test the boundaries of our situation by asking Chloe if she was up for drawing a line under our recent problems.

"How about we kiss and make up? It's been a while," I suggested in my most reasonable voice.

"Sorry. Not tonight, Paul," she answered knocking me back. "I'm *so* tired and stressed. Having sex is the last thing on my mind."

"That's a shame. We do need to move on from all this nonsense," I countered, trying to inject genuine disappointment in my voice, wondering if she might relent and cave.

"I don't mind if you want to sort yourself out," she piped up with a hint of enthusiasm, like she was pleased with herself for coming up with such a great idea.

"Sorry?"

"You know, take matters into your *own* hand."

"What, have a *wank*?"

"If you want to. I won't mind. I'm drained… And then you can be," she said, a smarmy smile on her face. "Of your frustrations," she quickly quantified.

An indignant fury took hold of me. I wasn't going to lie there and take this bullshit.

"Fine. I will." I threw the duvet back and got out of bed. "I don't need to beg you for my orgasms."

Halfway to the bedroom door I remembered my phone. I strode back, snatching it free from its lead in one violent movement.

"I need it for material," I grouched. "Something to get me going seeing as you're too tired to do it."

Storming out of the bedroom, I crossed the hallway in darkness to the main bathroom. A tug on the pull cord revealed the stark, clinical whiteness of the bathroom suite and its tiled walls. I shoved the door shut behind me. Naked, apart from Calvin Klein boxer shorts, I wondered whether I had the resolve to see such an act through. It was a bit embarrassing to embark on such a regressive course of action at my age, but then, why not? Fuck her. Or rather, don't fuck her. Get an adult site up on the phone, I reasoned, get going, do the business and come in the basin. Easy clean up. Back to bed with my honour intact. Sorted.

It had to be done. The last thing I wanted was to creep back into the bedroom and admit defeat, not after my proclamation about not begging for orgasms. With my determined face on, rather than my sex face on, I opened up the internet browser on my phone and typed 'Pornhub' into the search bar. A few clicks later and the combination of a strong wi-fi signal and superfast broadband saw HD pornography streamed on to my screen. My penis, rather satisfyingly, responded appropriately. Concentrating on the images on the phone's screen, held in one hand, I inched my boxer shorts down with the other, grabbed hold of my rigid penis and began a motion I hadn't performed in years. Ten strokes in, I nearly had a heart attack when, bolt-out-of-the-blue, the phone rang. Over the top of the video image of a pneumatic blonde getting pounded by an unfeasibly well-endowed man, Emily Winstone's name and number appeared. In a flustered panic, I frenetically swiped at the green phone icon to stop the ringtone.

"Hello, Emily," I answered shakily, my voice breathless and quiet, praying Chloe hadn't heard the ringtone.

"Hello, Paul," I heard her say. "Sorry it's so late. I hope I haven't disturbed you."

"No, not at all," I whispered, my heartbeat booming in my ears like I was stroke on a Ben-Hur galley slave ship .

"I can hardly hear you. Can you hear me okay?"

"Yes, I can hear you."

"Still struggling to hear you. Is this an inopportune moment?"

"No, it's fine. Chloe's asleep and I don't want to disturb her."

"Oh, gosh. Sorry. Are you in bed? You sound as if you've been running."

"No. Not in bed. Certainly not running. I'm in the bathroom."

"Oh. Shall I call back?"

"No, it's all right," I answered, thinking she might *never* call back. "I'm not up to much."

"What *are* you doing in there, then? You answered the call *very* quickly," Emily said in a voice tinged with playfulness.

"Cleaning my teeth," I lied, mortified to think she could ever know the truth.

"Do you always take your phone with you to the bathroom?"

"Pretty much. You never know when someone important might call."

"I can't argue with your logic there."

"Are you phoning about the interview?"

"Sorry?"

"The interview. About FE funding."

"Oh, no. I got let down on that. It never materialised. Shelved on space issues, I think."

"That's a shame," I said, noting my penis had done a pretty neat impression of the Wicked Witch melting.

"Don't be disappointed, I've got a far better proposition for you. Are you by any chance free this Sunday?"

"Funnily enough, I am," I replied, my spirits lifting. "Chloe's got to work all weekend, so I'm quite the free agent."

"Brilliant!" Emily exclaimed. "Steven and I were pencilled in to play on Sunday in a charity tennis tournament only he's had to pull out because of work as well. As such, I need a partner. Obviously,

92

my first thought was to ask you."

"Go serendipity."

"Exactly," Emily gushed. "It's a great tournament. You'll really enjoy it. Great fun. The vibe is thirty or so mixed pairs split into four groups playing at four different venues. The four group winners go through to the semis and the two victors are in the final. All the matches are played on various private courts dotted around the area and all the house-owning hosts provide loads of wonderful food and drink. We're due to play at Rupert and Aurelia Addington's place. Do you know the Addingtons?"

"No, I don't."

"He's a merchant banker. She spends his money. Absolutely amazing property. Makes our place look like a suburban semi." I raised my eyebrows at this. By further comparison I was currently in the bathroom of a squalid hovel. "It'll be the venue for one of the semis and for the final as well as our group matches because its court has the best playing surface and is in the nicest setting," Emily continued, painting a picture of property porn as opposed to the type I had been viewing. "Beautiful gardens. I'm sure Steven pulled strings to get in that particular group. The thing is, you see, as a group, semi and final hosting court we'll get to play there all day. With no driving off to another venue, we can totally crash out, relax and have a few drinks in between the tennis."

"Sounds idyllic."

"Oh, by the way," Emily remembered. "Bring a cozzie. They've got an indoor pool and everyone will have a dip at some stage or other."

"Wow!" I responded effusively. "Is anyone from the club likely to be playing?"

"Pretty sure not. There are some wealthy people at our club, but socially speaking, this is a different league altogether. We're talking very much the top end of society."

"You said it's for charity?"

"That's right. All the money raised from the entrance fees goes to a good cause. It's a couple of hundred quid per player, but seeing as you're stepping in last minute you're already paid for."

"Thanks very much. One issue, is Steven okay with me stepping in?" I asked, recalling our recent line call dispute.

"He'll have to be, won't he?" Emily replied bluntly. "He's the one who's let me down. What does he think I'm going to do? Play singles in a doubles tournament?"

"You certainly won't have to do that," I assured her. "I'll play with you."

"*And* partner me at tennis?"

"Sure," I managed to say.

"If you like looking at my legs, Paul, wait until you see the bikini I've bought for the swimming pool," Emily cooed.

"Stylish, is it?" It was the only question I could think of.

"Very. Hey, do you want to see a picture of me modelling it?"

"That'd. Be… Great," I laboured.

"I'll send you one on Snapchat, you naughty boy. Promise you won't go screenshotting it and show it to anyone else."

"I promise," I answered, mouth drying faster than a puddle under a Saharan sun.

"Cool. I'll send it in a sec. All the other boring stuff about the tournament times, postcodes, la-de-da, I'll send tomorrow. I'm getting a taxi so I can drink. You should too. See you Sunday, partner."

"Sure. See you Sunday… Thanks for thinking of me, Emily," I grovelled, unsure if she had heard my words so quickly had she hung up.

Within seconds I received a Snapchat notification. With trembling fingers I opened it and saw the selfie of Emily wearing her new bikini. The hand not using her phone had been placed, very provocatively, down the front of her bikini bottoms. The facial expression she wore spelt out the actions of a woman caught in the act of self-pleasuring.

"That'll do," I told myself. "Much better than Pornhub."

"All done?" Chloe asked as I gingerly eased myself back into bed. I had hoped she would be asleep.

"Yeah," I answered off-hand.

"You were gone quite a while."

"Hmm," I replied vaguely.

"Maybe we should have done the deed if it took you that long. Could have been a record."

You total bitch, I thought, saying nothing, rolling over and turning my back on her.

AD

Head propped on hand, I sat staring at my laptop screen, viewing my own Facebook timeline. The words, 'What's on your mind?' alongside the miniature version of my profile picture.

"Plenty," I told the screen.

I had to stop that. Talking to non-sentient, inanimate objects when alone in the flat. It was ridiculous such an action should irk me so much, an irritation clearly driven by my own sense of inadequacy and failure at being alone and not having a partner. Crazy really, seeing where technology was heading. Once I got shacked up with my Sexbot 3000 in a few years' time, I would probably think differently.

The gradual eroding of my soul via one-way conversations aside, the spinning orb of thoughts rolling around my head like a marble in an empty metal biscuit tin, did possess positives. The paperwork relating to purchasing the beach hut had been completed and all that remained was for me to pick up the padlock keys from the estate agent. My car, parked on the road directly outside the flat, pre-loaded to the gunnels with flat pack floor and wall units, a roll of heavy duty lino and enough screws, nails, tiles, tile adhesive and grout to revamp the hut's interior stood ready to go. The pre-cut worktop – new edge laminate strip in place – sat waiting in the hallway a few yards away, waiting to be lashed to the car's new roof rack. Tom, a fellow lecturer in construction, had prepared it for me because cutting and edging a three metre by 600mm wide rolled edge worktop, to the exact length required to span the two floor units, was well beyond my capabilities. When collecting the worktop and paying for all the other materials he had ordered in for me, I also borrowed a selection of Tom's tools – but not his best ones, as he was quick to point out.

"These boys will do you," he said, handing over an old-fashioned carpet bag of tools. "I'm not lending you my best ones to fuck up with your butchery. If you need anything extra, you'll have to buy it."

"What, like a mitre saw?" I asked, citing the most elaborate carpentry tool I knew off the top of my head.

"Like new Stanley knife blades," he replied. "If you come back with ten fingers intact and haven't broken any of my kit, I'll consider the venture a success."

"Will the worktop fit?"

"Of course the worktop will fit... Provided the wall's square," he backtracked.

"And if it isn't?"

"Then you'll have to ease the worktop off the wall and hope the tiling can cover the gap. Or let it in a bit."

I nodded, hit the denial button and put all my faith in my beach hut being a well-constructed, square-walled beach hut.

On the accommodation front, I had booked a small farmhouse room, bed and breakfast only, a few miles outside Southburgh – cheaper rates – for my three-night visit, the original intention to stay from Tuesday until late on the Good Friday. This plan now stood a distinct chance of being superseded due to the latest weather forecast. With dry, sunny and warm weather apparently set for the whole of the Bank Holiday weekend and into the following week, temperatures in the mid to high twenties – cue 'Phew! What a scorcher!' and 'It's 2018 all over again!' headlines – I now intended to stay longer. Maybe until the end of the Easter bank holiday weekend if I felt decadent enough.

Where I might stay for this extended break had become problematic. Everywhere was now booked solid. It appeared vast chunks of the country's population were looking to snatch a quick last-minute Easter break somewhere on the English coast. A happy home-based holiday indulged with a sly snigger aimed at those who had blown thousands to access guaranteed sun abroad. Something would crop up, I told myself, cross that bridge when you come to it.

Excited as I was by my first trip to the beach hut, the issue of Dad's sexuality continued to haunt me and play havoc with my sleeping patterns. A never-ending set of onerous night-time questions mentally churning as I lay flat on my back, hands clasped across my chest, eyes wide open and staring at a pitch-black ceiling. Ones concerning the exact nature of Dad's relationship with my mother, with me, with Malcolm and his other golf club cronies. Of course, this was without the other subset of angst I had on the go. The worries and anxieties caused by Graham's offer I couldn't refuse and the upcoming Ofsted inspection also clamoured hungrily for CPU resources. Working out a possible method of levering open Malcolm's closet, when the time came for it, a task appearing more impossible the more I thought of it.

Sitting facing the glowing screen, a dull sleep-deprived thud spreading across my forehead, I called it time for bed despite it only being nine. I wanted to make a prompt start in the morning to hopefully miss the worst of the traffic. Shutting down the laptop, I noticed a new Facebook friend request had popped up – a little red circle with the number '1' on it, imploring me not to leave. The last one I had received was from a woman called Katrina Creekmore who, when I clicked on her profile out of curiosity, asked if I wanted to see her cute pussy and big tits. The bit about hacking my account had been omitted. I had actually laughed out loud, the black humour coming from recognising the same profile picture from an earlier request that day. A Ms Cecily Xandra Flo who had asked, 'Hey, what's up? I am single, F19. Look For Someone Who Wants To Be Slap By My Big 38D Melons. Follow me. Looking for live sex tonight'.

"Haven't got the time, gorgeous," I said, closing the laptop down. "I've got to get up early tomorrow."

I really did have to stop doing that.

I was on the road by seven, surprisingly having slept a bit better than previous nights. On venturing outside, the dawning sky was cloudless, a faultless blue ceiling to a perfect day. Tying on the worktop to the roof rack, the air, although fresh, hadn't been cold despite the clear night. The morning promised a later delivery of the forecasted warmth. Driving, I felt good, happy to be on my way to the hut, my one agitation, unremittingly checked via anxious glances through the upper part of my windscreen, the sudden disappearance of a rolled edge worktop. Fearing my knot skills weren't adequate to secure the Galaxy Gloss hydrofoil strapped to my car, I maintained a constant vigil. I also kept it under sixty, in case my rope skills turned out fine but my roof rack fitting ones less so. The temptation to gun it downhill, to see if all held firm and I could actually take off for a few seconds, remained a massive no-go.

The early start failed to be the traffic-dodging panacea I had hoped for and progress took longer than expected. With two hours elapsed and less than eighty miles completed, I pulled into a service station for a caffeine intake, to stretch my legs and relieve my bladder. Sitting in the service station with a cappuccino and a chocolate chip muffin parked on the dirty table in front of me, I took refuge in my phone. One text notification from my mother wished me a safe journey and reminded me to send pictures of the hut. I texted back to thank her, telling her I was well on my way and had stopped for coffee. Before and after photos would follow in due course, I assured. 'Will I be able to tell the difference?' she immediately replied. 'I bloody hope so!' I messaged back.

With nothing else prompting me, I opened up my Facebook page and reluctantly clicked on the single friend request still showing. To my stupefaction, it was from a Jason Jeffries. I opened up his timeline and clicked on the profile picture. It was unmistakably him, a thirty-something-year-old him. JJ. I gawped at his face. The last time I had seen JJ in the flesh was nearly twenty years ago. Scrolling quickly through JJ's Facebook profile it appeared obvious he had only just set it up. There was nothing else on it other than the one profile picture. JJ had disappeared years ago and now, it seemed, for whatever reason, he was back. If it was him. And not an extremely clever scam set up by a hacker genius who had devised an elaborate one-off purely as a means of relieving me of my vast untold personal wealth. Yeah, right. I accepted JJ's request with no further hesitation.

Coffee drunk and muffin eaten, I made a visit to the loo before setting off. Back in the car, after an arbitrary waggle of the worktop to check all was still secure, I buckled up and decided to have one last look at my phone. The red circle of reward had lit up on Facebook Messenger. It had to be. It was.

'Hi, Paul, how's it going?' the message from JJ read. 'Yes! I'm back in the country! Got so much to tell you it's mental. Are you still playing tennis? We must meet up. I'm based in Norwich. Back coaching again. Where are you? Same place? Message me soon. Be fantastic to see you.'

Double thumb style, I quickly replied. 'Great to hear you're back! Tennis has been put on hold, I'm afraid. I've got plenty to tell you as well! Too much, unfortunately. Crazy enough, I'm in Southburgh all week. I'm doing up a beach hut I've just bought. You're really close if you're in Norwich. Why don't you come down to the hut for a day. The weather's going to be great. We can sit, eat ice creams, drink coffee and chat about old times.'

Messenger told me JJ was typing.

'Sounds cool. Got a few things to tie up. How about Thursday?'

I sent a thumbs up and then typed 'I'll message directions later.'

Jason replied with a thumbs up of his own.

Buzzing, I started the car. JJ was back! How great was that?

Arriving and then crawling through Southburgh in nose to tail traffic, everywhere was heaving. The small coastal town filled with cars, people, dogs, seagulls, the whole nine yards. No one was trapped inside a stasis pod this time, the transformation from my previous visit remarkable. Driver's window down, elbow resting on sill, warm air rushing in, I cruised, taking in the hundreds of families and couples happily mooching up and down the prom and street pavements. Everyone appeared ecstatic and surprised in equal measure, as if unable to comprehend their collective luck, to be outside in April wearing only shorts and tee shirts. En masse, they formed a colourful carnival, a life-affirming horde eager to take its chances with melanoma for an early-in-the-year fix of vitamin D. Off the streets, others were sitting on benches, grass lawns, walls, chairs outside coffee shops and garden furniture outside pubs, soaking up the heat like iguanas on rocks. They drank beer, coffee and soft drinks, licked popsicles, whippy ice creams or sat with sheets of white paper resting on laps, feeding themselves fish and chips, stopping only to lick the salt off their fingers.

On the beach, children were playing and running riot, tiny bundles of energy building their sand castles with buckets, spades and hands. Digging sand, shaping sand, throwing sand, kicking sand, running here, running there, transporting sand from one sandy place to another, their methodology only known to themselves. Other children were playing games, throwing balls, kicking balls, hitting balls with bats, paddles and rackets; throwing Frisbees, throwing Nerfs, screaming and giggling, the warming sun beating down on their bare sun-creamed backs.

A few brave souls were in the sea, filling buckets and loading water pistols to throw or squirt at siblings and friends. Pretend enemies whose bodies arched like contorted letter 'C's to avoid the watery projectiles sent their way. Some contented themselves by simply running in and out of the sea, or by daring each other to go in deeper. To go in above the bellybutton badge of honour. Every inch taken towards the horizon, an agonising, enthralling sting of icy immersion.

All young beach life had its guardians present. The parents and grandparents of those joyful protagonists, some of whom were supine, some sitting, some standing, watching and laughing at the antics before them, ready to step in at any sign of danger. Some felt compelled to join in, and when they did, they too acted like children as the touch of sand and sea regressed them to play out their memories of bygone seaside days.

The whole panoramic shoreline shimmered vibrantly, its mindset carefree and euphoric, a veritable utopia for toddler, teenager, adult and pensioner alike. Inching through the traffic, the mill-pond sea sat away in the distance, reflecting a million dazzling pinpoints off the benign ripples of its surface. Further still, sea and sky merged into a mass of blue. A beautiful benevolent blue. This was the superlative English seaside I had imagined on my previous visit. What fortune to be living it out for real on my very first trip.

Now. Where the fuck was I going to park?

I took a chance, left the car on double yellows and rushed into the estate agents to pick up the padlock keys. Back in the car quickly, I set off with the intention – rather the forlorn hope – of securing a parking space as near to the hut as possible. The main car park to the back of the pier would have spaces but was too far away to be practicable with all the gear I had to carry. With a helping pair of hands present, I could have double parked at the top of the steps leading down to the promenade, quickly dropped off all the kit, and left my helper to guard it while I went and parked elsewhere. On my own, not an option I was prepared to risk.

On the second hopeful run of kerb-crawling the coast road – looking for a parking space, not the purchase of sexual favours – lady luck smiled down on me and I spotted a couple getting into their parked car. Hazards on, I waited for them to go and slipped into the vacated spot the second they pulled off, breathing a huge sigh of relief. I had ended up three hundred yards from my hut, a result given the circumstances. Getting out of the car, I stretched my legs and soaked up the atmosphere and energy of the crowds around me. As much as I wanted, I couldn't switch to holiday mode and join them. I had work to do.

Over the next two hours, I performed the mundane back-breaking task of humping everything from the car down the concrete steps, along the promenade to place it on the hut's veranda. After the first run, I asked the family sitting outside the hut to the left of mine if they wouldn't mind keeping an eye on it while I fetched the rest. This simple request ballooned into a full twenty-minute conversation where, after their opening remark on how lucky we were, what with the fantastic weather we were having, they told me they came from Lincolnshire. The four of them, husband, wife and the two boys aged eight and ten had hired the hut for the entire two-week school break and were staying overnight in a nearby hotel. The mother moaned at how much more expensive it had been to book in the holidays, calling it a bloody disgrace and remarking it was no wonder parents pulled their kids out of school and sucked up the cheaper fine. Her husband nodded his head.

To save money, they had gone bed and breakfast because both the boys were fussy eaters and it was pointless paying for food if they weren't going to eat it. Their only worry, now they had found a restaurant catering to everyone's taste, was their boys' specialist dermatological sun cream running out. The father joking he hoped the weather would break just as he squeezed the last drop from the tube. But not really. Who would ever want fantastic weather like this to end? He was convinced it would be another summer like 1976 and 2018, what with global warming and all that. The mother said a friend of hers had paid over six grand to take her family to the Canaries for seven nights. She reckoned her friend would be 'pig sick' when she heard about the fantastic weather we were having. I nodded, saying I could well believe it and had thought much the same myself.

For my part, I confirmed I was the new owner of the beach hut, first visit – what a time to come, when we were having such fantastic weather – and I intended to upgrade it for the first few days of my stay. After completing the work, I told them, I would most likely stay on for a few days longer because of the fantastic weather. The husband and wife both strongly agreed and thought it an excellent idea. There was no way I should leave my newly revamped beach hut once all the hard work was done they chimed. I simply had to stay and enjoy it. You know, what with the fantastic weather we were having.

Good relationships established with one set of neighbours, I embarked on carrying my second, third, fourth, seemingly ad infinitum number, of heavy payloads from car to hut, weaving my ungainly way through the crowds. The strenuous nature of my undertaking reinforcing the fact I was one of only a handful of people on the prom on a mission. Everyone else appeared a free agent with ample leisure time at their disposal, swanning around, enjoying themselves, their biggest concern demolishing an ice cream before it melted. That or finding the public toilets because one of the kids was bursting/grandad's prostate was playing up again. My time will come, I self-motivated, already soaked in sweat, finally downing the last item from the car. Tom's carpet bag, the object I deemed most valuable because it didn't belong to me.

My first job, on unlocking the beach hut, was to take a photo of its gross interior. My 'before' shot to send to Mum later. From that moment on there was no hanging around and I cracked on with matters. Throughout the afternoon and into the early evening, I worked like a Trojan, pushed on by high enthusiasm. My only break, a tea time supper of fish and chips and a well-earned cup of tea. The near constant work regime only punctuated by answering the numerous well-intended, cheerful 'Doing it up, then?' questions-of-the-bleedin'-obvious from passing strollers.

For a start, I removed all the hut's old fitments, including the sulking stove – first item out – the hideously scuffed lino floor covering the last. The only thing I set aside and thought worth refitting was the red fire extinguisher, its tiny pressure dial's needle sitting neatly in the middle of the green safe-to-use zone. The tongue and groove floor of the beach hut, once revealed, looked sturdy enough, a relief the old lino hadn't hidden any nasty secrets like woodworm, dry rot, an illiterate allegiance to a Premier League football club or an inverted pentagram daubed in the blood of a sacrificed first-born child. After sweeping the floor with a dustpan and brush, sand really does get everywhere, I set about laying the new floor covering, the first to-do job on the refurb list. Tom had recommended this course of action and I had no intention of deviating from it, mainly for practical reasons, but partially out of concern for his tools taking on a mind of their own and assaulting me should I contravene their master's wishes. He had insisted the risk of damaging the new floor covering, while working on it, was more than compensated by the ease of laying it on a clear area with no awkward floor units to cut round.

It proved so, and despite my inexperience, I managed to trim the lino edges somewhere near a reasonable fit by the time the sun began to sink over the westerly town centre. As it turned out, I did have ample sharp Stanley knife blades to make the necessary cuts – several new ones were enclosed in the knife's handle – and, even better, I still had ten fingers after making them. So far, no stitches, so good. Lifting the edges of the floor covering back up, I stuck the double-sided tape I had brought with me to the floor and then, having peeled off the protective paper, stuck the floor covering down to the tape. Aching and now very tired, I clambered off my knees and slid my foot around the entire internal perimeter of the beach hut in one last attempt at maximising floor-to-tape-to-covering adhesion. Happy there were no edges curling back up like out-of-date sandwiches, I stacked everything new, plus the fire extinguisher, back inside the hut, closed the double doors and padlocked them shut.

As I set off to leave for the night, the pile of rubbish on the veranda, everything that had previously been inside, sat brooding, looking at me in a stroppy 'what ya gonna do about it?' manner. Nothing today, was my answer and my shoulders sagged at the daunting effort required to clear it. Maybe I would leave it until JJ arrived and beg him to help me.

That night in bed, ensconced in the unpretentious but cosy farm-house bedroom, I ached in muscles I didn't know I owned. The knocks and scuffs to my hands, ones I never noticed making during the adrenaline-fuelled frenzy of ripping everything out, were sore and throbbing. Every now and then, my hands would violently spasm in an attack of cramp, turning them into odious raking claws and I would have to ease my fingers straight by forcing them hard against a surface. Welcome to the world of full-on DIY, screamed the body of the white-collar worker. Despite my discomfort, I soon fell asleep, any mental worries I might possess completely usurped by utter physical fatigue.

Up early to get a prime parking spot close to the beach hut, I was down for breakfast – a bit stiff, but psychologically I was game – bang on its start time of seven. I opted for a full English, unusually, in the hope it would see me through to the afternoon. A tight schedule lay ahead as I wanted to get all the units in, the worktop fixed and, if possible, the tiles above it. That would just leave me the job of grouting on the morning of JJ's arrival. Standing in the way of this aspiration towered an intimidating wall of flat pack kitchen unit assembly. All that hardware 'A' screwed into arrowed holes in section of flat pack (diagram 1) bullshit and hardware 'B' – virtually indistinguishable from hardware 'A' but project ruining if used – screwed into arrowed holes in section of flat pack (diagram 2). As a joke, the one on you, flat pack section (diagram 1) and flat pack section (diagram 2) appear identical unless forensically checked for being handed. The giveaway difference something fantastically standout, like one single black dot signifying one drilled hole.

I hated building flat pack units with a passion. Chloe and I had bought new bedroom furniture shortly after getting married and my attempts at assembling it, for two whole weekends, register as one of the most frustrating moments in my life. And that's from someone who's been through a divorce with a solicitor like Furlington. The storage unit housing three soft close drawers was the nadir. A complicated piece whose assembly instructions appeared written in an impenetrable cryptic language and with a parts list as long as an orangutan's arm. The very first tool I needed, a 6mm Allen key, had been missing, either presumed dead or withheld by a malevolent minimum-wage factory packer.

Downing the last few mouthfuls of my tea, I sent JJ a message, the sat-nav post code for the car park behind the pier and detailed instructions on how to walk from there to the hut. 'From car park head towards sea and promenade. Walk in southerly direction along promenade with sea to left, pass pier, collect £200, carry on for 400 yards where you will come to set of concrete steps on right leading up to road. Do not climb and carry on. Eleventh hut is mine. I will be sitting outside knackered and bleeding, eating leftover tile grout from a bucket. If I've happened to slip into a diabetic coma, please resuscitate me.'

By the time I got to my car he had messaged back.

'Spot on. Will try and get to you by eleven. Save some of that tasty grout for me. I've been surviving on spaghetti bolognese made from broken racket strings and pigeon shit for the last six years. Hoping it's white grout and not grey, I've spent a fortune on getting these veneers. Re saving you, I once CPR'd a man to death, so don't get your hopes up.'

Southburgh life was starting to stir by the time I drove through its narrow roads. Delivery vans and lorries dropping off their cargo to various commercial enterprises, a few tortured middle-aged joggers wearing out their hip and knee joints and several Lycra-clad wannabe professional cyclists sped along the coast road on their two-grand carbon steeds, each one tête de la course. Bagging an early-bird-reward parking space only three cars away from the concrete steps, I locked up the car, bought a parking ticket and sauntered to the top of the steps, stopped, and sucked in the magnificence of the morning. A gentle breeze was wafting warm air up from the south west, a world away from the bitter north-easterly of my walk with Kevin. The sea flat, inviting and blue. Factor fifty, if you were fair-skinned, really would be a necessity. Winding my thoughts in and telling myself there would be plenty of time for eulogising later, I set off down to the promenade.

An old couple were already outside the third hut along from the steps. Him furiously reading a copy of the Daily Mail, her knitting Ronaldinho-style, needles a blur of movement, deceptive eyes looking elsewhere. Curiosity piqued, I wanted to ask what she was knitting but instead stuck to a bland greeting they both returned. Somehow I doubted she was knocking up socks for refugees, although that might have said more about me and my take on her husband's choice of newspaper. All the other huts up to mine were unoccupied, evidently the day still too early for an appearance by the Lincolnshire family.

Opening up, I scrutinised my floor-laying skills. Not bad. I rubbed the back of my hand under my nose. No point procrastinating. Flat pack time. Two hours later, the floor base units and the one wall base unit were built with only one meandering scenic diversion taken down a procedural-misinterpretation back road. A journey soundtracked by highly situation-specific Anglo-Saxon profanities such as 'fuck-arsing screws', 'shitting instructions' and 'where's the fucking M8 by 40mm roundhead bolts?'. At least no parts or tools were missing.

Another hour and a half saw the wall unit successfully hung with its full complement of doors in place. Twenty minutes of interminable twiddling had been used up getting the two doors to hang straight, close properly and have a sensibly-sized parallel gap between them. Starting to wilt through hunger and thirst, I locked up and went out into the sunshine, the heat impressive, hotter than the day before, the brightness blinding after working so long inside the hut. People were everywhere, the Lincolnshire family elsewhere. Standing on the veranda, I immediately began to unwind, the happiness of the surrounding throng passing to me by some manner of osmosis.

I turned right once stepping off the hut's veranda, heading in the opposite direction to the steps and the pier, on my way towards Kevin's legendary potable water tap. Noting it as I passed – a small, thirsty queue had formed to refill their virtue-signalling water bottles – I pressed onwards towards an establishment my estate agent had mentioned in equally glowing terms. Half a football pitch on, I arrived at an uncovered crazy-paving patio with eight wooden tables and chairs arranged on it. The patio fronted a homely café set ten yards behind it, one constructed from black shiplapped weatherboard with a cedar-wood shingled, shallow-pitched roof adding to its retro-charm. Inside the café were more tables and chairs and what looked like a busy kitchen. Perusing the menu and prices handwritten in chalk on a large blackboard trestle positioned on the patio's edge, I read 'Home-made lasagne - £8.99' which sounded appetising. Deciding to dine al fresco, I sat down at the one remaining unoccupied small table boasting only two chairs tucked underneath. Seated facing the sun, I closed my eyes, relaxed and absorbed the heat now beaming directly on to my face. The café's blackboard menu had stated 'Waitress Service'. Suited me, all I had to do was sit and wait.

"How can help?" a female voice asked a few minutes later.

Opening my eyes and pulling my head round to answer the accented voice, a stunning-looking young woman stood beside me. High cheek-boned, blue-eyed, generous-mouthed and with blonde hair pulled back in a long ponytail, I stared at her without answering for a time period she may well have considered bordered on sexual harassment. Even if I hadn't heard her voice, I would have ascertained by her looks she wasn't a local. At a guess, I would have said Ukrainian or Russian, if not, then definitely from somewhere out of the old Eastern Bloc. Flicking, I hoped, a furtive gaze lower, I glimpsed a curvaceous and well-proportioned body contained within an outfit comprising a simple white blouse, black leggings and trainers. Any number of super-attractive Eastern European sportswomen I had seen on TV over the years competing at athletic meets or tennis tournaments sprung to mind.

"Yes... Thank you," I stumbled. "Can I have the home-made... lasagne." My voice fell away in confusion as a doppelganger waitress brought food to a family of four on the adjacent table. A woman identical in every way to my waitress apart from the colour of her blue blouse. The blue-topped waitress caught my stare and returned it with practised nonchalance.

"Is twin sister, Svetlana," my waitress said impassively, having observed a reaction she must have seen, literally, hundreds if not thousands of times in her life. Probably every day of her life. "Am

Tatiana, white top. Svetlana, blue top," she recapped, smiling and showing off perfect white teeth.

"Where are you from?" I asked.

"Russia. Are here one year now. Haff get job together. Haff always get job together," Tatiana explained.

I nodded earnestly, as if listening to a matter of grave state importance. Behind the act, I drank in her beauty, just like I had when watching Emily Winstone play tennis. That same rush of desire and craving stirring deep inside. And, incredibly, there were *two* of them!

I took the 'after' shot and sent it with the 'before' one to Mum via WhatsApp. Pleased with what I had achieved – the two photos confirmed it – I plonked myself down in one of the two folding chairs I had bought an hour earlier and positioned directly outside the beach hut. Mission accomplished, deep breath and relax. I had finished everything on schedule right down to the grouting of the tiles. Time for a well-deserved rest and to unwind. In my head, I pencilled in a distant Beach Hut Phase 2 bill of work, due to commence this summer: the hut's external paintwork.

JJ was on his way. He had messaged me saying he had arrived safely in the car park and was walking southwards towards the hut. Sitting in the gloriously hot sun as the heavy prom traffic ambled by a fleeting cloud of unease passed over me, one I could only assign to apprehension. It had been a long time. Without doubt an awful lot of water had flowed under both our bridges. Would we still connect like we had as teenagers? I very much hoped so. The text message banter suggested we would, but until we had shared each other's company for a length of time, who could be sure? Convinced we both had a story to tell, I wondered whether JJ's documented the accumulation of as much life-damaging baggage as mine. Either way, more important was the aspiration our reunion might lead to an old lost friend becoming a new found one. Real friends had proved elusive over the last couple of years and a close confidant would undoubtedly make a welcome addition to my current sad, lonely existence.

On tenterhooks, I kept my eyes trained northwards along the promenade towards the pier, scouting the heads of the oncoming crowds, keen to catch a first glimpse of the best tennis player, for his age, I had ever seen play. It wasn't too hard to spot him when he eventually arrived, even at some distance, and despite the passing of many years I easily recognised him. Taller than nearly everybody around him, JJ hadn't changed a great deal, his hair remained cut in a similar style – long, foppish – although possibly a shade or two darker than I remembered. Now closer to me and less hidden by the crowds, JJ looked physically fit, his previously gangly body now fuller and more muscled, his stomach still washboard flat. On his back, JJ carried a huge red Wilson racket bag, worn like a rucksack, his thumbs tucked underneath its straps. I stood up from my chair and waved enthusiastically at him to attract his attention once he was less than several huts away. He saw my wild gesticulations, smiled and waved back.

"How you doing, man?" he asked, jogging the last few yards and offering out a hand which I pumped with vigour. "Looong time no see," he exclaimed scrutinising my face, I assumed, for signs of wear and tear. I couldn't see much on his.

"It is. Much too long. Good to see you, JJ. Glad you could come," I enthused, slapping his upper arm with my left palm.

Slightly self-conscious we were still handshaking ten seconds in, we unclasped hands and stepped back from each other, JJ's more muscular racket-wielding arm the classic giveaway of the serious tennis player.

"No worries," JJ confirmed.

"How long have you been back in the UK?" I asked, marvelling at the handsome and confident man before me, the one I had last seen as a rather gauche boy.

"Not long. Only a few weeks. Once I got back and started to sort myself out I thought I'd try and pick up a few of the good threads from my old life. You and others from the club, like Emma, Jennifer and Melissa. Haven't heard back," he said shrugging.

"I'm not really in contact with any of them anymore," I admitted.

"So, this is the beach hut, then?" JJ asked, changing the subject.

"Yeah. I only got the keys three days ago."

"If you were a famous rapper, you could call it your Bitch Hut," JJ joshed, a smile on his face.

I laughed at his joke. "It was a bitch putting together the flat pack units and that's about as close as it gets. All that old crap is what I took out," I said, pointing to the rubbish on the veranda. "I finished the new replacement units and tiling yesterday. I did the grouting early this morning."

"None leftover?"

"All used up. Your teeth are safe."

JJ walked up on to the veranda and poked his head inside the beach hut to check it out. "Looks nice. Are you a builder by trade?"

Pleased JJ had considered this a genuine possibility, I told him I wasn't, manual labour not being my thing, and I didn't exactly have a 'trade'.

"Not unless being a college lecturer counts," I told him. "I teach higher level BTEC business courses. Ten years now. Any limited DIY skills I might possess have been picked up along the way. I did have some help," I confessed, jerking my head towards the inside of the hut. "A friend who teaches carpentry at my college prepared the worktop."

"Have you always taught?"

"A levels, university, teacher training and then on to the real thing, that's my vocational story."

"Your dad's a teacher, isn't he?"

"In his early years he was, before he moved into administration.

112

He passed away a few years back."

"Oh, I'm sorry to hear that," JJ commiserated. "I think I can only remember seeing him a few times. I can remember your mum more, dropping you off and picking you up from tennis. He can't have been that old, can he?"

"No, not that old at all," I replied. "What have you been up to on the job front for all these years? Did you get close to making it as a player?" I asked, keen to shift the conversation away from Dad.

JJ pulled a face. "No. Nowhere near it. The big trouble with chasing a dream is how you cope when it blows up in your face and takes your fucking head off. Unlike you, I've done nothing settled. A bit of this, a bit of that, shit work mainly, some okay stuff in between. I have got back into tennis, though, playing and coaching over the last couple of years. It's the reason why I'm back. To see if I can get the coaching going and actually do something with tennis and my life. What I'd really like to do is coach talented youngsters and play competitively at a *decent* level," JJ explained. "A guy I know through a friend of a friend is the head coach at a good club in Norwich. He's offered me a lot of sessions helping him and they're paying me a few quid to play for them this summer. They want to get the club's first team up from regional level to national level if possible. It seemed a solid enough base to warrant coming home," he said, stepping back down from the veranda, taking the massive bag off his back and putting it by one of the chairs. "I'm hopeful it'll give me a starting point. They've got a couple of indoor courts and my aim is to set up a centre of excellence for local kids and push them on. Try and get the natural athletes into tennis rather than losing them to football and rugby. That's the plan, anyway," JJ said, his expression one of enthusiasm. "Incidentally, I've got a couple of bottles of beer in there," he said, eyeing the tennis bag. "I've only just bought them and they're still cold. Fancy one?" I indicated I did. "This weather's well nice, isn't it? Hot for the time of year. Crazy. How about we kick back, have a drink and seriously catch up on all the years we've lost?"

"Sounds perfect."

JJ extracted the two beer bottles from the voluminous tennis bag and with both in one hand he returned to the veranda, placed the edge of the cap from one bottle against the top edge of one of the old cabinet doors and smacked down on it violently. The cap flew off. He repeated the action with the other beer bottle and then returned, handing one to me.

"Little trick I learnt when I was going through one of my 'stages'," he said.

"What one was that?"

"Drunken alcoholic."

I wobbled my head up and down, digesting JJ's candour. It looked like we were in for a gritty, warts-and-all reunion. No air-brushed, my-life's-been-perfect social media bullshit here. Good. That suited me down to the ground. I had plenty to get off my chest. Most of it ugly.

"It's an awful long time, JJ," I commented. "I'm betting a lot has happened to both of us. Personally speaking, I think the one with the most fucked up story should go first."

"That'd be me, then," JJ opined.

"Mine's a blast. Especially my latest revelation," I warned, thinking I would tell him about Dad if we were being brutally honest and setting everything out on the table.

"Really?" JJ asked, his eyes narrowing. "Intrigue, man. I never had you down as that guy. Ordered, regulated, everything planned, that was you. Or so I reckoned. I'm looking forward to hearing it."

"Up until a few years ago, you'd have been bang on the money," I admitted, taking a swig of the cold beer. "Sorry. I'm not playing the ideal host very well. You are the guest. You serve first."

"Fair enough. Which end do you want?" I pointed to one of the chairs. JJ nodded and slumped into the other one next to his bag. "Fucking hell. Where to begin?" he demanded of the sky, his head angled upwards, the nape of his neck resting on the chair's back.

"How about from when you 'left' the club," I suggested.

"When they kicked me out?"

"From when they kicked you out."

"It was the moped riding that was the final straw," JJ confided, taking his first mouthful of beer. "When I crashed it into the net, it spilt some petrol from the tank and ruined a part of the Tarmac court's surface. I remember telling the club committee not to fret because it was a shit court in any case. I told them there were always loads of bad bounces and the whole court needed resurfacing, irrespective of the bit I'd fucked up. Didn't go down too well."

"I can imagine. So what happened next?"

"I was banned, sine die as they say, and within a month, proving that fate likes to kick you in the nuts when you're down, Dad lost his job. Not *lost* it exactly," JJ quantified. "He had to relocate. It all came as a bit of a nasty shock. The company announced plans to close his office with immediate effect. Normal bollocks about 'saving costs' and 'having to centralise'. They offered him the choice of redundancy or a relocation package to work at head office."

"Where was that?"

"Dublin. To be fair, it was a horrific call for Mum and Dad to have to make. In the end, they decided Dad needed to keep the job more than we needed to stay where we were. The redundancy package offered wasn't overly generous and the chances of Dad finding an equally well paid job seemed unlikely. Forced into a corner, they took the relocation route and within four months the three of us were living in Ireland. New house, new life and a new school for me. None of us knew a fucking soul apart from Dad, all of them his colleagues who'd taken the same option."

"That was the year you won a few rounds in the boys' singles at

Junior Wimbledon, wasn't it?"

"Yeah. My summer career high followed by my abrupt plunge into winter oblivion. Ironically, tennis was one of the reasons why Dad decided he needed to keep his job. He was funding me big time, putting a lot of money into my fledgling tennis career, paying for coaching, equipment, travelling and tournament fees. The LTA, the bastards, weren't helping at all. Dad hoped if he could just keep me going for another year I'd improve enough to the point where they would have to recognise my ability and give me funding." JJ's look turned wistful. "Never happened. All of us struggled in our new surroundings. Me the most. I never fitted in at school and the tennis infrastructure was worse in Ireland than it was in England, and that's saying something. I had to travel for miles to get coaching, hitting sessions, any sort of competition, and even then it wasn't great. Partly because of that and partly because I was so unsettled, my game stalled and my ranking dropped. I didn't get any better. Well, not enough to compete at the level I needed to play at. I became more and more disheartened and more and more unhappy. I've always had a mischievous streak in me and it soon developed into one a mile wide. I got in with the wrong crowd, got into drinking, got into girls and let everything slide. Tennis, education, my life. Mum wasn't fairing much better. She hated where she was too and home became a battleground rather than a safe haven as she and Dad argued, constantly, over the decision to move. The whole thing was a disaster."

Sitting in the increasing heat I listened, absorbed, to JJ's story. Despite the arguments and unhappiness, his family remained in Dublin, trapped by the common disease of having to earn money to exist, even if that existence in itself was woeful. Leaving school at eighteen with few qualifications and a strong disillusionment with tennis, JJ's disenchantment was magnified by hearing stories of other better connected players, ones he had beaten down the years, who had received LTA funding. This news only served to increase his feelings of marginalisation and of being treated unfairly, a mass of 'what if?' questions left swirling in his head. LTA funding would have meant he could have stayed in England, had better coaching and had access to hitting partners of top quality. Could he have made it as a pro if the LTA had stepped in? That was the big question, one he could never answer with any certainty. Statistically unlikely, for sure, but never having been given the chance was the towering issue. No satisfaction lay in discovering every one of the funded players failed to make the grade.

Having finished school and with zero desire to play tennis, JJ drifted in and out of casual work, spending most of his pay packet on his newly-developed love of booze. A bleak, depressing, two-year period of heavy drinking culminating in alcoholism, one used to blot out the pain of a failed tennis career, eventually came to an end when his then girlfriend, Darina, managed to sober him up. Now in a better place, in love for the first time and with a fresh purpose, they both ground out the long hours in their poorly paid jobs to save for a dream – backpacking around Asia for as long as their money lasted. Starting with flights to Bangkok, visits to Laos, Cambodia, Vietnam, India – 'never had the shits like it' – Indonesia and China followed before a tour-ending return to Thailand and a stay at Railay Beach. On the second night there, a 'misunderstanding' over a Thai sex worker abruptly terminated the relationship. The next day Darina left both JJ and Thailand, heading home for Ireland, her heart broken.

"A 'misunderstanding'?" I asked, quoting the word back to JJ.

"She thought I'd fooled around with this Thai sex worker," he explained. "She had invested so much time and energy in me, done so much for me and was so in love with me, it had all become a bit claustrophobic from my point of view. Consequently, I was toying with the idea, only toying, mind you, of expanding my sexual horizons. I was young and immature. Stupidly, I gave her the chance to doubt me."

"With reason?"

"Oh, yeah. *Totally* with reason. My toying went route one to doing. If she had known what I'd really got up to she would have killed me rather than just left me. There were two of them, you see. I *had* fooled around. Fooled around with *two* Thai sex workers. The thing was, I'd never done it with two women at the same time," JJ quickly continued, getting his justification in fast. "I thought if I didn't take the chance and do it now, while I was in Thailand, and remember it was right at the end of the trip and we were nearly out of money, I would *never* get the chance to do it." JJ's head moved in remorse. "I did love her and will forever be thankful for what she did for me," he said, his face hangdog. "It still didn't stop me, though."

"Did you regret it?"

"At the time, I did," JJ admitted. "The trouble was, I was more motivated by the regret I might experience if I *didn't* do it."

I laughed. "What was it like," I asked, sounding like a sibling quizzing his elder brother, "going with two women?"

JJ puffed out his cheeks, his brow creasing, as if I had asked him to explain quantum mechanics in a snappy soundbite. "The best way I can explain to someone like you," he began, which I thought a bit condescending, "is like this. You know how sometimes you're playing a tennis match and there's this one game when you play absolutely out of your skin? Where you play utterly fantastic?"

I nodded. "Sort of."

"The game where you hit winners from everywhere. From all over the court," he elaborated. "It's the game where you make a handful of brilliant strokes you would never normally produce. You're left thinking; 'Wow! That was amazing. Truly amazing!' Then you realise it's over. Finished. Really quickly. And you wonder if you'll ever be able to play like it again. You leave elated, yet somehow disappointed. Strange feeling."

"But at least you've done it. Played that way once," I countered.

That's true," JJ admitted. "There is that to it. I did have that brief memory to sustain me through the initial loneliness. Through the resulting carnage of Darina leaving me."

"Men, eh? Slaves to the sexual switch. The one we can't resist flicking despite knowing it's going to pop the main fuse. The one driven by a FOMO."

"Are you talking from personal experience here?" JJ asked, a look of doubt on his face.

"Let's hear all of your story before we start worrying about mine."

"Fair enough," JJ agreed and returned to telling me about the next segment of his life.

Darina might have left Thailand, but JJ stayed, eking out an illegal living working in bars and kitchens for the best part of two more years. Over this period of time he earned a little money, screwed a seemingly never-ending succession of naïve, female backpackers who were seduced by his local knowledge and easy charm before somehow managing to procure a year's working visa for Australia. Flying to Sydney, he initially stayed in an eight-to-a-room hostel – more women fell under his charm – and soon found a job within sports retail. Inside two months he was out of the hostel and sofa surfing around flats of the people he had got to know.

"Wherever I plugged in my mobile phone charger, that was my home," JJ said. "At the end of the first year, I found a farmer who signed off my three-month 'specific work' requirement. It cost me a thousand Aussie dollars, but fuck picking fruit in that heat in some rustic backwater miles from anywhere."

Around this time, one of JJ's friends, Ian, a guy originally from Birmingham who now had permanent residency, became involved with a local girl who was a tennis player. He mentioned to her how this guy sleeping on his sofa claimed to have played Junior Wimbledon and insisted she took him to her club to find out if it was true or not. Not having played in years, JJ turned up at the club and had a hit with her using a borrowed racket. Ava wasn't much of a player, but both she and the members could see, underneath the rust, that JJ had been a very good one.

"It all ended on a sour note," JJ explained. "Ava came on to me and, not being a person with enough willpower to look a gift horse in the mouth, I came on to her, as it were. Lots of times. Eventually Ian found out and I was off his sofa quicker than a Tsonga first serve."

"Where did you go next?" I asked, bemused at JJ's ongoing sex-fest travelogue.

"Another flat. Some Danish girl. Can't remember her name. She came into the bar where I was working, started speaking to me and when she found out I was English she told me how her parents had once bought her an M & S food hamper for her birthday. Bit weird, but there you go. Quick as a flash, I said I would have been more interested if it had been an S & M hamper. 'So you're into bondage?' she asked. I thought, why not, and told her I was. End of the evening she's a bit pissed, I'm a bit pissed, we go back to this flat she's renting, her parents were loaded and funding her big time, and I tied her up and fucked her. She loved it. I quite liked it too. Made me start thinking I would quite like to be tied up while she gave me a blowjob. Unfortunately, it turned out she was forever submissive. When I wanted to be tied up I had to do nearly all the rope work myself. She'd only chip in by doing my last free arm. Sort of took the shine off it, to be honest. Anyway, it didn't last long and I moved up to the Gold Coast. I met this older Aussie lady, late thirties, walking on the beach, and we hooked up for a few months. Think it was a bit of a rebound thing with her, she was always going on about her 'dick of an ex-boyfriend'. I didn't mind. We had fun, she was great in bed, and she paid for most of my food. When that ended due to my second year visa running out, I left her and headed back to Europe and spent a long time in Spain. I ran the pedalos on Benidorm beach before getting a promotion to the jet skis, sold timeshares in Malaga, did more bar work on the Costa Blanca, got a job onboard a big tourist-trip catamaran doing the mike commentary and did a bit of iffy drug dealing in Ibiza. It was mental. I was shagging my dick off," JJ exclaimed, wide-eyed with wonder. "I'd meet a girl at the start of her holiday, spend a week, ten days, sometimes a fortnight having it off with her and once she went home I'd get another. And when she went home I'd get another one after that. It was endless. Endless sex, sun and sea. In that order. Eventually, even the most surreal landscapes get a bit boring, so at the end of that year I shipped off to Austria and worked several winters as a ski lift attendant. In the summers, I would just concentrate on avoiding all the female German hikers who wanted to seduce me so they could piss on me in the privacy of their hotel rooms."

"Really?"

"Yeah. I draw the line at water sports," JJ said, a look of disgust on his face. "Anyway, the big step came when, one lunchtime, I met this ancient guy in a mountain restaurant. I was having Kaffee und Kuchen when he sat down next to me saying, 'Guten Tag', to which I replied, 'All right, mate?' Once he knew I was British he pounced on me, wanting to show off his perfect English to me and any poor bastard within earshot. He said his name was Horst. Horst from Leipzig in *East* Germany, he was very specific about that, and he was in the resort to 'partake in my love of Nordic skiing'. The old twat was showboating even at that early stage of the conversation. Before I knew it, over his bock beer, he started to backfill the gaps in my knowledge of his life story by telling me nearly all of it. He rambled on and on for what seemed like hours. To be honest, I just sat there and tuned him out, the only bits that stuck when he declared how much better life had been for him pre-unification. Counting each reason out on his fingers, he told me how he'd bene-fited from getting a free state-run education, how his family had

121

lived in a state-owned flat, how the Stasi had run a tight ship and how the East German women's track and field team had dominated world athletics, picking up gold medals and breaking world records for fun. I said, 'What, in between shaving?' but he insisted that was fake news. That it was all Western capitalist propaganda and Marita Koch had only ever taken vitamin tablets.

"When eventually, *finally*, he got to the last week of his life, I started to take notice. He mentioned a tennis hotel in the Salzkammergut area of Austria he had recently visited. It had indoor courts, good coaches, high quality cuisine and a ski area nearby. Customers came to the hotel to ski and play tennis in the winter and hike and play tennis in the summer. I asked him the name of it and, after he'd finally fucked off, found it on the internet. Looking at the website pictures of people on the hotel's indoor courts, I felt an urge, one I hadn't felt in years and years, to play tennis. Later that night, I sent off a bullshit CV by email and, unbelievably, got offered a coaching job, board included, to start the following month. The money wasn't great, but there were no outgoings, no living costs. First thing I had to do was buy a couple of rackets and some tennis clothes. I had nothing, literally nothing, to do with tennis in my possession."

"And you hadn't played?"

"Hadn't hit a ball since Australia. And that was only a gentle knock-up," JJ confirmed. "When I got to the hotel I met the head coach, Aiden. He was from South Africa, a good player, and I begged him to have a hit with me before I did any coaching. I came clean and told him I hadn't played in ages but could hit a ball. He was as good as gold, we had a hit and he kept my secret safe. He knew straightaway that I could play. It was then that I really felt the old enthusiasm return and knew I'd made the right choice coming to the hotel. A few sessions in with Aiden and I was cracking the ball cleanly. I couldn't take in how quickly it was all coming back. They talk about muscle memory and they're right, it was all still there. I only had to sharpen it up. After the first month or so I asked Aiden if we could have a proper match, after coaching. He agreed. A few of the guests stayed behind and watched, all the other coaches did. I'm sure everyone thought Aiden was going to wipe me off court. We played best of three sets and I beat him 6-4, 4-6, 7-5. My tennis mojo was *back*! I walked off that indoor court happier than I'd ever walked off any court, including a Wimbledon grass court. I stayed at the hotel for a few more seasons, practised hard with the other coaches when time allowed and thoroughly enjoyed it. It was a good crack. By way of a bonus there was a lot of clandestine adultery going on. Me and the other coaches bedded more than our fair share of rich MILFS, on holiday, away from hubby and the kids." JJ paused to look me directly in the eye. "You know, one of them actually gave me a handjob using an extreme western grip. She said she'd been trying it out to get more topspin on her forehands and needed the practice."

"You are kidding?"

"Only a bit," JJ confessed, wrinkling his nose. "Then, thanks to one of the coaches, the chance to return home surfaced and here I am. Sitting outside a beach hut in Southburgh with a coaching job in Norwich." JJ's face turned earnest. "You see, Paul, I've spent over ten years of my life drifting and now I want to make something of myself. Something in tennis. What I would most like to do is to help kids get a crack at the opportunity I never had. And I don't want it to be based on how rich their stupid parents are or how well connected. Like I said earlier, I want to be the guy who builds up my local tennis scene, gets into the schools and gets the talented kids on court. I know it might sound as if I've got delusions of grandeur but I truly want to have a go at changing the face of British tennis coaching."

"It could do with it. We're not exactly churning out a production line of top one hundred players. You go for it, JJ, you'll be great," I replied with complete honesty.

JJ drained the last dregs from his bottle. The beer must have been very warm by now, so distracted had he become relating his story. I had finished mine ages ago.

"That's it. The end. That's my update. You're up next." With a smile JJ cocked his empty bottle towards me.

The ball now firmly in my court, a wave of inadequacy rolled over me. My story felt small and parochial now I had listened to JJ's globe-straddling narrative. And the women! All the women he'd had. From a ménage à trois with Thai sex workers to affluent tennis mums via bondage, a host of young women with no baggage other than the sparse kit they carried on their backs and many a sun-seeking holiday maker. The number of them? Thirty? Fifty? A hundred? Two hundred? A thousand? There was no way I was asking but without doubt it must be a huge number by any reckoning. My life story featured five women. *Five*! A few early girl-friends, Chloe and Emily Winstone. I could push it to six, at a stretch, if I included my mother, but what man in their thirties could ever do that? Geographically speaking, my tale seemed equally stunted, taking part as it did within the confines of the UK and an area no further north than Peterborough and no further south than Guildford. If JJ was hailing ground-breaking political bulletins from the BBC World Service then I was on local radio, chatting about the trials and tribulations of a cat re-homing centre.

I rubbed my forehead with one hand and my skin felt sore and itchy. Maybe I was getting sunburnt. Too bad. Now was not the time for thoughts of self-doubt, self-recrimination or sun cream. Warts and all, however it made me appear. My story might not have the range of JJ's but it was definitely the most fucked up in its own bitter little way.

"I'll start at more or less the same point in time as you," I said, taking a deep breath and launching down the slipway of my life's voyage by sharing details of my formative years, of school, university and becoming a teacher. I only told JJ about Dad's death for the moment and of the Mother Situation created by it – JJ seemed unfazed by her new persona – not the questions hanging over his sexuality, before arriving at the momentous point of that missed smash.

"Ha! I bet you *were* looking at her legs as well, you dirty bastard!" JJ guffawed.

His words were the first signs of animation since I had started speaking. For the rest of the time JJ had sat impassively, a neutral expression on his face, his large body shoehorned uncomfortably into the folding chair. Was he judging me and my narrow life? It was hard to tell.

Declining to comment on his observation either way, I continued on the Emily theme until I got to the episode where I owned up to masturbating over the Snapchat photo she had sent me shortly after Chloe had refused me sex.

"What?" JJ exclaimed, his eyes boggling. "You hadn't had sex with your wife since you missed the smash?"

"Nope."

"And Chloe actually suggested you do yourself *and* made a derogatory comment afterwards about your past sexual performances? Wow! Okay…" I could see JJ mentally grappling with what I had told him. "So," he continued, chopping a tomahawk palm downwards, "this hot Emily, county standard player, right? Phones you up late at night when you're in the bathroom about to take your own sex life, and asks you to step in, last minute, to replace hubby in some *charadee* tennis tournament?"

"That's right."

"And this is after she's flirted with you weeks ago at the club after playing with you against this… *Steven*, by asking you for an interview that hints at something more? But the interview never materialises? She blames someone else for its non-happening?"

"Also correct."

"Going further back in time, you've kissed her once when you were both pissed and she's made a few saucy throwaway comments about how she's waxed her fanny for you after you drunkenly expressed an interest in it?"

"Got it in one."

"The culmination of all this possible-affair-in-the-making is you've started acting weird... and Chloe has started acting weird around the same time?" I indicated JJ had pretty much nailed the entire situation. "You keep quiet about the charity tournament. You keep it all to yourself and don't tell a soul because Chloe's 'working' and no one else from the club is likely to be there. You secretly go."

"I go," I confirmed. "By taxi. Because Emily said we would be at the same house all day and could indulge in a few drinks. I've also got my swim shorts in my racket bag because of the pool. I thought, alcohol, pool, her in that bikini..."

"The bikini you've already seen her wearing in the Snapchat photo. The one where you say she was fingering herself," JJ interjected, sounding ever more like a sleazy TV sleuth. "The one that got your SORN'd motor running in the bathroom."

"Yes."

"Why the fuck *didn't* you screenshot it?" JJ asked, a look of disappointment on his face.

"She told me not to."

JJ rolled his eyes. "Fine. What happened next?"

BD

"Thanks a lot," I said to the taxi driver, passing him a twenty pound note. "Keep the change." I was feeling magnanimous. And excited. And anxious. And a whole host of other emotions, ones I was incapable of processing accurately enough to isolate and identify.

The taxi pulled away behind me and from my viewpoint, one

taken between the two imposing brick pillars marking the gated entrance to the Addingtons' property, I gazed down a long gravel drive leading to a magnificent house set amongst immaculate pinstripe lawns. In a scripted moment, the clouds broke and the south-facing aspect of the timber-framed property became immersed in a shaft of sunlight, allowing its white rendering to dazzle spectacularly. Here was money. Big money. Serious moolah acquired – I refused to say earned – by Rupert, a merchant banker, one of a group of individuals culpable for the economic crash we had all paid so dearly for years ago.

They say crime doesn't pay, but from where I was standing as a left of centre college lecturer – politically, not in relation to brick pillars – it sure looked as if it occasionally picked up the tab.

If the Addingtons had sickening wealth, then at least my prayers had been answered in terms of the weather. On waking up and pulling open the bedroom curtains, I had thanked the god I didn't believe in for the arrival of a dry day and punched a silent, ecstatic fist into the air to celebrate. It had been my primary fear all week. That it would pour hard, the event would be cancelled and I wouldn't get to spend all day in the company of Emily Winstone. With that concern having faded, a new one had slipped effortlessly into its place – spending all day in the company of Emily Winstone and making a right pig's ear of it.

Taking an objective stance, my actions at home, ones replicated by Chloe's recent modus operandi, clearly indicated a marriage destined for a bad place. It wasn't too difficult to predict the ulti-mate black hole Chloe and I were headed for and the altercation, stress and bitterness sure to follow spaghettification. Subjectively, however, the prospect of one radiant day spent playing tennis with Emily Winstone, and the prospect of where *that* might take me, easily bleached out any blackness. So intense was her light – her image burnt on to my retinae thanks to a screenful of sensational Snapchat – it had all but rendered me snowblind to any future

127

marital denouement. When I blinked, I saw her image. When I closed my eyes at night, I saw her image. When I daydreamed and stared aimlessly at nothing, I saw her image. I knew I was acting crazy – truth was, I didn't much care.

The logic behind my reckless thought process lay in my total conviction in one single statement: one missed smash had put a death sentence on my marriage. Convinced of that now, despite considering it only a possibility until recently, my perspective had shifted to the point where I struggled to see any way out for me and Chloe. We looked finished, our marriage on the rocks and in the early stages of its death throes. Her 'overtime at work' schtick was certainly a falsehood, one affording her the space to conduct what I now presumed had to be an affair. The only bonus to this sorry state of affairs was me being given a free hit to go after Emily Winstone. Perhaps it was all I needed, all I wanted – an excuse to chase her.

From the moment Emily had asked me to play, told me of the format and described the social set involved, I realised I would be entering an exotic world in more ways than one. One where my annual salary might pass as average recompense for two weeks' work, for a start. The sight of the house, and all it represented, brought home with a jarring crunch the stratospheric level of prosperity enjoyed by the type of people I would shortly be playing tennis with. 'Ball', 'game' and 'different', were the words springing to mind. It wasn't fanciful to conclude that nearly every facet of their lives would be unrecognisable from mine.

All was askew, right down to the ridiculous level of monikers. In my thirty plus years of being alive, I had never heard of another Rupert – outside of an ursine, yellow-checked-trouser-wearing cartoon character and an openly gay film star – let alone talked to one or been invited to his house to play tennis. People like me didn't mix in the same social circles as people with names like Rupert, or his wife, a woman called *Aurelia*, for heaven's sake.

Although a boarding school product, I was still only a college lecturer called Paul, whose orbit never encroached the strange, alien world inhabited by the likes of the Addingtons. Today merely an aberration, a one-off, a free Disney fast-pass – no queuing involved – into the world of the one-percenters courtesy of Emily's invitation.

Once again, my tennis playing ability would be all I had on offer and I hoped to do myself justice in my one competitive area. A senior mixed doubles final groundhog day, where this time, crucially, Emily would be playing *with* me rather than against me. In theory, this made my task much easier because A) Emily was a very strong player, B) I was less likely, on account of her court positioning, to be distracted by her legs and miss smashes and C) she wasn't my wife. That said, it was all very well playing at a high level in a club match with Emily, but today was different. Not only out of my comfort zone socially speaking, the dynamic between me and Emily had become much more loaded thanks to the Snapchat photo of her posing suggestively in her bikini. Sending me a picture of herself on social media, with her hand on her crotch pleasuring herself, face contorted in ecstasy, quite reasonably to my mind, had taken things to another level entirely. It appeared, through her actions, that the possibility of something sexually illicit happening between us was strong. All I had to do was make sure I didn't blow it once again when on court.

I had witnessed Emily's competitive nature up close, none more so than when I played with her against her husband on a Friday night. Undoubtedly expecting to do well today, Emily was likely to be the strongest female player present and if we didn't end up victorious it would certainly be down to my failings rather than hers. One missed smash had effectively cut off sexual relations with my wife. The last thing I needed was another unforced error hindering my chances of *starting* them with Emily Winstone.

Although still fifteen minutes early, I started to make my way down towards the house. The two black wrought iron gates, hinged on the brick pillars and folded open down the drive, seemed welcoming enough, pointing their way to the house like giant signposts. Passing through the pillars, I noticed a slightly less inviting CCTV camera fixed to the left-hand one. Anyone in the house watching its feed wouldn't know me from Adam, but I hoped my tennis garb and racket bag would mark me down as a benign presence, as a friend rather than a thieving foe. Walking on, I employed a gait as far from 'shifty' as possible; head up, shoulders back, my stride full and purposeful.

Halfway down the satisfyingly crunchy gravel drive, I realised the house was even more spectacular than it had looked from the road and I recalled Emily's droll comment about it making Steven's house look like a suburban semi. The original two and a half storey timber-framed house looked to have been significantly added to over the years, with a large, sympathetic and tasteful extension on one side and a host of other outbuildings sited away from the main property. I couldn't see the tennis court and assumed it was at the back, along with the riding stables, artificial ski slope and eighteen hole golf course! I suspected the pool would be housed in one of the large outbuildings – a mini-Center Parcs subtropical paradise only without the middle-class hordes and their screaming kids – as I couldn't see the Addingtons slumming it with anything as tacky as an outdoor pool. They might be multi-millionaires, but this was Surrey, not California, and not even their affluence could purchase all-year-round hot weather.

Virtually at the house, I spotted movement in a ground floor window and a middle-aged woman began making wild, exaggerated 'round the corner' signs with her arm. Wearing tennis clothing, I thought that if she volleyed in the same manner anyone in the crowd better start ducking.

Dutifully following orders, I went around the side of the house and followed it to an open door right at the far end. The opening an entrance to one of those kitchens that makes yours look like a cockroach-infested shithole, despite having just spent twenty grand updating it. A full extension along the entire width of the original house, the kitchen was built in an exposed oak beam style, with a pitched roof, to mimic the original building's design. The external wall of the extension a succession of oak patio doors, all doubles, interspersed with fixed, full-length double glazed oak windows. Only two short sections of plastered brickwork, less than a metre high and finished with oak window boards, broke the pattern of full length glazing. The extension's returning ends, again full length oak windows, each had a single door opening. Peeking inside, an impressive oval breakfast bar with ultra-modern stools hogged the kitchen's central floor space. Fully enclosed with various drawers and cupboards on its straight sides, the breakfast bar had curved end panels and a granite worktop with inset sink, served by one of those specialist taps that dispenses both boiling and chilled water.

Entering the kitchen to set foot on the most impressive ceramic floor tiling, I perused the full length of soft grey units and high-end brushed steel appliances lining the original outside wall. My eye quickly fell upon an enormous double-door fridge, one capable of holding at least four adult bodies if stood upright. Might come in handy, I thought, should anyone die on court and the local morgue be pushed for space.

"Good morning, good morning. How are you? I'm Aurelia, your hostess for today," the woman I had seen earlier asked after she skipped energetically through the kitchen's entrance from the main house. "Have we met before?"

"Hi, I'm Paul and, no, we haven't met before," I answered, turning away from the fridge to face her.

Aurelia was upon me now and she placed her arms on me and fake kissed me on both cheeks. Once out of the social greeting, I could see she was wearing a L'Étoile tennis dress – cost, two

131

hundred quid minimum – and looked exceedingly well presented with perfect hair, make-up and a subtle all-over golden tan. Physically she was very slight – I doubted her dress size was more than a six – and age-wise I placed her mid-fifties. While hanging numbers on her, I suspected she used a racket whose head size was at least one hundred and ten square inches i.e. she needed all the sweet spot help there was going.

"Paul? Paul?" she asked herself, her brow creased. "Remind me, who's your partner?"

"Emily Winstone. I've stepped in last minute for Steven."

"Emily! You're playing with Emily. Of course, that's right she did tell me. I say, you've bagged the star lady player. Lucky you!" she simpered. "Do you work with Steven?"

"No. I play at the same club as Emily."

"Oh. You're a *club* player. Are you as good as Steven?" she asked, placing a hand on my arm.

"About the same," I answered, my earlier magnanimous mood holding. I'll give you that one, Steven, I thought. In the spirit of fairness, seeing as I want to give one to your wife.

"In that case, you two will do *very* well. Now. Can I get you a drink? While you wait for the others. Tea, coffee, wine, juice, a beer?"

"Tea please," I answered. It was too early for alcohol. Get a few wins under my belt, then I might think about it.

"What type? Earl Grey, Summer Berries, Camomile…?"

"Um, build… English breakfast," I replied, realising I would have to keep my wits about me to avoid flagging up any lack of sophistication.

After a riveting conversation where I quizzed her about the instant boiling water tap she had made my tea from, Aurelia excused herself from my company in order to complete last minute food preparation – either that or she had to empty the fridge of retirees from yesterday's social four to make room for the canapés.

Aurelia suggested I could go and have a look at the court, if I wanted, rather than hang around the kitchen. I said I would and with a cup of tea in hand and following her directions, I passed the indoor pool building – a quick look through the window, it looked fantastic – and with the stables and equine arena to my right, I walked on another hundred yards before arriving at the tennis court. There was, shockingly, no golf course or artificial ski slope. After next year's bonuses, Rupert?

The court had a hard Tarmac surface, painted green within the tramlines and coloured blue outside. Tarmac was not my favourite surface, I preferred the lower bounce of artificial grass, but nevertheless the court did look in excellent condition. I couldn't see the day being reduced to a lottery shoot out due to a mass of bad bounces, even if I could see the balls getting chewed up pretty quickly by the court's harsh surface. Both the tennis net and the netting cage around the court looked in perfect order, no holes in either, and the bottom of the court netting hadn't rolled up as if a cete of badgers playing a boisterous game of tag had bundled underneath it.

The court itself had been dug lengthways into an area of gently sloping ground and these grassy banks, to three sides of the court, formed a perfect little amphitheatre. Looking around, it was evident why the Addingtons' property had been chosen as the setting to host the final; incredible house, gorgeous surroundings, a well-maintained court, excellent spectator facilities and the additional bonus of a pool to frolic in post-tournament.

I dragged the sole of my tennis shoe over the court's surface in an attempt to assess its grip, bounce and speed. If any balls had been available I might have chanced my arm and secretly smacked a few serves down to see what the court played like. Not being an option and realising I might be getting a little over zealous to the point of becoming anal, I called time on my court visit and walked back to the house to see who else had arrived.

The full complement was the answer. Everyone due to play in our group had arrived while I had been inspecting the court and were milling around chatting in the kitchen and on the patio outside it. Aurelia clucked and fluttered around everybody making them welcome, her face decorated with a permanent smile as she cheerfully took drink orders, made and then distributed them. As she performed her hostess role with great charm and élan, Emily introduced me to all the other players, explaining how I was her 'saviour' for stepping in last-minute and replacing her unavailable husband. She emphasised the disappointment she would have suffered if she had 'missed out on playing against all you lovely people' and how good it was of me to partner her at such late notice.

Letting Emily do all the talking and hoovering up the credit for my purely altruistic appearance – yeah, right – I shook hands with the seven men and seven women who made up the rest of our round robin group. The age range of the men was decades-spanning with the youngest male shortly off to start his last year at university – Oxford, studying PPE. Boringly predictable, see you in the Tory cabinet in fifteen years' time – and a surprisingly ancient old boy who, if he wasn't aged the seventy-five years he looked, ought to be suing someone fast. When I greeted him, there had been no eye contact on my behalf as my stare had been inexorably drawn towards the massive fridge. Absolutely no drop shotting the old boy, I decided. In fact, best to hit everything straight back at him so he didn't have to move a single step. The last thing anyone needed was paramedic intervention – a 'one for the fridge' incident – sapping the day's vibe and, more importantly, scuppering my amorous intentions.

Conversely to the male players, all the women inhabited an age band comfortably covered by the term 'middle-aged' and, as a succession of wealthy, immaculately turned out, elegant, tennis-playing wives – none with a BMI over eighteen – lightly gripped my hand with heavily beringed fingers, I wondered if I had stumbled into some kind of Stepford Wives scenario. They all seemed so interchangeable, so hewn from the same identical social class they could almost be robots.

"Jesus Christ, I'm never going to remember who's who," I told Emily, once the greetings were finished and we had a little time and space to ourselves on the patio. "All the women look the same. Half of them are wearing similar tennis clothing and if they happen to use the same racket, I'll be totally stuffed."

"But you're a college lecturer. I thought you'd be *good* at memorising names," Emily gently teased.

"Yeah, well don't go telling them that. Not with those names. Allegra? Esme? I thought 'Octavia' was a type of Skoda," I said over-egging the pudding, even if my sensibilities had been jolted by the sheer affluence and breeding of everybody I had met.

"Don't worry about it," Emily replied, already on the expensive champagne. "And don't go over exaggerating for effect. I know they're all super-posh and super-rich but at least they're not bloody *Russian*," she said, picking up on the chip on my shoulder. "You relax. I'll keep you up to speed on the names front."

"Are any of them any good at tennis?" I asked, changing the subject.

"Not really. We'll win at a canter. The semis and the final will be a bit different," she added, knocking back the remains of her glass in one.

"Just out of interest, seeing as you've put us in the final already, how well can you play when you're pissed?"

Emily paused and weighed up my question. "Less well at tennis. Better still in bed," she answered, a smirk on her lips.

"In that case, do you want another one?" I asked, nodding at her empty glass.

Emily never had a chance to answer my question because Rupert Addington, a bulbous mass of a man poured into all-white

135

Lacoste tennis clothing – he was probably stealing weight off his wife at night when she wasn't looking – tapped his glass with a spoon and, having gained our collective attention, made his welcoming speech.

"Exactly the same as last year," Emily whispered sighing. "Poor Rupert. For someone with such wealth he hasn't much imagination. And he's getting fatter. Aurelia's so light and nimble on court, he's like a lumbering hippo."

After Rupert's speech and implored to do so by Aurelia, the sixteen of us decamped to the tennis court, a little flock of principally white-plumaged players bearing gaudy racket bags. Prince, Wilson, Head and Babolat the names rather than the usual day-to-day Gucci, Chanel, Hermes and Fendi the ladies might take with them. Once there, Aurelia announced the order of play from her previously written schedule, naming the first four players due on court and handing them a tube of new Slazenger balls.

"Best of seven games," she trilled. "Sudden death deuces with the returners choosing who receives. You can have a two-minute knock-up before your first match but after that it's straight in. We've got a lot of matches to get through and we need to keep things moving people! Winning pair report back to me after you've finished with the score. The couple winning the most games goes through. If two couples tie on games won then the head-to-head decides."

Sitting on the grassy bank in the pleasantly warm sunshine, I half-watched the best-of-seven-games round robin matches progress. Third one in and still having not appeared on court, I asked myself, if I had been standing on the grassy knoll instead of sitting on the grassy bank, which one of the players I might have assassinated for crimes against tennis. The answer: pretty much most of them, the playing standard sub-Friday night in most cases. That said, the true reasons for my tetchiness lay elsewhere. Standing on the patio earlier, I had envisaged me and Emily spending a lot of time together, chatting quietly and increasing the rapport and chemistry between us through rising levels of witty innuendo. One quickly escalating to a point of peak smut as our unresolved sexual tension rapidly came to the boil. The actuality, rather aggravatingly, turned out to be radically different. Since the one promising comment before Rupert's rehashed speech, Emily hadn't spoken directly to me and instead had continued playing the social butterfly, chatting and mingling with all the other players.

Her movements left me isolated and with the ordeal of making small talk, as and when it came my way, with individuals whose names I had mostly forgotten but who, annoyingly, hadn't forgotten mine. Perhaps they recalled my name so readily because it glaringly labelled me an outsider. Whatever the reason, already on the back foot from the off and feeling defensive, I stuck to the vaguest of generalities, trying to keep to the safe ground of tennis small talk – Nadal's forehand, Federer's incredible longevity, Djokovic's ability to do the splits, blah, blah, blah – while trying to avoid mentioning my job, the fact I didn't possess a second home in the west country, didn't ski, hadn't been to the Maldives, didn't have staff or a lawn mower you sat on.

Only when our turn on court came around, to play against Aurelia and Rupert, did Emily return and converse with me again.

"Nice and gentle," she whispered. "Just enough to win. We don't want to humiliate them. It's Aurelia and Rupert. Aurelia's the *thin* one," she mocked.

It was a reasonable enough request and I acquiesced, following Emily's lead on how hard to compete. As it turned out, Aurelia *was* nimble on court, Rupert a lumbering hippo. When we changed ends after the first game, I checked the court for fresh cracks where he had been standing.

By mid-afternoon, things had taken a turn for the better. With our group done and dusted Emily and I had nothing better to do than kick back, chill, enjoy the surroundings and wait for the other group winners to make their way to us. We had won our group – a clean sweep, worst victory 5-2 – already eaten a wonderful lunch and Emily was necking champagne, if not with quite the desperation of an alcoholic faced with impending prohibition, then certainly with relish. Alcohol and Emily were a big thumbs up as far as I was concerned. Last time she had been pissed in my company she had kissed me. And who could forget her earlier comment about how it apparently improved her performance in the sack? Not me, that's for sure. The only blight on the horizon, as far as I could discern, was the likelihood of her tennis deteriorating.

"Apparently it's not only the three group-winning pairs on their way here, *everyone's* on their way here," Emily languorously informed me.

"Going to be quite a crowd," I remarked.

"There will be. All coming along to watch us play." Emily took another mouthful of champagne and smiled at me. "Have you enjoyed it so far, partner?" she asked.

"It's been different," I confessed. "I realise I'm not exactly one of the clan."

"Everyone's been nice to you, though, haven't they? After I gave you the 'knight in shining armour' big up."

"Absolutely. Actually, considering how rich they all are, they're probably less snobby than some of the people at our club."

"*Everyone* here is filthy rich," Emily commented. "And they all know they're all filthy rich. There's no reason to have to constantly keep reinforcing it. It's not a competition. It's simply accepted by everybody as the natural way of things."

"Nice work if you can get it. Inheritance, entitlement, access to public school education and the Old Boys' Club," I pointed out.

"Easy, Vladimir," Emily chided.

"But, yes, I've enjoyed playing," I confirmed, moving away from the class warfare. "Thing is, how bothered are you about winning?" I asked, pulling a face at her glass.

"I won with Steven last year, so it would be rather nice to 'retain my crown'," Emily said, putting on a voice. "But Randolph wasn't playing with Camilla last year... so, bottoms up, I say." She drained her glass with an elaborate flourish.

"Randolph? Camilla?"

"Randolph Valentino-Smith. He's quite the player. Got a D1 scholarship in the US and played for several years on the ITF Men's Circuit, the third tier of the ATP Tour. He couldn't quite make the jump to the Challenger Tour so gave it up and came back to work for daddy's financial services firm." Emily looked disapprovingly at her empty glass and then up at me. "This is *strictly* between us two," Emily stated, her eyes widening. "Once I got wind of Randolph and his tennis-playing ability from one of Steven's work colleagues, we were at a social occasion together and she happened to mention him, I then asked her for his contact details. Once I had Randolph's number, *without* Steven's knowledge, I rang him and begged him to play today."

"How the hell did you pitch that?" I asked, thinking if Emily and I could win our group 'at a canter', as she put it, what was this guy going to do against such meagre opposition.

"I was, shall we say, 'persistent'. I thumped the 'good cause' drum and, rather more subtly, hinted at how good it might be for business. I told him there would be an awful lot of moneyed people around and he might make a few useful contacts."

"I can see why you didn't want Steven to know. Financial services. Helping out a rival firm and on *his* patch. Naughty, Emily."

"Who cares? Fuck Steven," Emily said, shrugging her shoulders, the tone of her voice changed in an instant, catching me completely by surprise.

Not wanting to push the matter, but secretly quite pleased her marriage might not be so sweet as well – two unhappy people thrust together on a tennis court, both seeking solace through sordid sexual satisfaction and solid volleying, that kind of thing – I asked, "And Camilla?"

"Good. Young. Only eighteen. Think she's in the senior top twenty for her county. Randolph said he didn't mind who he played with. I was only too pleased to pair him up with a strong woman."

"Enjoy the day, then?" I asked, my tennis pragmatism kicking in, despite being unable to fathom why Emily had deliberately invited such strong opposition.

"That's what I intend to do. Refill?"

"Sure. A bottle of Corona Extra for me."

Emily went to turn away before stopping and pausing. I could tell she was sizing up her options by her body language and the expression on her face.

"You know the Randolph 'how'," she said to me. "Interested in the Randolph 'why'?"

"A set-piece final?" I guessed aloud. "A chance for the losing players to see someone that good close up?"

Emily laughed. It wasn't a nice laugh. "I got Randolph to play with Camilla so I could cherish the look on Steven's face when they beat us," she said. "I know I can hold my own with Camilla, but Steven wouldn't stand a chance against Randolph. We'd lose and it would be. All. *His*. Fault."

"Right," I answered, unsure where to go with this insight.

"Steven's not fucking working," Emily hissed, stepping in close to me. "I *know* what's happened. He's found out somehow and the bastard's bottled it. Couldn't stand the thought of losing in front of all his friends." She took a deep breath and composed herself. "So, I'll have to lose with you instead. We'll go down fighting and I'm sure we'll enjoy the challenge. The only downside is I won't get to see Steven humiliated." Emily stopped and I saw her bottom lip go walkabout. For a split second I thought she was going to cry. "Sorry to put you in the middle of all this. I should have told you before.

It's complicated. Things have got a bit messy. There's a lot going on. Thanks for playing," she said, leaning in and kissing me on the cheek.

I watched Emily's desirable rear recede as she set about making the alcohol run to the large double-door fridge. The only clear fact to pop into my head, as I became submerged in her revelation, it appeared I didn't have to worry about unforced errors anymore.

As fate would have it, Emily and I didn't have to play against Randolph and Camilla in our semi. Stepping up our game, despite our joint booze intake, we played well and coasted home to another 5-2 victory against a young man partnering his mother. She was steady, but couldn't hurt us in any way, and he was a typical 'sprayer', one good shot followed by several half way up the court netting as he tried to knock the cover off every ball he hit. The swollen crowd of losing players, a sea of white set against a green screen background, sat and clapped and encouraged every point. A couple of Emily's blistering backhands received gasps of amazement as well as applause. A couple of my volleys were almost as well received.

"Well played," Emily congratulated me as we stood at the very top of the grassy slope, waiting for the second semi-final players to walk on court. "We've got to where I expected us to get to. Our 'seeded' position," she added, tongue in cheek. "In the final we go for it. One more drink each and let's see how many games we can get. Three would be a good effort."

"Sure. You never know, we might surprise ourselves."

"One other thing, Paul," Emily said, sidling up close to me, invading my personal space and completely ignoring my comment. "Can I count on your discretion?" she asked. "Like I did with that Snapchat I sent you?" I nodded eagerly. "Can I be sure what happens on a tennis charity tournament stays on a tennis charity tournament."

I felt my body engorge with hope. Images flashed before my

141

eyes, the ones I hadn't wanted Chloe to telepathically download from my phone.

"Of course, you can, baby," I said, giving it my best 'man of the world' swagger.

"You're so sweet and funny... Oh, look!" she suddenly declared, her head snapping round quicker than a motorist's passing a recent crash. "Randolph and Camilla have finally got here and are coming on court."

I, too, rotated my head to see them and suddenly realised exactly how sweet and funny a character I was.

"Maybe... he won't be as good... as he looks," I slowly mouthed, as I watched movie-star-looks Randolph begin his knock-up.

"You wait," Emily warned.

I did. I was right. He was even better.

We lost the final 6-2. Emily held her own with Camilla and Randolph wiped the floor with me, rather than with the intended victim, exactly as Emily had predicted. Randolph was simply too good, way above my standard, and he dominated every single point, sometimes by his mere presence as he intimidated me with his court movement and net poaching to hit harder, lower and wider, forcing me to miss in the process. In short, I got a free tennis lesson from a far superior opponent. A far superior, far better-looking, far sexier opponent.

As a heterosexual man, it can often be difficult to pinpoint what it is that women find attractive in other men. I'd had it in the past with Chloe, say, when watching a film, the 'You think *he's* good-looking?' conversation. It's not one we would have needed to have when discussing Randolph Valentino-Smith. I could very easily pinpoint what women would find attractive about him. No problem at all. None whatsoever. The fact he was also a rich, talented tennis player didn't exactly do him any harm or hinder him in the dreamboat stakes either.

Randolph was so attractive he easily fell into the category of the select group of men who are the answer to a certain hypothetical question. That question jokingly posed by one member of an inebriated group of straight men. The, 'If you were forced to have sex with one bloke, right? They're going to shoot you in the *fucking* head if you don't, *who* would you choose?' hypothetical question. (Incidentally, although there's no correct answer, there is one very, very, *very* wrong one. The name of anyone present.) Randolph was drop dead gorgeous. I could see it. *Everyone* could see it. *I* even fancied him. I could also see, with a sad, sagging heart, the distinct possibility Emily hadn't exactly told me the whole story.

"Emily's a cool player, Paul," Randolph slurred in a voice inflected with an American twang.

An hour after the final, the players left who fancied a swim, around ten of us, were in the subtropical paradise. I was standing by the edge of the pool next to Randolph, the others, apart from Emily who hadn't yet appeared from the changing room, were bobbing around in the warm, clear water. Randolph had a great all-over tan – it seemed a prerequisite for his social class – whereas, naturally, I didn't. I was two-tone and looked as if large parts of my body had been dusted down with flour by comparison. From my swim shorts' waistband up to my tee shirt neckline and down to the distinct lines cutting my biceps in half, I was white. So were my feet and the lower parts of my legs, the lines set exactly four inches up from my ankles and an inch above my knees, my swim shorts now blatantly exposed as shorter than the ones I had changed out of. It wasn't a cool look, the summer-tennis-player body's decal. Gratingly, underneath his golden colouring, Randolph's six-pack-sporting physique was equally as perfect as his looks and hair. Standing at his side, like one half of a 'before and after' clickbait advert for beach holidays and gym memberships, or him modelling high end male underwear while I was the man from JD Sports, I haemorrhaged self-esteem like a blown well head on an oil rig.

As acts of ridiculous masochism go, hanging around in swimwear rubbing shoulders with a brilliant tennis-playing Adonis sat pretty high on the list. Even so, I felt determined to tough it out, to put myself through the unnecessary purgatory in order to find out, for certain, what I desperately needed to know.

"She is that," I concurred.

"And fit."

"She *is* very attractive," I agreed, feeling uglier by the second.

"Here, I've got something to show you," Randolph said, pulling an iPhone out from his swim shorts.

"Don't forget and jump in the pool with that in your pocket," I warned as I watched him swipe at the phone. He was quite drunk. I had thought about pushing him in to see if he might drown, but had rejected the idea as pointless. Odds on he was also a fantastic swimmer. Fantastic lover. Fantastic you name it.

"Look at this, dude," he said, holding up the phone.

To my dismay, but not my surprise, I saw the same picture Emily had sent to me.

"Wow," I said, in a non-wow voice. Now I understood. I had, for want of a better phrase, 'been shafted'. Or 'played'. Played was probably the better option.

"I didn't come here for the tennis, Paul," he confided, slapping my arm cheerfully. "We've been sexting for weeks. I won't show you the picture I sent back. Modesty forbids."

Mentally I groaned. He had sent her a dick pic, I realised, as I tried to wrench my eyes away from Randolph's groin where they had subliminally alighted. And it would be massive. It went without saying it would be fucking massive.

"Hi, guys. How's it going?"

"Cool," Randolph answered, slyly pocketing the phone.

Emily had joined us. Pretty tipsy herself – tennis abilities down, shagging abilities up – now in the bikini she had sent to Randolph as a sexual calling card. The same one she had sent to me to make

144

sure she had a partner to play with and an excuse to hook up with Randolph. Emily's game plan may have morphed from its origins, but the outcome was still going to be the same. The marginal difference, as far as I could make out, her starting her fling with Randolph sooner rather than later.

"I'm going to swim a quick length and then make a move," I said, screwing my face up. "Got a bit of preparation for work to do tonight."

I read the autocue message scanning across Emily's eyes. 'Fall guy down. Repeat, fall guy down. Seduction is go. Seduction is go.'

"Okay, Paul," she purred, drinking in Randolph with gasping parched mouthfuls. "Thanks for playing with me. Don't forget what we agreed," she added, waving her eyebrows at me. She might as well have been waving her bikini bottoms above her head, spreading her legs and inviting Randolph to 'come on down'.

"Sure. No problem. Cheers, Randolph." I turned to shake the Adonis's hand. "Nice meeting you. Great play today. Awesome." I swivelled my eyes. "Might see you up the club sometime soon, then, Emily."

"Absolutely," she replied.

Feeling emotionally and physically shrivelled, I left them to it, dropping into the water and swimming breaststroke to the far end, not chancing freestyle, fully aware nothing looks more naff than getting halfway, tiring, and having to change stroke. At the far end, I pulled myself out of the water and went and got changed as quickly as possible. I left, surreptitiously, without saying goodbye to a soul. What did I care? I wasn't going to see any of them again. I simply needed to get out of that millionaire arena of mortification as rapidly as possible, now I had my answer.

Back with Chloe the following week, my own home started to take on the same humiliating vibe as the Addingtons' subtropical paradise. Worse, in fact. I stopped giving a toss about my phone but tellingly Chloe carried on exactly as she had before with hers.

Everything about our life together turned ugly and vile over the following months, as if viewing our doomed relationship on a huge 4K screen – lurid, defined and ultra-vivid, every pore, pimple and blemish visible to both our disgusted eyes.

Personally, I felt stripped of dignity, defiled and used, my confidence lower than at any other stage of my life. I felt duped, yet blameworthy. What *had* I been thinking? One fluky, right-place-right-time drunken five-minute kiss and the rest meant nothing. Only what I wanted it to mean. A harsh reality check, in the form of a tennis-playing god, soon dashed my hopes and revealed them as nothing more than deluded juvenile fantasy. One Emily was happy to encourage as and when it suited her, especially if disenchanted with Steven or when planning her subterfuge with Randolph. Like a fool, I danced to her tune, to every single note and, having served my purpose, had been dismissed with all the compassion of a gig economy worker.

Christmas Eve, convinced I sat at somewhere near rock bottom, Chloe knocked me deeper, my life journey forever downwards and heading right for the Earth's core. In a blunt, factual bombshell she coldly informed me she was packed, ready to leave and our marriage was over. She was moving in with her new man.

"Anyone I know?" I asked facetiously.

Chloe paused for several seconds. "Yes it is, actually. It's James."

Not someone from work, then. *James.* My best friend at the club.

Rendered speechless, I really hadn't seen that one coming, her second blow felt almost as vicious as her first.

"You might want to think about finding another club," Chloe 'suggested' as she walked out the front door. "It's going to be unworkable if you don't."

They were the last words she ever spoke to me, other than through a solicitor.

When I eventually recovered enough to phone James and asked

how he had the fucking gall to run off with my wife after twenty years of close friendship, he sounded unfazed and smartly flicked the blame back on to me.

"You shouldn't have missed that smash, Paul," he told me. "You started the doubts in her mind. No one else did that. Only you. You knew how much it meant for her to win and yet you still couldn't do it for her, could you? And all because you were too busy leering at another woman's legs." I started to protest, but James ploughed on, talking over the top of me. "*Understandably*," he shouted. "Understandably," he continued, in a quieter voice once I had backed down and shut up, "she felt vulnerable afterwards. Who wouldn't? She felt betrayed. Initially, she only came to me for support and as someone to confide in. From there on in, it just sort of happened. We didn't plan it, didn't set out to fall in love."

"No. I'm sure you never exploited the situation at all."

"Look, I'm only telling you this out of respect for our friendship. If it was anyone else other than you, I wouldn't have picked up," James said disrespectfully. "Chloe's told me all sorts of weird stuff about you. How you changed. How you started to behave really peculiarly after the final. Accusing her of having an affair with Steven. Acting odd indoors. She even told me how one night, after she'd tried to reconcile with you and begged you to give things one last go, you turned her down and made a big thing about going into the bathroom and masturbating instead." James's voice turned incredulous. "You're just not that guy who was my friend anymore."

"That's not true! That's not what happened! That's fucking bullshit and you know it," I informed him, furious at how Chloe had twisted things around.

"Look. I know you're cross and upset, so I'm going to hang up now. I'm sorry, mate. You really need to have a good look in the mirror... And look for another club while you're at it. Your name's shit up at ours right now. No one wants you there. Go somewhere else and do everyone a favour, eh?" James ordered before he hung up.

Unwilling to fight, more rationally unable to, I weakly conceded and not only left a wife of seven years, but also a tennis club of twenty. I didn't join another. Tennis had too many bad connotations. From the day of the charity tennis tournament I haven't hit a single ball. From the day of the missed smash, I haven't had sex with a single woman.

Part 2

Paul

"So how good was this Randolph, then?" JJ asked, the sun now well past its zenith and starting to dip behind the apex of the beach hut's roof.

"Is *that* your first question?" I retaliated, bemused and a little miffed. "I've just committed harakiri, the blood and guts of my life have slopped steaming on the floor, and your first concern is how good Randolph is at tennis?"

"Curious, that's all," JJ shrugged, batting away my objections. "Tactically, I'd have kept the ball on Camilla all the time."

"I couldn't keep the ball 'on Camilla all the time'," I sarcastically protested. "I could hardly return his serve or ground strokes. When I did get a look in, I went big every chance I got. And missed. Missed a lot. Maybe I need some coaching. When have you got a spare slot?"

"You just need to play."

"You had your period out. I'm having mine."

"Fair call," JJ agreed. "You *definitely* need to start having sex, though," he pointed out before pausing for a few seconds. "Christ, it's still hot, isn't it?" he remarked, changing tack, as if suddenly aware of his surroundings. "Unbelievable. If it stays like this up until June and then gets hotter, that'll do for me," he stated, scanning a beach still crammed with gambolling kids and attentive seniors. JJ leaned forward on his chair. "In all seriousness, I'm sorry for what you've been through, Paul. Not nice." More conspiratorially he asked, "Is now the time for the scores on the doors for the most fucked up story? I'm thinking a solid seven for yours."

"Not yet," I warned. "There's more."

JJ's mouth squirmed. "Is it freaky shit?" he asked, failing to conceal his expectancy.

I puffed out my cheeks, exhaling air. "Well, the next part does call into question my very existence and the reasons why I was put on this earth in the first place, so... yeah, I guess it is."

"Then go for it, man."

Acknowledging JJ's zest, I began the only recently discovered parallel theme to my car crash of a marriage. "Do you remember me telling you how, since Dad's death, Mum has turned into a cougar?" I began.

"Looking forward to meeting her," JJ confirmed, his eyebrows elevating.

"Puh-*lease*," I said, unable to stop myself smiling. "Anyway, moving swiftly on from your sick fantasy, when this promiscuous behaviour first started, Mum insisted there was a very good reason for it. One I didn't believe to begin with, if I'm honest. Now I think I do. I'm afraid for you to comprehend it properly involves knowing some background stuff. To do with work..." I added grimacing.

"No problem. The whole picture to get the context," JJ agreed, making a vague circular movement with his hands.

"Indeed. Therefore I implore you to sit forward on the edge of your seat, tense up, and hear the story of how my life's meaning, as opposed to my marriage, was shattered by a chance meeting with a Gas Safe heating engineer. One who currently may or may not be knocking off Mum. Probably is. Can't be certain."

"Major intrigue," JJ remarked. "Certainly sounds promising, freaky shit." JJ ran his hand through his foppish fringe. "One little thing before you get started. When you've finished, we get something to eat straight after, all right? I'm starving."

"It's on me," I promised. "I know just the place."

With JJ booked in for dinner at my expense, I told him about my college, Malcolm, his relationship with Dad through work and golf, the upcoming Ofsted inspection, Graham's request for me to impersonate the Director of Business, Catering and Sport and my three-hundred-pound suit sweetener. I then moved on to Mum's claim to have only had sex with Dad six times, during the whole of their marriage, and her subsequent desire to make up for lost time by embarking on a wild spree of midlife promiscuity a mere four months after his funeral. I detailed how my father callously spurned summer holidays with us in favour of golf club trips and how those formative summer holidays, happily spent with Mum and her parents, had shaped my deep-seated desire to own a beach hut. Lastly, I came to Barry 'The Bombshell' boiler man's theory that Dad had 'swung both ways' and my modification of it into the simple notion my father might have been gay, as opposed to bisexual or asexual. A gay man who had sought to hide his sexual preferences behind the façade of a heterosexual marriage and one 'I'm straight, here's the living proof' child. A notion I was determined to prove, or disprove, by extracting the truth from Malcolm in an, as yet, unspecified plan of Machiavellian cunning.

"Fuck!" JJ declared, encapsulating my sorry saga in one succinct exclamation. "Please tell me that's it and there's no more," he begged, a pained expression on his face.

I laughed acrimoniously. I wanted to ask what else there could possibly be, but kept myself in check. Self-pity is never an attractive trait at the best of times. Sitting outside my beach hut, it had to be an anathema.

"That's it," I confirmed. "'The End'."

"Thank god for that," JJ remarked with passion. "What a story! I'll have to upgrade you to a nine. You only needed an alien abduction with full probing chucked in to get full marks," JJ judged. "Shit!" he exclaimed shaking his head, still in a state of disbelief. "What a mess. When's the misery memoir coming out?"

"Never," I replied bluntly. "As for scores, I think I'll give yours an eight."

"You win then... but kind of lose," JJ said, thinking aloud. "No. *Have* lost," he corrected himself. "That's one horrendous story, Paul, but now's the hour to bounce back. They're always banging on about bounce-back-ability, whoever the fuck 'they' are, and now, aided by your beach hut, you can do. Onwards and upwards from now on, man."

"Spot on, JJ," I responded, pleased with his support. "It *is* onwards and upwards, despite this latest setback. I have to keep telling myself the corner *has* been turned. And on that thought," I motioned, getting out of my chair, "let's go and turn another one and get something to eat."

We put the folding chairs and JJ's racket bag safely in the beach hut, padlocked the doors and I led JJ the short distance along the prom to the café where I had previously eaten a very nice lasagne. We sat outside, bagging a table close to the promenade and still in the sun, the ones situated closer to the café now enveloped by the building's shade. We had walked and sat down in silence, both of us no doubt appraising each other's story. So much had happened to us, a little musing to absorb what we had both heard was only natural.

JJ's story continued to leave me in a state of breathless incredulity. His globe-spanning, freewheeling, peripatetic, wild, oversexed tale, one grounded in the sound anti-strategy of 'seeing what crops up next', was not one I could have ever embarked on. Unplanned, lacking in focus and with zero structure, his life path had been the direct opposite to mine – school, university, a job keeping me rigidly within the world of education, a handful of girl-friends and then one unsuccessful marriage, all occurring within a hundred-mile diameter circle. Our life experiences truly were poles apart.

Whereas JJ's story sounded an improving adventure, one where he conquered his early alcoholism and, eventually, came to terms with his failed tennis career, mine only succeeded in deteriorating at its end after having flat-lined through the thrill-free zone of domesticated life. That said, I did feel my tale harboured a much darker and more bitter sentiment. A lesson in how life can always hurl you a deadly curve ball however safe you're playing it.

Much more important than the evident contrasts in our lives was the sense of bonding I felt meeting JJ again. I felt comfortable with him, trusted him, even when revealing my most personal thoughts. The time we had spent apart felt more a matter of weeks than many years – always a sign of a strong friendship – and we still sparked off each other's sense of humour. Time, it seemed, hadn't distanced us and our camaraderie remained rooted in a relationship forged during teenage years. I felt extremely grateful for him to be back in my life. Pleased he had come to Southburgh to visit me.

"How can help?... Are back again," Tatiana stated, recognising me and flashing a friendly smile. "And haff friend," she continued, twinkling at JJ.

"Yes. Back again, Tatiana," I confirmed, feeling a bit self-conscious because I had behaved rather dopily the last time. "This is JJ. An old friend. We haven't seen each other for a long time."

"Is nice meet old friend from past," Tatiana declared, her head moving approvingly. "What drink are haffing?"

"A Coke, please," I replied.

"Same for me," JJ chipped in.

"And can we order some food as well, please?" I asked.

"Nyet. Is not allow order food same time as drink," Tatiana answered deadpan. Confused, I froze, sitting rigid like a shop window mannequin before Tatiana broke into a quicksilver giggle. "Am making joke. Can order food now. Is nyet problem. Are wanting lasagne again?" she asked me directly.

"Oh, right. Sorry. Very funny. You had me going there," I bumbled. "Yes, please. Lasagne for me."

"Once more copy and say 'same for me'?" she asked JJ.

"Same for me," JJ responded.

"Two Coke. Two lasagne... If get order wrong, is *free*. Is new management directive improve customer service," Tatiana said, spinning on a heel and heading back to the café.

Once out of earshot, JJ sucked in air. "Now, she is *lovely*," he proclaimed.

"That's not the half of it."

"What do you mean?"

"You'll see."

JJ didn't chase me any further for answers. "You know she likes you," he proffered instead.

"Do you think so?"

"Duh! Of course she does. Don't let the last two women in your life knock you back forever, man. She *likes* you. I can..."

A waitress in a blue blouse arrived at our table, silencing the conversation. "One Coke. One Pepsi," she said, putting the glasses on the table, her blue eyes darting at both of us but lingering on JJ. "Enjoy."

"Thanks," I said.

"Thank *you*," JJ echoed. "What the *hell*?" he declared once she was gone, the quiet volume of his voice not detracting from its intensity.

"To put you on the right track, she *hasn't* had a quick change of clothing."

"There's... *two* of them?"

I nodded. "Identical twins. From Russia, apparently. 'Tatiana white top. Svetlana blue top'."

JJ took a slow drink from the glass containing Pepsi and looked me in the eye. "Don't fancy yours much."

Tatiana and Svetlana

When visit café again, am please see him. Is nice looking man who haff honest eye, only with pain behind. Haff seen look many time in Russia, before vodka drinking start. Am feeling sorry and am wondering what haff make pain. When tell Svetlana are both agreeing is most likely because of woman. Svetlana say think is nice looking man too and both smile. Second time when visit café haff friend. Ferry good-looking man. Ferry confidant. Haff much excite. When take order for drink, am making joke is not possible order food at same time and am also saying if order wrong, meal is free. Am thinking on feet, as expression go, and after am haffing quick conversation with Svetlana. Am saying man from other day is back with good-looking friend.

"Must check out. Are two good-looking man, on own, with nyet wife, nyet girlfriend, nyet screaming brat in café," am saying.

"Da, will check out," Svetlana say. "Will take drink. *Wrong* drink."

Is routine haff use before, share waitress duty for check out good-looking man.

Me and Svetlana haff plan. Is plan meet two nice man. Not one nice man for me and one nice man for Svetlana, but two nice man. Is ferry complicate and cannot be change. Plan not ferry likely am thinking when only job can find in Southburgh is waitress where haff serve family, family, family all of day. Always family and child with many disgusting dad who look me and Svetlana with tongue hanging out when wife not look. Me and Svetlana haff many secret telephone number note from disgusting dad which haff come wrap in five or ten pound note. All say same thing in different way. 'Ring me for some fun', or 'Fancy a threesome? Call this number' or 'Hook up with me. Either one of you, your both sexy'. Am smiling, pick up big tip, never phone. Am not Russian prostitute. Svetlana not Russian prostitute. And know grammatical mistake when see one.

"Friend attractive and know is attractive," am saying Tatiana when return kitchen. "Am thinking might be fun and am liking man haff confidence. Haff nyet arrogance. Not other from long line narcissistic dad think can buy waitress with five pound note. Am thinking haff one evening, if one nyet good, never see again."

"Agree," Tatiana say.

"Tatiana, are thinking want go out on date? Are finding Russian identical twin attractive?" am saying, make joke.

Tatiana make face of deep concern, like enemy of Putin living in UK. "Am hoping is possible," Tatiana say.

Are laughing. All of man fancy Tatiana and Svetlana. Is not arrogance, is fact. Is story of life. Is blessing and is curse.

JJ

I knew something was going on right from the minute the one in the blue top, the Russian waitress named, Svetlana, brought us the two drinks. Making a big song and dance of pointing out one was a Coke and one was a Pepsi after her sister, Tatiana, had said we would get a freebie if she got our order wrong. Blatant. Paul hadn't clocked it because he was too busy hiding behind his towering wall of insecurity. With good reason, I suppose, straight off the back of getting so seriously shafted. Mind you, even if he hadn't recently suffered such a shitty divorce, I don't think Paul would have been much better. From what he had told me and from what I had seen first-hand, it was pretty clear he hadn't much of an idea when it came to women.

When he first began telling me about Emily, I knew it would end in tears. It was *so* obvious, right from the off, that she was only jerking him around. The things she said and the OTT way she said them, using him as an entertaining distraction to rile up her dick of a husband. I mean, seriously, what was Paul thinking? As a better-than-average club tennis player only better-than-average looking, earning a college lecturer's salary, he was never going to cut it with a woman like Emily. Unlike Randolph Valentino-Smith. That was the only bit in Paul's story where I would have liked to have stepped into his shoes. His tennis shoes. To have had the opportunity to play with Emily against Randolph and Camilla. I reckon we would have taken them. Then maybe Emily would have slept with me rather than with Prince Randolph. Apart from that, Paul could keep his life. So rigid. So boring. Like living in a straitjacket.

Paul never stood a chance with Emily. Fact. He allowed himself to become totally obsessed with how she looked and how she played tennis, that's all. Not a crime, just dumb. He had got caught in a lust-bubble of his own making, one that was always going to pop at some stage or another, and when it did, he discovered his wife was already in one of her own. One that wasn't going to pop. With James, a supposed friend. Not that I would ever dare criticise – screwing around with another bloke's wife or girlfriend – been there, done that, got the tee shirt *and* been on the end of the death threats.

Top and bottom of his story, marriage Game Over, with only one drunken snog and a risqué Snapchat to show for it. Not what he was hoping for. Horrible as it was, as a tennis player, I did kind of like his story in a perverse way. The notion one missed smash could completely fuck your marriage – the first domino to go down that takes all the others with it. It made an impression on me and I promised myself, there and then, as I listened, if I ever got close to someone who played tennis, I would never, *ever*, play mixed doubles with them. History's always shown how keen it is to repeat itself. Why give it the chance when you don't have to?

The possibility Paul's old man had been a closet gay was a worse cross to bear, to my mind. Now that is cruel, wondering if your dad only wanted you as a shield to hide the fact he liked sticking his you-know-what you-know-where. I had nothing against

157

him being gay, only in the manner he had strung everyone along and effectively ruined his wife's life. Fair play to Paul's mum, though, for wading through the wreckage and getting on with it and owning the situation. I thought it showed her in an extremely positive light. I also thought it strange how she had never considered her husband's disinterest in her might have been down to him, rather than allowing everything to reflect poorly on her. Poor woman couldn't see the wood for the trees, I suppose. As opposed to the wood she hardly ever saw her husband get for her.

It was a pity Paul didn't seem able to grasp the initiative back as easily as his mum. His alternative beach hut-based plan of re-energising, reorganising and recommencing the next phase of his life seemed pretty flaky to me. Disregarding the scary thought of a single guy, in his thirties, owning a *beach hut* you had to wonder why the fuck he would want to look back and try to recreate the past? Why would he want to relive the holidays that framed the issues he had with his dad? It didn't make any sense to me and I marked it down as a product of his confused thinking. The plan evidently didn't appear to have made much difference so far. His ace hermit crab impression in front of Tatiana and Svetlana, where he visibly shrank back into his shell at the first sight of an attractive female, only served to prove it. No wonder the poor bastard hadn't had sex since his missed smash.

He needed help, that was a cert, and I was up for being the guy to give it to him. He had always been a good mate at the club and used to back me up and defend me when I had one of my crazy turns. Meeting him again, I realised nothing much had changed on that score. I still liked him and got a strong impression he still liked me. Back in the day, as kids, we were as different as chalk and cheese, apart from both loving tennis, and it seemed weird how our life stories had so accurately confirmed it. Maybe that's the reason why I liked him so much. Because he *wasn't* like me, competing for the same tiny bit of space as me. I'm the first one to hold my hands up and admit I couldn't be friends with someone like me. There would be far too much jostling and squabbling for the centre stage spotlight.

After we had eaten the lasagne, I told him now was the moment to reintroduce himself to the female half of the species. Time for us to make our move on the Russian twins.

"Make a move? Do you think they'll be interested in us? They're outrageously attractive," he asked, all wide-eyed and worried, the angst whooshing out of him like he was a freshly opened can of tennis balls.

"Paul. Don't you get it? They're *already* interested. The ploy about getting the order wrong was the bait. They're waiting to see if we go for it." I could see he was still unconvinced and tried to reason logically with him. "Paul, have both of them waited on any other table, apart from ours, since we've been here?"

Paul flexed his shoulders. "I don't know. I haven't been looking."

"Well I have. And they *haven't*. Trust me. Svetlana, blue top, came over to check us out after Tatiana, white top, gave her the heads up. My take is Tatiana liked the look of you from the other day and she got Svetlana to serve the drinks so she could check me out. They're looking for a double date. Trust me."

Paul's face had turned to the hue of off-white laundry, only he looked washed out with stress rather than soap powder. "Okay..." he started uncertainly. "But what if you've got it wrong? What if Tatiana likes you and Svetlana..."

"You are *fucking* kidding me?" I butted in, not believing my ears. "What difference does it make who prefers who? They're *identical* twins! They could swap blouses in the kitchen and pass themselves off as each other and we'd never know. You could have sex with one of them twice, or both of them once, and probably never notice. If you got lucky. Then they could discuss who was the best in the sack."

"They wouldn't do that, would they? I'm not sure I'd be too happy about that. I don't mind you scoring my life story, but that's a different ballgame altogether."

I tried to hide my exasperation. "Look. With your recent love life, appearing on www.comparemyride.ru *after* sex is the last thing you need to worry about," I joked. Paul fell silent. I threw my hands up in frustration. "I'm *kidding*, okay? They *wouldn't* do that... I wouldn't have thought... not put a review up... I bet they have swapped over at some point in the past to see if they could blag it, though. You'd just have to, wouldn't you?" I said getting side-tracked. "You know. When they were little, I'm talking about," I added, not wanting to freak him out more than he already was.

Paul started grinning and the colour gradually came back to his cheeks. "I didn't mean that," he gently explained. "You jumped in too quickly before I had a chance to explain. I was going to say what if Tatiana likes you and Svetlana doesn't like me. Or Svetlana likes you and Tatiana doesn't like me? What if they both like you and neither of them likes me? The mechanics of a *double* date when they're so close?" Paul queried.

"Tatiana *likes* you," I reiterated, dismissing the other permutations before my head got giddy. "I know your confidence is a bit dented, but what about 'The Plan'?" I asked, hustling him. "This is the start of it. Right here, right now. And I'm not talking Fatboy Slim."

Paul laughed at my musical reference. "I know, I know. I've got to take the plunge at some point," he admitted. "And it would be nice to be able to..."

"Stop masturbating," I cut in. "Exactly. If your mum can get back in the dating game at her age." As soon as the words left my lips, I knew I had hit him with a zinger. The poor bastard actually winced. "Sorry. Bit below the belt. But come on. You know what I'm saying is true."

"Yeah, but doing is a lot more difficult than saying. It's the fear of getting hurt and rejected again," he admitted with candour

"I know, man," I empathised. "Let's get the ball rolling and see where it takes us. Yeah? If it doesn't work out for both of us, we ditch them. Deal? I promise I won't go solo," I added before I could stop myself.

Paul gave me a bit of a look before slowly nodding. I nodded back and I called Tatiana over to our table the next time she was close.

"How can help?" she asked.

"Do you get a fee for every time you say that? You ought to," I teased.

"Nyet. Is part service."

"I'd like to get the bill, please," I told her, pseudo-serious face now on. "The food was good, only I'm afraid we do have one tiny problem we're not happy with."

"Oh?" she questioned, pretending as if she didn't know what I was talking about. "What is problem?"

"We ordered two *Cokes*. You gave us one Coke and one Pepsi. You got the order wrong. *And* you did say that if you got the order wrong there'd be no charge and we'd eat for free."

"Is true," Tatiana admitted.

"How about, to save making things awkward, we pay the bill in full and you and your sister agree to join us for a drink once you've finished work? Think of it as a small contribution to the thawing of UK-Russian relationships."

"Is possible," Tatiana conceded.

"But only if you don't bring any novichok," Paul unexpectedly chipped in.

"Haff use up nerve agent on customer not leave tip," Tatiana replied.

"Perfect," I said, liking her sassiness. "What time do you finish?"

"Seven."

"Great. We'll meet you at Paul's beach hut shortly after seven. It's fifty yards that way," I instructed, pointing back along the promenade. "You can't miss it. It's got a massive pile of crap on the veranda. He's been giving his beach hut a makeover," I explained. "If you're lucky he'll show you his grouting."

"What is 'grouting'?" Tatiana enquired.

"That'd be telling. I'm JJ, by the way."

"Are paying bill, JJ?" Tatiana asked.

"Nah. Paul will settle up. His treat," I answered, getting up to leave them. "Is there a loo in there?" I gestured towards the café. Tatiana nodded.

As I left them to get to know each other better over a credit card machine, I walked inside and spotted Svetlana clearing some dirty dishes from an inside table.

"See you just after seven, Svetlana."

"Haff arrange?" she asked, her lack of surprise convincing me I had called it right.

"All sorted," I confirmed.

"Haff wife or girlfriend at home?" she asked, her look cutting me in half.

I shook my head, unconcerned by her directness. "I've only recently arrived back in the country. I've been on a world tour of women. Didn't bring any back."

"And friend?" she asked, apparently accepting my answer as gospel.

I laughed. "Divorced, only a few weeks ago. He's actually *frightened* of women at the moment." A look that may have signalled self-congratulation flickered across her face. "You and Tatiana? Anyone significant?" I reciprocated.

"Nyet."

"How long have you got left on your visas?" I asked, throwing it out there seeing as she seemed keen to see everyone else's cards face up on the table.

Svetlana's face hardened for a millisecond and then eased. "Nine month."

"You are both gorgeous. It could work out," I replied, keeping my face leer-free.

Svetlana tilted her head and hauled down the corners of her mouth before heading off to the kitchen with four food-caked plates.

Paul

I managed to pay Tatiana for the meal and drinks without coming across as a complete cat-owning, undiscovered-flea-trapped-under-the-foreskin, lone-killer psycho. I think. Once she had departed with a credit card printout receipt and unnecessarily precise directions to my beach hut, I relaxed sufficiently to remember I was meeting her again, socially, in less than a couple of hours time. An interaction so much more loaded than the bill-paying episode I actually felt my knees weaken – a reaction I had always previously dismissed as a tired literary cliché. Better not risk any upright sex positions on a first date, then, I crudely thought, before a massive reality check kicked in. I was getting way, way ahead of myself, just as I had with Emily. At least this time I'd had the nous to recognise it, so slow progress of sorts at least.

Pulling slowly away from Sex Central terminus, my train of thought shunted into some buffers – sex-bed-sleep. No! Where were we going to sleep tonight? What with the earlier engrossing catch-up conversations, the meal and JJ's vocal sparring to secure a double date with identical Russian twins, it had completely slipped my mind, and no wonder, where we were going to stay for the night. When I voiced my concerns to JJ as we left the café – don't look back, he warned, it looks terrible – he suggested both of us should sleep in the hut as driving anywhere in search of accommodation after a few drinks was a definite no-no. JJ also mentioned he fancied hanging around with me for longer, possibly over the entire bank holiday weekend, especially if things panned out favourably with Tatiana and Svetlana. Pleased as I was at the prospect of spending more time with him, I informed JJ sleeping in any of the beach huts in South-burgh was strictly forbidden. In response, he burst into laughter, mocking my unwillingness to violate authority, an area of activity he, apparently, had always specialised in. Consequently, with me capitulating rapidly, we rushed off to buy a couple of cheap airbeds to sleep on before the shops shut.

In actuality, we didn't have much choice. I knew everywhere was booked solid and sleeping illegally inside the hut was a lot more appealing than kipping under the stars on the beach or shoe-horning ourselves into a car. As JJ pointed out, with the door pulled closed the chances of detection were slight and considerably less than being on the beach. Even so, as someone unused to disobeying laws and directives, it did worry me. Time to regain the spirit of recklessness that had seen me accept the mission of hoodwinking Ofsted inspectors, I decided. In comparison, this was nothing.

The atypical traditional British seaside shop we found – expensive, relatively free from souvenir tat and boasting a nice line in designer slides – stocked everything a kid could ever need, or think they might need, to have fun on a sandy beach. It also housed an amazing assortment of flotation devices, ones capable of enabling any youngster to be swept out to sea by an off-shore wind and feature on an early evening regional TV news slot. Our required 'lilos', as my mother used to call them, sat amongst inflatable unicorns, swans, dolphins, pizza wedges, flamencos and staid, old-fashioned swim rings. I picked up a couple of the cheaper PVC airbeds, ones that would have been half the price on Amazon, tucked them under my arm and went to pay.

"Better get something to pee in," JJ whispered discreetly, stopping me in my tracks. "Like a beach bucket," he said, indicating towards a vast assortment.

"Do the spades come with them?" I asked back in an equally quiet voice. "So I can shovel our shit straight out the door on to the pavement while no one's looking and then blame dog walkers."

JJ gave me a languid look. "I wasn't thinking of crapping on the floor, more in the public toilets. The bucket is just in case we get caught short at night after drinking alcohol," he explained, shooting me a 'get-what-I-mean?' look. "We don't want to make our presence any more obvious than necessary. Running out of the hut to whizz on the beach would be a bit of a giveaway, don't you think? And pissing up the side of your neighbour's hut is never good form."

"Very true," I conceded. "The only thing is… I don't *really* fancy having to urinate in your urine."

"Then we'll get *two* buckets, my squeamish buddy. I'm buying a green one, to match the colour of my piss seeing as I've been OD'ing on asparagus. What colour do you want?"

"Red… I *must* book that doctor's appointment."

Laughing, JJ grabbed a round green bucket and then reached out for one of the red ones.

"*Not* the matching red handle," I pointed out with overbearing severity, grabbing his forearm tightly. "I want the one with a *white* handle that's a *castle*-shaped bucket."

We both started giggling.

"I might still get a spade to be on the safe side," JJ declared, picking out a lurid pink one. "In case the weather breaks, we get heavy snow tonight and have to dig ourselves out in the morning. It'll double as a handy weapon as well. If we happen to get invaded by marauding Somali pirates whose GPS has gone down."

"Not forgetting we can always use your rackets for snow shoes and hand weapons as well."

"No. We're *not* using my rackets because, firstly, wearing them as snow shoes will ruin the string tension and, secondly, any blood-letting will ruin the grips."

"Why *did* you bring your rackets?" I enquired, being serious for a minute.

"I thought we might be able to find a court and have a hit."

"Oh, right."

Acting two decades under our real ages, we paid a very unimpressed shop owner and carried our purchases back to the hut. Once inside, we each blew up an airbed – I felt so light-headed I thought I was going to faint – and laid them on the floor with our respective buckets next to them. To finish, JJ hung the solitary spade on one of the hut's coat hangers.

"There. One spanking paddle, two Eazi-Clean wipe-down beds, a couple of cum collectors and one seriously scary dildo," he said, cocking his head towards the red wall-hung fire extinguisher I hadn't thrown out. "From beach hut to sex dungeon Suffolk-coast style."

"Don't for Christ's sake say any of that to Tatiana and Svetlana," I begged. "They'll run a mile."

"Or *will* they?"

"Probably two," I insisted. "To be honest with you, I don't think it's a good idea to let them see inside at all. As a sex dungeon or as a hotel room. Too 'loser' either way. Let's lock up and wait outside. And don't mention the grouting."

"Fair enough."

Padlock secured, we stood and chatted on the promenade as the evening gradually turned from twilight to darkness. A waxing moon slowly rose into a perfectly clear sky and as I stared at it, hovering above the seaward horizon, like a massive cliché, I thought if ever a night had been designed for romance then, surely, tonight was the night.

"Be yourself, Paul," JJ suggested, as the time approached seven. "Relax and enjoy being in the presence of attractive women on a warm, beautiful night. Everything is going to work out fine."

As much as I appreciated his support, when I first saw the twins, I soon doubted it.

"Oh, great. Which one is which?" I asked.

Tatiana and Svetlana/Svetlana and Tatiana were approaching the beach hut in changed clothing but with unchanged hair styles. One was wearing skinny black jeans and a casual tee shirt while the other was wearing a navy and red strappy summer dress. Both looked amazing.

"We don't want to get off to a bad start by muddling them up. They must get so fed up getting mistaken for each other."

"Don't fret it," JJ softly assured. "Let them make the first move. Remember, Tatiana likes *you*."

"Good evening, Tatiana and Svetlana," JJ said, cunningly not moving his head a single inch. "We were thinking, we're more than happy for you to suggest a pub, seeing as you're the local experts. Even if you are from Russia."

"Local knowledge dangerous thing," said the twin in the dress.

I didn't really have a clue which one it was to be honest. Pushed to bet my life on it, I would have said Tatiana despite not having a single reason to base such an assumption on. One thing JJ and I did both recognise, whichever twin had said those words meant it as a joke. She hadn't made a malapropism.

"That's good," JJ retorted instantaneously, "I could do with some danger to spice up my life. You're a bit of an adrenalin junkie as well, aren't you, Paul?"

"Totally," I confirmed, feeling anything but.

"Harbour Inn. Is nice pub," said the same twin, gravitating fractionally towards me.

I took my cue and started to walk alongside her while JJ manoeuvred himself to the side of her sister, the twins side by side with us flanking them.

"Busy day, Tatiana?"

"Can tell already?" she asked.

"Not really. What we call an 'educated guess'."

"Am understanding," she confirmed. "Da. Ferry busy. Am expecting worse tomorrow and weekend. Many people with weather."

"Yeah. Us Brits do tend to go a bit mental when we see the sun," I commented, keeping the small talk bumping along as we strolled.

Underneath the surface of banality, I was pumped with nervous energy. How on earth had this woman, from such an unknown and little understood part of the world, for me anyway, fallen into my sphere of influence? JJ was the answer. Without him it would never have happened. Back in the game? Not yet, but not as far out of it as yesterday.

"Am hearing haff divorce," Tatiana unexpectedly asked.

I was genuinely surprised. "Er... yes. That's right. How do you know?"

"JJ say."

"Oh."

"Is nyet problem. Haff pain, can tell. Is normal. Am helping," she said, a warm look on her face.

"Thank you," I responded not understanding.

"Am walking pub let buy drink," she explained, taking my hand and entwining her fingers with mine. "Is start."

The instant her hand took hold of mine, I felt a straining at the fly of my trousers time-travelling me back to teenage years and my first girlfriend. To an era when any female touch, however innocuous, triggered the same base response.

"You're right," I admitted, trying to remain unflustered. "It is a start."

During the remaining walk to the Harbour Inn, I discovered Tatiana's age as twenty-five – both had been delivered by natural birth – they came from a town called Podolsk, some twenty miles south of Moscow, and had no other siblings. Other than that, she seemed slightly reticent to reveal much else from her past and seemed far happier to let me do the bulk of the talking. Much like her, I felt unwilling to retread the monologues previously voiced to JJ and knew all too well discussing the subject of an ex, on a first date, made for a universally recognised error. Instead, I briefly touched on recent events, the successful World Cup Russia had hosted and the ongoing diplomatic problems between the UK and her country. When she asked what I did for a living I told her I taught, as a college lecturer, and used to play a lot of tennis.

"Maria Sharapova," Tatiana responded.

"Yes. There's been quite a few top Russian female players over the years."

"Am remembering Anna Kournikova."

"Good player. Even better looking," I said, hoping I didn't sound overtly sexist about a female who had never shied away from using her appearance as a marketing tool.

"Many beautiful Russian woman," Tatiana stated, a glint in her eye.

"I realise that now."

Leaving my compliment hanging, I asked Tatiana if she had much interest in popular culture, in books, films and music. She admitted she wasn't much of a film buff, hardly ever read, but did enjoy music. Older rock music primarily, from groups as far back as those from the late sixties. She had her father's taste in music to thank for it, she told me, letting out one of the few details of her past. Her father had been a high-ranking bureaucrat who travelled extensively to the West after Gorbachev's glasnost policy of reform started, one who frequently returned with a bag of CDs after every trip. It was a genre of music I quite enjoyed myself and I pondered on whether to make a cheesy reference to 'Stairway to Heaven'. Wisely, I binned the idea before it had the chance to escape from my mouth.

On arrival at the Harbour Inn, the pub was predictably busy and incredibly hot inside, despite all the windows and doors being flung open, the latter held in place by ancient cast iron balance scale weights. The evening had hardly cooled from the earlier heat of the day and the air remained obstinately static – as if thickened and out of a massive jelly mould – refusing to do anything more than wobble, a cooling breeze only noticeable by its absence. Staying indoors seemed sacrilege on such a wonderfully warm night, so with drinks purchased after a long wait we opted to sit outside the pub, making do with the grass lawn adjacent as all the external tables and chairs were occupied.

The first thing I noticed, as we sat cross-legged on the dry grass as a foursome, was how many people kept staring at us. And by 'us' I mean Tatiana and Svetlana. Individually, Tatiana and Svetlana would have secured many an admiring glance, collectively, however, they were more than the sum of their parts. Heads of both sexes constantly turned to double take, literally, the blonde-haired doppelgangers. If the twins seemed unconcerned, they were probably used to it, I wasn't and it made me consider how many men, and probably a fair few women, must have hit on them – I shuddered to think from what age – over their lifetime. A constant incoming barrage of wannabe sexual partners, forever testing and probing and pushing and hassling for a chance sexual encounter. Superficially empowering, you might think, before reflecting how energy sapping and tiresome fending off such advances might become.

Witnessing the phenomenon first-hand, another facet of their lives struck me. The strangeness of a life where many rites of passage, particularly when young, were always taken in the company of an identical person at your side. And how, in that process, the likelihood of individual identity became ever more compromised, getting lost or blurred and forever merged into a collective singularity in the eyes of the world. Surely, an incredibly frustrating experience. Even more so when your looks made you stand out like a sore thumb. And yet here they were, at twenty-five,

170

nearly two thousand miles from home, still attached at the hip. Perhaps their bond was all-powerful, or maybe their dual path through life had created an inherent weakness, one where each still needed the other as an emotional and psychological prop to function on a daily basis.

Whatever the case, a plethora of questions, all ones that simply had to have been endlessly asked of them, formed uselessly in my brain. From impersonating each other – as touched on by JJ – to other formulaic staples such as reading each other's minds, experiencing each other's pain, finishing off each other's sentences, knowing something was wrong when apart and liking the same food, clothes, music, men – the list went on and on – right down to the bizarre issue of whether their periods had synchronised. How could I ask any of those questions without eliciting a jaded, weary response or, worse still, causing an affront? I couldn't – and with nothing else in my locker, I let JJ and his seemingly bottomless bag of entertaining anecdotes take the lead and do all the heavy lifting.

"Another drink, Tatiana? And what about you, Svetlana?" I eventually enquired once their glasses were empty, careful to virtue signal my recognition of their precious individuality.

Queasily, they both nodded simultaneously and ordered the same drink.

At the bar, JJ turned to me after placing our order. "FYI, their visas run out in nine months."

"Meaning?"

JJ rocked his head from one side to another. "Not sure yet. They might be looking for a way to stay in the UK. Whether they see us as a potentially convenient vehicle for achieving that aim, I've no idea."

"What, like through a fake marriage?"

"Fuck knows. I haven't a clue how it works with someone from Russia. I'm guessing they're on a short term work visa, it runs out in nine months and then it's back home unless they can sort something."

"Might be fun to find out what they've got in mind."

"Getting the taste for it now, are we?" JJ asked, smiling and giving me a nudge. I nodded. "I'm up for seeing what occurs. Svetlana told me the score back in the café. She wasn't exactly trying to hide it."

"Onwards and upwards, then?"

"Why the hell not?"

When we got back outside, the twins had changed places. I didn't think anything of it so went and sat down next to Tatiana.

"There you go, Tatiana," I said, handing her a vodka and orange. To her side, Svetlana burst into laughter and then Tatiana started too.

"Am Svetlana," Tatiana stated, her bosoms wobbling with mirth under the thin material of her strappy dress.

"*Seriously*?" I asked, very confused.

"Da. Tatiana there." She pointed to the twin I had been calling Svetlana all evening. "Is time swap."

Bemused, I saw *Tatiana*, in her skinny black jeans and casual tee shirt, pat the ground next to her. "Come, Paul. Sit with Tatiana. JJ, is time for Svetlana," she said, holding out an open palm towards the twin in the strappy dress.

As JJ and I swapped over as instructed, he whispered to me, "Oh, man. What the fuck have we got ourselves into?"

For all the confusion and consternation, he sounded genuinely excited.

JJ

"How did you sleep?" I asked, lying flat on my back, my eyes staring at the gloomy apex of the beach hut's roof, the dawn light sneaking through the tiny window behind me.

"Not very well," the self-pitying voice to my right admitted. I heard Paul move and pictured him propping himself up on his airbed with an elbow. "I kept waking up and thinking of them."

"Yeah. It is a bit of a mind fuck."

"Plus sleeping on a cheap airbed, on a beach hut floor, hardly adds up to a Premier Inn Good Night Guarantee."

"What time did they say they were off work this evening?" I asked. I was itching to see them again, well eager for the next instalment of whatever it was they were playing at.

"Tatiana said five. If it was Tatiana and she wasn't pulling a double double bluff on us. Like when a penalty taker looks at the right corner, to make the goalie think he's going to stick it in the left corner, but is actually going to put it in the right corner, only he knows the goalie knows that, so puts it in the left corner... I think that's right," Paul explained, looking flummoxed. "Anyway, that's not half as confusing as them."

"To the goalie's right, or the penalty taker's right?" I asked.

"What?"

"Nothing. So, we've got until five to kill. What's the plan?"

"Apart from trying to untangle my brain? Clear the rubbish and get a shower. Change my clothes. So I'm clean and presentable for the next bizarre instalment of 'Double Dating Identical Twins'. I reckon we should pitch the whole thing to Netflix."

"A swimming pool!" I blurted in a flash of inspiration, turning on my side towards Paul. "We can find a local pool, pay to go in and use the showers."

"That'll work for me. A hot shower might help ease my stiff neck," Paul complained, sitting upright and starting to roll his head from side to side.

"What you really need is Tatiana to ease your stiff dick."

"Tatiana or *Svetlana*?"

"Either one would do it."

"It is *weird*, though, isn't it?" Paul said. "I mean, come on, you're the expert with women. You had plenty of them on your world

173

tour. What's the crack with these two? Originally, I had them down for prizing their individuality," Paul continued not waiting for my answer. "Yet when I offered to buy them a drink, they both ordered the exact same one in exactly the same way. And then owned up to impersonating each other. After that I chucked the towel in. Way over my head."

"If it's any consolation, they're a first of a kind for me, too. Maybe it's a self-protection thing aimed at weeding out crap boyfriends. For both of them. Can you imagine how many pairs of guys they've had hitting on them over the years?"

Paul nodded. "Loads."

"Precisely. Whatever's going on, I don't think we'll arrive at any answers on our own. I reckon we need to park that bus for now."

"Agreed. What I do need to do is move the car. If we can get the rubbish on board before the parking ticket runs out we could go and get rid of it. If you don't mind helping."

I stood up positively. "Let's do it. One thing about sleeping in here on these fucking things, you definitely don't want a lie-in," I said, toeing my airbed. I pulled out my phone to see the time. "Oh, look. Emma's just sent me a message. That's cool. I'll tell her I'm with you. Just about to play at being an unpaid waste disposal operative… Done. Right…Seven thirty. Load up, dump the rubbish and grab a bite to eat after. Somewhere I can charge my phone. I've only got fourteen percent battery left and the shock of it dying might kill me. We'll have to nip back to my car and renew its parking ticket. I've got a bag to pick up. I brought some extra clothing on the off chance of staying longer. You ready?"

"As I'll ever be," Paul answered, getting slowly to his feet.

I cracked open the beach hut's door and poked my head outside. It was seriously bright, the low sun shining directly in on me, forcing me to squint hard while my eyes adjusted. It was going to be another hot one.

"All clear," I proclaimed back into the blackness of the hut.

"Better empty the buckets first. Not unless you want the place to reek of urine."

Over the next couple of fun-filled hours, after Paul had rinsed out two buckets of pee in a freezing North Sea, we shifted the rubbish from the hut's veranda up to his car and somehow managed to cram all the shit into the boot, across the dropped back seats and on to the roof rack. Paul was paranoid about the stuff we had tied on the roof rack working loose, continually walking around the car, forever testing the rope and everything held down by it.

"Come on, man. Time to make a move. Knock the OCD on the head. It's getting busy. It'll be horrendous at the pier car park if we don't go soon," I chivvied.

"I'm a bit worried something might come off," he replied, waggling the old worktop for the nth time.

"Yeah, I get that," I told him. "Leave it. It's only three points for an unsecured load. Let's go."

By the time we got to the car park behind the pier, without shedding a single chunk of laminated sawdust, the traffic was pouring in and we had to wait fifteen minutes to get through the entrance barrier. Once past it, Paul parked alongside the ticket machine and I did some more queuing, this time on foot, for another twenty-four hour ticket. Having bought it, I jogged to my car, replaced the old parking ticket with the new one, retrieved my overnight bag and phone charging lead and then legged it back to Paul's vehicle.

"Found it?" I asked getting back in, the bag placed between my legs, the only space left for it to go.

"Only four miles away. It's in the sat-nav."

"Okay, pedal to the metal time. Let's go and join all the other sad fuckers with nothing better to do than visit the local tip on a hot, sunny bank holiday."

The recycling centre turned out as dire as I thought it would be and was predominantly filled with expensive SUV owners piously placing their crap in the correct skip like they were saving the planet single-handedly. For our part, we were in and out in twenty minutes before driving off and spending a couple of hours at a fraught, turbulent McDonald's where we charged ourselves, charged our phones and eyed an endless parade of fat, pasty individuals with tattoos. Afterwards, we took a much-needed hot shower in the small leisure centre we found online, a twenty-minute drive away. Its pool bafflingly filled with lilywhite swimmers who had an aversion to sunlight.

By three in the afternoon we were back sitting outside Paul's beach hut, arses parked in his comfort-free chairs, the longest leg of our morning's work not finding a parking space and being forced to commute into town on foot. By then everywhere was hot and rammed, absolutely full to the brim with well-to-do families dressed in Jack Wills, Abercrombie and Fitch, Hugo Boss and Tommy Hilfiger clothing. Accompanying them were more Labradors than you could wave a stick at and say 'Fetch!'

The children were mostly little replicas of the type I used to beat at tennis when I was younger. The ones who had more coaching and nicer tennis gear than me thanks to their affluent parents. Kids who used to have the front to cheat on line calls but would blubber like a baby when I beat them, their parents laser-beaming pure hatred at me for having the temerity to win. Like I was a devil child. Maybe I was. Maybe I'm now a devil man. It did sort of surprise me how bitter I could still be, now I was back among them again. All those years away from the country and they were still here. Nothing had changed. The circle of wealthy life continued.

"If I see another pre-teen on an iPhone, I'm going to get one of my rackets and drive volley it clean out of their hands," I told Paul, sounding off my thoughts. "Spoilt little bastards."

"I *need* an ice cream," Paul replied in a brat's voice. "A Magnum."

"Look out. Ugly baby alert at two o'clock," I warned, spotting one in an expensive buggy. "Fuck having to Instagram pictures of that to your friends."

"They say love is blind."

"Welding goggles are more effective... Here we go. Convoi exceptionnel," I quipped, a family now in front of us, a mum and dad pushing two grandparents, each in a wheelchair – the grandmother's chair with a lead tied to it, ubiquitous chocolate Lab straining on the other end – followed by two small boys on bikes fitted with stabilisers. "It'll be 'carnage on the prom' if one of those wheelchairs hits a dropped wallet and causes a multiple pile-up," I remarked, caustically. "There'll be blood and fruit smoothies everywhere."

"Are you always so snippy about people's perceived wealth?" Paul asked.

"Weren't you when you played in the charity tournament?" I counter punched, feeling a little annoyed at being called out.

"Not so much snippy, more uncomfortable," Paul responded thoughtfully. "It was more the feeling of being an outsider, of being unused to mixing at that social level. On a broader take, of course inequality bothers me. I know I went to boarding school but it wasn't an especially posh one. I'm a fully paid-up left-leaning academic. You have to be, it's in the fine print of the job contract. The charity tournament people were proper one-percenters. The bulk of the people here aren't in that league."

"You reckon?" I asked scornfully. "Did you see the cars at the tip? Second-home owners up from London, the lot of them."

"Possibly."

"And how much did you pay for your hut?"

"Seventy-six grand."

I snorted air down my nose derisively. "For a pile of glorified kindling? And that's not stinking rich? Seventy-six thousand pounds for a wooden hut used a handful of weeks a year." I leaned across and gave him a friendly punch on the shoulder that came out much harder than expected. "You fool. Think how much one-to-one coaching with me you could have had for that sort of money at forty quid, no, make that *fifty* quid an hour."

"It wouldn't be enough. Not to beat the likes of Randolph Valentino-Smith, anyway," Paul replied rubbing his arm, wincing and trying to hide how much it hurt.

"If we get to have that hit, I'll tell you how much I could improve your game. For nothing."

"Very generous, but I'd be rubbish. I haven't picked up a racket since the charity tournament."

I pointed up to my face. "The coach's all-seeing eye penetrates the rust."

"Cast it on Tatiana and Svetlana when you next see them," came Paul's reply. "You don't have to tell me how good they are. Just what game they're playing would suffice."

Paul

I was drunk. And I had double vision. No wait, there would be *four* of them. Not double vision, then. I was sticking with the drunk, though. I hadn't been drunk for ages. Not since the last time. We had been to the pub again, got through a fair few rounds and then moved on. To here. Anything could happen here, I thought, trying to fathom out the two of them sitting on the cheap, scuffed velour upholstery across the tiny, scratched table. Tatiana and Svetlana. Dressed identically. They had let us decide which one was which. And they had kept moving and swapping places all evening, on purpose, like a magician hiding a ball under cups. Maybe everything to do with them was sleight of hand.

"Sod this," I had said to JJ earlier when we were buying drinks at the bar. "I'm calling whichever one I'm talking to Tatiana."

"Good idea. Me too."

Already pissed, JJ had been supplementing his alcohol intake between pub-bought rounds by constantly swigging on the bottles of vodka Tatiana and Svetlana had brought with them. They had enthusiastically joined him while I refrained, freaked by FOVIBO – fear of vodka-induced blacking out.

JJ's thigh was pinched tight against mine and it reminded me of the time I sat down too close to Emily Winstone. Not a good omen. The four of us were squashed around the tiny table of an ageing static caravan, the model type 'Mirage' – according to the name-plate above the door – and I wondered, as my head passed under it, if the sign would turn out to be prophetic. The caravan was Tatiana and Svetlana's home, permanently sited within one of the less salubrious caravan parks on the outskirts of Southburgh. We had been invited back. Whether for coffee, to play Monopoly, to have sex, to talk about Putin's gammy right arm, to get murdered and diced up – our vital organs hawked on the dark web within minutes – I had no idea. And in my current state, cared even less. Potential outweighed apprehension. I was pissed and up for a night of Russian roulette.

"Paul," the one sitting directly opposite me said.

"Tatiana," I replied, squinting as I tried to focus on her beautiful high cheek-boned face.

She reached over the table and kissed me tenderly on the lips.

"Paul," the one sitting directly opposite JJ said.

"Tatiana," I replied.

She reached slightly further over the table and kissed me tenderly on the lips.

"JJ," the one sitting directly opposite me said.

"Tatiana," JJ replied.

She reached slightly further over the table and kissed him tenderly on the lips.

"JJ," the one sitting directly opposite JJ said.

179

"Tatiana," JJ replied.

She reached over the table and kissed JJ tenderly on the lips.

"Paul. Am Svetlana," the one sitting directly opposite JJ said.

"Svetlana," I replied, squinting as I tried to focus on her beautiful high cheek-boned face.

She reached slightly further over the table and kissed me tenderly on the lips.

"Paul. Am Svetlana," the one sitting directly opposite me said.

"Svetlana," I replied.

She reached over the table and kissed me tenderly on the lips.

"JJ. Am Svetlana," the one sitting directly opposite JJ said.

"Svetlana," JJ replied.

She reached over the table and kissed him tenderly on the lips.

"JJ. Am Svetlana," the one sitting directly opposite me said.

"Svetlana," JJ replied.

She reached slightly further over the table and kissed JJ tenderly on the lips.

"Paul. If want Tatiana," the one sitting directly opposite me said.

"Haff also want Svetlana" the one sitting directly opposite JJ said.

I looked blearily over to JJ. I needed guidance. The trouble was, so did he.

"JJ. If want Tatiana," the one sitting directly opposite JJ said.

"Haff also want Svetlana," the one sitting directly opposite me said.

JJ looked blearily over to me. He needed guidance. The trouble was, so did I.

Eventually, in response, JJ wiped a finger under his nose and slowly shook his head. "You Nas!" he said, laughing under his words, as if the twins were joshing him. "How about I sing a song?" he asked, completely out of the blue, scanning our reaction, a manic smile drawn on his face by a talentless Picasso-fixated

180

artist. "Na na na na, na na na na. Hey hey. Which one is which?" he chanted, bursting into an old Bananarama cover I instantly remembered. "Is it Svetlana? Or Tatiana? Hey hey. Who kissed my lips?"

"Na na na na, na na na na. Hey hey. Which one is which?" I enthusiastically mimicked, grinning from ear to ear and taking on the lead singer role. "Is it Svetlana. Or Tatiana. Hey hey. Who kissed my lips? Perestroika," I started off again. "Saw two daughters. Hey hey. Which one is which?"

"Does it matter? Does it matter? Hey hey. Who kissed my lips?" JJ responded, now clapping along to his own words.

In my head, another variation popped up like an internet advert. "They're doppelgangers. They're doppelgangers," I started singing, now clapping along as well. "Hey hey. Who kissed my..."

The one sitting opposite me swung a bottle of vodka down so hard on the table it shattered into smithereens, its glass spraying everywhere. Shaken, JJ and I shut up instantly and the caravan went deathly silent. The only noise I could hear internal, a booming heart overdubbed by a rasping breath. I stared in horror at the razor-sharp shards strewn across the table and then at the few pieces sitting in the folds of my crotch. A hint of sobriety returned, enough to realise Tatiana and Svetlana weren't drunk despite guzzling the majority of the vodka. Adrenaline flooded in. If not for a lack of leg room, my knees would have been knocking. Nauseously, I felt the whole caravan teeter on the edge of revelation, its full length wallowing slowly up and down, like a slow-mo seesaw ride, ready at any moment, to plunge downwards from its unseen fulcrum, taking all inside with it silently into the abyss.

The one sitting opposite me still held the jagged-edged broken bottle neck in her hand. One thrust of that in my jugular and I would bleed out in minutes.

"You want know story..." the one sitting opposite to me asked in a soft, non-aggressive voice.

"... Of two little Russian girl who haff same beautiful look?" the one sitting opposite JJ finished off.

I turned and looked at JJ as he turned and looked at me. I pictured us trapped in an old music hall act, one where the two protagonists play out the movement and reflection of each other in a non-existent mirror. As we both nodded our heads in sync, a smile of approval appeared on both the Nas' kissing lips.

Tatiana and Svetlana

Am born first, before Svetlana, by sixteen minute, in year 1993, so am 'Big Sister'. At time, Russian tricolour haff replace Soviet hammer and sickle flag for only two year. Father haff say from early age and all through life, "Is time of great change... Tatiana. Of great opportunity," he keep saying, always looking Mamochka for confirmation. Am seeing her move lip on all occasion. Am not stupid. Father cannot tell if am Tatiana or Svetlana.

Mamochka say always know am Tatiana and little sister is Svetlana. Is story haff heard many time how on day of birth make mark on Svetlana for telling difference because is impossible tell difference otherwise. Are identical. Mamochka admit. Haff also paint toenail, was other method, or dress in different baby clothe. When are older, haff make Svetlana haff short hair style while am haffing hair stay long. After Svetlana haircut, when first look each other, is strange. Is instinct something not right. Are not liking haff different hair style and different look, is not how should be. Are ferry upset. All of first night of haircut are crying and scream and, when Mamochka come see what is problem, make Mamochka promise cut hair same in morning. Mamochka ferry tire and worry because Father haff good new job and need sleep. Mamochka give in if promise be quiet and go sleep. Mamochka promise next day Tatiana haff hair cut same. After hair cut same Mamochka promise never do again and say can always haff same hair style. Me and

Svetlana say if not cry and scream all night, every night, and, while on subject, also say must always haff same clothe as well. We *must* haff same clothe. Mamochka agree, is not happy, but never run risk and break promise.

Mamochka always ferry proud of me and Svetlana when growing up. "So beautiful. Both so beautiful," she say all of time. Everybody who see when are out say same thing. "Such beauty. Such striking blonde hair. So pretty. Must be so proud," people are telling Mamochka. And then ask which one Tatiana and which one Svetlana. Mamochka insist, tell everybody, family, friend, acquaintance and stranger always know. Even when in same clothes with same hair, Mamochka always know. Is bullshit. Me and Svetlana know haff not get name right all of time now hair and clothe are always same. Is right sometime and is wrong sometime. Is nyet big thing, but as time pass and get older are wondering more why Mamochka can only tell sometime. Is Mamochka, after all and all mamochka should know name of child.

Am born second, after Tatiana, by sixteen minute, in year 1993, so am 'Little Sister'. At time, Russian tricolour haff replace Soviet hammer and sickle flag for two year only. Father haff been saying from early age and all through life. "Is time of great change... Svetlana. Of great opportunity," he keep saying, always looking at Mamochka for confirmation. Am seeing her move lip on all occasion. Am not stupid. Father cannot tell if am Svetlana or Tatiana. Is not only parent suffer same problem.

When me and Tatiana little older, am thinking eight year old, on hot summer day, when alone in bedroom, Father at work, Mamochka in kitchen, we take off all clothe, stand in front of bedroom mirror and compare body see if can find reason why Mamochka only tell difference between Tatiana and Svetlana on some of occasion. Perhaps is possible hidden distinguish feature can only see from certain angle. Experiment show look exact same, haff same height and, check on scale, haff same weight. To half kilo.

Are checking arm, leg, back and bottom, try discover clue set twin apart. Are looking for birthmark, for mole or freckle all over body. Are looking at shape of head and all feature on head, of hand, of foot and tooth. Are looking at eye, eyebrow and way of hair growing. After much time, finally realise and discover is nyet possibility Mamochka can tell from physical appearance. Haff move on way are walking, way are talking, way gesticulate, way move all of body. Is impossible know. Haff seen with own eye in mirror. Do all thing exact same way in exact same time. Are identical in every aspect. Am smiling at Tatiana. A secret smile for a secret find. Is obvious now in hindsight, but are only young at time. Mamochka haff no clue. Mamochka only guess. Sometime guess right, sometime guess wrong. On day of secret am starting make diary of Mamochka success hit rate.

"We know secret," am telling Mamochka as say goodnight in bed, "how are telling apart."

"We found secret," Tatiana say from bunk bed.

"Is no secret," Mamochka say. "Am Mamochka and can tell difference between own daughter. Is possible are confuse."

"Nyet, Mamochka. Is ferry bad thing say. Am knowing am Tatiana and am knowing since haff same haircut and wear same clothe, cannot tell difference between own daughter," Tatiana say.

"Are only guessing," am saying. "Am knowing am Svetlana, but when are saying am Svetlana are only guessing. Are not confuse. Is ferry bad thing say."

"Nyet. Is not case," Mamochka say.

"Da. Is case," Tatiana say.

"Da. Is case, Mamochka," am saying.

"Well, are ferry clever girl," Mamochka say, stroking forehead, voice ferry strain. "Am sorry. Am apologise. Is own fault, though. Only haff happen because want same haircut and same clothe. When baby am making…"

"Da. Are knowing story, make mark, paint toenail, haff hear

184

hundred time before," Tatiana say.

"Am just saying," Mamochka say. "Daughter haff understand is not secret for anyone else. Is our secret. Is for nobody else. Understand."

"All am understanding," am saying, "is situation massive mistake for Mamochka make."

"*Promise*," Mamochka say, ignore statement.

"Can promise," Tatiana say. "But only if Mamochka promise always give Tatiana and Svetlana what want."

"Svetlana?" Mamochka say.

"Can promise," am saying. "But only if Mamochka promise always give Tatiana and Svetlana what want."

"*Mamochka?*" am saying same time Tatiana, put Mamochka on spot.

"Promise," Mamochka say.

"Why haff not tell Father?" Tatiana say. "Haff seen haff no clue and is always look for answer when Mamochka haff no clue either."

Mamochka lip thin. "Father haff been away from home much more because new job. Most time in house is only Mamochka, Tatiana and Svetlana. Father most important one in family, is thinking," Mamochka say. "Because new job and money earn. Haff change attitude and think am only low housewife in eye now. Perhaps am liking fact cannot tell difference between own daughter and is haffing always ask. May haff good job as bureaucrat, but looking after Tatiana and Svetlana is *my* job. Is job cannot do good as me. Is why must keep secret and never tell. For sake of Mamochka self-esteem. For sake of family."

"Is job reason why Father not home now?" am saying.

"Am hoping so," say Mamochka, strain ferry much on face.

First day senior school ferry strange. We haff move house now into nice area of Moscow, in Yasenevo District, thank Father and promotion in GRU, Military Intelligence Service. New school much bigger than old and many older boy and older girl stare as walk through entrance. Is scary and in all lesson is *teacher* who also stare. After one day only, headmaster contact Mamochka for way of telling difference, is saying is impossible for teacher and if cannot tell difference then maybe haff put in separate class. Is something Mamochka haff promise will never happen from start of schooling as pay for keeping secret.

"Haff make promise, Mamochka," Svetlana say. "Never tell secret and in return haff promise never haff wear different clothe, haff different haircut or go different class. If make go in different class will never go school again and haff tell Father of secret."

"Same!" am saying.

"But teacher must know. For work. For test. For ask question," Mamochka protest. "Haff always complain for not knowing daughter, but seem determine make life hard as possible for everyone, even Mamochka. Am sure sometime lie which one Tatiana and which one Svetlana."

"Remember promise!" are saying at same time, ignore Mamochka observation.

"Take ribbon," Mamochka say, haffing idea after being on end of severe browbeat. "Put ribbon in hair before enter school. Can take out once school finish and is only for classroom if want. When first go in classroom tell teacher, 'Am Svetlana with ribbon,' or 'Am Tatiana with ribbon.' Is for lesson only. If want, can take ribbon out in playground. Is only for teacher. But maybe is good idea make new friend," Mamochka say with hope.

Am looking at Svetlana and can tell think is good idea. Am thinking same. Is good idea. Are agreeing wear ribbon in class but not in playground. Why haff need for friend when haff Svetlana and Svetlana haff me? Next day, take ribbon for school and Svetlana wear for first lesson and tell teacher "Am Svetlana." For second lesson, am wearing ribbon and tell teacher "Am Svetlana". Are changing true identity often. Am Tatiana in Mathematic and then am Svetlana in History. Svetlana is Svetlana in Mathematic and then Tatiana in History. Are moving class and change ribbon when are hiding where nyet one can see. Next time, in same lesson, are changing again. Are not wanting give any teacher chance know which one Tatiana and which one Svetlana, despite possible is tiny. Are wanting teacher think, 'Both girl are exact same. Is impossible tell without ribbon.' Is ferry much what want world think. Teacher. Pupil. Everyone. In classroom, am always sitting next Svetlana as haff ask Father tell school must happen. Word of Father now take more serious than word of Mamochka and am thinking school are frighten Father. Am thinking is ferry good Father haff promotion and is big shot in GRU and haff much clout.

Am not sure when first impersonate Svetlana. Feel natural as when am Tatiana or when am Svetlana. Svetlana say same. Perhaps haff something do with Mamochka mistake when young, guessing name and calling own daughter by name of twin sister. Understand haff contribute issue by insistence of look same all of time, but am often wonder if insistence of look same all time is subliminal issue cause by Mamochka not know difference of own daughter. Theory is like chicken and egg. One chicken and two egg.

In beginning, when not proper selves, are always making sure careful name work correctly and swap paper if necessary before hand in, in case teacher spot difference in handwriting or level of work. When homework begin, practise and copy, copy, copy make everything same. By end of year exam everything is good and haff nyet need worry over work. Handwriting is identical. Standard of work is identical. Everything is identical.

First year senior school, Svetlana haff first period one day after am haffing mine. Haff arrive puberty little late and Mamochka haff warn what expect. Are not haffing fright of sight of blood or monthly pain, are haffing fright of how body might change. Are haffing fright of growth spurt, up and out, of breast and pubic hair, things which haff chance make difference. Are worrying, lose sleep over coming month and is much check, check and check of body.

Thank luck star haff ferry good fortune and share DNA make grow same rate. Haff same height, haff same size breast and haff same shade pubic hair as colour of hair on head. Haff not single pimple, and complexion stay perfect as before. Situation stay same. Nyet one can tell which one Tatiana and which one Svetlana. Only difference now when look in mirror, is see young woman rather than young girl.

As teenage year arrive, boy, young man, man and dirty old man are sniff round me and Svetlana all of time. Are sniffing me and Svetlana like randy tom cat sniff female cat in season. It never stop. Wherever go. Whatever do. 'Hello, girl! Want haff walk with me and friend?' 'Hello, Blondie. Want go for coffee? Haff cigarette? Score drug?' 'Hello, gorgeous. Want fuck me and friend?' 'Hello, sexy. Want make threesome?' Am linking arm with Svetlana and laugh. 'Nyet way. Haff boyfriend already.' Am lying. Haff not. Haff never.

All of boy want me and Tatiana and because this all girl are jealous. Father has job where often travel West so haff good music CD, good Western fashion and also make-up. This make boy want more and girl hate more. Are haffing nyet girlfriend, but are also haffing nyet boyfriend. Is different now as haff sexual drive as are older. When haff sixteen year of age, me and Tatiana haff big frustration and big curiosity of what is like sleep with boy, haff boy cock inside body. Is problem as haff always done all thing together, at same time, sometime as self and sometime as each other. How can do with sex and boy?

In past, for two year now since fourteen, haff play game instead, where Tatiana close eye and pretend am boy while am kissing and touching body and making come with finger. Haff done same for me. Next progression was when haff bought sex toy together for fifteenth birthday present. Mamochka not know as haff careful hide toy and haff share toy use on own or on each other when Mamochka out. One day, after haff done Tatiana and

Tatiana haff done me, Tatiana say, "Why not do same with boy? Find nice boy are liking and are both sleeping with him?" Am asking Tatiana if mean together as threesome or at different time. Tatiana say is interest and not sure, but soon decide different time is best. "Best part is then boy not haff know," Tatiana say "If are not telling and take care haff no chance find out." Am thinking is best for many reason.

Boy choose is nice boy. Eighteen year old and more grown up than other. Is handsome and intelligent who haff name, Alexei, and is top student in school. Is boy who always treat me and Tatiana with respect and is ferry polite, never make cheap cat call or sexual harass. Other bonus is always buy vodka when ask. Alexei never make crude remark when talk, always friendly and haff good sense humour. Alexei make me and Tatiana laugh ferry much. When next talk with him, after make joint decision Alexei boy for sex experiment, one day when haffing coffee in café, am making bulk of conversation as in plan. Am flirting big style, and agree meet him later in evening on own. Little does know, is not Svetlana who go!

Tatiana go first, on first date, and then am going on second date and so on. After each date, are telling each other, in big detail, what haff happen, what haff said and how far haff travel on journey toward haffing full sex "We haff first kiss!" Tatiana report after first date. "We haff first kiss!" am saying after first date. "Alexei haff now fondle breast, too!" am saying, after second date. "Haff rub Alexei dick through trouser!" Tatiana scream, hand cover mouth as if cannot believe what haff done. Am asking, always, how haff done thing like this and haff ask what Alexei haff done and exactly how feel. Is imperative haff consistency of action and accurate knowledge response for maintain deception Alexei only with one woman.

"Alexei haff put hand inside of knicker and finger inside of me now," am saying after date. "Is not as good as you, Tatiana, but am sorry for saying is ferry much more exciting with Alexei."

Tatiana haff nod head in agree and say think same as well. Is first time other human haff effect bigger than sister haff on other sister. Is radical moment.

"Haff wank Alexei off," Tatiana admit. "Haff unzip trouser, take cock out and hand do this," Tatiana say, make up down motion with hand. "He haff come all over me! Will haff wash clothe before Mamochka see."

"Show exactly how haff hold cock," am asking Tatiana. "Show on sex toy."

A few day later, Tatiana confess Alexei haff lick pussy and on next date am haffing him do same for me. When Tatiana say haff suck Alexei cock am not haffing ask question as Tatiana make demonstration on sex toy.

Alexei haff go through every progress level twice, and end on even number, before haff chance move next level. Is only way me and Tatiana haff same identical experience. Alexei haff not remark on logical even progression toward boss level of penetrate sex. Am thinking is haffing such good time, haff not notice.

Tatiana lose virginity first. Is turn as haff always go first. Is fair as is 'Big Sister'. Am always second, but some of time second is advantage as am discovering loss of virginity take longer than Tatiana.

"Not fair!" Tatiana say, laughing.

Is meeting Alexei tomorrow so is nyet problem. Problem come in few week when Tatiana say think might haff fall bit in love with Alexei and, although love me more, haff jealous when am spending time with him and haff sex. Is big problem haff not consider. Am liking Alexei as well, am not sure is love, but am haffing also feel of slight resent when is with Tatiana. When one haff fun, other is left indoor and haff nothing do. Situation nyet good.

Because am loving Tatiana more, am saying can haff Alexei and am find someone else on own. Word 'on own' haff make cry.

"Svetlana. My Svetlana," Tatiana say, holding body tight. "Am never making do anything on own. Are me and am you. Are one. Am seeing Alexei tonight and will tell is over."

Am sad lose Alexei but mood soon pass as see situation as valuable lesson haff been learn. Lesson learn is clear: One man is nyet good and so answer haff be two. Me and Svetlana laugh with nyet humour and say must search internet for identical male twin who want marry identical female twin. "Or," Svetlana say. "We haff make own way in world." Am shock Svetlana suggest idea although am knowing is only alternative. Frighten alternative. Haff big discussion, every night, try decide what best, for week after week. In end, when is time for university decision, make compromise and try make own way in world to small extent. Not go different university, is too big step, instead go same university on different course. This mean spend time in different classroom all on own and always be Tatiana and Svetlana as separate identity.

When time come, is ferry strange situation. Is ferry uncomfortable in lecture and is ferry difficult for keep concentration and stay calm. Is when vodka haff help ferry much, but gradual, over month, effect get weak and haff manage attend lecture when are near sober. As time haff pass and first semester end haff survive, but only because am knowing am meet Svetlana after. Svetlana say same and haff always same feel of panic when apart. Am telling Svetlana live on own apart is impossible. For few hour, is possible, for longer, nyet way. Svetlana agree.

Outside classroom, are stay in same accommodation and attend social event together. At social event try meet nice pair of man who are good friend, who are both liking. Is difficult, as even man who are ferry good friend soon want take out on own as couple and not as foursome. Is bad enough when not in classroom with Svetlana, go on date without make situation worse and haff panic attack when try. Also, when haff secret swap identity, often is case am not so keen on man, or Svetlana not so keen on man as although are identical twin haff slight difference in prefer of man type. Whatever

191

situation, if one of man is nyet good then both haff take walk, as expression go. In end, haff make decision foursome is only show in town and despite beauty, pair of man come and go quick as cannot deal with situation of always in four.

Soon haff reputation as ferry unusual woman and all man at university start avoid like plague. By end of first year, man only look, but not try make conversation. Are still wanting, thank beauty, but haff impossible reputation now and haff too much baggage for man try start relationship. Even new fresher soon hear story and leave alone. Most beautiful girl at university haff nyet boyfriend. Is strange, but understand as are knowing are unusual. Sometime, after ferry much vodka, are going out in city for one night stand with two man who only want same. Sex with nyet string. Haff positive effect on sexual frustration, but is nyet long term solution. Back home for summer with Mamochka, and occasional Father, before second year commence, are thinking hard for resolution. Is possible break identical twin bond and live as individual? Answer: Nyet with capital letter. Or haff find, somewhere, anywhere, two man who haff ability accept as are. Together, interchangeable, as one.

One day, in middle of same summer break, Father make surprise and say are going on special holiday Sochi on Black Sea coast. Is saying haff been invite by important oligarch stay in beautiful apartment on coast and also attend party on luxury superyacht is owning. Superyacht moor in marina for all of holiday and is wonderful example of wealth create by former state run company of gas industry, although Father say is best not mention. Father say is all connect with job, and insist on not ask detail – is wise never ask detail in Russia of Putin – but still me and Tatiana excite haff chance go. Mamochka haff less enthusiasm even though Father haff bought Mamochka many new expense clothe and shoe for wearing and haff also book facial, hair, manicure and pedicure. Mamochka pretty, but haff hard life when young. Year are written

192

on face with hammer and chisel and also suffer shy in company of people not know well.

"Am haffing something special for... Svetlana," Father is saying, looking at Mamochka for confirmation.

"What is present, Father?" am asking, think is other point for Mamochka success hit rate.

"Here," Father say, hand me one of expensive box haff in hand. "Am haffing same present for Tatiana. Haff not forget," Father say.

Am opening up box and am taking out ferry expense necklace. Necklace spell out name and haff 'Svetlana' written in cursive attach ferry fine chain. Is made beautiful white gold, but haff keep bubble ball of horror in stomach from showing on expression.

"Try on, Svetlana," Father say.

Am trying on and look down at name rest above cleavage. "Is ferry beautiful," am saying. "Ferry expense. Must haff cost many ruble. Thank you, Father. Is so precious, am thinking is only for special occasion," am saying, take off necklace and put back in box.

Father smile disappear, but voice stay warm. "Wear on night of party on yacht," is only word Father say.

"Yes, Father," am saying.

"Tatiana," Father say, give box Tatiana.

Tatiana take present and put on necklace haff 'Tatiana' written in cursive attach ferry fine chain. "Is beautiful," Tatiana say. "Am agreeing with Svetlana, is only for special occasion. Me and Svet-lana will wear necklace on night of party on yacht."

"Haff thought haff tattoo?" Father say, from left field. "Look ferry sexy on young girl."

"Are not liking them," am saying quickly. "But are liking new dress and shoe for party on oligarch yacht."

"Only if not same dress and shoe," Father say ferry fast.

"Can be same dress and shoe," Tatiana say. "Especially if wear necklace."

"Da, okay. Will give Mamochka money," Father say with sigh.

"Party ferry special night. Many special people on yacht. Special people, who haff connection and money. And son..." add Father with knowing look in eye.

Am giving Tatiana look. Maybe son of oligarch more open to unusual relationship with identical twin.

Holiday apartment is ferry nice, food from expensive restaurant haff great taste, weather and beach magnificent. All haff fantastic time and even Mamochka haff relax by end of week. On night of party, me and Svetlana haff make big effort look as best possible. Both haff identical red dress, cut low front, low back and high on one side. Shoe haff ferry high heel. Me and Svetlana haff same lipstick and eye shadow, same foundation, same length false eyelash. Are looking in mirror and only backward writing on beautiful necklace set apart. Haff made feel queasy cannot impersonate when want so haff do next best thing. Am wearing necklace spell 'Svetlana' and Svetlana wear necklace spell 'Tatiana'.

Big black car take family Pavlov on journey fantastic superyacht in marina. Father wear expense black suit with white shirt and black tie and take Mamochka by arm board superyacht after are arriving. Me and Svetlana follow behind. Are many people already on yacht. Are many old man and some young man. Are many young woman and some old woman and am thinking is typical Russian elite patriarchy. Some of young woman haff look and body as good me and Svetlana. Is shock. Are usually most beautiful woman in room by much distance in school, in university but not, are seeming, on superyacht moor in Sochi marina. Are two, however, and despite fact haff lot beautiful woman in Russia, most who seem be on superyacht, are making more head turn than other.

As evening progress, me and Svetlana move from Mamochka and Father company into group young man and woman. Am not particularly like man ferry much as all haff ferry high opinion of self and haff head size of bushel basket, as expression go. One man, small height and ferry thin, who haff tell by other is son of oligarch who own superyacht, has exception ferry big head. Haff group crony who laugh at all joke when not funny and hang on all word like is famous Russian hero Yuri Gagarin or Georgy Zhukov.

"Haff question for Tatiana," Oligarch Son say Svetlana "As are second in alphabet," refer necklace spell 'Tatiana'. Group of crony laugh at rubbish joke, Svetlana manage smile. "How much are thinking cost superyacht?"

"Haff nyet idea," Svetlana say. "Many ten of million US dollar?"

"Are wanting me show beautiful bedroom suite?" Oligarch Son say.

"Nyet, thank you. Am fine here with Svetlana," Svetlana say.

Oligarch Son make gracious smile. "As wish. Get drink instead. What are liking?"

"Vodka and orange," say Svetlana.

"For you... Svetlana," Oligarch Son say, check necklace.

"Same," am saying.

Oligarch Son snap finger and waiter run like life depend on it. Oligarch Son whisper waiter who look Svetlana and nod. Am haffing strange premonition Svetlana in some kind danger, which am thinking silly, but neverless haff guard up. Drink soon come and soon more drink come after glass empty. Drink come every fifteen minute on dot. After hour of drink, am dancing with Svetlana, throw shape on floor with group of crony and Oligarch Son. If am saying self, me and Svetlana are ferry good dancer, ferry sexy when dance together thank year of practise in front mirror. All man like ferry much and me and Svetlana centre attention much disgust of other glamorous woman. When stop, haff other vodka and orange as two man start haff conversation and stand in way of see Svetlana. Although am relax, am still on guard and say after few minute please excuse as must visit bathroom. Am leaving man, make circle and spy Svetlana from distance where are hide from other eye. Across superyacht dance floor, am spotting Svetlana finish drink and sudden become woozy, unsteady on feet. Oligarch Son in flash put arm round Svetlana shoulder and call assistance from member of crew. Nyet one in group of crony take notice or are haffing look of surprise when crew help woozy Svetlana off dance floor as Oligarch Son follow. Am knowing Svetlana not drunk. Nyet way haff enough vodka and orange disappear down Svetlana neck make drunk. Immediate am thinking drink haff been spike. Decide must follow Oligarch Son from distance and see what occur.

Svetlana haff been take down lower deck by crew. Heart thump and stomach sick, am secret following, hide in nook of corridor like am playing part in Hollywood film. Haff great luck and nyet one see as am watching crew take Svetlana into cabin as Oligarch Son make surprise move and disappear other place. Is odd haff not gone in room with Svetlana and crew but decide haff wait outside. In few moment, crew come out room and disappear down superyacht corridor. Am thinking haff short window of opportunity enter cabin before Oligarch Son come back.

As am entering cabin, am seeing Svetlana on bed. Am soon shaking her and talk her, but seem haff nyet ability move or talk and haff only little conscious. Am sure Svetlana know am at side and haff come help. Am also sure haff ferry little time and decide desperate plan for stopping horrid act Oligarch Son haff plan. Am quick take off Svetlana necklace and next am pulling off bed and gentle lie on floor other side from door. How manage swap Svetlana necklace with one on own neck with hand tremble so much am never knowing. Once haff done, am looking for object protect self. Am seeing small bronze statue on wall shelf, am grabbing and am quick lying on bed in Svetlana place. Am hiding statue under body and am closing eye. Am waiting. Waiting for loathsome Oligarch Son.

Ten minute pass, then hear door open and stomach start cartwheel.

"Fucking provincial bitch," Oligarch Son say as come in room, closing door and lock. "Haff turn down in front of many friend. Is big mistake, fucking whore. Cannot turn down now. Haff take little blue pill and dick now rock hard for long time. Cunt and arse in for big screw now."

Am feeling Oligarch Son climb on bed as anger rage inside what haff plan for Svetlana. As push body onto back and feel hand start pull knicker down, am opening eye and lash with statue. Am hitting Oligarch Son in head as hard as can with base of statue. Am Big Sister protecting Little Sister from arrogant thug. Head has nyet room for consequence, haff only ferry much anger in mind. Am hitting only once. Once enough. Statue make sick thud as smash into Oligarch Son skull.

Am off bed ferry fast and wrap Oligarch Son head with jacket, stop blood spill on floor. Am trying keep calm as consequence *are* in head now. Oligarch Son unconscious and with force deep breath haff grip on situation as realise nyet one disturb room for while, door is lock, and haff time make next decision. First am getting water from bathroom and splash Svetlana face. Am encouraging get up, am shaking and slapping face, and am managing move little sister into bathroom. With Svetlana head over toilet, am putting finger in throat and make sick. It work and Svetlana sick. Am putting finger down throat again and again. Svetlana sick again and again. In between retch noise, am hearing bad news as Oligarch Son start groan. Haff think of solution fast. Am sure haff only one and am starting run bath.

First coherent thought how strange am feeling. And haff disgusting taste in mouth. Slow, eye bring world in focus and am shock by vision. Tatiana hold head of Oligarch Son under water in bath, pushing hard as body make strange twitch and jump. After time, body move nyet more. Is clear Tatiana haff drown him.

"He haff spike drink! He want rape when unconscious," Tatiana explain after am asking what on earth is doing. "Haff move off bed when asleep, swap necklace and take place. Haff hit with bronze statue when haff start rape and haff now finish job. Oligarch Son dead, Svetlana."

Is ferry much take in, but am gradual feel strong and head is clearing.

"What now?" am asking.

"Are throwing over side after making look like haff commit rape. Are staying here on bed, Svetlana, and in morning when wake up are saying are remembering haff been rape. Am soon as possible return group of crony like nothing haff happen. Is only way."

Head is in whirl, but trust Tatiana haff make good plan. "Okay," am saying. "Must make look ferry realistic."

Me and Tatiana pull Oligarch Son from bath and lay on back on floor. Tatiana undo fly of trouser and take out cock. Is still stiff!

"Quick! Haff not much time before Viagra stop," Tatiana say, take emergency condom from dress and put on Oligarch Son cock. "Sit on cock, Svetlana. Sit on hard. Much bouncing. Haff ferry rough sex. Oligarch Son not haff plan make gentle love."

Is crazy thing Tatiana ask, but am seeing logic in plan for get away with murder and create watertight alibi. Am also thinking what Oligarch Son not haff in life, can now haff in death. With Svetlana in charge. Is big difference. Haff pay ultimate price for horrible intention.

Am riding dead man cock for five minute and am thinking not much different from live man. Am thinking is only less noise and last longer. Am doing ride ferry hard, ferry violent. Is painful.

"Now in arse," Tatiana say.

"Serious?" am asking.

"Is what Oligarch Son say. Screw cunt and arse," Tatiana say, pull face.

"Haff nice way with word. Is man of charm," am saying.

"Am sorry ask such terrible thing, Svetlana. But perhaps Oligarch Son haff tell crony or crew intention what want do. Is chance corroborate action and make alibi ferry tight... Wait. Can see if find something help," Tatiana say and look through bathroom cabinet. "Haff much fortune," Tatiana say, hold up tube. "Haff find KY Jelly."

"Is lucky day," am saying.

"Lucky? Haff drink spike, man haff plan rape…"

"Duh! Am being sarcastic," am saying. "Smear jelly on cock and soon finish job is better."

Tatiana do as ask and am riding dead man cock in different aperture five minute more. Am doing ride ferry hard, ferry violent. Is painful. Ferry painful. More painful than first ride. Once finish, Tatiana take condom off Oligarch Son cock and hide in knicker for later disposal. Then bruise inside thigh and inside arm with finger of steel, forcing Oligarch Son hand into skin of mine. Tatiana then tear knicker, rip dress and stretch out shape. Tatiana rake Oligarch Son fingernail over all body, scratch everywhere and make sure skin under nail. Once satisfy am looking like haff been victim ferry rough sexual assault, together are dragging body of Oligarch Son over cabin door lead outside balcony and, with bare cock still outside trouser, are heaving over railing and into sea. Body of Oligarch Son clatter off hull as drop in sea. Haff fortune cabin below area where all guest are drinking and side of ship face out seawards. Nyet one witness plummet and nyet one hear body of Oligarch Son crash off hull into water.

Next, me and Tatiana clean room, clean statue, clean bathroom, clean everything. Everything back perfect. Next are putting on correct incorrect necklace and am climbing back into bed. Tatiana lean over me once in bed and are kissing ferry rough, smear lipstick all over face and give love bite on neck. Is like old time before Alexei.

"When morning come, must act in ferry much distress," Tatiana warn. "Am going back group of crony and saying am not knowing where are. At end of party, when catch up with Mamochka and Father, are leaving yacht and am saying perhaps haff meet nice young man. Be strong, Svetlana. Are soon back together. And when are back together, are leaving. Leaving Russia forever. Together forever. Am loving you, Svetlana."

"Am loving you, Tatiana," am replying.

"Am loving you, Svetlana," Tatiana say as leave room.

In morning, after nasty night on bed with nyet sleep, think, think, think of what haff happen, all hell break loose. Oligarch himself find in bed but haff not find son. Haff red eye and tear when come in room because haff rub eye for correct effect when hear pandemonium outside door. Am screaming at oligarch haff been abuse after drink haff been spike. Am showing him bruise and scratch on thigh and arm, torn knicker and ruin dress. Face can already see. Am saying want doctor because inside haff much pain. Am saying haff been rape and sodomise, am saying want Mamochka and Father. Am saying want Tatiana. Am saying want police. Oligarch only agree doctor and when doctor arrive, after examination, he haff confirm act of violent sex in vagina and rectum. Is nyet semen, but am quick to point out Oligarch Son haff wear condom. Oligarch admit son always ferry wary of unprotect sex and catch STD, especial from woman not know. Is bigger stroke of luck than KY Jelly and am thinking is time strike while iron hot and am on roll, as expression go. Am starting crying and scream again and saying haff been rape, haff been rape, haff been rape, haff been sodomise, haff been sodomise, haff been sodomise over and over. Am hysterical. Am beyond counsel or pacification. Am class act.

Later in day, body of Oligarch Son is fish out harbour, with droopy cock poke out of trouser. Am casual suggest must haff take own life after enormity what haff done hit home. Am suggesting couldn't live with self after heinous deed.

Head wound, is decide by doctor, is from hit hull of superyacht as fall. Is blood on side of superyacht and damage to head ferry consistent with incident of such nature. Is more good luck and now oligarch ferry much on back foot. Heart is broken, oligarch declare, as haff more love for son than even US Dollar. Haff great emotion as say although son now dead, haff great wish not involve police and haff beg not press prosecution.

"For sake family name and family business, Tatiana. Am begging," oligarch plea. "Haff not suffer enough with loss of son?"

Am thinking, nyet, is all of Oligarch Son make. If haff not decide spike drink, still be alive. Family haff not suffer half enough in Svetlana opinion. Am insisting must haff conversation with family before am making decision. Oligarch haff nyet real option and despite much protest eventual allow Father come aboard superyacht. Father haff come on own, haff forbid Mamochka and Tatiana accompany after oligarch call and explain situation.

Father first word is agree with oligarch is best not press prosecution. "Is not changing anything for better, Tatiana. What haff happen, haff happen. Is bad but past set in stone. Cannot change, can only change future. Nyet prosecution best future for all concern."

Am thinking is ferry big stitch up, as expression go, and oligarch declare haff more love for son than even US Dollar is pack of lie. As despicable Father sit on bed, am phoning Mamochka and say haff fury with Father after what haff said. Mamochka say on phone must press prosecution and Father only think self and job and connection powerful Russian elite. Am agreeing and nodding is true. Am thinking Mamochka only try worm way back in with twin daughter and only think of self. As look Father am seeing sycophant man, as listen Mamochka am hearing pathetic woman. In moment decide am cutting Mamochka and Father from life forever. When speak with Tatiana, is thinking same.

Few day after death of Oligarch Son, with much negotiate, compromise haff been strike and Father and oligarch win. Police haff not been involve. Am making nyet press for prosecution. On other side of fence, me and Tatiana haff also win and haff get away with murder. Nyet prosecution of Oligarch Son is only in exchange for many, many US Dollar, deposit in Swiss bank account, for life-change experience haff suffer. Much money haff been place in joint account Tatiana and Svetlana Pavlov. Is much US Dollar, but not ferry much for billionaire oligarch. In end think haff let off light.

When summer break from university haff finish me and Tatiana haff already decide leave Moscow and haff book flight West. Mamochka haff little energy for argument with decision and accept defeat. Mamochka haff take easy route and stay with Father despite big disagreement over prosecution. What make matter worse, Mamochka haff discover Father haff affair with wife Dutch ambassador who haff meet at Golden Earring reunion gig when on GRU business in Amsterdam. Mamochka haff moan and criticise and cry but haff not courage of conviction in leave Father.

Me and Tatiana haff decide only people in world can trust is each other. As recrimination boil over in massive family row on night leave for West, me and Tatiana give back necklace, say can stick up arse while still in box. Is only box, haff keep necklace as worth much money. Are not stupid. In effort make dramatic contempt gesture equal, are telling Father of Mamochka pathetic secret. Are putting Father in picture Mamochka not as good mamochka as like think haff been. Are telling few home truth and suggest part reason me and Tatiana not like stupid name necklace lay Mamochka useless upbringing. Mamochka using own daughter as weapon against Father for own ego not conducive for happy home. Haff also inform Mamochka haff make big psychological damage on me and Tatiana. Is no wonder want swap identity when own Mamochka haff call name wrong half of time for almost twenty year and Father haff no clue either.

Next day, early, are taking taxi Moscow airport with visa haff for Germany. Are heading West for taste of European democracy, McDonald's, Starbucks, Nike and Coca Cola. Haff plan meet two man who haff desire share life with identical twin. Man never materialise even in West and, after many year, many different country and many man, where are always work hard help preserve oligarch nest egg for rainy day, are ending in Southburgh, work in seaside café. Haff not meet right two man in UK and haff only many dirty dad proposition.

One day, early in season, haff chance make double date with Paul, who haff beach hut, and old friend, JJ. First date haff been good and on second date, also good, haff decide ask Paul and JJ back caravan for explain situation better and perhaps haff session make love. Before haff chance finish point explain mechanic of future relationship, man are starting sing silly song. Tatiana haff much frustrate and hit vodka bottle on table almost hard hit Oligarch Son on head with bronze statue. Haff desire effect stop song, but now feel haff make full explanation for mechanic of future relationship. In silence, Tatiana start tell Paul and JJ story of ferry pretty identical Russian twin.

Paul

I reckoned I must have cut the underside of my chin on the shards of glass resting on my lap, given how low my jaw dropped during the process of hearing Tatiana and Svetlana's story. I had definitely sobered up, that was a given. With a brain like a sponge immersed in a concentrated cocktail of incredulity and desire, I turned towards JJ to see his reaction to the Nas' story. His head swivelled towards mine way out of sync – a second's worth of delay, winching us out of the music hall act – and as his features met square to mine, I felt my body recoil. Like an inexperienced shooter pulling the trigger of a powerful hunting rifle I recoiled, jolted backwards by a pair of eyes glittering with unrestrained and highly inappropriate glee.

"*You,*" he began, levelling an index finger at me exactly as my mother had once done, "have just been *owned* on the crazy fucked up life story. That's a *ten!*" he stated, his voice drenched in euphoria. For the second time that evening the caravan went deathly quiet as JJ's face turned quizzical with a side dish of frustration. "Who the fuck are Golden Earring?" he asked.

"Again!" I exploded, unable to believe my ears. "Is *that* your first question? What the hell is *wrong* with you?"

JJ looked slightly crestfallen. "What's your first question then, *Paxman*?" he asked, fighting back.

I had a list. A mighty long list. All incrementally adding weight to the crucial teaser of whether what we had heard had any semblance of truth to it or not. It wasn't only the mangled syntax, with barely a plural or correct verb tense in sight, bafflingly mixed with many fluent English words like 'woozy' and 'cursive', phrases like 'window of opportunity' plus all the 'nyet problem' and 'nyet one' nonsense and the Father/Mamochka handles that jarred, it was the detail itself. There seemed an awful lot of hurdles to clear before happily breasting the winning tape of belief.

The first one was the secret where, allegedly, a mother couldn't tell her own daughters apart and was reduced to blind guessing – surely the most heinous of mothering taboos imaginable – an act which, they claimed, contributed to psychologically damaging both girls and tipped them towards a lifetime of identity swapping. Once Tatiana and Svetlana realised they truly were physically identical – discovered at an early age when trying to find a giveaway feature that never existed – and that their mother was winging it, the three females then signed up to a convenient conspiracy of silence. One suiting the twins' overpowering desire to remain individually unidentifiable and the mother's wish to lord it over the father. The one lever of power she could exert within their lopsided marriage. At the end of their story, this pact seemed to have been conveniently forgotten and it was Mamochka who was left to shoulder most of the blame for any psychological damage her crap parenting had supposedly caused.

Nevertheless, with a mother committed to addressing the twins by guesswork throughout their formative years, and never being corrected, a father who didn't have a clue, and their increasing longing to look, dress and appear alike, Tatiana and Svetlana's shared path was allegedly set in stone. Two lives always to be spent together, identities wilfully swapped, forever bent on deception, and not a single shrink around to help when you most needed one.

With the twins older still, the tale moved on through the self-pleasuring, incestuous years to Alexei, the world's luckiest sap, fumbling his way through a painting-by-numbers teenage sexual rite-of-passage – albeit with *two* different girls at the same time – with him not realising it. When the relationship falters, because one falls in love with him a bit more than the other, they dump him because of the strain it puts on their relationship. Next, it's off to university with Tatiana and Svetlana trying and failing to separate, if only for a few hours at a time. By now, virtually undatable and hated by every other female, they head off into the city for a succession of sex-only one night stands, the only way they can quell their frustration.

Quietly running in the background to all this is the father's job, one gradually elevating him up the social and bureaucratic ladder in a country slowly unwrapping itself from the confines of communism. Finally, he gets to the point where he mixes with the newly created mega-rich elite and this progression culminates in a holiday at an oligarch's invite. Clearly, the father had designs on his glamorous daughters marrying into money, if only to further his own career. That said, not even the most pessimistic of dads could have envisaged such a sordid ending to a party on a super-yacht. Unless you were making it up.

The attempted rape by an oligarch's son onboard a superyacht, leading to his murder, as one sister stepped in to save the other, was perhaps the most outlandish part of their tale. The necrophilia wasn't dead boring to listen to (ha-ha), but would his penis have really still been hard? Admittedly, I wasn't particularly au fait with the effects of Viagra on a corpse, but the question still had to be asked. And, if so, would it have gone 'droopy cock' by later the next day? I mean, how soon *does* rigor mortis kick in? And while we're on a forensic line of questioning, wouldn't a post mortem have revealed the unusual nature of the blow to the head administered by Miss Tatiana, with the bronze statue, in the luxurious cabin? And that the lungs of 'Oligarch Son', his body dragged from the Baltic Sea, were filled with *bath* water? Where was the condom? Did anyone question the significance of the cabin door not being locked, as the oligarch's son would have undoubtedly left it? Hadn't anyone noticed that the tube of KY Jelly had been tampered with and checked it for prints?

The complete lack of investigation mystified me. Mafia state or not, even in a country like Russia, could anyone believe a dead body would be so contemptuously swept under the carpet? Okay, maybe, that point not so unbelievable. Scratch that worry entirely. Possibly par for the course. Maybe anything was possible if you chucked enough hijacked-state-industry filthy lucre at it.

Which brings us neatly to the pay off. The sum deposited into a Swiss bank account, which all felt a tiny bit thriller novel. Was money going to end up at the heart of the next part of their story? Were Tatiana and Svetlana no more than a couple of chancers from Essex with fake names and dodgy accents? Women more likely to have something in common with the Moscow State Circus than Moscow itself. A couple of low grade crooks who were determined to tap me and JJ for a few grand in order to access the oligarch's bribe? Was that the real truth of the matter? We were being set up and scammed? In real life, rather than by email or on the internet. How quaint. How old-school. How, in all of my life, I had never, *ever*, wanted, so desperately, to be utterly wrong.

I actually *ferry* much liked them. Both of them. And ferry much fancied them. Both of them. And ferry much wanted to be 'haff session make love'. With both of them, even if it was to be on a one-at-a-time basis rather than as a threesome. Because having sex with both of them, one at a time, even if you didn't have a clue which one was which, certainly looked to be on the cards as it appeared to be a prerequisite, given their joined-at-the-hip mentality. To be actually part of the deal. On *their* part. What a twist! That was usually the boringly predictable *male* fantasy with sisters.

Here's the thing. Would I notice the difference if it did ever come to fruition? Or would I turn out to be just as gormless as Alexei? And their useless mother. And their hapless father.

"How much did this oligarch put into your Swiss bank account? You know, apart from many, many US dollar?" I couldn't stop myself asking.

"Don't worry about him," JJ butted in, alarm splattered over his face. "He's recently divorced and been rubbed down with cynical sandpaper and given two coats of paint from the Dulux 'Bitter and Twisted' range..." JJ stalled. In the quietness I could hear his brain ticking over. "Do you *really* want to have sex with both of us? *Both* of you... With *both* of us?" he clarified.

"Finally, a question that makes sense. Nice one, JJ. Took that time to get from your dick to your brain, did it?"

"Got a long way to go."

"Great. A game of penis Top Trumps. With only two cards in the deck."

"Nyet arguing! Am showing!" the one sitting opposite me exclaimed, rising and leaving her seat.

A few moments later one of the Nas – as good a name as any – returned with a laptop, booted it up and made a host of keystrokes. Once completed, she rotated the laptop so that its screen faced me and JJ. The screen showed the Credit Suisse Current Account details for a Ms Tatiana and Svetlana Pavlov. The account contained one hundred and eighty-three thousand, two hundred and nineteen US Dollars. There were very few transactions, mainly withdrawals and one headline deposit of an original sum of exactly two hundred thousand US Dollars dated 19th August 2014. A BACS transaction from the account Gazcom Général. The rest were interest accruements.

Beside me, JJ let out a low whistle. "Think how many cups of coffee you'd have to serve to make that kind of money."

"Story is true," said the one sitting opposite JJ.

"I bet it makes your mouths water every time you log in," I proffered.

"Are not Pavlov *bitches*," said the one sitting opposite me, catching me out with her depth of knowledge. "Give account detail, Paul," she then demanded. "Is final irrefutable proof."

Doing as instructed, I took out my smartphone, logged into my current account and gave her the sort code, international account number and account name.

"Will make transfer of ten US dollar."

The one sitting opposite me made more keystrokes on the laptop and after a while a verification text pinged to the phone of the one sitting opposite JJ. More keystrokes took place.

"Is done. Refresh page on phone."

I refreshed the page on my phone and there was the deposit, in sterling, in my account, from T & S Pavlov. I showed it to JJ. One of the Nas spun the laptop screen around so we could see it. There was the ten dollar transfer to Paul Chambers. They had one hundred and eighty-three thousand, two hundred and nine US Dollars left.

Like an unbeliever seeing the light, doubt flooded from me. "I'm *so* sorry. I apologise for my scepticism," I grovelled. "As much as I don't like it, JJ's right. I have been scarred. I'm sorry for not accepting your story as the truth. It's very strange," I turned to JJ, "I've only caught up with my best friend's life story a couple of days ago and thought his was crazy. When I told him mine he thought it bested his... But yours... Yours tops both. You're right, JJ, it *is* a ten."

"Defo," JJ confirmed.

My grudge-free words must have done the trick.

"Is fine. Is time for next step. Come, JJ," the one sitting opposite JJ said, holding out a hand.

JJ took it and squeezed out from behind the table, glass shards dropping from him as his long legs straightened.

"Come, Paul," the one sitting opposite me said, holding out a hand once JJ and her sister had left the tiny living area.

"One quick question. Why do you make yourself distinct at the café? Why not both wear a white top or a blue top?" I asked, staying put and not reaching out to her.

She laughed like she was laughing at the antics of a small child. "If think am wearing white blouse every day, or blue blouse every day, haff other think coming," she answered. "And don't want complete freak customer."

I nodded. It made sense. "One last question. What shall I call you?" I asked. "I can't keep calling the one I'm talking to Tatiana." It suddenly seemed very important.

"Na. Are both liking Na. Song ferry funny… only maybe didn't show at time. Is perfect name."

Yes, I thought, as I finally clasped her hand and she led me to one of the caravan's bedrooms, it was perfect. Perfect for us and perfect for them.

As she led me by the hand through the dingy caravan, I felt the relief from letting go of my doubts being rapidly replaced by the rising excitement, and the definite apprehension, of impending sex. As Na softly closed the door, I agonised over the perceived prowess of her previous lovers in addition to the realisation I was about to sleep with either a murderer or a necrophiliac. That last thought vanished from my head as I realised it no longer mattered to me. I didn't care. Now I had accepted their story, I could view the incident differently. Not as a brutal act, but rather one bathed in heroic love and the all-consuming tenacity to protect a sibling. If I had ever had a brother or a sister, let alone a twin, I would have wanted them to be as fiercely protective of me.

"Is first time since divorce?" Na asked, catching me off guard with her directness. I saw little benefit in lying and nodded my humiliating affirmative reply. "Is nyet problem. Haff sex toy if finish quick."

Unable to work out if this made me feel better, or a whole lot worse, I ridiculously enquired whether it was the same toy mentioned in their story.

"Nyet. Is new one. Haff multi-speed vibration and pulse setting."

"That's nice," I remarked, as Na seductively unbuttoned her blouse. When she started to kiss me, sensuously and passionately, I knew my long period of abstinence was soon to be over. Not *too* soon, though, I pleaded.

JJ

I awoke lying flat on my back, my eyes staring at the gloomy caravan ceiling, the dawn light sneaking through the tiny window adjacent to me. Instead of a whining, sleep-deprived Paul on an airbed in a beach hut to my right, Na was next to me in one of the caravan's tiny double beds. Fast asleep, her breathing remained calm, slow and regular. This was pretty much the exact opposite to all the mental shit going on in my head. Thoughts swirled. Images leapt. Questions scatter bombed. Top of the list, the one demanding if the woman next to me was the one who had taken my hand across the table last night.

I had definitely had sex with that one. Great sex. Top five on the all-time list, for sure. In the aftermath, we never spoke much, we were too exhausted, so we cuddled, soon both falling asleep. Hours later, I wasn't sure how many, in the black of the night, she got up. I heard her. Heard footsteps. Heard the toilet flush. When she came back to bed, I pretended to be asleep.

"JJ," she said, nudging my arm. "Haff wake up?"

"I have now."

"Good," she said, her hand moving down to my dick, starting to tug me off.

I didn't need a second invitation. In seconds I was hard and ready. I felt her wetness with my finger and we went for it, doggy-style, hammer and tongs. During the most intense action, the phrase 'Don't come-a-knocking if the caravan's-a-rocking' would well have captured the moment. Again amazing. But amazing with the same woman? I couldn't be sure. Couldn't be sure it was and couldn't be sure it wasn't. It didn't bother me at all in terms of it being freaky shit or a bit out there. I didn't care, unlike Paul had to begin with, whether their back story was legit or not. What difference did it make? The whole thing with them was way too exciting to consider binning it over something as dumb as an iffy past. Messed up to fuck or not, I didn't care about it one iota.

What I did care about was knowing which one of them was currently in bed with me. A bit drunk earlier, I might have sung, 'Does it matter? Does it matter? Hey hey. Who kissed my lips?', well, now I realised it kind of did. I wanted to be able to tell. I've had sex with hundreds of women, occasionally several on the same day, sometimes pissed, sometimes out of it on something and I always, always, knew who I was doing it with. Last night I didn't. And it was bugging me. I didn't want to be bracketed with that idiot, Alexei, or the Nas' parents for that matter. What I needed was a way of finding out, or, easier still, Paul finding out a method for me. I could picture him cracking it, being a bit of a dark horse and picking up on some elusive detail I might miss. Perhaps we might be able to pool our knowledge, fit it together bit by bit and try and suss them out that way.

There was *one* other problem. Bit unnerving. Couldn't deny it, though. Despite all the women over all the years, not one had ever made me think she was 'The One'. Not even Darina, when I was young, in love and relatively wide-eyed and innocent. Even back then I had convinced myself something more sexually exciting was

211

out there, nagging at me to go find it, provocatively dressed in a PVC basque, lying on a distant patch of verdant green grass somewhere. As of this moment, for the first time ever, I was actively reconsidering that viewpoint. My age? My coming back home after all my travelling? The notches on my belt finally catching up with me? Getting embroiled with a pair of identical Russian twins with my oldest best friend? Probably a combo of all four. Whatever the reasons, I found myself thinking if I hadn't ever found 'The One', then maybe now I had found 'The Two'.

My only concern, as the lovely Na slept soundly next to me, the frightening prospect of losing her and her sister. Getting dumped was not a concept I had previously spent much time brooding over. Experiencing it for the first time, alarm started to grab me. I was on fresh ground here, all right. No wonder it completely fucked men over. Men like Paul.

Paul. He had better have managed to keep his end up, I ruefully thought. Kept them(?) happy. If not the pair of us might be out on our ears in a shot. Staring at the grubby caravan ceiling, a creeping realisation loomed up on me. It was *exactly* like playing a game of doubles! Sex doubles! One where you rely on your partner to play well in bed rather than on court.

Paul

The morning after the night before stated, unequivocally, I was back in the game. Twice in one night! Oh. My. God. I could categorically state, on oath, I had never had sex like it in my entire life. Absolutely the best ever by some distance. The energy. The technique. The enthusiasm. The no holds barred. The sex toy. Wow! Wait till I tell Mum – so wrong on *so* many levels – she'll be proud of me.

I think it had gone as well as I could have hoped. I mean, you don't pick up a racket after not using one for nearly two years and start hitting winners from all over the court, do you? I had tried to keep mine out of it for as long as possible, in case it broke a string on the first stroke, so to speak, and had dragged out the foreplay as long as possible. The toy had been handy – as Na had suggested – and so had other methods. She/they seemed to have [both] enjoyed it by the way they were caressing my hair while I was down there.

I'm not stupid. I knew the Nas would make notes, comparing, ready to swap details at a later date. Like they had with low-watt-light bulb, Alexei. Not a club I wanted to be a member of. A guy wholly duped by the women he was having sex with. To be fair, that isn't. JJ and I had been spoon fed the deal, the only ambiguity from last night being whether or not the inevitable switcheroo had taken place. The Na who had come back to my bed – I heard her get up, a bit of scrambling about and then a toilet flushing – may not have been the one who had left it in the first place. I would have to ask JJ what he thought, whether he had heard anything or noticed his Na get up in the middle of the night.

Shortly after hearing the flush, whichever one of them it was returned to bed and on climbing in asked, "Haff wake up?"

"I woke up when you first got up."

"Good," she said, her hand moving down to my penis, working its skin up and down in a rhythmical motion.

Next thing I knew she was down on me, her soft, hot, flickering tongue working its magic, soon taking what felt like all of me inside her mouth. I pulled her lower body towards me and she expertly positioned herself sixty-nine style. It's all we did. It was amazing. I was first, predictably, but I made damn sure she came second. Impending tongue fatigue or not. I knew I had to do my bit in the crazy game of sex we were playing. Knew I mustn't let JJ down. Not only did the dynamic of a Nas relationship rest on two men capable of stomaching the shared space/shared identity schtick, it also needed both women to be equally attracted to both men. By definition, the two Nas had to fancy the two men, want to spend time with the two men and be happy to sleep and have sex with the two men. If one of the men fell from favour, then I had no doubts both would be gone in a flash. And if it turned out I was the cause, thanks to poor sexual performance, then I could easily see how JJ might never forgive me. To use a music analogy, after our little sing-song in the caravan, I imagined I would be about as popular as a Lost Prophets' track playing at an anti-paedophilia fund raising event.

From the moment Na had started to unbutton her blouse, I rationalised I was unlikely to be able to match JJ's size, power and endurance so had to be the one playing an alternative game. Employing the subtle little chip and drop shots, the wrong-footing deft touches, the ones hopefully as delightful and effective in their own way as JJ's massive ground strokes pounding away from the baseline. Maybe it was why they had invited us back in the first place, why they had told us their story. Because JJ and I were different. Different in nature, different in physicality, different in attitude and different in bed. A difference that might well appeal to two women who so wanted to be the same.

I hoped so. My conventional marriage hadn't turned out to be a bed of roses and I couldn't see me entering into another one any time soon. If ever. Maybe a freak show liaison was the only type left for me.

Tatiana and Svetlana

Svetlana haff suggest haff first go with JJ. Am thinking is because then haff second go with Paul.

"Are thinking what haff happen with Alexei?" am asking, pull leg.

"Nyet. Am only make suggestion. Is nyet problem if want haff first go with JJ."

"Coin?" am asking, take UK pound from purse.

"Coin," Svetlana agree. "Can call."

"Okay," am saying, flick coin in air. "Head." Coin land head.

"Is Big Sister coin. Haff double side," Svetlana say, only half mean it.

"Are swapping in middle of night?" am saying, put ground-work in place.

"Is best," Svetlana agree. "Haff many drink in pub, take own vodka, invite back caravan, explain situation and haff sex…"

"If man want," am saying, make old joke.

"Only if man want," Svetlana say, make lips into pout.

Plan from day ago. One maybe never happen when JJ start song and Paul join. Situation back under control after am breaking empty bottle on table. Until Paul ask question. Question cause by pain lose woman. Am bit surprise as am thinking desire of sex with ferry beautiful Russian woman stronger in head than desire for evidence of ferry beautiful Russian woman story. Am making bigger disclosure than like with account transfer, but haff come so far and think worth risk. After transfer, can see Paul acceptance and haff move next stage of evening.

As coin dictate, am taking hand of JJ and lead bedroom in caravan. Am excite. Am wondering how good is in bed and how big is cock. Am hoping is big, but am also hoping is not too big. Otherwise can be pain in arse. And make jaw ache.

JJ technique like saying of despise British Prime Minister, Tony Blair, 'Penetration, penetration, penetration'. Hard, fast and in many position. Am liking. Is no fanny around as expression go and am thinking is joke there somewhere. When am meeting Svetlana at predetermine time in night, are swapping and am going now in bed with Paul. Haff only oral sex and is nice. Is trying ferry hard impress. Is different, but end result is same. Haff two orgasm in one night. Am ferry happy.

215

After Tatiana and JJ leave am taking hand of Paul and lead other bedroom in caravan. Am excite. Am wondering how good is in bed and how big is cock. Am hoping is not ferry small, am hoping is not ferry big, am hoping most love-make is not disaster. Can see haff worry over time elapse since last sleep with woman and ask if case. He haff confirm and haff try put mind at rest by saying sex toy can give happy ending if finish quick. Paul haff ask whether is original sex toy, for Stalin sake, and am saying nyet and explain haff multi-speed vibration and pulse setting. He is liking, say is nice, and am thinking, finally, can start now and am unbuttoning blouse.

Paul ferry unselfish lover, am haffing show how set multi-speed vibration and pulse setting but is nyet problem, and he haff use toy and tongue for long time. When am close haff put cock inside — as turn out is not small or not big, is average — and use toy same time. Haff almost come together! Is good sign. Paul haff same notion, am thinking, as seem also ferry happy. Think big weight off chest now haff sex again.

When am meeting Tatiana at predetermine time in night, am whispering Paul is good with tongue under cover of flushing toilet. Tatiana say JJ haff not much interest in oral sex, saying like hard, fast penetration, penetration, penetration. Both ferry excite, swap and go in different bedroom. Am asking JJ if awake and put hand on cock as underline intention. JJ haff quick response, am ready too, and is soon haffing from rear. Is as Tatiana say. Is hard and fast. Is different from Paul. Is good. Am liking. Am liking ferry, ferry much. Am haffing best of both world. Haff two orgasm in one night from two different man. Is not something am sniffing at.

Paul

The next four days in Southburgh, following on from the first night of tempestuous sex with the Nas, were happier than any others I had spent there, comfortably surpassing those of my fondly remembered childhood. Truth be told, they were probably the best days of my entire life, or at least felt like it, so great was the rush. The weather stayed perfect, hot and brilliantly sunny from dawn till dusk, my personal disposition mirroring the unobscured orb radiating life-enhancing light from its ever-blue backdrop. F22 all the way, Grandad. Although marking time to some extent, the hours I spent with JJ flew by as we sat outside the beach hut chatting, laughing, watching the world – and its dog – go by. I could tell JJ resided in an equally good place because he stopped sniping at the endless procession of well-heeled consumers passing to the front of the beach hut. So magnanimous his nature, he even took to petting canines, indulging many a Labrador on extendable leads of varying hues who came up to him in the hope of finding food. More astonishing still, he engaged their masters in the pleasant, if anodyne, conversations typical of those spoken between dog and non-dog owner. At least it saved him from having to engage the by-passing hordes in 'what wonderful weather we're having' conversations for a couple of minutes.

The only time JJ slightly bristled was on the morning after spending our second night with the Nas, when I knocked him back over trying to discover which one was which. I was feeling so euphoric, all inclination to isolate the elements of Tatiana and Svetlana now seemed irrelevant, of no consequence and of little value. I was more than happy with the status quo, back in the game and getting more into it with every passing day, my confidence and well being growing exponentially. Let sleeping dogs lie nicely covered my modus operandi regards finding out their identity.

"I'm really not fussed about it," I told him candidly. "I'm more than happy with the situation as it is. Ecstatic, in fact. Ignorance *is* bliss. Don't fret over it, is my advice. Maybe one day, in the fullness of time, if we're still with them, we'll be able to tell them apart. In the meantime, why not look at it as a doubles four made in heaven? We're in the ultimate, times two polyamorous relationship. One that's turned me into a shameless Pollyanna. No mean feat considering my starting point. Why rock the boat?" I asked. I could sense JJ's rising irritation, but before he could voice it I went in for the kill. "Of course, you could simply *ask* them. If it means that much to you. Or get them to wear those necklaces. *If* you could get a signed guarantee to say they'd be wearing the correct one and wouldn't swap."

I saw JJ mentally take a massive step back and his agitation quickly withered. "Nah. Fuck that. Avoid the Kryptonite for now."

Deflated, JJ slumped back into his not-quite-big-enough folding chair, his eyes set to sea. His face had tanned over the time he had spent in Southburgh, making his hair appear lighter – or maybe the sun had bleached it – and he looked all the more handsome for it, if that were possible. My old junior tennis friend, I marvelled. Back in my life in a way I could never have imagined – given the time to write a thousand contrived scenarios – since his initial contact on Facebook. I wondered, briefly, if I might be living in a dream, destined to wake up in heart-rending disappointment, lying in a tiny pool of my own body fluids. No, not this time, I concluded. It was reality, all right. One grounded in bizarre fantasy.

JJ must have caught me staring at him in his peripheral vision. "What?" he asked, his face cracking into a wide grin.

"Just running over what's happened since we've met up, that's all."

"You'd have got good odds."

"Lottery winning."

"You've done well, though, son," JJ stated. "I'm proud of you."

"Thanks, *Dad*," I answered a bit caustically, feeling slightly demeaned.

"No, I mean it. Fair play to you. It can't have been easy, what with your…"

"Extended period of abstinence?" I offered, pulling no punches. "After, to borrow a phrase from football journalists describing an inept fullback marking a skilful winger, enduring such a 'torrid time'?"

"Exactly."

"I knew I had to keep my end up," I admitted, smiling at the double entendre, any hint of annoyance gone. "To keep us in the game."

"Had to make some good strokes," JJ confirmed, raising his eyebrows and grinning.

We both laughed. "Fancy a Magnum and a walk on the beach?" I asked.

"Why not."

By the absolute, very last day JJ could stay – one day after the previous absolute very last day JJ could stay – it had become part of the regime, taking a morning walk across the hot sand, paddling in the freezing, foot-aching water, while eating a Magnum. Big, chunky, chocolate-covered Magnums. In the afternoon, we would visit a pub, sip cold beer and pass the hours in delirious content-ment while waiting for the upcoming main event. The time when the Nas finished work in the café and the four us could reunite. Once in their company, we would walk and talk, hands clasped as two pairs – never knowing whose hand we were holding – and go to other pubs, eat meals and quaff more cold beers, the Nas only ever demolishing vodka and oranges, in sync, their drinking capac-ity perfectly matched. At night, in their caravan, we would make love, invariably twice. Inevitably accompanied by night-time, swap-over shenanigans. We presumed, we never asked. In the morning, JJ and I would walk the Nas back to the café and then return to the beach hut, open it up, set up the chairs and plonk ourselves in them in the sun, the cycle of Southburgh life recom-mencing. A video stream, on loop, of sun, sea, sand and sex. An R18 version of Groundhog Day. Incredible times.

On JJ's absolute very last day he insisted, rather than go for our morning walk across the beach with Magnums in hand, we swap the ice creams for rackets and have a hit at tennis. He had Google searched and found public courts a short drive away, had multiple rackets and some new balls in his large red Wilson tennis bag. I, on the other hand, only had no acceptable excuses. To be honest, I felt relaxed not making any. With my demeanour so upbeat, stepping back on to a tennis court seemed of no consequence after everything else I had conquered.

"Don't hold back," I joked as I felt the weight of one of JJ's rackets in my hand, turning to walk to my baseline.

"Don't worry, I won't."

For the next hour, in the growing heat on a horrid, uneven, black Tarmac court, JJ ruthlessly worked me over. It wasn't a hit, it was a lesson. JJ snapping out advice during every rally. If, until a few days ago, I'd had a dated mental picture of him as a talented junior, it had now rapidly been superseded by an in-the-flesh assessment of an extremely potent senior. What a player! Way above my level in an exact repeat of the last time I had been on court with Randolph Valentino-Smith. By the end, I was saturated in sweat and due for an extended stay under the caravan's shower, our default route to cleanliness before and after our Nights of Nas.

"Enjoy it?" JJ asked as I handed him back his ball-striking weapon, my legs shot and heavy.

"Yeah. I did," I replied genuinely. "I'm very rusty, your racket's a bit heavy for me and not as powerful as mine, so it took a bit of getting used to. And I'm not fit enough. Apart from that, great."

"Remember to try and get your grip round a bit more on your forehand and backhands, like I told you. You'll generate more spin and be able to hit harder. The fitness will come back the more you play."

"Where and when am I going to be doing *that*?"

"When we play and practise."

"Play and *practise*. For what?".

JJ's face flashed with anger. "James and Chloe did the dirty on you and fucked you out the club, but you're not the only one that's happened to," JJ said pointedly. "So... to show how we're not men who can be trifled with, I've entered us in the club's half centenary Open Men's Doubles tournament this summer. We'll show them, partner."

"What!" I exclaimed. "When?"

"Emma told me about it. It's in June. How about we go back and kick a few arses? Walk away as winners *and* take Tatiana and Svetlana with us. Imagine going there with them. Our new girl-friends. That'd feel real good, wouldn't it? That'd stir up a scene. Put a few noses out of joint."

"Well..."

"There you go then. Put in the effort, practise hard and we go back to our old stomping ground ready to wipe the floor with all comers. And we double blow them away with our new, stunning, identical partners."

"You're making a pretty good job of selling this to me."

"You *know* you want to."

An image of JJ hitting Steven with a massive smash blossomed in my mind – what a delicious irony – followed by one of Chloe and Emily's jaws falling quicker than a moon ball on seeing the Nas. There was no doubting how good that would feel.

"I'll pay the entry fees," I offered.

JJ

An hour into my journey back to Norwich, the lorry in front of me braked hard and I had to slam on the anchors to stop myself ploughing into the back of it. That pretty soon snapped me out of auto pilot. Thirty miles covered and I couldn't recall a single detail, my head stuck in the clouds above Na Na Land. Pulling off slowly as the lorry started to move again, life felt strangely precious. Much more so than usual. It dawned on me, there and then, how I didn't want to end up a grim traffic statistic and never see the Nas again. The incident actually gave me the willies and I overtook the lorry at the first opportunity, ridding myself of the horrific vision of me and my car plastered all over its tailgate.

Suddenly hyper-aware of my own mortality – not something many could accuse me of, given my numerous past dumb escapades – made me realise how wrapped up with the Nas I had become. Had I fallen in love with them without realising it? A near accident only flagging it up a few minutes earlier? Mental shrug. Clueless me, not having had much firsthand experience of romantic entanglement, although all the pointers I imagined someone might experience, if seriously loved up, seemed present and correct when I stopped and thought about it. Not wanting to leave them. Check. Missing them after leaving them. Check. Wanting to be back with them as soon as possible. Check. Missing having sex with them after, let's check, five hours. Check. Especially not wanting to get smeared all over the back of an Eddie Stobart vehicle. Check. Picturing spending the future with them and not feeling terrified, trapped and trussed in the straitjacket of overwhelming commitment. Check. I shook my head in disbelief, eyes fixed firmly on the road. Wowza. Powerful stuff.

Only it wasn't quite as straightforward as that. Spending my future with the Nas meant spending my future with Paul. How the hell would that work? All move into one living space together forever? Four of us in a rented flat – unless the Nas splashed their oligarch's-son-rape-silence cash as a deposit on a semi. Two pairs cohabiting with the added spice of sharing each other's partner, the women swapping beds, clothes and men, me and Paul just swapping them. If we were to ever marry one of the Nas, Paul would not only be a best friend but also a brother-in-law who was sleeping with my wife and I would be his best friend and a brother-in-law who was sleeping with his. We could end up in a documentary. Louis Theroux asking me and Paul what it was like to be married to, and sleep with, two identical women. Us caught gormless to camera saying we couldn't really say exactly because we couldn't tell them apart. After years of trying.

I had often wondered when it would all come to an end. When it would stop. When I would *want* it to stop. The chopping and changing. Jobs, countries, women. Getting my tennis mojo back and returning home to a coaching position I viewed as long term had been the start. Meeting the Nas possibly the end. Chuck in the age factor – early thirties, should know better by now – and you had all the ingredients to knock a nomadic, commitment-averse, womanising existence squarely on the head.

Of course, there might be another slant to it. A less pragmatic take on my situation might cite my meeting Paul, and then the Nas, as merely a case of the stars lining up. Of it being destiny. Fate. My horoscope from a week ago reading: 'Those born on the Libra/Scorpio Cusp of Drama are ruled by Venus and Pluto. A potent combination of flamboyance and sexuality and never more so than this month. With a full moon rising in Gemini, look out for a hot, new romance with twins. If your best friend's a Leo and can share, chances are they'll be keepers'.

Strange how it could happen so quickly. All my years of winging it, avoiding it, only to fall for two women in the space of days. A pair of Russian twins I knew virtually nothing about. Mind you, I hadn't known much about any of my previous women and they hadn't got to me like the Nas. Obvious why. They never had the associated buzz of danger. The excitement. The jeopardy that clung to the Nas like a second skin. Scary on the one hand, yet on the other, the Nas' mystery and peril combo the perfect antidote to any concerns over settling down. Shacking up, if it ever came to it, with Paul and the Nas was never going to be boring. They might end up drowning one of us in a bathtub, or flinging one of us over the side of a pedalo, rather than a superyacht, but it was never going to be anything short of a thrill-a-minute ride. One I was more than prepared to stump up the price for a ticket.

I knew Paul was up for it. We had discussed it sat outside that beach hut of his. His conventional lifestyle choices had let him down big time and the way he saw it he had nothing to lose in going way off-piste. As it had turned out his crap plan, as I had originally thought, of spunking thousands on buying a beach hut to reorganise, recharge and restart his life had been spectacularly successful. For him and me. Go Paul. I could tell he was loving it and why not? I could see his confidence growing daily. All that old negativity falling off him. I was well happy for him. That went for his tennis, too. I would pretty soon knock him into shape and teach him how to play doubles properly.

Of course, the raw mechanics of our foursome meant there was little point in denying serious admin still lay ahead. Even somebody as off the cuff as me could see that. Me coaching in Norwich, the Nas waitressing in Southburgh and Paul teaching at his college all presented distancing issues of their own. The 'how' and 'where' being problematic rather than the 'why'. Still surmountable, though, if we really wanted it to work. I did. So did Paul. We had voted to stay in. Into the Nas. On the face of it, the Nas were into us, the only concern the nagging doubt over their ultimate objective, should there be one. There existed the chance me and Paul might be getting set up for a fall, well, a couple of visas at least, and, once they had them, they would be off. I couldn't worry over it. I would take my chances. Couldn't stop myself. I was besotted and happy to admit it. I loved them, or at least thought I did, perceived myself to be in love with them. I certainly loved being with them. Loved the way they talked and loved the way they swapped identities, despite wanting to crack the code one day. I loved having sex with them, that was a given, and loved the intriguing fascination of their dark back story. I would have liked to know more, but no matter how many times me and Paul asked they refused to elaborate further. 'Haff tell story once, is no reason tell twice' they would say.

Another huge part of my infatuation with the Nas was based on my admiration and respect for them. How they had looked out for each other to the max. How, when it came down to it, they were prepared to go to any lengths necessary to get the life they wanted. Blurring identities. Murder. Sex with a corpse. Staged rape blackmail after stopping the real thing. Bailing on their parents and telling them a few home truths. Leaving home and not going back. Surviving, finding work and saving their hard-earned nest egg. Say what you like, you could never accuse them of being snowflakes. Pity in a way, they say no two are the same, and all you need is a microscope to spot them.

Tatiana and Svetlana

Am phoning and message JJ many time and is nice talk. After am phoning and message Paul and talk. Paul and JJ are also phoning and message me and Svetlana. Haff give two number each and haff random swap phone with Svetlana. Is old habit hard of breaking. Are arranging meet Saturday after JJ haff finish morning coaching and is going pick up me and Svetlana in car and take Paul flat. Is not much room in flat, Paul say, but haff two bedroom. Haff decide visit Paul as weather in Southburgh now awful. Hot sun only memory and haff much rain since. Café haff been ferry quiet after Easter holiday and weather break. Not many customer. Is bad as haff more time think how much am missing Paul and JJ. Time haff pass ferry slow.

Am packing weekend bag in caravan Friday evening when Svetlana return with shopping. Am asking if haff got nibble for journey.

"Da," Svetlana say, empty content of bag-for-life on table. Crisp, apple, Mars bar and Yazoo chocolate drink.

"Which one are liking best?" am asking, throw curve ball at little sister. "Haff over week consider."

Svetlana wrinkle face, pack of Pink Lady in hand. "Am thinking Mars bar."

"Are knowing what am talk about," am saying, roll eye.

"Is difficult. What are thinking?"

"Am asking question first," am insisting.

"Cannot choose," Svetlana decide after gap like judge on X Factor. "Am liking both same."

"Same," am agreeing.

"Is definite best boyfriend ever haff. Work well."

"Am thinking is best opportunity will ever get," am saying.

Svetlana nod head. "Same... If day ever come, which one marry?"

"Coin?" am saying.

Svetlana pull face like arse haff been smack. "Are using *my* coin. Can haff call."

Am heaving shoulders. Only different last name. Is nyet big deal.

Later in evening am putting new battery in multi-speed vibrating sex toy when phone chirp notification. Is WhatsApp. Haff end-end encryption so is safe. Is Alexei and ask how are going. Am saying fine. Is asking if any progress and am saying haff make good progress since last talk. Is then asking which one am talking and am saying wouldn't like know. Smiley emoji from Alexei and comment say nothing haff change. Is long time ago am saying back. Alexei then say GRU still haff poor standing in Moscow and struggle rebrand after debacle of Salisbury attack. Alexei wonder what the fuck Anatoliy Chepiga and Alexander Mishkin haff been thinking at time. Am saying nothing, only reply with sad face emoji. Haff been good in one way, Alexei say, haff promotion now General Igor

226

Korobov haff die and replacement haff new broom mentality, although, as is par for course, haff more pressure and stress with upgrade. Agitprop and dezinformatsiya ungoing operation. RT, Sputnik and manufacture of deepfake news take much energy, much organisation and many Russian ruble. Alexei complain haff many spinning plate keep in air. Haff hear this whine ferry many times before and am saying sure Alexei career on upward slope and sure can cope. Haff not feather in cap from part in Chechen contract kill of Putin enemy Boris Nemtsov? Alexei say pseudocide of Ukrainian journalist Arkady Babchenko, avoiding Russian-paid assassin, haff been bit of black eye and counter feather in cap. Am saying perhaps Alexei better off do nyet more navel gazing as is bad for health. Carry on do job well as Alexei haff always do job well. Is impossible control all of world and media. Alexei say haff try tell Putin that. Am laughing if am knowing is not funny. Say is late and am contacting with fresh news when happen. Alexei send thumb up emoji and say sleep well, Svetlana, and please pass message Tatiana. Am not responding. Is lucky guess. Half of time anyone right. In little girl diary, haff keep note of Mamochka success rate. Forty-eight point two percent. Is no wonder haff leave home young.

Paul

I slumped into my settee exhausted, yet energised. I had done it. Survived the week. And what a week it had turned out to be, a real insight into the mad, duplicitous world of management. With my week's stint as an acting director put to bed, I could finally relax and look forward to spending a good part of the weekend with JJ and the Nas. I had booked cinema tickets and a table at a gastro pub as highlights of the two-day itinerary. Tentatively, I had also pencilled in a visit for the four of us to see my mother. That was a suck it and see option, a visit I would quickly erase if the vibe felt wrong, despite it being one I presently wanted to keep – partly for Mum to see JJ again, more for me to show off Tatiana and Svetlana. (I had been messaging Mum fairly regularly and she knew JJ was back in my life and I had mentioned, rather vaguely, how we had met 'these couple of women' while in Southburgh. What I hadn't mentioned was the possibility of us popping by.)

I could picture my mother – my new mother – approving of our unusual four-way sleeping arrangements, given her fresh take on all matters sexual, and knew she would love to see JJ. My doubts in visiting her lay elsewhere, in whether it was too early and, more to the point, too creepy to be throwing in the 'meeting the parent(s)' scenario at such an early stage.

A ten-minute sit down, I told myself, then time to crack on and buy the food at the local supermarket for the meal I intended to cook tomorrow evening. JJ planned to pick up the Nas by two tomorrow, he had just messaged me, which meant I would then have ample time to prepare the meal and get everything ready for their arrival. For the short period of down time I had allowed myself, I let my mind run over the events of the past week, looking back on them from the viewpoint of a man coming to terms with his rapidly changing circumstances.

The Monday morning meeting in Graham's office at the start of the week, with the other proper directors of the college, had been an eye opener, to say the least. Graham set out his vision and line of attack for the Ofsted visit with great zeal and his usual profanity, chewing up the scenery with a speech littered in reference, militaristic imagery and a call to arms based on creating a siege mentality. There were plenty of odd contradictions in his words, but if anyone else noticed them then they kept their mouths firmly zipped. Exactly as I had.

"Good morning troops," he began, once we were all shoehorned inside his office at the ungodly hour his red-flagged email had stipulated. Graham put a knee up on his desk, clambered on top of it and stood upright on its surface. "Welcome to the bunker! The war room!" he boomed, stretching out both arms, his embrace towering above everyone in the room. "Praemonitus praemunitus!" he declared. "Forewarned is forearmed! We are indeed indebted to our courageous Vice-Principal, Malcolm Green," Graham waved a strident fist of solidarity in Malcolm's general direction, receiving a sheepish face in return, "for the prior knowledge of this week's Ofsted inspection. Wednesday and Thursday are the days to note in your diaries, gentlemen." I glanced around at the all-white patriarchy surrounding me and saw he wasn't kidding. "Bring it on, I say. We *will* be ready. As Francis Bacon so aptly wrote in his book, Meditationes Sacrae and Human Philosophy, 'knowledge is power'. In our case, the power to see Ofsted packing, their list of requirements satisfied and a 'Good' judgement on our educational establishment securely in the bag. After… Normality. Back to the priority of teaching students. That is our business. Never let us forget we are here to prepare our students for the vocational demands of life. While Ofsted, and its small-minded, bureaucratic box-tickers, live only in a nether world of meaningless statistics and data-based judgement." Graham's eyes were like the shards of a broken bottle on a floor. Clear, sharp and ready to cut the unwary. "I don't have to remind you of the uncomfortable truth, as far as they're concerned, that they'd be far better intentioned spending their time inspecting the fucking *government* rather than us. If Ofsted want to see student attainment on the rise, they should be inspecting how the government is cutting funding. Inspecting how the government is pushing casual contracts to try and save money. Inspecting the government's desire to privatise tertiary education. Inspecting the government's ridiculous insistence on English and math GCSE re-sits. They ought to be inspecting why, for over a decade, lecturers have suffered inflation-ravaged salaries. Why lecturers have suffered increasing paperwork demands yet decreasing lesson preparation time. But no.

We're the ones put under the magnifying glass. We're the ones copping the flak for poor successive government educational policy. We're the ones charged with turning government inadequacy into a meaningful and educational experience for sixteen to eighteen year olds." Graham paused and walked to the side of his desk before turning and walking back to its centre. He wasn't a popular principal – his bullying and explosive temper had seen to that – but his rousing speech had pushed a lot of the right buttons and the man could sense it. For a brief second, I thought he was going to launch himself into us and crowd surf, or alternatively, if he had misjudged the mood of the room, smash on to the floor as directors parted like the Red Sea did for Moses. Neither occurred. Graham remained on his podium. "'Be stirring as the time, be fire with fire'," he cried from his heightened stage, thrusting an outreached arm towards the ceiling's central strip lighting. "'Threaten the threatener, and outface the brow of bragging horror'. To quote Philip the Bastard from The Life and Death of King John," he explained, his voice quieter and more reserved. "And that is what we shall be doing, colleagues. Fighting fire with fire. Out-manoeuvring the enemy. Out-witting them with cunning, strategic pincer movements. Putting *our* fucking tanks on *their* fucking lawn. All of this… Without them realising it." Graham's countenance turned to an expression of appeal. "Do not doubt we have the justification to do what is necessary. Through our integrity, we have earned that right. Never let us forget, we are in this *together*," he stressed. "We mind each other's backs. We are loyal. We are as one. Against the common enemy, we do what must be done." Graham halted and sucked in air, his chest expanding to maximum capacity. "Because if we don't," he warned, "the bastards might label us 'Requires Improvement'. Or, if petty vindictiveness takes them, the nadir of 'Inadequate'." Graham let us brood on the odious thought. "And we all know what sort of shit-show that'd be."

It was quite the opener.

The first manifestation, in practical terms, of what Graham's speech incurred, specifically speaking, was quickly spelt out. To my unease, directly to me in person.

"Paul, Director of Business, Catering and Sport," Graham said, singling me out with a pointed finger. "Nice suit by the way. Make sure those Football Academy heathens on BTEC Sport are off site for the duration. I don't need eighteen arseholes with zero academic interest hanging around my college waiting to kick off at any moment. Fuck them out of it somewhere. Don't care where. Hire another coach for them. A fifty-two seater," he said, laughing at his own joke.

If struck by the simplicity of the plan, I could see the merits and plausibility of its effectiveness. Graham obviously thought it a winner and students other than those under my jurisdiction, who were also seen as problematic, were subjected to similar tactics. The Director of Health and Social Care and Hair and Beauty was told to arrange out-of-classroom trips for two of his groups and Construction's notoriously 'difficult' – read 'violently anarchic' – plumbing class were off-sited as well. With a slight tweaking of emphasis, duff lecturers were made invisible – rather than duff students – and several known 'weak spots' were gifted the poisoned chalice of two days' sick leave, allowing competent staff to take over their lessons. A level maths, right across the board, was deemed to be on a week of student assessment, thus avoiding the terrors of any actual maths teaching taking place during the Ofsted inspection. The paperwork and tests cleverly set in motion the day after Malcolm had originally told me he'd had word of the Ofsted visit.

For the rest of the teaching staff, of which, not forgetting, I was one, a different deal ensued.

"Any of *your* lecturers," Graham spat, staring us down individually, "who are 'too ill' to come in on any days of the Ofsted inspection must, and I cannot stress this seriously enough, phone me on the morning by seven a.m. to explain why. Anyone who doesn't phone and doesn't show and doesn't die by the end of the day will wish they fucking had." Graham waited for his threat to sink in. "Right. On to students with poor attendance records. You know who they are. If you don't, find out. Get on to the bastards and scare the bejesus out of them. Send taxis to pick them up. Get Student Support to go round to their squalid houses and drag the fuckers out of bed, if that's what it takes. I want attendance up here," Graham insisted, forgetting his temporary levitation and banging his hand so hard on the ceiling it drew blood from his knuckles. Undeterred, Graham pushed on. "During this visit it is *imperative* we project and portray an ambience desirable, suitable and conducive to learning. All areas of the building need to be serene for the entire length of the inspection. Tranquil. An oasis of calm. Everything under control. Like a swan. Us paddling like fuck under water if needs be, effortlessly gliding above. To help facilitate this desirable state of affairs, Malcolm will be the college's nominee and will meet and greet the lead Ofsted inspector. Once he has made 'first contact' with the alien overlord, Malcolm will do his damnedest to get a feel for, or better still, get a look at, what areas they'll be prioritising. As soon as he knows, he'll pop out a text to the relevant director. Needless to say, all of you must have your phones on, notifications on and about your person at *all* times. All day and all night from now on. Carry them everywhere. In the car, in the toilet, in bed, on the job. Be vigilant. 24/7. Anyone not responding to a text… Let's not go there," Graham suggested. "As soon as you get word an inspector is coming to a specific area get down there and sweep it clean, making sure none of our wonderful students are engaging in mischief, like having sex in the corridor or smoking weed in the toilets." Graham slapped the back of a hand into the palm of his other, the sharp crack reverberating around the room. "Paperwork!" he barked. "Make sure *all* staff are properly prepared to have an inspector sit in on them. Make sure they have everything required and up to date with lesson plans at the ready. Lessons must start on time with lecturers in class five minutes early, *not* drinking fucking coffee. Registration completed within the first ten minutes." Graham clapped his hands together, like a football coach on the sidelines, and moved to motivational mode. "Let's make sure we're organised, troops. Crank it up to the max. Let's get through this fun event as best we can. It's to *everyone's* advantage we see this out." Motivational mode ceased, Graham's eyes flung out daggers like a circus knife act on amphetamines. "One last warning. If I find out any member of staff has spoken ill of the college to any inspector... God help them." Graham strafed us with laser beams of intimidation. "You'll all be getting an email later today. In it contains our line of attack. Our message. The face we want to project. Read it, memorise it and preach it to every member of your staff so they're well prepared for any Ofsted inspector they come into contact with... Excellent... Now... Don't just stand there!" he heckled. "Get on with it! Fly, my pretties, fly!"

As we crowded out of Graham's office, I sought Malcolm and gestured him to one side.

"Christ. I hope for your sake your source is spot on," I told him, dreading to think what might happen if Ofsted turned out to be a false alarm.

Malcolm made his signature move of smoothing down his comb-over. "They're booked in to The Royale Hotel for Tuesday and Wednesday night. Confirmed over the weekend," he simpered.

"The Ofsted inspectors?" I asked, surprised to hear they used the same hotel as my old tennis club.

"Our spies are everywhere," Malcolm replied, a twinkle breaking surface in his watery eyes.

"Blimey. Wheels within wheels."

"Welcome to management."

By morning break, on reflection, I decided the whole situation was laughable. Like when the Queen visits and everything gets a deep clean, a lick of paint and the homeless are dragged off the streets, put in a skip for safekeeping and later released. The whole escapade a ridiculous charade with one side digging while the other backfilled the holes, all of it a stinking, nonsensical pile of mass misdirection where every signpost imaginable got swivelled through one-eighty degrees. That said, I wasn't about to start swimming against the tide, not with a possible future promotion hanging in the balance. Financially, after the divorce and beach hut purchase, I was stuck at base camp, sherpa-free, with no crampons and not a single bottle of oxygen to my name. Any chance of climbing higher, especially now I had two Nas to entertain and impress, massively upstaged any restrictive moral quandaries I might harbour. This was my chance to impress, and I intended to grab it with both hands. Up that greasy pole and onwards. Cynically, I appreciated how much my changed mindset made me so much more suited to a life in management. Sitting with my first coffee of the day, the possibility crossed my mind I was experiencing some form of early midlife crisis. That or I was finally growing up, like a fledgling locust, hardening my political and social views rather than my wings.

Official notification of Ofsted came on Monday afternoon along with Graham's email. I had two – lucky me – one for my role as a lecturer and one as a temporary director. The latter riddled with cloak and dagger tactics between its lines, sometimes blatantly in them, spelling out Graham's intent, the former only a simplistic call to arms. Neither shocked nor outraged, now I had seen matters from both sides of the fence, I realised this was how the world had always turned.

By way of response, the teaching staff collectively spasmed, as if hundreds of frozen popsicles had dropped down their collars and slid vertically over their naked spines. The long awaited storm, finally sighted, grew large on the horizon. Upper management bullied and cajoled middle management. Middle management bullied and cajoled lecturers. Lecturers cajoled students, and when that failed, resorted to either threats or bribes, whatever they thought it took to secure a deal on good behaviour for two days. The truly irremediable, staff and students, were sidelined as Graham had planned. I played my part and organised the deletion of BTEC Sport from the process of Ofsted inspection. By late Wednesday morning our graceful swan act still held firm, all sleight of hand apparently remaining undetected by the outsiders. Then, slap bang in the middle of a class, I got a text from Graham.

'Incident in carpentry workshop. Get there ASAP and sort! John [Director of Construction] tied up with Ofsted inspector in Painting and Decorating. Carpentry next!!!'

Leaving my class with the charge to undertake independent research – probably on Instagram or TikTok – I ran to the carpentry workshop to find one of the students had nearly taken the top of his finger off with a wood chisel. Tom, my friend and beach hut worktop fabricator, the lecturer in charge, had wrapped the boy's finger with a rag in an attempt to staunch the bleeding.

"Hospital job?" I asked softly in his ear so the boy couldn't hear. Tom nodded. "Graham texted to say you're next on the list. They're with John in Painting and Decorating at the moment." I warned, running the predicament through my head. Ambulance plus paramedics equals pandemonium, I concluded. "I'll take him to A&E in my car. What's his name?"

"Luke."

"Come on, Luke. Come with me. Let's go and get you sorted," I told the boy, pulling a huge wad of paper towel off the wall roller. "No blood on the seats," I warned, passing him the paper.

Apparently, we missed the inspector by six minutes. I lost the best part of six hours of my life in A&E. Most of it spent having sporadic, monosyllabic conversations with a grumpy trainee carpenter.

"Throbbing," he complained at one point.

"We've been here for four hours, Luke. So's my head," I answered.

Once Luke had finally been stitched up and given a tetanus jab, I took him straight home and then returned to college. It was gone seven by the time I knocked on Graham's office. He was in a meeting with Malcolm, the two poring over a laptop when I went in. I explained what had happened.

"I didn't bother to text you," I informed Graham. "I thought you'd have more than enough on your plate. Besides, everything was under control. Tom let me know his inspection had gone fine," I added casually.

"Nice work, Paul. Good option," said Graham nodding appreciatively.

"How's your day gone?" I enquired.

"Some departments are stacking up issues like a fat fuck on an all-inclusive holiday piles food on a plate, but overall we're getting there. One more day to hold it together," came Graham's terse reply.

First thing Thursday morning, a female Ofsted inspector came to see my department. (So much for Graham's promise to keep me 'low profile and well under the radar'.) An elegant woman in her fifties, she seemed pleasant enough on first meeting her. Until that moment, my status had been virginal regards direct interaction with Ofsted inspectors, although I had been observed in the past. As we introduced ourselves, the woman came over as nothing other than professional and evidently not as one of the demonic monsters characterised by Graham's Monday morning clarion call. Even so, I recognised she had a job to do and was initially wary of opening up to her and stuck rigidly to the 'on message' script Graham had put in his earlier email.

As luck would have it, we were due to visit my department's most senior lecturer – another of Graham's ingenious timetable manipulations? – a lady named, Ellen, and, as I both hoped and expected, she knocked her lesson right out the ball park. Poised and with paperwork perfect, she started bang on time, had the class under her full control and asked interesting questions of her students affording them the time to answer, never once committing the cardinal sin of wading in with answers of her own. By the end of the half hour we spent with her, all her students had learnt something. As a fair to middling lecturer myself, I could see Ellen was top drawer, as did the Ofsted inspector.

"Very good lesson," came the uplifting feedback as we walked out of the classroom.

From there we moved to a catering class and, having relaxed a little, I ran a little bit of pre-planned spiel by the inspector concerning the popularity of cooking on TV, how this had positively affected our uptake numbers, and brokered a few considerations on the proliferation and status of the phenomenon AKA 'Celebrity Cook'. Some of it ran off the rails slightly and drifted perilously close to flirtatiousness – no offence detected – something I would never have dreamt of attempting in a work situation, let alone with an Ofsted inspector, at any time prior to meeting the Nas. By the time I left her, I had convinced myself I had won her over and her report would be favourable.

Free from my chaperone duties by twelve, and with no lessons to teach until the afternoon, I opted to roam the corridors rather than hole up in the staff room. It turned out to be a fortuitous decision as I caught two boys embroiled in a heated argument outside the on-site Subway food outlet. Hearing the verbal confrontation from a distance echoing down the corridor, I increased my walking speed to a jog and arrived nicely in time to see the first blow thrown, a wild, swinging right-hander that missed its mark by a distance.

"You fucking prick!" the would-be recipient of the punch bellowed, charging his attacker, head down like a raging bull, ramming him into a wall.

"Oi! You boys! Pack it in!" I shouted, the two of them now a single, writhing mass of testosterone-fuelled BO, poor skin, bad haircuts and black skinny jeans.

Astonishingly, my voice had sufficient authority and menace in it to instantly cut through the red mist enveloping the two protagonists and they stopped fighting immediately. Freeze-framed in cartoonish mid-grapple, I went for admonishing them with the official go-to weapon of the lecturer. Sarcasm.

"Now, I enjoy a good cage fight as much as anyone," I began, my tone withering, "it's just that I'd rather be watching Connor McGregor in a pay-per-view UFC bout. Not witnessing two clueless teenage adolescents falling over each other in my college corridor when there's an Ofsted inspection on. If you insist on wanting to have a go at getting each other in a rear naked choke, I suggest you do it somewhere more suitable, where you can be properly supervised. Now get out of my sight and start behaving like a couple of grown-ups before I change my mind and put you on a disciplinary." The two boys disengaged themselves from each other, their anger evaporated. "What do you say?" I asked, giving them evils.

"Sorry, Sir," they both mumbled.

"And?"

"Thank you, Sir."

"Right. Off you go. And don't be so stupid again. Talk to each other if you have a problem. It's a lot less painful and it'll get you into a lot less trouble," I advised, becoming more friendly, watching them disappear down the corridor.

"The master at work," came a voice behind me.

It was Graham. Someone, probably a member of the Subway staff, had alerted him to the fight. (Re the link between the historic number of scuffles outside Subway – for whatever bizarre reason, I was no psychoanalyst – see also the attraction between iron filings and an electromagnet.)

"Thanks. Johnny on the spot, that's all."

Graham sidled up to me, both hands plunged deep into trouser pockets. "A word of advice, Paul. Never be coy or underplay your hand if you've done something well... or if you've done something disastrous, for that matter. Go big, whether it's boasting or blame-shifting. So big your inflated ego crushes all others next to it." Graham eyed me earnestly. "Rule one of management. Just for you. Free of charge... You got a spare minute?"

I looked at my watch. "Next lesson's one-forty-five."

"Let's get something to eat and a drink. My treat," Graham suggested, his head nodding at the Subway entrance. "Then we'll go somewhere quiet. The Fuselage."

The Fuselage was part of college lore. Used by students on Travel and Tourism courses, it comprised a small room whose walls contained a mock fuselage depicting a commercial airline's interior, complete with genuine seats, overhead compartments and dummy windows. Within this true-to-life set, students were taught cabin crew skills as they played out their respective roles with fellow students often taking the part of passengers. Described to me by others – I had never been inside – as tight and confined to a point bordering claustrophobic, its special status derived from other areas of activity outside those of academia. As one of the more controlled areas – few people had access to it – and its very specific and limited use, The Fuselage was the closest place to a 'safe haven' within the entire college building. Rumour had it, senior staff used it as a 'chill zone' when wanting to avoid flak and other colleagues. Further rumour had it senior staff also used it as a 'room', in the 'For god's sake, get a room' context. In short, legend had it, The Fuselage was seen as the default option for those tricky moments when unresolved sexual tension at work simply *had* to be.

With a Chicken & Bacon Ranch Melt and a cappuccino each in our hands, Graham led the way and on arrival opened the door with his security pass. Passing through the doorway we came to a very narrow area filled with clutter – a small table, a few chairs, two filing cabinets, aviation posters on the wall – before walking into what was a very plausible recreation of a modern short haul airliner. Boarding the 'plane', to my left I spotted, in its non-use position, a foldaway chair of the type used by cabin crew during landing and take-off. Opposite it were storage lockers for flight meals and hot drink despatching equipment. A couple of strides on, we reached the narrow corridor splitting the two-banks-of-three passenger seating configuration. Along the furthest fuselage wall there were six rows of seating with only three on the nearest due to the space taken up by the entrance opening and lockers.

"I've paid for extra legroom," Graham told me, walking down the aisle to the front of the plane where an all-white bulkhead complete with a large flat screen – presumably for training purposes – marked the extremity of the fuselage.

"How does the pilot get out?" I asked once we had sat down in the front row seats boasting extra legroom.

"Don't worry about him. He's happy enough. He's got a thing going with the female autopilot," Graham answered, taking a sip of his coffee. "First things first. Have you got the receipt for your suit on you?"

"Yes," I replied, fishing it out of my wallet. "Two hundred and eighty-nine," I confirmed, showing it to Graham.

Graham passed me a brown envelope. "There's three hundred cash. Keep the change."

"Thank you very much," I said, pocketing the money.

"We haven't only come here for the making of a marginally inappropriate financial transaction," Graham explained. "I wanted to congratulate you on how well you've done stepping up as director for the visit," Graham continued. "The Ofsted inspector you showed round was very complimentary. The question is; how would you feel about making it permanent?"

I nearly choked on my Subway sandwich. "Really?"

"Really. You've done all that we've asked of you and more. Malcolm and I have discussed it at length and I told him I thought you'd be the perfect fit. He agreed. Not only that, it adds to the ethos of the college to promote from within rather than dragging in an external candidate. Now, obviously, we'll have to advertise and interview, yadda yadda yadda, but the job's yours if you want it. I'll see to that. Personally. Capeesh?" I capeeshed. "Excellent. Any questions?"

Clamping down on my desire to ascertain what my new salary would be, I asked a question more in keeping. "What's the latest from Ofsted? How are we doing?"

"We're doing good. Good is the word because 'Good' is the Ofsted judgement we're going to get," Graham revealed, a look of satisfaction on his face.

"We're home and dry?"

Graham nodded. "Malcolm's with them now going over the last batch of statistics. It's a done deal. That should knock back a few of the more vociferous management critics, like those UCU whingers and the fucking sticking-their-noses-in-where-they're-not-wanted governors. To summarise the situation, Paul, good for us and good for you. I'm not saying it won't be a steep learning curve," Graham commented. "But it's one I think you'll soon master."

"What can I say?"

"How about 'thanks'?"

"Thanks, Graham. I really appreciate this."

"No worries, you've earned it. By way of an introduction, the senior management team are having a quiet celebratory drink on Sunday evening. Be nice if you could come along and mix with your future peers. We can't disclose your promotion officially, not until we've undertaken the due process, so you'll only be there on the basis of your having helped out during the Ofsted inspection. Look on it as an early opportunity to work out which members of the senior leadership team you'll end up despising," Graham said, a sardonic look on his face.

"Sure," I answered, reeling at the speed of it all. Me invited, socially, into the upper tier and on more money.

"I'll text you a time and venue," Graham said, tucking into his chicken and bacon melt. "Fancy something stronger?" he asked, licking his fingers and pointing toward the drinks trolley parked in front of the other bank of front row seats.

"Absolutely," I answered, not wanting to refuse.

"What have we got here?" Graham asked getting up and rummaging violently at the back of one of the trolley's drawers. "Bombay Sapphire gin. Smirnoff Red Label vodka. Johnnie Walker Red Label whiskey. Mount Gay Rum. What do you fancy?"

"Smirnoff, please," I answered, thinking of the Nas. Graham passed me the miniature bottle, taking a Johnnie Walker for himself. "I thought they'd all be fake, like everything else in here."

"Most of them are. Old bottles filled with water. I get catering to put a few real ones in a secret little compartment right at the back. My secret stash."

"Nice. I've never been in here before," I admitted, craning my neck round. "It's quite impressive."

Graham nodded, a lewd grin spreading on his face. "The Room of Requirement, I call it. Like in Harry Potter. I bet these seats could tell a few tales, don't you? I bet they've seen a few spillages in their time. And I'm not talking tea, coffee or water masquerading as booze, either. I reckon DNA testing could make for some interesting blackmail opportunities."

I laughed, thinking maybe Graham and Susan's DNA was splattered in here somewhere. "I think it's fair to say I have heard a fair bit of speculation over the years."

"It'd be a lot worse if some of the male cabin crew students got in here more often," Graham suggested, cracking open his homophobic review book.

An idea flitted into my head. It was a dangerous one but I felt I

242

had to run with it. "Do you mind if I ask you a rather delicate question?"

Graham's eyes lit up. "Go on. I'm in a good mood."

"Have you ever got the impression Malcolm might be gay?"

Graham guffawed. "Malcolm? He's a fucking old-school wet lettuce sporting a comedy comb-over who's got useful contacts, maybe. But not gay. Stake my life on it." Graham's expression morphed to one of perplexity. "I thought he was an old family friend?"

"He is. My gaydar's crap and I wanted a second opinion, that's all," I fudged. "I can't pick him out or pigeonhole him for all the years I've known him. His wife left him years ago, he's never had another relationship that I know of and I've always wondered why. He never mentions anything to do with his social life, desire, attraction, that type of thing. Women or men. Perhaps he's not interested."

"In sex? Ha!" Graham scoffed. "If life has taught me anything it's up there as one of the biggest drivers. The one constantly receiving software updates to keep it functional. Along with money and power. I'm rather devoted to all three as it happens," Graham candidly admitted. "Everyone, okay, overstatement, *virtually* everyone has their thing. Malcolm might spend every night tossing himself off while perving over 1950s big band album covers, for all we know. Doing a 'Duke Ellington' might be his special euphemism. I'd wager the old bastard still has something that stokes his fire. Even at his age."

JJ

The Saturday morning elite tennis coaching session had gone well, although I have to admit my mind hadn't always been fully focused on teaching teenagers how to split-step before volleying or to wrist snap when serving. The Nas were up next and the thought of spending time with them had a diversionary effect on everything going on in my head. Excitement and yearning were building in me, creating pressure, bringing me to the boil and a point where I would surely pop. No prizes for guessing the rupture site. Or for what type of fluid would burst out.

A couple more promising juniors had joined up, taking the group number to twelve. Word was getting out. The parents of the two newbies – all four played tennis themselves – were ambitious for their offspring and I sensed they might be the type to get a bit carried away with the hope their kid might turn out to be a Grand Slam winner. During my brief induction speech, I stressed the ground rules to them: no pacing around the courts like caged tigers, no shouting encouragement or instructions during sessions or matches and definitely no home coaching. As I pointed out, it would only undermine and confuse what I was trying to instil in their children. My way or the highway, people. Since coming back from Austria and working predominantly with juniors, rather than adults, I had quickly discovered nothing pissed kids off more than receiving conflicting advice. I had already had a few 'my old coach never told me to do it like that' scenarios, ones I quickly stood on and scrubbed out like Nadal removing a mark from a clay court.

"That's why he's your *old* coach and I'm your *new* one," I would say, or, if the father had been interfering, "That's why I'm called, 'Coach', and he's called, 'Dad'."

Going back to the parents and my rules, they all signed up like the poor behaviour I mentioned had never once crossed their minds. Yeah, right. Whether they would stick to it, time would tell. The best answer lay in getting my elite group's status so high and well respected, no parent would dare compromise their kid's chance of staying in it. Early days, but I was working on it. The next step, looking much more long term, was reaching out to the kids who were sporty but whose parents didn't play tennis. These were the ones I needed to convert; the footballers, rugby players and athletes, trying to persuade them to pick up a racket. This meant getting into schools and putting in a major amount of groundwork. It would take time and I am, by nature, an impatient person. Not a good combo. Still, I reasoned, if I could mature so quickly in other aspects of my life, I didn't see why my tennis coaching should be any different.

Leaving coaching after changing and showering in the club-house, to save time, I started driving to the Nas way too fast, not wanting to die in an accident apparently a less pressing motivation than shaving a few minutes off the journey time. Even someone as impetuous as myself soon saw the massive contradiction in that theory and I backed off accordingly. It seemed as if it was just one epiphany after another when driving to or from the Nas. Arriving at their caravan site, nicely in one piece, they were out to greet me before I had a chance to get out of the car. They must have been looking out for me, from a caravan window, seeing as I had messaged them while, fessing up here, still driving. My actions proving it's impossible for me to give up all my bad habits at one once.

Hyper-excited and bubbly, both the Nas greeted me with kisses and hugs, their faces alight and glowing. Ditto my feelings exactly. I would have stripped off and made love to both of them on the grass there and then, in the rain, given half a chance. Instead, I cracked a few jokes about how long it had been since I had last seen them, how they both hadn't changed a bit and then accused them of fucking up the weather.

"Haff done nothing! Is JJ fault!" one of them said laughing.

God, I loved her. And the other one.

Like we were eloping fast before their scrap-metal-dealer dad and his shotgun came home from a hard day's stripping lead off a church roof, we quickly threw their two cases in the boot, locked up the caravan and got in the car, the Nas opting for the back seats. We set off to Paul's with the sky slate grey above us and the temperature in the mid-teens, the contrast from the last time I had been at the caravan park remarkable. For the first half hour we gabbled away, the animated conversation between the three of us only fading once we were well on our way, the drudgery and boredom of the journey eventually taking its toll. Occasionally, above the noise of the car, I could hear the odd snippet of Russian as the Nas conversed in their weird, yet to me, strangely fascinating language. Wishing I could understand them, I wondered how long it would take for me to learn a smattering of rudimentary Russian off the internet. Too long, was the honest, lazy answer. I had been all round the world, lived in many countries, and had only ever spoken English throughout. Like the vast majority of Brits abroad, my conversations were with foreigners whose command of the English language was invariably better than my abilities in their native tongue. Sometimes, embarrassingly so, their command of the English language was better than mine. Full stop. And that's never a good time to pull out your phone and start Googling 'backhand' in German, believe me.

Ten miles or so later, their chit-chat stopped completely when they both nodded off, one Na head leaning on the other Na shoulder. As I drove on, I couldn't stop myself checking them out in the rear view mirror every few minutes, their reflections like one viewed in a funhouse distorting rear view mirror, its speciality duplication. Every time I looked, a tingle of excitement ran up my back and made the hairs on my bare arms stand up. What exactly was going on in those two heads? What *did* they have planned for the long term? More pressing, what did they have planned for tonight when caught in the unfamiliar layout of Paul's flat? Would the sex switcheroo still be on, and if so, how would they work it? If I hadn't been driving and super motivated not to have an accident, I would have rubbed my hands together at the prospect.

When we arrived at Paul's shortly before five in the afternoon, he invited us into his flat's one living space to a table decked out with candles, glasses, cutlery and place mats, bottles of red wine, the works. He said he had spent all afternoon preparing dinner and we were to be eating in. He asked the Nas to take their seats and beckoned me to come help him.

Once inside the poky kitchen and out of earshot, Paul whispered what he had in mind.

"I've cooked home-made lasagne. We'll serve it to them. It'll be role-reversal from how we first met."

"That's a brilliant idea," I said enthusiastically, noting the empty bottle of wine on the worktop, one undoubtedly consumed by a stressed chef. "I know what. Got a pen and paper?"

Paul found my requested items and, with the menu written, I went back out to the Nas seated at the table.

"How can help?" I asked, doing an impression of their accent, epically failing to keep a straight face. "Is menu." I plonked the sheet of A4 paper on the table, the words 'Home-made lasagne - £Free' scrawled on it.

The Nas couldn't stop laughing. They absolutely loved it and jumped up to embrace Paul when he brought in the steaming tray of lasagne once they had 'ordered' it, saying how thoughtful he had been and what a wonderful idea it was. I looked on with affection. Not only of the Nas, but also of Paul – in a BFF macho male kind of way, naturally.

After dinner was over – the Nas praised Paul's lasagne as superior to the one served at their café – we sat together, all four of us squeezed on the sofa, wedged in tight, glasses of wine in our hands, chatting away like old friends. A scene physically reminiscent to the first night in the caravan when we had sat pinched around its small table, only in an emotionally different zone completely. Even if we had all moved on massively, the Nas' constant conundrum jangled and, thanks to sitting on the end of the sofa, I had no idea whether I was jammed up against Tatiana or

Svetlana. Our thighs so close you couldn't slip a fag paper between them. Despite my not knowing, I had to concede, in the big scheme of things, it didn't matter. Paul was right.

"I've got us cinema tickets to see a late film tonight," Paul told us, his words a little slurred. "It's an action adventure, nothing too taxing. Should be fun. Tomorrow, I've booked us Sunday lunch at a nice pub I know. Sunday evening, once you've left, I've got to go and meet my college principal and his senior team for drinks because... I've been promoted!" he gushed, raising his glass in a toast to himself.

We all congratulated Paul on his unexpected promotion and he briefly explained how his upgrade to a senior position had come about thanks to a successful Ofsted inspection. I could see how chuffed he was and felt pleased for him. He *was* turning his life around. All hail the power of the beach hut.

"Haff told parent?" Na asked.

Paul shook his head, explained how his father was no longer with us and, maybe because of the amount of wine he had drunk, without any prompting, began to tell the story of his parents' strange relationship and how he had holidayed in Southburgh years ago when a child. A topic he had never mentioned before when in the Nas' company. Once finished he asked the Nas about their parents.

"Haff not speak parent since leave Russia," Na declared, her face void of emotion. "Is nyet problem. Haff no desire talk parent. Are not part of life. Is true, Svetlana?"

"Da, Tatiana. Is true."

The significance of their words hit me like a doubles partner's misplaced first serve in the back of the head. Paul's face indicated likewise. The Nas had self-identified *and* were wearing different outfits. For the moment, until they could remove or change them out of our sight, we knew which one was which. *If* they were who they claimed they were. Even so.

The Nas seemed amused by our shock. "We haff talk," Svetlana said.

"Are happy for JJ and Paul know," Tatiana said.

"Some of time," Svetlana added.

"Maybe one day can tell," Tatiana suggested.

"We're working on it," I chipped in.

"Are you telling us the truth?" Paul asked. "This isn't like with the necklaces on the superyacht?"

"Da, is truth," Tatiana confirmed.

"Da, is truth," Svetlana confirmed.

"If one of you ever had an accident that left a scar, then we'd know you apart *all* the time," Paul spouted. "And what if one of you put on weight, lost weight, aged differently or got pregnant? You're young and identical now, but something, at some point, eventually, will mark you as different. Has to. You can't be the same forever…" He let his theory hang for a few moments. "… What about your parents, JJ?" he asked, turning to me. "I don't remember you mentioning them at all now I come to think of it. And I can't remember asking after them. I'm sorry. Very remiss of me."

"There's not a great deal to say other than we drifted apart. I kept in contact with them for a bit after I first left home with Darina. From then on the messages gradually dwindled away before stopping altogether. I haven't spoken to them in years. Truth is, I don't think I've ever forgiven them for moving to Ireland and wrecking my tennis chances. I'm not saying I'm right, I'm just saying, that's all."

"Tell me and Svetlana, JJ. Tell what haff happen lose parent," Tatiana directed.

I nodded, making it Paul's turn to listen to a story for the second time, a shortened version of my fledgling tennis career.

"Six parents. Five alive and I'm the only child left talking to one," Paul declared solemnly once I had finished.

"Visit Paul mamochka tomorrow. Am wanting meet her,"

Svetlana suddenly stumped up.

"Da," Tatiana agreed.

Out of the corner of my eye, I saw Tatiana raise an eyebrow at her sister and the two squeezed themselves, like a couple of corks from a bottle, out and up off the sofa. Without a further word, the pair headed into one of the bedrooms.

"Shit! You don't think I've upset them, do you? Too much saying they won't be identical forever?" Paul whispered, alarm in his voice.

Before I had a chance to answer, the Nas did it for me. They were back in the room. In matching bra and panties, and nothing else. My eyes did the stalks thing. There was no telling them apart now. Every luscious curve identical, every lustrous strand of hair indistinguishable, their lacy lingerie uniforms uniform. It really was uncanny just how perfectly alike they were, more so eyeing them virtually naked alongside each other.

"Haff make too much talk," Na said.

"Is time for action," the other Na said.

"Paul haff cook dinner, so haff won first choice," Na said, moving a hand over the middle of her toned stomach and then over her sister's.

Paul looked over to me. I had zilch to say so blanked him and kept staring out to an imagined point on a non-viewable horizon, expression frozen, like one of those crazy heads on Easter Island.

"I know!" Paul exclaimed, Eureka light bulb floating above him. "I'll toss for it," and he pulled a coin from his pocket. "Heads, Na to my left. Tails, Na to my right."

Paul flipped the coin, caught it in the palm of his right hand and slapped it on the back of his left. The reveal was mine to call.

"Heads," I proclaimed. "The Na to the left has it. Well, has, Paul... Oi, did you two swap places when we weren't looking?" I asked because the Nas were giggling.

"Nyet. Haff not swap," Na to the left said. "Are laughing

because haff use coin same way."

"It's all good," Paul declared. "Let the coin decide, I say. Let fate be the arbiter. No one can take umbrage that way. How else could I pick? You are the same, and I love you both equally." The split second after his words had escaped, Paul clamped his hand over his mouth like he had hastily told a vicar to fuck off during a christening ceremony. "Too much too soon?" he asked me crestfallen.

"No, man. It's fine," I told him. "I'm with you all the way."

"Come, Paul. Haff bedroom," Na to the left suggested, holding out a slender arm.

"Haff sofa, JJ," the other Na suggested, sidling over and undoing the belt on my trousers.

Tatiana and Svetlana

Haff ferry nice time at Paul flat on Saturday evening. He haff cook lasagne and with JJ serve me and Svetlana as we haff serve them on first meet. Was ferry funny and ferry good idea. Am liking much. After meal am revealing identity as Tatiana and then am hiding again when strip down new lingerie only. When ask Paul choose who want haff first, is using coin. Like we haff! Is hilarious and me and Svetlana haff big laughter, not only because similar use of method in make decision, but of secret swapping place when Paul and JJ not look. Is game from childhood never grow old. In moment after coin decision, Paul and JJ are letting slip are in love with me and Svetlana. Is good news as make next stage more probable. Neverless, thank coin choice, am haffing sex with JJ before film and with Paul after film. Am saying am in love with JJ as said am in love with Paul. Svetlana say same when haffing sex with Paul before film and with JJ after film. Am not sure if am in love or not, Svetlana haff same feel, as is first time haff been ferry close with two man. If not love, am imagining is ferry close.

251

Breakfast am asking if intend visit Paul mamochka before lunch in pub. Paul happy say da and phone mamochka for arrange visit. After call on mobile, Paul say mamochka haff ferry much excitement see JJ again and meet 'new girlfriend'. Am thinking is nice meet last parent standing. Am asking JJ if go mamochka house in JJ car or in Paul car and is finding ferry funny. Am not understanding JJ hilarity and am letting matter go.

Is only short journey of half hour in Paul car and are soon knock on door of nice house in nice neighbourhood. Door is answer by attract woman in expensive clothe who look more young than am expecting.

Hi, Mum," Paul say. "You may remember this not-so-young-now man, JJ. And this is Tatiana and Svetlana. We met in the café where they work, just along the prom from my beach hut. They're from Russia."

"It's *so* lovely to meet you all! I'm so glad you had time to pop round and see me." Paul mamochka say. "JJ! Look at you all grown up. My word, what a handsome man you've turned into. And you two beautiful ladies, Tatiana and Svetlana… Sorry, I don't know which one… Paul didn't…"

"Is nyet problem," am saying. "Am Svetlana," am lying. "Haff issue all time."

"I'm sure you do, my dear… Crikey, you really *are* exactly the same, aren't you?" Paul mamochka say, look ferry close me and Svetlana. "Which one of these two lucky chaps is your boyfriend, Svetlana?"

"Both," am saying.

"Oh… And you, Tatiana?"

"Same," Svetlana say.

"Gosh. How wonderfully modern and exciting," Paul mamochka say, arch eyebrow. "Sorry, please excuse my manners. Let's not stand here on the doorstep all day. Come in, all of you. I'll get the kettle on. My name's, Linda, Tatiana and Svetlana. If I wait for my son to introduce me properly, I'll be waiting forever."

Am liking Paul mamochka, Linda, ferry much in only few minute of meet. Haff great energy and big personality, can tell. Are following into living room for something is calling 'elevenses' and Linda say make self comfortable while make drink and open many biscuit. Is not long Linda return and fuss over all in room like mamochka hen, hand tea and biscuit out, ask question and say again how cannot believe how handsome JJ haff become and how gorgeous me and Svetlana are looking.

"So," Linda say sitting in armchair, dunk Rich Tea biscuit. "How do you boys know which one of these two beautiful ladies you're sleeping with? Do they let you know? Can you tell? Or do you do it by roster?"

"Mum! Please!" Paul say, haffing big embarrassment. "*Jesus* H Christ!"

"Don't be such a prude, Paul," Linda say. "Tatiana and Svetlana said they were the girlfriends of *both* of you. I hardly think it bothers them me asking the obvious question."

"You'll have to excuse my mother," Paul say me and Svetlana. "Now she's single again, she's officially obsessed with... anything like that."

"Curious, that's all," Linda say.

"Paul and JJ are not knowing," Svetlana say, answer Linda question. "Cannot tell difference."

"We are working on it," JJ say. "It is true, though, Mrs Chambers. We never know which one's which at any given time. Let alone in bed."

"To be fair, Tatiana and Svetlana did make it clear when they set out the ground rules," Paul say, more relax now.

"We only know which one's which when they tell us. *If* they're telling the truth, that is," JJ say, make wink.

"What a... fascinating relationship. Do you mind me asking if you were telling the truth a minute ago, Svetlana?" Linda ask me.

"Nyet," am saying.

"So you're *not* Svetlana?" Linda say.

"Nyet."

"You're, *Tatiana*?" Linda is asking again.

"Maybe," am saying, rotate hand back and forth as am laughing. "Is situation how are liking from when little girl. Are liking identity ambiguous. Reason is complicate."

"Is ferry complicate," Svetlana say, back up big sister. "Is issue of childhood."

"I understand completely," Linda say. "Do you know, Tatiana and Svetlana, when I was a little girl, I always dreamt of what it would be like to have a twin sister. Not one who necessarily looked exactly like me, but one who was always there for me and there with me. I thought it'd be wonderful to have someone to talk to, confide in and ask advice from when there was a problem. As I grew into womanhood and married young, that wish seemed ever more desirable and relevant. If I'd had a twin sister, I'm sure I would never have put up with my miserable marriage for so long. She would have empowered me to leave."

"Is true," am saying. "Haffing twin is powerful relationship."

"Ferry powerful," Svetlana say.

"Paul say are haffing big problem in marriage when husband alive," am saying, show interest in life of woman am liking.

As answer, Linda put flesh on bone what Paul haff say about father and golf infatuation. Is ferry interesting story of strange man who haff not want haff sex with woman or go on holiday with wife and son. Cannot imagine what is like haff man who haff not wish haff sex. Ferry strange.

"Am thinking only reason man not haff sex with woman, is man not like woman," Svetlana say.

"I think it's certainly safe to say my husband never found *me* attractive," Linda say.

"All of woman," Svetlana say.

"All women?" Linda say.

"Da. All of woman," Svetlana say.

"Haff not thought before?" am saying. "Haff not thought husband like man instead?"

"Well, no. I haven't... I didn't. Ever," Linda say, ferry confuse. "I always thought it was my fault... Until Peter died that is and I've discovered other men who *do* find me attractive. At least I've finally managed to put my old life into the place where it now belongs, the dustbin of history."

"'Dustbin of history', is quote of Leon Trotsky. Tell Menshevik departing 1917 Congress of Soviet," am saying.

"Was it? Well I never. I didn't know that," Linda say, impress with knowledge of famous Soviet politician and Marxist theorist.

"Da. Is true," am confirming.

"Paul haff ask work friend if father gay man," Svetlana tell Linda.

"Did you? What, Malcolm?" Linda ask Paul.

"I did," Paul say.

"When?" Linda say.

"A few weeks ago." Paul say. "It was difficult finding the right moment to broach the subject. Pressing someone on whether their dead colleague was gay or not, isn't your typical workplace topic. The first time *I* thought Dad might have been gay was shortly after I came round when Barry was fitting your new boiler. When I brought my new suit to show you. He was the one, of all people, who first got me thinking. Sitting in the car afterwards, I was shocked to the core, I don't mind admitting. Like you, Mum, the idea had never crossed my mind. It didn't feel great, wondering whether I'd only been planned as a diversionary device to hide my father's true yearnings."

Linda face now drain of colour and ferry pale. "Poor you. Thinking Peter only wanted you as a card to complete his fake Happy Families set. How awful," Linda say, now ferry upset.

255

"What did Malcolm say?"

"He knocked me back. Denied all knowledge of anything and wouldn't say a bad word against Dad. He more or less accused you of lying."

"I *never* liked him. Odious man," Linda say.

"Thing is, by then I'd come up with the theory Malcolm might be gay himself. That the pair of them might even have been lovers. That is until I spoke to Graham, our principal, he's worked with Malcolm on a daily basis for over six years, and he thought otherwise."

"I need something stronger than this," Linda say, put down tea. "JJ. There's a bottle of vodka in the cabinet over there. Be a darling and bring it over."

JJ get bottle of vodka and give Linda who pour straight in cup. Linda must haff see look on face and wave bottle. Am not needing second invite and pour vodka in cup. Svetlana do same. Paul and JJ not want, say is too early. Is never too early for vodka.

"That's better," Linda say, as drink vodka. "Who's Graham, again? I'm losing track."

"The principal," Paul say. "He was so impressed with my new suit and how I acted when wearing it, he bought me a Subway sandwich and coffee and invited me to The Fuselage…"

"The Fuselage?" JJ say. "What the hell is The Fuselage?"

"Good question. For once, JJ," Paul say, smile at JJ. "The Fuselage is a mock up used for flight cabin crew training. And it doubles as a college staff sanctuary, a sort of hidey-hole. Anyway, after inviting me to The Fuselage and then permanently promoting me, more about that later, I asked him if he thought Malcolm might be gay. He said no. He said he didn't think so."

"I really can't keep up with this," Linda say, hand rub forehead. "What are you saying now? That we're back to square one? Peter liked women, only not me? That you weren't a child conceived out of a desperate need for social deception?… And you've been *promoted*?"

"Definitely promoted, the rest I'm not sure. What Graham did say, and it was only a throwaway line that resonated, was he thought something, something sexual, must still stoke Malcolm's fire. After considering it, and it's only a hunch, I wondered if that was the case then maybe it had also stoked Dad's fire. Was 'it' what they got up to when they were away on their 'golfing' holidays?"

"Bottle please," Linda say, drink straight from neck after Svetlana give.

"Malcolm at meet which are attending in evening?" am asking Paul. Haff see shatter look on Linda face and decide help.

Paul nod. "Yeah. He'll be there."

"Are wanting try know truth of husband who haff not want haff sex with you?" am asking Linda.

"God, I don't bloody know. I suppose it would help eliminate Paul's horrible situation of being the son of a lie. Like all those children of 'closet queen' politicians from years ago," Linda say. "Of course, it might only confirm it. What do you think, Paul?"

"I'd like to know," Paul say, "one way or another."

Am looking Svetlana and am using twin telepathy. Am knowing answer without word. "Nas will find out if is possible," am saying. "Will make honey trap in pub. We as beautiful woman, JJ as beautiful man."

"Then haff cover every base," Svetlana say.

"Oh, yeah. Don't mind me," JJ say. "Stick my name down on the volunteer's list without bothering to ask."

Svetlana move and sit on JJ lap, run hand through hair and touch face. "JJ make good gay man. Haff good bone structure. Haff need only little make-up, change of hair and clothe."

JJ protest haff shrink. "All right, then. But only because it might help Paul and Linda out... mind you, I'm not growing a moustache."

"What, in eight hours?" Paul say.

"Is fine, JJ, and," Svetlana say, in ferry sexy voice, "if play part can haff like man tonight."

Am turning head as Linda make cough and splutter. Am not understanding why is one choke on vodka. Is my turn in JJ bed tonight.

Haff enter pub on own. JJ sit at bar for hour now and haff arrive ten minute after Paul meet senior staff for Ofsted go well celebration. Tatiana stay in car for playing next part if all thing go accord plan. Many head haff turn as walk from door and take seat on stool at bar, from where keep eye on Paul and comrade. Am wearing ferry slut outfit and much make-up. Tatiana wearing same ferry slut outfit and much make-up. Are always saying not Russian prostitute when get tip with secret phone number from dirty dad in café, but tonight is look are going for. Am expecting much attention from man, more than usual, but haff interest in one. Paul haff show online photo of subject, Malcolm — is disgusting old man — and if haff any interest in woman will see if can make take bait.

Early in evening at Paul flat, me and Tatiana haff put eyeliner on JJ, do hair and pick clothe wear. Is wearing tee shirt and rip beach short of Paul, are ferry tight clothe, and haff borrow Linda clip-on earring for right ear. Is old stereotype show is gay man, but is from time of man Malcolm age. Am especially please with JJ hair, which haff change from foppish fringe into quiff in style of Georges Remi Tintin. Haff also use spray colour of Linda and make quiff red. Quiff like red flag symbol of gay man, not red flag symbol of socialist revolution. From stool at bar, JJ only few yard away and am impress how much look like gay man. JJ try hard act like gay man too and see haff order Appletini, which sip in flamboyant movement of body. Am thinking now in role, is possible relax and start enjoy act. Am also thinking JJ not last thirty second on Friday night in Omsk before face crush by fist of homophobic thug. Neverless, if Malcolm haff any interest in man will see if can make take bait.

Haff consider JJ only happy and try hard in role as is think only of special reward which haff offer as incentive for part in honey trap. Haff nyet problem offer reward of special sexual favour as, one, am knowing Tatiana quite like and, two, haff always prefer carrot instead stick when motivate comrade on mission. Am not like some from past could mention; Joseph Stalin, Vasily Blokhin, Genrikh Yagoda, Lavrentiy Beria name but few.

Pub busy, mainly couple, with few group of man who cannot keep eye off sexy woman at bar. Man in couple also cannot keep eye off sexy woman at bar, but is sneak look, like dirty dad in café. Is compliment am not need as know look good, even if appearance seductive upgrade from usual. Am not needing aggravate of extra attention when haff more important task. Am making mental shrug, is par for course when set honey trap. Ugly woman much use as chocolate teapot in honey trap operation as expression go.

Of all attention, first man who haff ask if want drink is Paul comrade. Am thinking is Principal Graham, from Paul description and also from attitude and language of body. Am thinking Graham think is alpha male and is principal in all walk of life, not only work, and when ask if want drink haff much pleasure in cut dead.

"Nyet. Haff drink, thank you," am saying.

Principal try alternate conversation. Am still showing nyet interest. In end, when see am not for turning like despise British Prime Minister, Margret Thatcher, alpha male return with tail between leg and face like bulldog chewing wasp as other expression go. Can see Paul haff hide smile on face from principal as come back and haff much pleasure in see balloon of self-importance pop. As watch principal, am trying find eye of subject of honey trap. Think haff succeed for split second and am sure haff notice so am making brief smile. Is ferry subtle and haff done like is mistake. Haff tell JJ is tactic must try perfect and we haff practise in Paul flat. Am warning is no good sit look sexy only, must make proactive move and introduce self by method seem reactive. As if subject make first move and initiate contact. Is all in manual, but am not saying this.

Am continue mind own business, with occasion accident-on-purpose glance at Malcolm, when ferry annoying other man stand in way and try make conversation while friend stand at side like lemon. Or is gooseberry? Am not sure which fruit for situation.

"Excuse me, you don't happen to have a plaster do you? Because I scuffed my knee falling for you," man say.

Is such bad line from internet deserve five-year stretch in Siberian Gulag.

"Nyet," am saying. "Is best ask behind bar as possible haff first aid box. Hope haff not rip cheap trouser," am saying, look down at leg.

"These are Levi chinos," man say, as if is special.

"Da," am saying with sneer. "Is what am meaning."

Haff trepidation take sarcastic route when deal with unwant man, but haff learn lesson from past and is always best be cruel be kind. If nice, man always, always, always get wrong impression and think is in with shout of get hand in knicker. If horrible, man soon get message and save all concern much hassle.

Is only after third vodka and orange Malcolm arrive at bar. First impression is want take scissor and cut long strand of hair that fold over head. What on earth is thinking? Is not hiding, is make attention of bald head.

"Good evening, young lady," Malcolm say, as lean on bar.

"Hello," am saying.

"Ahh. Not only beautiful, but not local, either. Ukrainian? Russian, I'm guessing?" Malcolm say.

"Da. Am from Russia," am saying. "Haff ever visit?" am asking, get small talk off ground.

"Yes, I have. Twice, in fact. Once for pleasure and once for work purposes. I took the Trans-Siberian Railway from Moscow to Vladivostok many, many years ago and attended a conference at Saint-Petersburg State University in 2013, if I recall correctly. Very impressive city and the university building was splendid. And…

um?" Malcolm say, search for name.

"Tatiana," am lying.

"Ahh. Tatiana, what a lovely name. From the Roman family clan name Tatius."

"Da," am saying, surprise at knowledge.

"As I was about to ask, are you on holiday or over in the UK working, Tatiana?" Malcolm say.

"Am working," am saying. "Am working girl."

"Oh, I see. Anything interesting?" Malcolm say, as attract barman with wave of many ten pound note and start order list of drink. "Would you care for one, Tatiana?"

"Da. Thank you. Haff vodka and orange," am saying.

"A vodka and orange as well, please," Malcolm say.

Once barman go make drink can continue set trap. "Work interesting all of time. People pay and am making dream come true," am saying with sexy voice, as move body and wipe pretend mark from bare leg. Is move give Malcolm chance look down blouse.

"I'm sure you do, my dear," Malcolm say, eye stuck on breast as barman start put drink on tray.

"Da. Am doing often. Am ferry good... Haff dream?" am saying.

Malcolm Adam apple bob. "Yes. I have been known to do my fair share of dreaming. Very special dreams, though. Quite specific."

"Is nyet problem. Haff cater for many taste in time," am saying, ferry casual and relax.

"And how much would it cost me to have you make my dream come true?" Malcolm say, voice down as whisper.

"How long dream take?" am saying.

"I think an hour would suffice."

"Is one hundred," am saying. Is ferry cheap for how sexy look tonight and am bit upset sell self so cheap. On other side of fence, am not want price be issue.

"It will have to be at my house," Malcolm say. "It's only ten minutes from here by car. Is that a problem? Do you have transport

261

and satellite navigation at your disposal?"

"Is extra fifty for home visit," am saying. "Haff take taxi."

Malcolm give vodka and orange barman haff prepare. "There you are, Tatiana," he say, let creepy finger touch hand as give glass. "I'm happy with your terms. It's been a while since I've 'treated' myself and tonight has been a celebration of work success, so what better way to end it than with you. Can we arrange to meet after my social engagement ends?"

"Is possible can wait," am saying. "for extra twenty. Is quiet night. Am thinking not get offer from man there, for start," am saying, nod head at JJ, who quick look away.

"Yesss," Malcolm say slow, haffing look of repulsion on face. "The gay male community are sadly rather oblivious to your particular fleshly charm."

"Daaa," am saying, mimic voice pattern and look of repulsion for hope start rapport. "In Russia, gay man never dare dress blatant in public. Would be like ask for brutal beating."

"I'm sure, you're right, Tatiana. Mr Putin's not exactly a champion of the LGBTQ community, is he?"

"Nyet," am agreeing.

"Even if he did turn a blind eye during your World Cup and order the hoodlums off the streets..." Malcolm look over shoulder at group of comrade. "Please excuse me, Tatiana, but I do really have to get back to my fellow colleagues and take them their drinks. Can I give you my address and then meet you there in say an hour or so. If you'd prefer that to staying here, that is. As I'm sure you're only too aware, protocol dictates we can't leave together." Am nodding is best. "Fine. Let me nip into the gents', write my address out on a piece of paper, and I'll leave it here on the bar when I come back to collect the drinks."

"Will need deposit," am saying. "Think are trustworthy man, so am only needing fifty."

"I think I've enough cash," Malcolm say in fluster as pat pocket.

"I'll have to get the rest from a cash point on the way home."

"Is best. Must haff cash up front before any of dream begin," am saying, keep up illusion of hard-nose prostitute. "Give fifty now and one-twenty at house."

"Of course."

Malcolm do as say and am soon pick up fifty pound and note of address off bar. Am thinking is like waitress with ferry good tip. After drink vodka and orange in one, am leaving pub and walk toward Tatiana in car.

"You haff make contact with subject?" Tatiana say, as am opening door.

"Da. Was ferry easy. Haff make contact and haff make contract," am saying, please with use of English as show Tatiana fifty pound. "Haff use prostitute before," am saying, as join Tatiana in back seat. "Is not first time, can tell. Haff make arrangement meet house later. Am not sure what is wanting, but is not wanting JJ. Haff no interest even when am pointing out in conversation tangent. Haff look of disgust when look at JJ. Nyet fake news on face."

"Is good. Make easy life. Is better are dealing with subject than JJ. Haff done well, Svetlana," Tatiana say, before face haff sudden look of concern. "Am wondering, while on subject of JJ and think ahead, did pack anal lubricant?"

"Da," am saying. "Is not KY Jelly. Am ferry kind sister."

"Thank ferry much. Haff forgive me," Tatiana say, making joke.

Are both laughing ferry much.

"Oi! What's so funny?" say small voice, knuckle knock on window. Is JJ. Am noticing haff already pull off earring. "In, JJ," am saying. "Haff many thing tell."

JJ get in driver seat of car – is JJ car, not Paul car – and am telling what haff happen.

"Shit! You're not actually going to go through with it and meet the dirty old fucker, are you?" JJ say, alarm in voice.

263

"Duh! Da!" am saying. "Is one hundred-seventy pound cash and possible answer for Paul màmochka why husband not haff want haff sex. Of course, are meet dirty old fucker."

"Are going?" JJ say.

"Da. Both go and check keep other safe," am saying. "Like school, like university, like oligarch superyacht. Like whole life."

"Only is less danger than oligarch superyacht," Tatiana say. "Is only weak, old man and nyet oligarch crony. Is nyet problem for Pavlov twin."

"Okay," JJ say. "If you're sure you can handle it and you definitely won't be in any danger. Do you want me to come along as extra protection?"

"Aaahhh, nyet thank you," am saying at same time as Tatiana, ferry much like JJ concern for safety.

"Relax. Is nyet problem," Tatiana say.

"Really is nyet problem," am saying.

"Problem now is organise," Tatiana say, in business voice. "First must find Malcolm address on sat-nav and send Paul message say meet in car when haff park out of way. Malcolm must not see four in car or is kiss of death."

JJ find Malcolm address on sat-nav, move car out of way and message Paul information. Then haff wait. Is forty minute when Paul phone and say meeting haff finish. JJ flash headlight when see Paul, and Paul run and quick get in passenger seat.

"All right, everyone?" Paul say, slight out of breath. "What's happened? What's the plan now?"

Am explaining what haff happen and what plan happen next. "JJ drive house. Malcolm haff stop for cash and are sure arrive first. Once arrive, can park small distance away and me and Tatiana walk back. JJ and Paul wait all time in car."

"What, go back on your own?" Paul say.

"Da," am saying, same time as Tatiana.

"You don't have to go through with this if you don't want to,"

Paul say.

"Am wanting," am saying.

"Am wanting," Tatiana say.

"Are you sure you'll be okay? I couldn't bear it if anything was to happen to you," Paul say. "Not when you're risking it for me and Mum."

"Aaahhh, thank," am saying at same time as Tatiana, ferry much like Paul concern for safety.

"Enough. Step on pedal, JJ," Tatiana say, "haff not time for sentiment now."

Haff enter house by back door and Malcolm give rest of cash in kitchen. Am counting note and say must use bathroom before start. Malcolm explain where is and am leaving kitchen but not go bathroom. Instead, am quiet let Svetlana in back door before return like nothing haff happen.

"Come with me, please, Tatiana," Malcolm say.

As control queasy feel stranger know proper name, am expecting go up stair in bedroom. Instead go in room down stair with many book on both side. At end by door haff blackboard on wall with big desk in front. In front big desk haff many small desk in row. Am thinking is like school classroom, school classroom in house. Apart from name thing, am fairly relax as know Svetlana haff follow and wait outside door. Big question is what dream Malcolm want make come true. Soon know answer when speak.

"Welcome to my classroom. It's where… where I want you to be my headmistress," Malcolm say, voice wobble, sweat on forehead and pink bald head. "A very strict headmistress who has no time for naughty boys whose work is not up to scratch. There's several capes over there. And canes. If you wouldn't mind…"

Am knowing exactly what want and show am understanding. Am walking over and put on one of cape as am now in charge. Am dominatrix. With back turn, am undo one more button on blouse. Haff no bra, so am showing much breast. Am choosing cane, turn

265

and am strutting back, like model on cat walk. Am start quite enjoy self.

"Is what want?" am asking, tap end of cane on palm.

"Oooh, yes please, Headmistress," Malcolm say, voice like moan.

When at desk, am lifting leg and place black high heel shoe on surface. Am knowing Malcolm can see knicker and wait for eye settle. Once haff let haff little look, crash cane on desk like crash bottle on caravan table and like haff said crash bronze statue on Oligarch Son head.

"What are doing out of seat, boy? Sit down!" am screaming. Malcolm haff scramble in seat at desk in front row and am giving more order. "Get out pen and paper and write ten fact on Storming of Winter Palace. Nyet talking."

Malcolm lift lid on desk, take out pen and paper and make start. Am taking leg down and sit in swivel chair, stretch both leg out straight and wide under desk. Am thinking Malcolm can see much knicker when peek under big desk from seat. By look of glance, am sure is case. As sit, am bending cane in hand while watch Malcolm write. Malcolm eye move from paper and look between leg ferry often. Can tell am driving wild as face get more pink and haff more sweat. Haff always haff power over man because of look, but now haff Malcolm in palm of hand. After ten minute of look and write, look and write, look and write, only pupil put up hand.

"Da, boy?"

"Please, Headmistress. I've finished."

"Bring," am saying.

Malcolm bring paper and put in hand, which accident-on-purpose drop on floor. Am getting up from chair, turn and bend on straight leg pick up paper. Am wearing ferry short skirt and know Malcolm look at ferry pert arse. When pick up paper, as am facing door, can see Svetlana look round corner, tongue move over top lip. Think am also turn on sister little bit and am remind of many orgasm before Alexei. Once haff paper, turn face Malcolm. Is standing with hand behind back like good schoolboy while read answer. Can see sick bulge in trouser and decide read paper twice as use up more time. Am surprise at Malcolm answer, haff good knowledge, is obvious educate man, but, as ferry strict headmistress, is nyetwhere near enough.

"Is poor work, boy," am saying, screw up paper and throw in face. "Haff not mention February Revolution. Haff not mention direct by Nikolai Evreinov. Haff not mention set design of Yury Annenkov. What haff say for self?"

"Sorry, Headmistress. I'll try harder next time," Malcolm say. Is grovelling, but can tell is loving. Am liking also as power is special thing. Is why Russian leader always try ferry hard keep.

"Are always making excuse, boy. Always make big promise. Never make happen. Must haff punishment," am saying. "Get on hand and knee and clean shoe with tongue."

"Yes, Headmistress," Malcolm say, fall at feet.

"Must not touch skin," am warning. "Shoe only."

Is disgusting look down on Malcolm bald head as lick shoe. Haff much sweat on pink scalp and grease hair is plaster on top like grey footbridge over sea of skin. As think am wishing Malcolm haff wear gimp mask, feel wet tongue on top of foot.

"Evil child!" am screaming. "Haff said only shoe! Sit back at desk!"

Am waiting, ferry cross, as Malcolm get off hand and knee and sit at desk. When in seat, walk ferry slow and stand next desk. Am bending down and speak in ear.

"What haff make think can lick foot?" am saying, ferry soft. "Did not ask lick shoe clean only?"

"Yes, Headmistress."

"Are thinking is good idea disobey?"

"No, Headmistress."

"So why are doing?"

267

"Sorry, Headmistress."

"Is nyet good say sorry now. Haff already disobey. Why are disobeying, am wanting know?" am saying.

"I couldn't stop myself, Headmistress."

"Why?" am saying.

"It was too much, Headmistress."

"Too much?"

"Yes, Headmistress."

"Am not understanding 'too much'."

"Too much temptation. You're too beautiful."

Am so close Malcolm now, can smell sweat from bald head. "Is no excuse. No boy haff right disobey headmistress," am saying. Am standing up straight. "Put hand on desk," am saying. "Nyet," am shouting. "Palm of hand up." Am waiting Malcolm turn hand. "Are ferry naughty boy," am saying and swish cane hard on both palm. "Ferry naughty," again am caning hand.

Malcolm make cry of pain and am thinking is also one of pleasure. When look, haff two mark across centre of hand.

"Hand on head," am saying. "Stand in corner face wall. Now."

Malcolm struggle from seat, is not ferry easy for old man with hand on head, and walk into corner.

"Nyet move muscle," am warning, as take other cape and cane from corner of room. "Am now haff go haff wash. Cannot bear haff disgusting stain of naughty boy on body. Will haff wash whole leg in soap water," am saying as walk other side of door. "Is Svetlana turn," am saying ferry quiet to little sister. "Haff fun... Must undo button," am reminding.

Svetlana undo button, put on cape and take cane.

Am walking back in room as Malcolm stand in corner like prisoner of war.

"Take hand off head," am saying. "Nyet turn round."

As Malcolm obey, long strand hair come off bald head and hang over ear. Am surprise how long as is past collar. Malcolm quick put

268

back, wipe hand over bald head and smooth hair flat like cover up big secret. Am thinking is worse than despise ex-President of United States, Donald Trump, with ridiculous antic of hair. Neverless, is ferry interest react and haff give idea for possible discover truth of Paul mamochka husband secret.

"Hair is long, boy," am saying. "Am certain is too long obey school rule. Hair must not touch collar. Are thinking rule of school is thing can disobey?"

"No, Headmistress. That's not true at all. My hair doesn't touch my collar..." Malcolm say, as start move head.

"Nyet move muscle!" am shouting. "Are arguing, boy? Haff see for self how long is hair."

"No, I'm not arguing, Headmistress. But look for yourself. Please. Please can I turn round and show you?"

"Da," am saying.

Malcolm turn and show hair plaster over bald head with proud look on face, like haff best haircut in world.

Am standing at front of class with both hand on hip, not impress, cane rest against desk.

"Come, boy," am saying.

Malcolm walk toward and arrive at desk with sick bulge in trouser. "You see, Headmistress. My hair is above my collar," Malcolm say.

"Are ferry certain, boy. Are sure stay in place?" am asking.

"Yes, Headmistress."

"Nyet more lie, boy," am shouting. "Haff already see not stay in place."

"But that was only because you made me put my hands on my..."

"Quiet! Nyet more argue. Will make test see if hair obey rule. Bend over desk," am saying, point at one haff sit earlier.

Malcolm face twitch and do as say. Is ferry eager. Is knowing what come next. Is what always want come next from ferry start.

Haff make wait for end of hour. Is all part of game. Is climax.

Malcolm haff bend over desk. "If hair stay in place, is nyet problem," am saying. "If fall down... will haff cut hair off."

"I'm sorry, Tatiana," Malcolm say, start get off desk. "Can we just break off for a second. Rather remiss of me not to have given you a safe word..."

"Quiet!" am screaming, as push Malcolm down. "Nyet talking! One!"

Am taking ferry big swing and thrash cane over Malcolm buttock before can say other word. Malcolm make cry of pleasure and pain. Am knowing is painful as hit with cane ferry hard. Am also knowing is what haff want from start. Am also knowing threat cut off hair is what not want. Am wondering what is most big desire.

"Two!" Am thrashing cane over buttock again.

"Argh."

"Three!" Am thrashing cane over buttock again.

"Aarghh."

"Four!" Am thrashing cane over buttock again. Malcolm make groan this time and whole body start shake.

"Aaarghhh."

"Five!" Am thrashing cane over buttock again.

"Aaaarghhh... Aaaaarghhhh... Aaaaaarghhhhh," Malcolm cry, as body start convulse.

"Six!" Am shouting, as make last stroke hard of all.

"Aaaaaaarghhhhhh," Malcolm scream as head and body shake like five-litre emulsion can on paint mix machine. "Oooooowwwwhhh-hhh. Oooowwhhhh. Oowhh," Malcolm groan.

With last jolt of head from orgasm, strand of hair not stay in place and hang from head like grease grey ribbon.

"Tut-tut-tut," am saying. "Stand, boy. Off desk." Malcolm slow get up from desk on ferry weak leg of custard. "Turn," am instructing.

Malcolm turn and face with hair hang down from ear. Sick bulge in trouser haff go, but is replace by wet patch. Haff come in pant.

"What this?" am asking, as lift grease hair on cane right in front Malcolm cross-over eye. "Is almost touch shoulder, boy, let alone collar. Hair not stay in place as promise. Haff alter ego cut off."

Is cue enter and am walking in room through doorway with scissor haff find in kitchen. Once see what Svetlana haff in mind, haff rummage through drawer and discover tool for carry out threat. As walk near Malcolm, am making menace snip-snip-snip with large scissor.

"Are ferry naughty, boy," am saying. "Haff disobey *my* alter ego and haff now pay cost. Are soon modern day Samson.

Malcolm is ferry confuse. Is keep looking me and Svetlana with look of stupefaction.

"Is not perfect dream?" Svetlana say. "Haff *two* headmistress?"

"I... I don't understand. What's going on? Who is she?" Malcolm say Svetlana.

"Is barber," Svetlana say.

"No! No! Please, not my hair. Don't cut my hair," Malcolm say, as wipe hair back on head.

"Serious?" am saying, as arrive Malcolm and Svetlana. "Are worrying over tiny hair? Are bald. Small strand make nyet different and fool nyet one. Make matter worse. Am doing favour," am saying.

"No, no. Please. Not my hair," Malcolm say. "Safe word. Whatever is the safe word you respond to, I'm saying it. Please. Please, can we stop."

"Haff one last chance, boy. Am needing name of other boy like you. Who like same thing."

"Ah... Yes... All right. I understand what you want. I do. You want more contacts? More customers who will pay for your considerable skills? I can do that. You want more, I can give you more."

"Da," Svetlana say. "More name of naughty boy. Is what are wanting. Write on paper. You haff many?"

"Of course. Certainly. I'll write them down. And their mobile numbers. There's quite a few. You can ring them. Say you come highly recommended by me... b... b... both of you," Malcolm say with stutter.

Like frighten rabbit, Malcolm write list of dozen naughty boy. Once finish, snatch from hand and look down list. Name mean nothing. Is nyet Paul surname.

"Haff miss any naughty boy? Are all there? Are sure list extensive?" am saying.

Malcolm ferry confuse, he look me and Svetlana like are ghost or omnipresent demon. "Yes. All there. Everyone I know... Sometimes we would meet here, all of us, for a special 'class'." Malcolm say, slight lose look of terror. "It doesn't happen often. I don't see many of them regularly now. All of us are waning with the passage of time. You wouldn't understand, being in your prime. It's called 'getting old'."

"So haff miss *nyet* one?" Svetlana say, ignore stroll down memory street.

Malcolm face now turn ferry sad. Tear roll gentle down cheek as mind in poignant moment. "Well... Only one," Malcolm say with mist in eye. "Because he's no longer with us. The one who introduced me to the class a long, long time ago. The one we all recognised as our Head Boy. My best friend and closest work colleague. The man who I held in my arms as his life drained from him on the seventeenth fairway of our favourite golf club."

JJ

At the time I'm not sure how Paul viewed it, to be honest. He didn't comment one way or the other, just sat there in silence, eyes glazed, an air of half-formed horror stamped all over him. I kept quiet too, no way was I going to start popping out questions, trying to discover answers to the thoughts charging around his head. Well, not for a while anyway. When the Nas came back to the car and told us what had happened, it well rattled me. Not so much the fact Paul's dad had been revealed as a perverted sexual submissive seeking domination as a regressed schoolboy, more by the method and lengths the Nas had gone to in order to find out. My first instinctive thought – typical of me – the endless exciting possibilities the Nas' performance opened up regards role play in the bedroom. The second, more considered one, where had they perfected the technique to pull it off? I mean, how credible could it be to believe a pair of complete novices, waitresses no less, could rock up, plan and then complete a perfect honey trap operation after passing themselves off as, firstly, believable prostitutes, and then, moving smoothly up to the niche end of the sex workers' scale, convincing dominatrixes?

The whole episode had a different feel to their Oligarch Son story, where they had concocted their actions on the fly in answer to the grim situation they found themselves. This time it had been planned. A little voice in the back of my head said, 'Identical, beautiful, blonde Russian twins, working abroad with a stash of cash in a bank account obtained in well shady circumstances? Gotta be the obvious thing, JJ'. The obvious thing being the surreal, but gritty, world of espionage, double agents and under-cover surveillance with a splash – probably on a door handle – of nerve-agent-inspired, state-aided assassinations. A world they might have been introduced to because of what had happened that night on the oligarch's superyacht. Had someone found out the truth and thought, wow, these girls are something else. Someone from the Russian intelligence services – their dad, possibly? – who could see they possessed the raw talent to move into field operations.

Only possibly. When you said it out loud, actually voiced the idea, and remembered they were still waitressing in a tiny café in the back of beyond in Suffolk, only fifty yards from Paul's overpriced beach hut, it sort of reined in the theory. Made you think, nah, not buying it.

Still, whatever. I had originally wondered what the hell we were getting ourselves into on our first date with the Nas. Impersonating a gay guy sitting in my car, listening to their successful mission, wearing eyeliner, with coloured hair, squeezed into a pair of Paul's old, ripped beach shorts, so tight they threatened to cut off the circulation to my nuts, I saw little reason to change my viewpoint. Far from bothering me, I felt enthused. Whatever they had lined up for me and Paul, I was absolutely a willing participant. More than willing. Better than being bored any day of the week in my book. And that was *before* the sex I took part in that night of Malcolm's entrapment. In the brief post-orgasmic moment after doing it like she had promised, I couldn't have cared less if they were a pair of sleeper agents whose next mission was to shoot another state-enemy oligarch's son in the face, in the street, in broad daylight. I would probably even pass them the gun.

Paul

Not pretty – file under 'Towering Understatement' – having to listen to the Nas' story, told in their weird shared way of one of them starting off, the other taking over and alternating until the end. Initially, I felt exactly as I had when they had related their Oligarch Son tale, the only difference this time I desperately wanted to *disbelieve* it rather than wanting it to be true. The final line had crushed any hope. The line where Na relayed Malcolm's description of how my father had died in his arms. I had never mentioned that to either of them, or to JJ. Conclusive irrefutable proof, therefore, that my father enjoyed a female-dominant/male-submissive sadomasochistic fetish fixated within the confines of a rigid pseudo-educational setting. Maybe it would have been better

274

to have found out he was gay. Or liked fucking chickens. Anything other than what I had just heard.

With the realisation of the indisputable facts, my brain floundered over the pros and cons of the Nas' revelation and what to do with it. Not that I could see any pros, to be honest. If any were present they were buried at the bottom of a huge pile of cons, well away from the grasp of my reasoning. The main issue was what would I tell Mum? If I were to tell her anything at all. Could she handle a truth so unsettling, so shocking, so utterly vile and sordid? Sitting next to a 'gayed-up' JJ in the passenger seat of his car, our blonde, Russian, identical twin girlfriends in the back seat dressed as a couple of whores, I quietly slipped that one in the pending tray – my mind continuing to seek refuge in thoughts of mundane clerical work.

What really freaked me was the schoolboy stuff and Malcolm's assessment that Dad had been the instigator, and the ringleader, of their little clique of like-minded deviants. I recognised quite a few names on the list of shame the Nas had handed me, all golf friends of Dad, and managed to raise a rueful black-humoured smile as I linked submissive sex acts to a submissive sport – one forever in thrall to its codes of etiquette, player behaviour, byzantine rulebook and rampant, hypocritical misogyny. An old boys' club where women aren't welcome yet whose members secretly desire complete female subjugation. Of course, I could be missing the green with that analysis. Maybe everyone on the list had gone to boarding school, been bullied by matron, and the golf link was only a consequence rather than a driver, if you can forgive the puns. The feted clubhouse a next stop safe house for those moulded by the harsh, parentless, loveless environment of a private boarding school.

In my self-absorbed bubble, I vaguely heard JJ start the car and at least felt grateful for dodging the boarding school bullet with 'fetish' written on it. *Not* like father like son, thank god. As the car pulled away, I moved with it to wondering how I would ever manage to look Malcolm in his watery eyes again. Or stop staring at his horrendous comb-over. Or at his office desk. Or at the crotch of his trousers – the list of no-go areas seemed endless.

During the journey back to my flat no one spoke a word to me. In a world of my own, I frantically searched my memory for any clues, any hints, where past words or deeds might have suggested Dad's kink. I couldn't think of any. Whenever and however it had started, wherever it had taken place, Dad had managed to conceal it from both Mum and me. While we visited the Suffolk seaside with Mum's parents, Dad was undoubtedly being disciplined to within an inch of his life, and no doubt revelled in every second of it. In between those spank-fests, work, golf and a few sly thrashings on the side must have kept him ticking along. Mum and I remained, to all intents and purposes, unloved throughout. I was too young to realise anything was wrong within their marriage and remained bedazzled by Dad's propaganda. Mum, on the other hand, slowly sunk without trace as her husband's disinterest gradually killed her. While Dad hid his perversion from us both, Mum hid the distress it caused her from me. What a sorry picture of complete and utter domestic catastrophe.

Mum, I'm sorry for ever doubting you. Dad, fuck you. You complete arsehole. Retrospectively, I'm glad I never played golf and it pissed you off. Thank heavens for tennis. Good old middle-class, what-now-post-Andy-Murray, hopelessly ineffectual LTA, Wimbledon-debenture-ticket flogging, all-white clothing, strawberries and cream, clapping the umpire for saying 'no flash photography' tennis. A sport that, in the UK anyway, was dragging its knuckles across the grass only a little less heavily than the sticks in a bag mob. I looked over at JJ, quiff of red hair sticking up proudly in an act of non-conformity, and hoped his efforts might help change British tennis from the ground up.

That night, after the most amazing sex I'd had in my life – both the Nas were hyper on returning to the flat, as if the drug of success had pitched them somewhere closer towards nymphomania and upped even their high grade sexual game – I wondered what Dad had ever seen in pain as a sexual reward. An unyielding cane as opposed to soft pliant flesh? It was beyond me, abhorrent in every sense, an aberration that sickened me to my core.

"Next time, can do different way," Na said softly, as we lay cuddling in bed.

"Sorry?" I asked, winched from my thoughts.

"Different way. Ferry excite love-make."

"What? Do you mean... not sure how to phrase this... up the... you know?" I asked, gently probing her suggested mode of probing.

"Da. Haff done before?"

"No. Never."

"How are saying, is first time for everything."

And then it hit me. For some reason it just flew into my head.

"Sometimes I know how to tell you apart," I replied. "It's Tatiana who goes first when you tell one of your long stories. It's always Tatiana who goes first."

"Are knowing who am now?" Na asked, a slight edge to her voice.

"Not a clue."

"Is start am supposing. Not ferry helpful."

I kissed her on the forehead. "It doesn't matter anymore. Not now. To me or JJ. We're over the intrigue, we're just happy to be with you. Both of you. Thanks for finding out the truth about Dad. It was very kind of you. A bit grim, but at least I know the truth."

"Nyet problem. Am please can help. Are telling mamochka?"

"Not sure. I'll have to think about it. It's a terrible thing to have to tell her."

"Haff good think," Na said, resting her head on my chest, taking hold of my hand and squeezing it tightly.

JJ

The world keeps turning, that's what they say, and they're right. The Nas' revelation about Paul's dad never stopped our little world from revolving. It kept spinning from one amazing weekend right on to the next and the next and the next one after that, pulling us in tighter rather than flinging us apart, consolidating us like we were space dust merging into a newly-formed planet. All the time growing and spinning, spinning and growing, gyrating in space a little closer to an event beginning to weigh heavy on my mind. The doubles tournament I had entered me and Paul in at our old tennis club. Under my insistence, within our tight, restricted weekend schedule, we had started to cram in even more practice than we had previously. Emma, who was keeping me up to speed on all matters tournament via social messaging, had confirmed Randolph Valentino-Smith's rather late entry with James as his partner. I had previously made Emma promise to keep our entry under wraps as the notion of me and Paul rocking up unannounced to confront *them*, and all they represented, was just *soo* delicious it made my heart sing.

My surprise at Randolph's participation could never match the corresponding elation I experienced on getting the news. I was over the moon. Euphoric. The one bit of Paul's story where I had wished I could have been him *was* going to materialise. In a men's doubles match rather than a mixed. Incredible. I *would* get the chance to see how good the Moneyed Chump – AKA Randolph Valentino-Smith – was at tennis. Where it mattered. On court, up close and personal and not through a third party. The problem, I hold my hands up and freely admit it was very much *my* problem, was Randolph encapsulated everything I loathed about his sort of tennis player. Affluent background, easy access to all the tools you needed to make it, obvious talent, yet he still hadn't made the grade. He had given up. When the going got tough, he had chucked in the towel and slipped back into the safe haven of working for daddy's financial services firm. His hunger, or rather the lack of it, had killed his chances. I, alternatively, would have killed to have had those chances. Instead, I got cut off from all funding and turned to booze. Sure, we had both ended up in the same place, but swap us around, give me his deal, and I reckon I would have made a whole lot more of it. I felt angry and anger, if you can't control it and weaponize it on a tennis court, can be a very destructive ingredient. For you, that is. Not your opponent. I knew, when the time came, I would have to be very careful my rage didn't swallow me up whole and catastrophically affect my game.

When I messaged Emma about Randolph and asked why he had entered, she answered, 'Randolph new squeeze of club member, Emily, who has recently dumped hubby. Word is Randolph very good player and very good looking!' Emma told me, apparently unaware of my knowledge of him. 'So am I', I wrote back with a laughing emoji. 'Make sure you seed us 1 & 2. So we can meet in final. And still keep it quiet we've entered. I want it to be a BIG surprise when we turn up on the day'. 'Think I can swing that. And don't worry, no one will know you've entered', came her response. I sent a smiley face and three thumbs-up emojis I was so overjoyed.

Game very much on! It had to be like that, us meeting in the final. The whole day building to a supercharged crescendo. And not only in terms of tennis strengths. Let's be honest, underneath the surface, once everyone found out who was playing, and with who, there was going to be a shed load of shite nicely piled up and ready to hit the fan.

If Paul had felt the pressure of playing with his wife against another married couple in a final, then our prospective seeded match up would see him on familiar ground – only on super-strength steroids. Not only would Paul be facing up to James, his ex-wife's new lover and partner, he would also be facing up to

Randolph – a richer, better looking, better-tennis-playing charadee-tournament nemesis – the new lover and partner of, Emily, who had used him as a pawn to snare Randolph. Add in my desire to crush Randolph like a bug and my chip-on-the-shoulder-the-size-of-a-flagstone enmity of spoilt, rich kids and you had enough serious shade occurring, a million watt floodlight would struggle to cut through it. Flip it to their viewpoint, James hating Paul and under intense pressure from Chloe to smash her ex, Randolph's entitled tennis ego wanting to impress his new county standard lady, and 'messy' was severely undercooking it. I don't know about on-court coaching, we might all need on-court psychoanalysing.

I decided to strategically withhold all this info from Paul for the time being. The guy had been through enough of late what with the revelation of his dad's gross fetish. No point in freaking him out right now. Not when I could leave it a month and freak him out closer to the time when, hopefully, I would have coached the fuck out of him and made him a much better doubles player. The last time he had played at his old club he had lost the match, lost his wife and lost his life. Not gonna happen this time, I swore to myself. Not on my watch.

Six weeks after discovering the sick secret of Paul's dad, Paul's promotion at college officially got its rubber stamp and he moved out of the classroom and into management. Graham, his principal, had been as good as his word.

"Management, eh? Just like your old man," I kidded as we were about to step on court for the friendly doubles match I had arranged, the Nas watching on from behind the side netting, drop dead pretty in the warm sunshine, undoubtedly putting off our opponents with their glamorous mirror image presentation of desirable female flesh.

"Don't," was all he answered.

We talked about Paul's dad properly for the first time in the changing room of the clubhouse as we showered and changed after we had finished playing. We had won four and three and were well on our way to becoming a very good, solid pair. Paul told me how hard it had been, initially, to interact with Malcolm and hide his new-found, appalling knowledge of the man. Only now, weeks down the line, was he finally, sort of, coming to terms with it. The promotion had further helped cement his self-esteem, he thought, and with the continued runaway success of our joint relationship with the Nas, he felt he was now somewhere near back on track. Near enough in as strong a place mentally as he had been before the Nas' honey-trap mission.

I casually asked if he was going to tell his mum. He told me he had put off making any decisions about his dad's secret until he could cope with Malcolm at work and the stress of the promotion issue – the interviews, going up against other candidates, the perpetual worry Graham might pull the rug out from under his promise – had been finalised. With those boxes ticked, he admitted all his excuses for non-action had evaporated.

"I've been fobbing Mum off for ages. I can't keep doing it," he explained

"Then I think you should let her know. Your dad hid his sicko stuff from your mum and she hid her misery from you. Break the Chambers mould. Tell her. You can't be carrying that type of crap around forever."

It was like I had given him the nudge he needed and Paul agreed, promptly asking me if I would accompany him. I said I would be only too pleased to go with him and so, the next weekend, when it was my turn to bring the Nas to him, we went and saw her. By that time Paul had decided the Nas should come too, reasoning we had collectively found out, so should collectively inform. After we sat Linda down in her living room with a stiff drink – her go-to tipple of stress, vodka – and pre-warned her of the ordeal ahead, Paul got the Nas to tell their story once again. As soon as one of them started, a strange smile briefly formed on his lips, which I thought a bit odd, seeing as what horrors were to come next. At the time, I presumed it to be an anxiety smile, one attempting to hide the discomfort he felt at letting his mum in on his father's shitty secret. When the other Na finished off, delivering the crucial bit about Malcolm holding his dad on the seventeenth fairway, Linda's living room fell silent.

"Thanks, Svetlana," Paul said, shooting me a glance, cracking the silence.

I got his look and at once understood. It wasn't only the silence he had cracked. Somehow he knew which one of them was which. He had done it! Just as I suspected he might.

"Thanks to the Nas' efforts, Mum, at last you know why Dad was so indifferent to you. It was *nothing* to do with you. Never was. It was *never* your fault. His gratification lay in different areas. Miles from where you were. I'm sorry, very sorry, for not believing you. I hope you can forgive me."

Linda, who had somehow managed to bottle it all up until that point, burst into tears and the four of us rushed to console her. Group hug time.

"Of course I forgive you. Paul. Oh, dear. Oh, dear," she kept saying. "Oh, dear me. I feel quite physically sick."

Eventually she calmed down and managed, after some gentle encouragement by the Nas, to take a large slug of vodka from her glass.

"Thank you my darlings," she said to Tatiana and Svetlana. "How brave of you to do that for me," she remarked, the blood slowly coming back to her cheeks. "I can't quite take in what you did. So brave. So audacious." Linda drained her glass. "Let's never mention the vile old toad again, shall we?"

We all nodded, and in an instant, Peter Chambers was written out of all our lives. If you can believe in such bold, melodramatic statements. I doubted Paul or Linda could ever completely wipe Peter and his fetish from their minds. Every now and then he would drift back in, if only for a hideous second or two.

We stayed with Linda for an hour or two before we left to go back to Paul's. For me it couldn't come fast enough. I was gagging to speak to him alone. The second I got my chance, I asked him how he had cracked the Nas' code.

"Is it anything to do with anal sex?" I asked.

"What! *No!*" Paul reprimanded, his face screwed up, a mixture of shock and horror. "It's when they talk. Whenever they tell one of their long-winded stories it's always Tatiana who starts off and then Svetlana goes next."

"Is that it? You haven't worked out how to tell them apart all the time?"

"That's it. And no, I haven't."

"That's not very helpful."

Paul laughed. "That's what Na said."

"Which one?"

"I don't know."

I shrugged. "Oh, well. It is a start, I suppose."

"Na said that too."

"Which one?"

"The same one who said it wasn't very helpful. The same one I *still* don't know who it was!"

"Ok. I get it, I get it," I said, trying to calm him down. "I suppose it doesn't matter. Although I think I would like to be able to tell one day. So I'm not in the same boat as Alexei." I paused, another question forming. "Anyway, going back to, you know, that *thing*, have you done it with one of them up the...?"

"Yes! Yes I have, thank you very much for asking."

"And you *definitely* don't think it's anything to do with that? Not anything to do with one of them taking it up the arse on the superyacht and getting a taste for it?"

"*No!*" Paul answered stridently. "For god's sake, no. 'Getting a taste for it'? What? When she's faking rape by having violent sex

283

with a corpse to fabricate an alibi to get away with murder?" Paul shot me a contemptuous look. "Jesus Christ, JJ. What *are* you thinking?"

I felt a little pissed with him for that. For being so aggy. The real truth, I was feeling pissed with myself because it did sound a ridiculously awful and crass thing to say once Paul had spelt it out in such vivid terms. Despite this, I couldn't stop myself from retaliating and dropping Randolph and James playing together by way of a massive, nuclear distraction-bomb.

"Shit!" Paul exclaimed, jaw slack, anger gone in a snap. "Are you certain?"

"It's what Emma's told me. I can show you the message," I confirmed, pleased to have shifted the conversation away from my tasteless theory.

Paul slowly shook his head, his eyes aimed at the ground. "I can't *believe* Emily's with Randolph and blown Steven out. They've hardly been married five minutes. *And* he's playing with *James!*" Paul lifted his focus to me. "Jesus, JJ. That's serious baggage all round. The two women who shafted me have joined forces. And so have their men."

"Exactly," I said, positivity cranked to eleven. "It's the perfect chance to fuck all of them over big style. Revenge is a dish best served two straight, man."

"There's going to be *so* much hate," Paul stated, still coming to terms with the news. "I don't think I can do it, JJ. I really don't think I can handle it."

"You'll be fine," I assured him. "This is your big chance to get even. Look at what else you've achieved. This tournament will be the cherry on top."

The look on Paul's face changed from anxious to urgent. "I *need* more coaching, JJ. *Coach* me! For fuck's sake coach me, JJ! Coach me to within an inch of my life," Paul pleaded, a tinge of panic in his voice.

"Don't worry. I will. Before and during. You'll be fine."

"Urgh!" Paul turned away in disgust.

"What's up now?"

"Nothing. Words. Words I'd used thinking about what Dad had got up to, that's all."

"Punching those volleys away at the net when I'm serving, that's what you need to be thinking about," I warned him, not taking a sniff of pleasure in seeing my prophecy come true. "And getting your returns in. Making lots of first serves…"

"The Nas. We'll need the Nas to come and support us. Nobody else will be," Paul stated, cutting in, an edge of frenzy to his voice. "What with the lies James and Chloe have been spreading throughout the club. I'm not exactly going to be Mr Popular and welcomed back with open arms, am I? You neither, come to that. A lot of the older committee members who voted to chuck you out are *still* there. Hanging on like the zombie undead! They've been hating on you for years, too."

"We're fucking toxic. So what?" I retorted, upping my insouciance. "We'll get hazchem decals for our tennis bags. We'll develop a siege mentality, us against them, like your principal did for Ofsted. And we'll get the Nas to cheer us on. They won't take any crap from anybody. They're our secret weapon. What else do we need?"

"A few easy early rounds to get into our stride?"

"You'll be fine," I assured him once again, trying to focus the tiny knot of anger already forming in my stomach into something positive. Throwing me out the club just for riding a moped on their crap hard courts. The bastards. I'll show them.

Tatiana and Svetlana

In Paul car travel old tennis club and am thinking is tension with

285

Paul and JJ. Haff practise tennis ferry hard and see if are good enough win tournament. Am hoping is possible as know how much Paul and JJ want happen. Is also more than tennis tournament and day haff much hidden agenda thank many reason. Paul haff tell me and Svetlana how Chloe, wife of past, blame Paul lose tennis match because look Emily leg. Is time when begin end of marriage, where old wife haff start affair with Paul friend James. In same moment, Paul think Emily want haff affair after kiss, but haff turn out only pawn in Emily game of chess annoy husband and snag Randolph. Big success it seem and Emily now with Randolph – apparent ferry attract man – on permanent basis after haff leave husband. Am thinking is gold digger and haff only swap rich man because new man more rich. Am not judge, am just saying, is all. In game of musical chair, James and Chloe also couple, so is ferry charge atmosphere if haff play James and Randolph in final. Is good chance haff play in final as James and Randolph number one seed, Paul and JJ number two seed. Am thinking situation is like TV soap opera or plot in crazy book. Like newspaper article on man and woman from Jeremy Kyle TV show where headline say, 'Could not make up!' When haff tell Paul what am thinking, say, 'Like your Oligarch Son story, then?' and think, da, haff fair point, only proviso is story ferry much indicative of culture in two ferry different society.

Am interest see Paul ex-wife and Emily woman. Am not normal concern of look of other woman, but today is contest. Is not only me and Svetlana man against Chloe and Emily man, is me and Svetlana against Chloe and Emily. Is war of man on court and is war of woman off court. Is ferry nuance situation, is war play out under civil code, is ferry subtle typical English situation where word haff two meaning and where hide insult in friendly comment. Neverless, as haff tell Svetlana, if Chloe or Emily haff too much of what cat lick arse, as expression go, will slap bitch in face. For all social air and grace, am not take any shit from two slut like that.

Last night is first night haff tell Paul and JJ cannot haff sex. Haff tell must haff good night sleep as is well know fact sex make leg weak next day. Haff promise special reward if win, thing haff not done before. Look on Paul and JJ face ferry funny as try think what am talking about. Think haff done all way, but is not case. Haff say, win tournament and are finding out. Am doing bit help boost morale and inspire, am thinking. As haff think haff say before, am prefer use carrot instead stick when motivate comrade on mission.

Is conscious decision wear necklace father haff give, although am wearing one in beautiful white gold haff 'Tatiana' written in cursive attach very fine chain. Same Tatiana, although, obvious, is wearing one in beautiful white gold haff 'Svetlana' written in cursive attach very fine chain. Am also wearing different clothe Tatiana as both are thinking is much like when in café and are not want freak customer. Can see are identical, haff necklace like name badge and wear different clothe. Is close as ever come fit in with society identity norm. Is much as can stand as haff nyet chance swap. Am Tatiana all day and Tatiana is Svetlana all day. Thing do for love!

Am wearing most expense and elegant clothe in wardrobe for tournament. Tatiana same. Is ferry different look from night of honey trap as are not wanting conceit English tennis club membership think are Russian prostitute or from seedy Russian date website. When me and Tatiana haff look in mirror see reflection of ferry glamour woman if say so self and am thinking is nyet way Chloe and Emily as hot, however attract Paul say Emily suppose is. Is first front in war off court, win battle of glamour look. When win battle of glamour look, start win over enemy man as cannot cope when face with beautiful woman. Is man weakness from all time. Is simple divide and conquer strategy. Second front is play game of barb comment behind mask of chit-chat when face Chloe and Emily and other woman from club. Am sure trouble come when see me and Tatiana with Paul and JJ and, certain as sun set in west, woman bitch about good look and nice clothe as are jealous. Haff much fear man want more than self. Haff good reason for fear, is first front tactic!

Am knowing today are being outnumber by enemy, are surround in fact, but is nyet problem as are use tough situation. Not affect me and Tatiana. Haff queue for bread for six hour in minus ten centigrade and walk school in two-metre snow, not like some can mention who haff not want walk in Salisbury slush. Is in Russian DNA, most of time, stand much hardship, except, seem, when try cover up fail assassination attempt. Collapse of communism, Western sanction, Battle for Stalingrad is usual benchmark for Russian stoic response. Haff tell Tatiana, Chloe and Emily can bring on and give go if think are hard enough. Am not take any shit from gold digger or pathetic insecure English woman who think husband miss smash because is looking woman leg. If want make fight, ferry soon find hell hath no fury like Russian woman, as paraphrase expression go.

Paul

Pulling up outside the tennis club, my heart was paradiddling like an ADHD drummer after downing six energy drinks and a double espresso. Getting out of the car, my legs feeling weak and jelly-like despite not having had sex last night – double loser – I experienced a major wobble. Had I the mental strength to deal with the upcoming double barrel of buckshot coming my way? Two balls of heavy gauge lead pellets aimed point blank at my torso in the form of serious social and tennis confrontation. The soap opera plot; ex-wife, Chloe, now in a relationship with ex-best friend, James, who was partnering Randolph (likely final opponents), a man who had previously thrashed me at tennis and was now in a relationship with the stunning, Emily, a one-time infatuation who had used me as a vehicle to get in his bed. Add into the Five Go Flighty mix, JJ's anger at how I had been blown out of the club, how *he* had been blown out of the club, his pathological desire to tennis-best rich-boy Randolph – a man pushing most of his hate buttons – and all ingredients for a stomach-churning dish were evidently in situ.

Convinced I would be faced with major hostility from Chloe, James and most club members – how else could it pan out? I hadn't been around to counter their drip feed of poison – I felt disinclined to be the one distributing olive branches and attempting to mend fences. I still harboured far too much rancour for that. Not solely for the damage to my private life, but also for how the pair of them had terminated my tennis life. Callously unplugging it from the life support system of the club.

With Emily and Randolph, things were slightly less clear cut. Sure she had dangled me on her piece of elven string, manipulated and toyed with me, but could I hate her for it? My inner jury was out, partly because I recognised the grief garnered from chasing her was partially self-inflicted, even if, and I'm sticking with this one, she had started the ball rolling by kissing me. Your Honour, I rest my case. As for Randolph? Well, he was simply better. Better looking, better player, better job, better prospects and a better catch. He had got the girl, no surprise there, but hadn't intentionally humiliated me – save for on court – simply because he never saw me as a love rival. A bit galling, but hardly malicious.

As for the mechanics of Emily and Randolph becoming a couple, factually I was in the dark. Steven was a deeply unpleasant man and the schadenfreude I derived on hearing Emily had ruthlessly dumped him for Randolph was the only fly of satisfaction caught in the vile web we had spun. The whole mess was a gigantic shit-show, one, up until now, I had been removed from for some time. Scarily, that state of affairs was soon to end. Worst case scenario saw nerves paralyse me on court, causing JJ and me either to not make the final or lose it. If that denouement materialised, then my tiny hit of pleasure, caused by Steven's loss would pale into insignificance compared to that experienced by Chloe, James, Emily and Randolph.

With a sense of an escalating force easing my temples apart, and with stress levels rising, I looked over at JJ across the car's roof. His demeanour helped steady my ship, the expression on his face hewn from a mindset of assured, controlled intensity. When the Nas slid out the back seat – body language calm, relaxed and languid – like a couple of identikit supermodels, positivity coursed back through me, purging self-doubt and lowering my mental psi. I *can* do this, I realised. The Beach Hut Plan had worked, been successful beyond my wildest expectations, and, thanks to it, I had answered the questions concerning my father, become reunited with my mother, earned a work promotion and gained a relationship with three amazing people – one as unconventional as it was thrilling.

Feeling happier and more at ease, I moved to the back of the car and started to focus. All logical appraisal insisted the day hinged on one single objective – winning the tournament. All else was secondary. Forget the side show of multiple personal animosities, today JJ and I were in the results business. Like Premier League managers. As he had rightly said, it was payback time. Revenge *is* a dish best served two straight. All we had to do was hang tough, power through, be victorious and smugly hand out the R-word platters to the losers. Really smugly, like when you get shown to a table on a Saturday night in Nando's.

"The guy beating out my heart's rhythm has been on the Red Bulls and coffee," I confided to JJ as we took our racket bags out the boot of the car.

"Absinthe makes the heart go arrhythmia. So I don't doubt energy drinks and caffeine would do a similar job."

I pulled down the boot lid and slammed it shut, any negativity, hopefully, safely trapped inside. "Are you feeling nervous?"

JJ shook his head. "I'm pumped rather than edgy. Just got to keep the temper in check, that's all."

I sucked in a big lungful of air through my nose, steeling myself. "Entrance as planned?"

JJ nodded. "We walk in all smiles," he reiterated, now addressing all three of us. "And say exactly what all the pros say at any tournament. How great it is to be here and how wonderful it is to be back. Even if, like them, we don't necessarily mean it. I think we can stop short of saying it's our favourite Slam of the tour, though," he added sarcastically.

"Happy with that, Nas?" I asked.

"Da," they casually said in unison, not fazed in the slightest.

"You look stunning," I confirmed, taking further strength from them, once more amazed at the fantasy reality I was sleeping with both of them. "Tatiana, you're with me and Svetlana, you're with JJ. As discussed," I said, addressing them by virtue of their necklaces, glossing over the conundrum of whether or not they were the person their jewellery insisted.

"Da. Come, Paul." Tatiana took my hand. "Make entrance like ferry big movie star. Make big statement intent."

Clasping her hand tightly, like I had on our first date when we strolled along Southburgh's promenade – possibly, fifty-fifty call, as ever – we walked down the narrow hedge-lined pathway towards the club. Emerging on to the flat patio area fronting the clubhouse, we found a crowd already gathered there – competitors, partners and friends of competitors, club members who had only come to watch. A few heads started to turn as we were noticed and then, like a murmuration of starlings in flight, others rapidly followed. Whether they were people who knew me, or bizarrely, even the minority who didn't, it appeared to have no bearing on the collective reaction. Everyone ended up staring at us like we were returning royalty – in a newly-formed republic.

Male eye pupils subconsciously dilated. Female lips consciously passed sly comment. The one dog present started to bark. Nobody said hello. Lynch mob glaring on, I felt frost form on my newly-acquired stubble, a deliberate choice designed to indicate my radicalised persona to anyone paying close enough attention to notice. Whatever rumour had been spread concerning my departure from the club, there was no denying it must have been both malign and malevolent. And spectacularly successful. My shock return to the club seemingly as welcome as a violent burglar in shit-caked shoes ascending a white-carpeted staircase to steal a valuable family heirloom.

For a short time, I encountered the dubious rush of being one half of a deeply unpopular Stardust Couple. It lasted precisely five seconds. Until Svetlana arrived with JJ – taller, more handsome, bigger racket bag, exactly the same woman on his arm – when the looks and the epitaph quickly shifted to them, the Chambers' brush of animosity tarring them by association.

"Jason Jeffries?" I heard a croaky voice enquire as the four of us stood soaked in a hosing of disdain.

Out of my peripheral vision, as I had been absorbing the crowd's frosty response, I had noticed an elderly man – a bona fide, coffin-dodging, zombie-undead committee member – come shuffling out of the clubhouse. Having had his dirty old man's eye caught by Svetlana, he had then clocked JJ and hailed his question. Hobbling over on ancient legs, he offered JJ a liver-spotted hand. Up close, I recognised him as the club's life president, a man whose playing days were long over and whose position was largely ceremonial. The club had probably wheeled him out from his care home to preside over their milestone event. The idea being his longevity and decade-spanning club association added figurehead gravitas to the day's proceedings. It was why he wasn't aware of the crushing animosity towards us. The old sod had been out of the loop for donkey's years.

"It is," JJ answered, receiving the mottled hand and pumping it enthusiastically.

"Good lord. I haven't seen you here since you were a junior. I take it you're playing today?"

JJ cranked his head toward the huge red Wilson racket bag on his back. "Sure am. Great to be back. So many happy memories," JJ emphasised, sticking to the script.

"And this delightful young lady is your wife?" Coffin Dodger asked, diverting his attention to Svetlana. Whip-smart she responded to his outmoded assumption by sending him a smouldering look capable of disarming a battalion of paratroopers.

"My partner, Svetlana," JJ corrected. "But only off court."

"Shame," Coffin Dodger proclaimed, wistful look on his fourscore-ravaged visage. "Pleased to meet you, Svetlana," he continued, the wizened hand out again, pressing flesh. "So who's your partner *on* court today?" he asked JJ, finally crowbarring his scrutiny off Svetlana.

"Paul. Paul Chambers," JJ answered, wafting a hand my way.

Coffin Dodger looked at me with a slight quizzical backwards movement of his head. Like I had just stepped off an alien spaceship holding up a giant placard saying 'Take me to your leader' – in Cantonese.

"... Yes. Of course... Paul. Paul Chambers," he announced after a bit of satellite delay. "Are you still a member?" he wondered, dappled paw extended.

"I left a few years ago," I replied, handshaking with a rictus grin. "Wonderful to be back."

"Excell..." stalling mid-word, like a poorly-maintained vintage car, Coffin Dodger's gaze had alighted on Tatiana. "...ent," he finished, starting-handle-cranked mind spluttering back to life.

"My partner, Tatiana," I informed. "But only off court."

Too bamboozled to speak, Coffin Dodger stuck out his default-action, sun-damaged claw, shook Tatiana's hand and stepped back, appraising the Nas several times in a state of befuddlement. "Splendid," he muttered. "Absolutely splendid."

"That wasn't so bad. Friendly enough considering everyone

else's reaction," I whispered, as Coffin Dodger tottered off. "Bearing in mind, if I remember correctly, he *was* on the committee that booted you out," I remarked to JJ. "Strange how he remembered you, but not so much me. Probably got a touch of dementia. It's generally accepted the older memories are the ones that last the..."

"Least of your worries, man," JJ interjected.

I followed JJ's look to see James and Chloe arriving, closely followed by Randolph and Emily. Chloe and James hand in hand – conservative, a little self-conscious – Randolph and Emily with arms wrapped around each other's waist – loved up and wanting everyone to know it – an even starrier Stardust Couple than the version she had been in with Steven.

With the boring Coffin Dodger interlude now consigned to history, the crowd's interest perked up with the introduction of the home favourites, the Geiger counter of toxic fallout now clicking harder than the day Chernobyl went pop. Competitive tennis was one thing, rarely was it spiced up with such weapons-grade biliousness, all uncomfortably green-screened to a post break-up 'who's winning now?' backdrop.

Time obligingly halted as the eight of us stood opposed, one line of four versus another line of four, the shock of my appearance written large across the faces of Chloe, James, Emily and Randolph, like the family of a fratricidal son unexpectedly seen out on parole eating a chocolate ice cream in the sunshine. As the centrepiece, I felt the full wrath of their hatred pour down on me and as I stared back, determined not to waver, recognition surfaced that here, in the flesh, were the people who had moved heaven and earth to ransack my life. As I vowed not to weaken and doggedly held their look, their attention wavered, dithered and then, finally, shifted. Like fist fights to the college Subway and iron filings to an electromagnet, the Nas dragged the limelight from me. I should have known better. Wherever they went, whatever the setting, the Nas were always the headline act.

On best Wimbledon behaviour, the crowd stayed hushed. No one attempted flash photography and not one distracting feathered creature landed on the space between us as our protracted rally of silence played out. On what I imagined to be something like the twenty-third stroke, a winner – read 'zinger' – killed it dead.

"What are looking at, idiot woman?" Svetlana suddenly snapped, aggressive and unrestrained.

"Haff not seen better look beautiful Russian woman before, ugly tramp?" Tatiana sneered.

Whatever everyone had been expecting to happen next, it wasn't that. At that instant, in Surrey, at a tennis club – where the atoms of English social mores bond most tightly – an East European subatomic particle beam blitzed them apart. Although mentally geared up for a metaphorical dogfight, even I had been sideswiped by the Nas' brutally uncouth response and I'm ashamed to admit my socially conditioned disquiet must have manifested itself on my face.

"Paul, is nothing," Tatiana told me dismissively, loud enough for everyone to hear, the mass of bystanders now teetering on titillation thanks to witnessing such a public washing of filthy laundry. "Haff only tell truth to pig-ugly woman."

To my astonishment, Emily untangled herself from lover-boy Randolph and stepped forward, face crimson and incandescent with rage.

"Don't think I don't know it was you who told Steven those lies about me and Randolph," she hissed vehemently, her attention now very much back on me.

"That's a double negative, Emily," I heard myself say, instead of asking what the hell she was on about. "No wonder you never got commissioned to write that academic piece for your 'trade magazine'. Screwfix must have had second thoughts."

"You're an unspeakably vile man, Paul," she sniped. "What

time does the lease on your escorts run out? I can't imagine they'd be here with you if you weren't paying for them."

Mortified, I switched from Emily's maleficent beauty to that of the Nas and saw them smiling cruel curls of perfectly applied lipstick.

JJ

First impressions after the surge of anger I felt at the Nas getting dissed, and at how quickly things had turned majorly hateful, were as follows. Chloe; not bad looking, a bit straitjacketed, the type of woman I could easily imagine marrying someone like Paul. James; a bit of a non-entity, the type of guy I could easily imagine ending up with someone like Chloe when her marriage to someone like Paul had ended. Emily; feisty, fit, very fit in fact, factor in her tennis prowess and definitely the type of woman I could imagine Paul lusting after when married to someone like Chloe. Randolph; absolutely the type of dick I had imagined, with his unearned wealth, suntanned good looks, talent and utter lack of work ethic. Just the type of guy I could easily imagine someone like Emily wanting to off-the-radar shag when paired in a charity tennis tournament with someone like Paul.

Riled by Emily's nasty insinuation, a fresh objective formed in my head. One where despite her being the most openly aggressive towards us, she ended up fancying me and wanting to screw me. In spite of herself, that was the crucial bit. In my head, I pictured a future her intensely agitated by how I had made Randolph look a chump on court, yet secretly desiring me because of it. If she hated herself for it, so much the better. Amazing. Times *have* changed. I *actually* had zero interest in her, not now I had the Nas, only as another means of on-court motivation. I wanted her to want me because she could never have me. This learning curve I was on!

296

Shit! Whoever said love was a powerful thing certainly knew what they were on about.

"Come on," I said to Paul and the Nas, walking forward to end the standoff, sick of the goldfish bowl situation. "Let's go sign in. I don't need to listen to another word of this."

Cutting through the crowd, and the atmosphere, we checked in at the organiser's table situated within the clubhouse. Emma's HQ from where she was running the show. It really was long time no see and she seemed genuinely pleased to meet me and Paul again. I thanked her for staying true to herself and for being the only one swimming against the tide of club opinion. And for seeding us.

"Not been the warmest of welcomes so far. To say the least."

"There's been a lot of… conjecture going around," Emma answered. "I don't take any notice of it. It takes two to tango. All I've heard is one side of the story, not that that seems to bother most around here. I mean, there's no way Paul's as horrible and disgusting as he's been made out and you weren't *that* bad as a junior, JJ."

"What's been said?" Paul asked perturbed.

"You don't want to know," Emma answered.

"I do," Paul insisted.

Emma let out a sigh and lowered her voice. "*Don't* say I didn't warn you. Basically, the story Emily put around was how she partnered you in some tennis charity competition and throughout it you kept hitting on her. Pestering her to have sex. Constantly. She said she found it very upsetting and you were extremely pushy about it and even got angry when she said no. She said you didn't seem to be able to comprehend the fact she never found you attractive in any way, shape or form and that she was a happily married woman. She said in the end your behaviour bordered on abusive. She said you seemed to think you had a right to some form of sexual reward because you'd stepped in to partner her as a last-minute favour. She said she could only assume you made the retaliatory accusations out of pure spite and bitterness at being rejected."

"What! None of that is true!... I did play in a charity tennis event with her, that bit is true. *Not* the other stuff." Paul waggled a mystified head as it all began to sink in. "What retaliatory accusations?"

"The ones you made directly to Steven. The ones accusing Emily of having an affair with Randolph. The ones you bombarded him with. Emily said this caused a massive upheaval at home, what with Steven eventually being convinced, overwhelmed by your constant litany of lies. She said their marriage went into freefall, all because of you. Became irreversibly damaged. Feeling emotionally fragile, Emily sought out Randolph to explain and, as the two innocent victims in the sorry saga, they began supporting each other through the entire harrowing ordeal. Over time, it became a bit more than that and they tentatively started dating, once it became evident Emily's marriage was over. Now they're a happy couple looking to the future and trying to put the matter behind them. In spite of all you did."

Paul stared at Emma, incredulity oozing from every pore. "And everyone at the club *believes* that, do they?" he asked.

Emma nodded. "Pretty much. She tells a good tale does our Emily. She can turn the old waterworks on in a flash that girl."

"So nobody thinks she actually *did* have an affair with Randolph, Steven found out, and *that's* why their marriage went down the tubes?"

"Not really," Emma replied, pulling a face. "Because it all sort of ties in to what Chloe's been saying about you. She backed up Emily by saying you'd started acting a bit strange after losing the mixed doubles final to her and Steven. Calling Steven all the names under the sun in the car going home afterwards. And blaming her for mistakes she had made in the match. By all accounts, you were so horrid it made her cry, even accusing her of having a fling with Steven at the awards night. She said she was so upset by it all she vowed there and then to never partner you on court again. With hindsight, Chloe thought perhaps you had developed an unhealthy jealousy of Steven and an infatuation with Emily. As for the charity tennis thing, she said you never once mentioned you were due to play with Emily, you kept it very hush-hush, and your behaviour shortly before the tournament bordered on weird. It all got very personal, to be honest. Chloe even told everyone how one night, shortly before the charity event, you preferred to masturbate rather than make love to her. An offer she had selflessly made in one last desperate attempt to get your marriage back on track."

I couldn't stop myself and let out a splutter of laughter, knowing the real truth behind the incident.

"Sorry, man. That's awful. Terrible thing to say," I apologised, holding up a hand.

"So how come Emily asked me to play with her? How did she explain that?" Paul asked.

"Couldn't get anyone else at short notice after Steven's unavoidable work commitment cropped up," Emma responded. "She said she needed someone who was a half sensible player and you were the only one left after trying several others. Besides, at that point she still thought you were a normal guy and hadn't got you marked down as a sexual predator," Emma continued. "She thought you'd enjoy it, mixing with a different social set. In the end, all you did was moan about them too, saying they were 'a bunch of stuck up twats'. Worse still, she said you'd used the loo in this fantastic country house and left the toilet seat up."

"What?" Paul asked.

"A joke. I made that bit up. Not the rest, though. Sorry," Emma explained, scrunching her shoulders and smiling. "James and Chloe have spun a very similar tale to explain how they ended up together. Emotional support in a time of crisis caused by, let me see, oh yes, you again, Paul, all leading to something more. You've been quite the catalyst on the new partnership front by all accounts."

"Let it go, Paul. There's no way you can win the spin war now,"

I warned him. "But we can win the war of spin. Top, side and under. Emma, any chance we can have a can of balls for a hit?" I asked.

"Sure. I'll get you some." Emma fetched a can of Head balls and handed them to me. "Good luck," she said. "Give them all a tennis lesson, JJ. You too, Paul. I know you're not like that. Unfortunately for you, virtually all of the club membership have been seduced by Chloe and Emily's version of events. You disappearing off the scene compounded your guilt in many eyes and you know how the club likes a good gossip. You've been trending for months and months."

"Thanks, Emma. Appreciate that," Paul mumbled, still away with the fairies.

Can in hand, I asked the Nas if they would be all right on their own for fifteen minutes. They both laughed, and with their blessing I shoved Paul out the clubhouse to find us a free court. It turned out to be the one where I had crashed the moped a lifetime ago.

Now covered in artificial grass and with the underlying base no doubt resurfaced, all physical remains of the bike's leaking petrol tank were long gone. Despite this, I still had to take a quick time out and lent on the net of entanglement – another replacement – and thought of the young me, dreams still in place, pro career a possibility, realistically just the first telltale signs of things starting to go awry. It was a poignant moment, one I didn't dare dwell on for too long. Clearing my head, I remembered there were a couple of rehearsed points I needed to drum into Paul. Even more so now Emma had revealed the ugly details of his character assassination.

"Forget all that shit Emma told you," I stressed, grabbing him by the jaw and jiggling his head roughly. "Those two women are a right couple of pieces of work. They've certainly done a number on you, man. In the current #MeToo climate you never stood a chance. You're a white, middle-class bloke and you fucking did it! Just like they said you fucking did it! But, ask yourself this, does it matter?"

"Well, yes. It's awful."

"But does it matter if we win? And the Nas are here to see it? You don't *need* this place anymore. Don't need the people here anymore. You've moved on."

"No. Suppose it doesn't," Paul conceded. "And I have moved on."

"Exactly. Delete it. Don't burn a single calorie worrying over what's been said. It's lies. The Nas know it's rubbish. I know it's rubbish. Total bollocks." I gave Paul a jolting jab to his upper arm. "Winning is all that matters. That'll more than set the record straight. Now. You good?" Paul nodded an affirmative I thought I could believe. "Nice. Listen. A few prepared words. First up, I don't want you apologising to me today."

"What do you mean?"

"No saying 'sorry' every time you miss a ball. It really pisses me off when people do that. I know you're not missing on purpose. No one misses on purpose. Apology not required."

"Sure. Nyet problem."

"Great. And another thing. If we're ever forty-love down, don't even think of saying 'good game to win', all right? That's even fucking worse. It makes you sound like a parrot. 'Pieces of eight, pieces of eight'. 'Good game to win, good game to win'."

"Okaay. Anything else?"

"If I go fucking mental at any stage, for whatever reason, ignore me. Concentrate on your own game."

"Got it. On the other hand, if *I* go mental, do everything in your powers to talk me down and land me," Paul countered.

"Nyet problem. On line calls we back each other up. And we don't play two on anything. I don't play two, okay? Ever. If they can't decide whether it's in or out, it's in. Same goes for our calls. Obviously we call fair. Overly so. Give our opponents the benefit of any doubt. Might help us win over the crowd."

"Good call."

"Perfect. You know… this feels mad being back here on this court again," I tried to explain. "Stranger than a fucking Eurosport ad… Sorry… That's it… I'm rambling. No more past. Game head on. Last piece of advice, try and remember everything we've worked on. Keep hitting. Don't just poke it back. Right from the off. We play the same way right through the group stages and into the final. Positive, positive, positive. We try and crush everyone, even if we're coasting. And we celebrate big. Every point. High-fives, fist pumps, plenty of 'Come ons!' That'll get up everyone's nose and put them off. You're a much improved player, Paul. Time to show it. Let's do this for the Nas. Coming all this way to support us. Getting that sort of shit chucked at them by that lying bitch Emily… And," I said, my top teeth grasping at my lower lip to stop a leer, a look I've always detested, "we get to find out what our sexual reward is *when* we win."

"Yes, I know! I wonder what…?"

"Back burner. Tennis time!"

We hit for ten minutes or so and as we did I noticed Chloe, James, Emily and Randolph, among many others, watching and getting a sneak preview. No doubt weighing up how good and how much of a threat I was, confirming one way or the other the rumours they had heard. Word must have filtered out I was back. With Paul it had been obvious, but many may have struggled to recognise me. Once I realised I was under the microscope, I went for a few showboat strokes, a couple of crunched forehands down the line, one big backhand cross court, a couple of overly flash stop volleys. I reckoned I impressed, timing everything perfectly as I did, the ball locking on to the centre of my racket. Like what you see, Emily? I thought, striking another clean one. Knickers wet yet? This was great fun. Did everyone in love feel so empowered?

Knock-up done and dusted and with other pairs waiting their chance, me and Paul vacated the court and found the Nas setting up base camp on a section of grass alongside one of the other courts. With a few minutes of the knock-up remaining, I had a quick wander and sized up the opposition. Most of the players I saw were around Paul's standard, but a handful looked better. Watching Randolph hit, he did look a cut above and somewhere on a par with me, the crunch being how his game would hold up when put under pressure. It was all very well looking good, and being good looking, in a knock-up, or when winning easily, like he had against Paul, but how would his technique hold up under fire? I was determined to launch a blitzkrieg on him and find out.

Twenty minutes later than scheduled, the first round robin matches started, our first match coming in the second batch of fixtures. The round robin consisted of four groups of six pairs, best of seven game matches, top four qualifying via most games won. Semis were a one set shoot out and the final a best of three, the last set taking the form of a championship tiebreak to ten points. Watching the match closest to us, Svetlana touchingly asked where the umpire was and I told her there wasn't going to be one, not even for the final. I clarified how the players umpired themselves, each pair calling their own lines with the score kept verbally. She wasn't impressed.

"What if cheat? What if say ball out when ball in?"

"All club tennis is played that way," I explained. "It can be a nightmare with kids, but most adults call honestly most of the time. Although the temptation to call a base line ball long sometimes gets too much, and that's the one that looks most in from your opponents' viewpoint at the other end. Cue argument. As soon as deliberate bad calls start, that's it. No point in playing. Errors are different. Anyone can make a genuine bad call and if they do you have to suck it up because there's no Hawk-Eye. To be fair, sometimes it is hard to tell when you're concentrating more on hitting the stroke. The usual cop out when players aren't sure, or if there's a disagreement, is to 'play two'. Play the point again. That's all right, but if you're playing to a good standard with experienced players it

303

shouldn't be necessary. Call it out or play it as in. End of."

"I hope it wasn't too uncomfortable for you earlier. Emily had no right to insinuate what she did," Paul chipped in, changing the conversation. "She can say what she likes about me, but not you two."

"Haff make note in little black book," Svetlana said, tapping her temple.

Paul

Despite my club reputation turning out to be a whole lot worse than I had expected – no mean feat – JJ and I negotiated the round robin games unscathed, winning our group by a considerable margin. The closest we were pushed, a 5-2 victory, the heaviest defeats we inflicted, two butt-kicking bagels. With me playing in the deuce court, JJ taking responsibility for the big points in the advantage court, we played aggressive tennis from the off, both of us serve-volleying all the time, including on second serves. JJ had done a fair amount of work with me on trying to pep up my second serve, to get a bit more action and zip on it, and it had definitely helped. After the group stage neither of us had dropped a single service game and my confidence had grown. JJ's suggestion of channelling anger as a focal point to drive my will to win had also helped, that and his constant tactical cajoling.

During all our matches, the Nas clapped and whooped every single point we won – and the ones we didn't. Shamelessly, they cheered our opponents' unforced errors and pushed the envelope of acceptable tennis crowd behaviour to its limits by applauding our opponents' double faults. Like a two-woman football crowd giving the opposition a hard time, they were loud, partisan and tribal. If not quite at the stage of rushing the netting to make lewd hand gestures and offer explicit profane advice on where opposition players could stick their racket handles, then they weren't far shy of it. The backlash against the Nas' inappropriate behaviour for watching tennis, as far as JJ and I could discern on court, was zero. Nada. Not a soul tried to counterbalance the Nas' support and boost whoever we were playing against. No one cheered our unforced errors, our forced errors, or even the clean winners that sailed past us come to that. Our two beautiful, identical Russian twins easily managed to browbeat an entire English middle-class crowd.

Make no bones, I loved it, the Nas getting under everyone's skin like they were a couple of giant ticks. Any smidgen of embarrassment I had felt at their prior verbal outburst had long dissipated. Emma's revelation had put paid to that. Siege mentality indeed. Us against them. We were here for revenge and now I wanted it more than ever.

Late afternoon, we played the first semi-final and were pitched against a couple of seasoned ex-county players in their forties, who were both technically solid and possessed good serves. As is often the case in a tight men's doubles match, especially on a relatively quick artificial grass court, everyone held serve twice, but in the ninth game we broke to take a 5-4 lead. JJ's down-the-line backhand winner eliciting a frenzied response from the Nas. At the end change, one of the opposition asked, rather sarcastically, if there was any chance the Nas were with us.

"They're our partners," JJ answered.

"Are they identical?" the original questioner enquired, squinting into the distance.

"They are," I assured him.

"So identical we never know which one of them we're fucking," JJ stated matter-of-factly.

I think that image buried deep in our opponents' heads because JJ held the next game to love. They never made a single return between them and we eased into the final 6-4.

"Nice tactic," I observed, as we walked off court. "Throwing in the old 'sexual imagery' ploy during an end change."

"Nice serving, you mean," JJ corrected.

Thanks to the Nas' vocal support and us securing a place in the final, we were ruffling more club member feathers quicker than a job-and-finish turkey plucker at Christmas. Yet, in spite of Emma's proclaimed level of dislike the club had for us – apart from dear old disengaged Coffin Dodger – Emily's outburst remained the single act of open belligerence for the whole day so far. For all the supposed antipathy, only muted angry looks came our way. Words were undoubtedly spoken, but not to our faces. Inactions I laid firmly on the doorstep of restrictive English middle-class mores.

"Who do you want to win?" I asked JJ as we traipsed over to watch the second semi.

"James and Randolph. And you have the cheek to say I'm the one who asks dumb questions."

I took his point. This was the duel JJ had been waiting an awful long time for. Being robbed of it by our adversaries falling at the very last hurdle was not the desired storyboard.

Throughout the entire length of James and Randolph's semi-final match, the Nas stood right behind Chloe and Emily talking loudly in Russian. I had to admit it did sound quite intimidating, specifically so when they both sporadically broke out into cold laughter. The type of laughter I imagined a hired killer might make when describing, to another hired killer, how the brains of their victim had splattered up the wall when shooting them point blank in the head. I'm not sure why their conversation and the tone of it conjured up those pictures, obviously I couldn't understand a single word of it, but it just did. If it unnerved me, then it definitely put the frighteners on Chloe and Emily, who resolutely set their eyes forever forward, never once daring to look round, like they were in a cinema and their seat was being constantly kicked by the resident armed psychopath.

Highly unsociable as it was, I rather enjoyed it, watching my ex-wife and ex-infatuation getting psychologically worked over by the two new women in my life. It appeared the Nas were endlessly adaptable on whatever stage you placed them, whether faking rape and murdering an oligarch's son, dressing up as hookers, acting as dominatrixes to spank elderly schoolboys, posing as boorish tennis fans and, not forgetting, when impersonating each other. Not a bad CV, if ever there existed an employer who needed such a skill set.

James and Randolph won, much to JJ's relief, a tight match they squeezed out 7-5 against a pair JJ rated marginally stronger than our semi-final pairing.

"The cracks are starting to show, man. Randolph got way tight in that one, the flat track bully. This is going to be so sweet taking them apart," JJ commented as the four of us stood in a semi circle, waiting for our call for the final.

"He still looked pretty good to me. It won't be easy."

JJ jabbed a finger into my chest, his eyes firing up in an instant. "We *fucking* take them, okay? Any chance we get to smash the ball at them, we do it. Bodyline. Let the fuckers know we mean business."

"Easy, JJ. I know Randolph embodies nearly everything you despise, class, tennis opportunities, attitude, I could go on, but calm it down. Remember what you said to me? Anger into controlled aggression."

JJ blinked rapidly a succession of times and then jerked his head up and down in a burst of staccato movements. "Slap me," he stated.

"Sorry?"

"Slap me. Hard. In the face."

Before I could respond, Tatiana stepped in and cracked JJ so hard in the face, the slap resonated like an echo.

"Thanks," he said appreciatively. "Fuck me, my ears are ringing."

"Fighter who lose control, lose all," Tatiana warned. "Are both black belt in judo, so know what talk about."

"Genuinely? You've not mentioned it before," I said, unsure if she was exaggerating.

"Haff learn keep self safe. Against man who always pester for sex," Tatiana explained, widening her eyes at me. "Am making fun," she insisted, as my mouth swung open to protest.

"There's so much we still don't know about you, isn't there?" I asked.

"Is funny, am thinking same," Svetlana said. "Prefer masturbate than haff sex with…"

"Finalists to court number one please! Finalists to court one!" Emma's voice proclaimed over a loudhailer, cutting Svetlana short.

"Let's do this!" I said, fist-bumping JJ.

"Let's go!" JJ reiterated.

"Come on, boy!" the Nas piped in unison.

We both made to head off only for them to stop us dead in our tracks, taking hold of each of us in turn, kissing us like we were teenagers under a pier.

Walking on court it was difficult to wipe the smile off my face, although I think I managed the lipstick. I hoped a lot of people had seen it. That would give the haters something else to bitch about.

JJ

I couldn't remember feeling more alive when stepping on to a tennis court, seeing James and Randolph waiting for us at the net, two lambs ready for slaughter. I felt good, upbeat and hyper-motivated, the challenge I had long awaited only moments away. Revenge and a chance to set the record straight, it felt, on all those who'd had better tennis chances than me. Two birds with one stone, three if you counted trying to seduce Emily into wanting me

308

through the medium of swinging a racket.

After a couple of peremptory handshakes, I thought it best to set out our stall early doors. When Randolph called 'rough' correctly when we spun for choice of ends or serve, I looked down my nose at him and said, "That's the only thing you will win, fella."

"We'll see," he replied in his best sneer, but his stare dropped quickly from mine.

"I'm now officially living rent-free in his head," I told Paul as we walked to our base line. "I reckon there's every chance he'll bottle it if we can get at him. James looked well nervy too. If you can, first return, drill one at him. Aim between his eyes. I'll do the same. Make the fucker think he's like one of those little yellow ducks in a shooting gallery."

What happened next turned out better. First point of the match, Paul mishit a major forehand frame-wrapper with loads of top on it that sailed over James's head and kicked off the court for an unclean winner. Setting the mood music even further to the dark side, neither of us apologised for the fluke. Somewhere to my left, I heard the Nas cheering as loud as they could. A perfect start. Second point, serving to me, Randolph missed his first serve, rolled in a kicker second and I creamed my return at James, the ball smashing him right in the chest before he had a chance to move his racket.

"Yes! Come on!" I screamed and went over to fist bump Paul as the Nas clapped and cheered.

Love-thirty. Paul missed his next return but I made the most of another second serve, hitting deep to Randolph's backhand as he had stayed back. He went at Paul with a backhand topspin down the line that had nothing much on it and Paul put away a comfortable volley. Fifteen-forty and a very early break point. The next shot Paul played was a great one. Randolph got a good first serve in down the tee on to Paul's backhand, one he managed to block at full stretch to Randolph's feet as he came into volley. Randolph's volley was defensive and, gambling by going across, I poached it and punched away my own volley winner.

"Come on!" I shouted, giving it an extravagant Nadal-style fist pump as the Nas responded off court. Playing to the crowd, I blew them a kiss.

From there on the first set wasn't in much doubt as the Paul and JJ mean machine steamrollered our opponents deep into the artificial grass surface. After the first end change, I held serve, we broke James, Paul held, Randolph held, I held and then James held to get us to a rapid 5-2 lead. Paul had a bit of a wobble serving out the set, but after a couple of deuces he got us over the line to take it 6-2. Cue the Nas making loads of noise while we both fist-pumped and high-fived. We were on fire.

During the half hour it took us to go a set up, the home crowd tried to politely get behind their favourite pair. It had been an uphill struggle for them, getting vocally bullied by the Nas and with little to feed on thanks to Randolph and James playing inconsistently, thanks to the pressure we were exerting on them. Our power play constantly took the net from them and harried them to either pass or lob us. Shots they couldn't come up with. I was keen for it to stay that way. If there was to be a reaction in any way from our opponents, the start of the second set would see it.

One of tennis's unique attributes, a quality that makes it so watchable and so interesting, is the way it's scored. It's based on a system where little clusters of actions are completed and then incrementally banked. The scale of loss or victory within these banked packages, the game and the set as they're termed, are relatively inconsequential to the overall result. In a best of three sets match, winning one set 6-0 doesn't count any more than winning 7-6. In either scenario, the loser can draw a line under his loss and start afresh in a next set. In a sport like football, a 4-0 half time lead, as opposed to a 1-0 lead, for example, has a huge impact on the result; a one set to love lead doesn't, even more so in a Slam, where it's best of five. Within a single set, the same concept applies and games can be clawed back one at a time because each one stands as its own separate entity, the possibility of winning it in as little as four points never changing, irrespective of what's happened before. As a consequence, piece by piece, it's possible for a player or a doubles pair to dig themselves out of a fairly big hole, unlike in other sports, where a single continuous accumulative scoring system makes it far more difficult.

Currently, me and Paul were sitting pretty in the driving seat, admiring the view with James and Randolph bundled up in the boot, hands cable-tied and gaffer-tape over their mouths. That said, the match was far from over. We had to guard against them gradually turning it around, game by game, and taking the next set. The following ten-point championship tiebreak decider a lottery, a penalty shootout where anything could happen and fast.

"Well played, Paul. Let's keep it going. No backing off. We can't afford to let them back in it," I stressed. "Let's try and get an early break."

Staying for one more game before the next end change, due to the first set finishing on an even number of games, Randolph served and held to fifteen, going for broke, serving big and flat. Fuck you, I thought, and did the same on my service, pinging down two aces and a couple of unreturnables, the last one Rick O'Shea'ing off Randolph's racket frame and clearing the netting. Some kid caught it and everyone clapped, only for him to epic fail throwing the ball back, taking two more swings of his skinny arm to get it over the netting. As the ball successfully arched over, everyone clapped that.

"Fucking hell," I remarked slyly to Paul. "It's worse than Wimbledon. Thank fuck it's not raining and Cliff's not here."

Still, emphatically one all.

James held his next serve to thirty and Paul held his after one deuce, locking us at two all, no breaks of serve, the games better

311

quality, more contested and more energetic now James and Randolph had upped it and ironed out the errors. As Randolph prepared to serve, I could sense the crowd's increasing involvement. They might all be idiots who had fallen for the lies Chloe and Emily had bandied around, but most were players capable of appreciating a high standard match when they saw one. I was convinced the tiny incident with the kid had helped, distracting the crowd away from the nastiness underscoring what was essentially a grudge match. They were immersing in it for the right reasons now and, not to blow smoke up my own arse, enjoying viewing a player of my standard at close quarters on their own courts. And Randolph, of course. Two young guns slugging it out with decent partners. Almost in spite of themselves, they were getting into the tennis. I wondered whether Emily was any closer to getting into me.

Next game we made no impression on Randolph's serve other than to earn a few more brownie points with the crowd. At forty-thirty and with me and Paul camped at the net, Randolph hit a fizzer of a topspin lob that landed incredibly close to the baseline or might have clipped it. I wasn't sure but immediately put out my arm, hand flat, to indicate the ball was good however much I wanted to call it out. The crowd clapped Randolph's shot, perhaps ten percent of the applause directed at my honesty.

My next service game was the best of the match in terms of all round quality. I kept winning the points serving to James, one rally a right pinball affair where all four of us faced up at the net, yet losing them serving to Randolph. On a roll of brilliant service returns, he ripped the ball down at my feet on three separate occasions as I backed up my serve with a volley. I made all three, but couldn't do much with them, giving Randolph enough time to unleash booming forehands at me and Paul where we both struggled to control the ball, forcing us to make weak defensive volleys that eventually got put away as our position in the rally deteriorated. At deuce, in a repeat of the game's pattern, I won the next point serving to James and then served a slice serve down the tee on to Randolph's forehand. He read it and crunched another great return at my feet, only this time, instead of volleying cross court at him like I had before, I angled my racket face to make a much more difficult down the line winner. One that completely wrong-footed the edging-over poacher James. The Nas weren't alone in clapping that shot. Three all in games.

In the handy book of tennis commentator clichés, it's called the 'vital seventh game'. In my opinion, whoever coined the phrase ought to be taken to a field somewhere, made to stand against a dry stone wall and be shot at by a ball machine on full power. Whatever. Agonisingly, despite two break points, we couldn't take it, Paul unfortunately missing both chances by going at the ball too hard, not by choking, sending both shots long.

"That's all right. You were positive. Come on, let's go," I cajoled, trying to give him a boost as he shook his head in despair. "Don't for one second think of apologising," I warned.

Possibly still reflecting on his two missed chances, Paul misjudged a couple of makeable returns from James on his next service game, dumping two volleys into the net. On the advantage side, Randolph continued his high standard of play hitting two clean service return winners, the sound of the ball coming off his racket like gunshot. Paul's service game passed in less than a few minutes as he brutally lost it to love, the first time he had been broken all day. The crowd, sensing a massive change in fortune, started applauding and cheering as Randolph gathered a couple of balls to serve at 5-3 up. The Nas did their best to counter it, shouting out 'Come on Paul and JJ', which although not rolling off the tongue quite as nicely as 'Roger', 'Andy', 'Tim' or 'Borg', still lifted my spirits.

I beckoned Paul over for a quick mid-court confab, slowing everything down and giving Randolph the chance to mull over the difficulties he might have to face serving out the set in a tense match.

"Make them play as much as you can. They'll be tight. We *have* to make returns," I told Paul, equally concerned he might be starting to mentally buckle.

Opening point, Randolph put in a first serve Paul couldn't handle, his return going well out. Second point, Randolph went wide to my backhand, I hit a backhand cross court return, he made a solid volley back and I whipped an almost half volley topspin lob over James for a winner. The Nas liked that one and I let out another massive 'Come on!' to let everyone know I wasn't going down without a scrap. Fifteen-all. Randolph missed his next first serve and followed it up with a safe-mode kicker to Paul's backhand. Arm tight, Paul prodded it back, a sliced floater high over the net. Expecting a punched volley winner down my line or down the middle, Randolph edgily pushed his forehand volley long, the ball ballooning over the baseline by a couple of feet. Over the top of a few groans, the Nas went wild with excitement.

"Vamos!" I shouted, changing things up a little.

"One get out of jail card used," Paul cracked as we fist-bumped.

Fifteen-thirty. Unsettled, Randolph took a bit off his next first serve to make sure he got it in. Big mistake. I was all over it like a rash and cracked a forehand winner down James's line. If he blinked at it, that was about it. Him not getting creamed scant consolation for the evil look Randolph had given him for not covering his tramlines.

"Yesss!" I cried, giving it the clenched fist again, Paul likewise on the other side of the court.

"That's huge, JJ," Paul congratulated me as we high-fived..

"Have you been taking a sneak look in the showers?"

Taking my position halfway across the advantage court's service line in preparation for Paul to receive serve, I caught Emily looking at me. 'Penny for your thoughts,' I mouthed to myself, returning her gaze.

Break point on fifteen-forty, Paul cannily blocked Randolph's wide serve over James's head, forcing Randolph and James to cross as Randolph ran and hit a backhand cross court ground stroke from close to the baseline. He should have gone down the line at Paul or maybe lobbed, perhaps his ego wanted to take me on or maybe his brain addled, either way a poor shot selection. Closing the net down, I played a cute stop volley into the space James had vacated. Game to us and back on serve at 4-5. I didn't shout after the stop volley, only looked at Paul and waggled an elevated clenched fist at him. The Nas kindly provided the backing vocals.

The next two games after the end change were short and sharp. Suited me. I served out to love for us to draw level at 5-5, one ace and three missed returns, a game that rapidly put James back under the spotlight. With our opponents seemingly at sea, we snatched James's serve to thirty, making a couple of outright winners and dominating play at the net. 6-5, Paul's serve to come, and only a regulation hold away from wrapping matters up.

"Forget where we are score-wise. Treat it like any another service game," I told Paul at the end change as we swigged our drinks.

"Easier said than done."

"They're gone," I said dismissively.

"You reckon?"

"Not quite but pretty much. Try not to give them any cheap points. Make them earn everything."

First point, I made a premeditated move, went early, and cut off James's cross court service return with a sharp volley down the middle, a winner greeted by an explosion of joy from the Nas.

"Keep doing that," Paul enthused as we touched hands. "I'm not fussed if I have to play a second shot. I'm not proud."

Second point, I feinted to go across, but stayed put. Randolph saw my initial movement and went down the line and there I was,

315

waiting, cigar on, to punch away a simple winner. Thirty-love. Pressure off a little, Paul made a good deep volley behind a first serve as I stood my ground at the net, unable to intercept James's cross court return. Lacking time due to the depth of the ball, James tried to lob me, I got back underneath it with a quick backpedal and smashed it away to create three match points. On the first one, Randolph went shit or bust and hit a massive forehand return Paul could only net on the volley. Second one he served a double. Forty-thirty.

"No panic. Stick it on his backhand and this time I'll go across," I instructed, making out my words were ones of encouragement.

Paul got a decent first serve in and I left it to the last moment to go, wary of being passed down the line. My backhand volley down the middle, done at full stretch, although good, was never going to be a winner. With good speed, Randolph scrambled back to the centre of the court and hoisted up a difficult, deep lob that I conservatively smashed at James who had retreated and joined his partner at the back of the court. Behind the base line, on the defensive, James could only answer with a lob of his own. A much easier, shorter one. As the ball looped slowly up in the air, on Paul's side of the court, only three yards or so over the net, I pictured *the* perfect way for the match to end. Paul stepping in to put away an easy smash, laying a myriad of demons to rest with one ironic swing of his racket.

A fast action shutter crashed down on the scene. Fuck that. He might miss again.

"Mine!" I shouted, stepping over to pummel away an easy smash, the ecstasy of the Nas echoing in my ears.

Tatiana and Svetlana

Haff nice day out, watch Paul and JJ win tennis. Haff enjoy cheer on and get up nose of club member who only haff answer of dirty look. Make change from dirty dad in café, am supposing. Is disappoint not haff big confrontation as haff set mind and body for event. In end, all notion knife in back conversation haff not happen. Am thinking Western democracy all snowflake, haff not heart for fight and Russia roll in tank whenever like. Neverless am impress cruel story Emma haff tell make by Chloe and Emily and am admitting as piece dezinformatsiya is ferry clever. Is perfect blend small truth and much lie. Haff say Svetlana, am wondering if pair might want job as Sputnik writer, which make Svetlana laugh. Most fun part day when stand behind Chloe and Emily and tell fairy story, The Unsmiling Tsarevna, in native tongue. Is story Mamochka tell me and Svetlana when little girl so haff many unhappy memory, perfect for scare fragile English rose.

Paul and JJ haff get glass trophy for win from ferry old man. Am saying Svetlana look old like Russian man. Svetlana say big different being *is* old, not just look it. Da, am agreeing, is not strength of Russian male, number of year under belt. Most drop like fly when hit seven decade. On way Paul flat in Paul car, haff start think of reward haff promise Paul and JJ for win tournament and haff nerve. Svetlana same. Haff not done before. Is step in dark even if usual do sex with light on. In back seat haff secret toss coin who go first. Paul haff win. Me and Svetlana not sure if is better man go first or second. Haff nyet clue as haff nyet previous experience. Will haff see.

At flat haff order takeaway dinner and while wait Deliveroo, Paul and JJ haff shower. After eat meal, me and Svetlana haff shower and all sit in small living room on sofa drink vodka and orange, me and Svetlana, Corona Extra, Paul and JJ. Paul and JJ haff much pleasure keep go over what haff happen at tennis tournament, remember many shot and incident from day and can tell are ferry please with self. Is much laughing. Am happy, Svetlana same, elephant in room is reward. Are quiet and only smile at joke while knock back vodka and orange.

"Are you two all right?" Paul say, when penny fall on floor. "You don't seem your normal selves. Has anything happened we should know about?"

Am thinking is nice haff notice and now is time bite bullet and show elephant. "Is reward," am saying. "Is ferry special. Haff not done before and haff nerve."

"Same," Svetlana say.

"Wow!" JJ say. "That's the last thing I would have expected. You two being nervous over making love."

Paul and JJ haff look each other and is pause. "Are you going to tell us what it is?" haff say together.

"Who are thinking, are me and Svetlana?" Svetlana say, try hide nerve behind joke.

Paul and JJ smile but expression say are waiting hard for answer.

"Da. Okay. Am telling," am saying.

Is silence.

"Yesss," JJ say, hand wind invisible handle.

"Is threesome," am saying, pulling cloak from elephant by let cat out bag.

Is big look of worry on Paul and JJ face, like waiter haff spill red wine down Putin white shirt.

"Is no need panic," Svetlana say, roll eye. "Are meaning one of Paul and JJ with me and Svetlana. Paul turn first, JJ second. Haff flick coin in car."

Paul and JJ haff breathe ferry big sigh relief.

"No offense, JJ, but thank Christ for that," Paul say.

"*Same*," JJ say.

Am lying awake in JJ bed, JJ asleep. On reflect, is better man go second for first try threesome with identical twin. JJ haff luck of coin but am thinking Paul never know different, and if did, am sure not bother. As haff tell Paul, two tongue better than one and think

318